I0556083

Valiant Light

A Demon Trappers® Novel

Other Books
by Jana Oliver

Briar Rose
Young Adult

Dead Easy
Young Adult Mystery

Tangled Souls
Paranormal Romance

Time Rovers Series
Time Travel/Alternate History Romance
Sojourn
Virtual Evil
Madman's Dance

The Demon Trappers Series
Young Adult Urban Fantasy
U.S. (U.K.)
The Demon Trapper's Daughter (Forsaken)
Soul Thief (Forbidden)
Forgiven (same title)
Foretold (same title)
Grave Matters (same title)
Mind Games (same title)
Valiant Light (same title)

Vertias Series
Writing as Chandler Steele
Romantic Suspense/Thrillers
Cat's Paw
Killing Game
Broken Dreams

Valiant Light

A Demon Trappers Novel

Jana Oliver

 Nevermore Books

Published by
MageSpell LLC
Porto, Portugal 4050

This novel is a work of fiction. Names, characters, places, and incidents are the product of the author's imagination and are not to be construed as real. Any resemblance to actual persons, living or dead, events or locales, is entirely coincidental.

Valiant Light
A Demon Trappers® Novel
ISBN: 978-1-941527-14-6
Copyright © 2017 Jana Oliver

Cover Image/Art: Yocla Designs
Angel Wing Graphic: Used with permission of
Macmillan Children's Books

All rights reserved.
No part of this book may be reproduced or transmitted
in any form or by any means now known or hereinafter
invented, electronic or mechanical, including but not limited
to photocopying, recording, or by an information storage
and retrieval system, without the written permission of
the Publisher, except where permitted by law.

Demon Trappers is a Registered Trademark of Jana Oliver

To Carrie Fisher

Who lit the way for so
very many of us

Acknowledgements

I have been writing Riley and Beck's stories since 2008, over nine years. At this point they're like family, I know them so well. For an author, it's been a unique pleasure to chronicle their journey as they've overcome obstacles that would have broken most of us.

When I look back at where they were in the first book to where they are now, both emotionally and in terms of skills, the growth has been incredible. And yet, despite all their kickass ways, they're still the kind of people you'd like to share a beer with. Or in Riley's case, a big mug of hot chocolate.

Ironically, the original series proposal I submitted to St. Martin's Griffin for the first few books had hinted at a Riley and Ori pairing, but the instant Beck showed up in the first draft, I knew the Fallen angel had just lost out big time. Though that wasn't the norm at the time (Young Adult paranormal romances were big back then) I went with my gut and the results speak for themselves.

Since the second book in this series, my guiding light has been the Amazing Mollie Traver (www.mollietraver.com). Now a freelance editor, she ensures my grammar is correct, that I haven't screwed up some portion of the Demon Trappers' canon, and that the characters remain true to themselves. The series' success is, in part, due to this lady's efforts and she will always have my deepest gratitude for all her hard work on my behalf.

Clarissa from Yocla Designs (www.yocladesigns. com) helped craft the final three book covers and they rock. And as always, I must send a special thanks to Macmillan Children's Books (London) for allowing me to use the gorgeous angel/demon graphic.

Bretagne Brackett created a seriously kickass promotional campaign for this book that just blew my mind. Using her experience as my intern, she now works for a major multimedia company and I have no doubt she's dazzling them as well. My thanks are inadequate, trust me.

I also owe my thanks to my fellow authors in the Feisty Five critique group—Berta Platas, Michele Roper, Carla Fredd and Maureen Hardegree—for all their support over these many years. And a hug and kiss to my spouse, Harold who is always there no matter how tired and grumpy I am after long hours hunched over a computer.

There is no way I can thank all my readers who have followed Riley and Beck's journeys as eagerly as I have. This series exists because of you. Bless you for letting me tell their story, for it is one I will always cherish.

"The measure of human character is our reaction to dark times. No one can sidestep darkness. It is the throne upon which light sits. If a soul has not known sadness and struggle, there is no chance of overcoming, no cherishing the dawn."

~ Rabbi David Wolpe

"When the going gets weird, the weird turn pro."

~ Hunter S. Thompson

Chapter One

March 2019
Atlanta, Georgia

Riley Blackthorne wasn't alone in this dark and desolate Georgia pasture. No, she had a companion out here in the middle of nowhere, a friend. In this case, a necromancer—one who wore an extremely worried expression.

That's not good.

Senior Summoner Mortimer Alexander was a little shorter than Riley's five-seven, rather wide, and currently covered in a black hooded robe. Not only was the garment a decent barrier against the chilly night air, but its color announced that this man was a *serious* magical threat.

"You ready to do this?" Mort asked.

"Sure, why not? How hard can it be?" Riley replied.

Her companion winced.

On the magical power scale, Riley rated a light blue robe, as she was just a beginner—albeit one with a bit of talent. Which is why this "let's test your magical wards" exercise had made her uncommonly nervous. It would be like a robin trying to defend itself against an eagle. The raptor almost always won.

It hadn't helped when Mort had suggested she leave off her robe and wear dark clothes. Something "washable," he'd said. Having seen his magical wards decimated by a much stronger necromancer, Riley knew why he'd made that suggestion. She was in for pain, and probably an epic nosebleed.

She took a deep breath, trying to relax. And failed.

Mort fiddled with his robe, nervous as well, then lowered his hands by his sides. They were already beginning to glow a brilliant blue. At any other time, Riley would have thought that was cool, even pretty, but soon that magic would be racing toward her.

"Do your best," he said. Then he cast his spell.

A second later Riley was on her back staring up at the stars, trying hard to catch her breath. It'd been like being body-slammed by a semi.

Mort had insisted that learning how to ward against an attacker's spell was much like training for a marathon. The first time you ran five miles, you whimpered in pain and prayed to die. However, each subsequent run was a little less horrific as your body grew accustomed to the strenuous exercise. In this case, if Riley "exercised" her magical wards regularly, her ability to protect herself would grow stronger.

Riiight.

As her breath evened out, she stared up at the glorious night sky. The last time she'd seen stars this bright was in Scotland, the evening she'd battled a necromancer. It'd been the day after she'd turned eighteen. She'd lain on her back on the cold ground and stared up at the heavens. The stars had sat embedded in the velvety black sky, and there'd even been a meteor painting a lacy trail of white in its wake.

That night, and the attack by a necromancer, had taught Riley a bitter lesson: If she wanted a future with Denver Beck, the man she loved, she'd have to embrace magic. That certainly wasn't the path she'd ever envisioned. She was the daughter of a master demon trapper, and her family had trapped Hellspawn for centuries. But her interactions with Hell, and especially with Lucifer, had made her the ultimate bait for those who just couldn't resist summoning evil.

Which was why, instead of finalizing plans for her upcoming wedding, she currently lay on her back, every muscle aching.

A face came into her line of sight, then a hand. Riley rose to her feet with Mort's help, sure her chest was on fire. Looking down, she saw that her navy sweatshirt was lightly singed. Luckily, she'd worn one of her old ones.

"We'll do it again," he said, trudging back to his spot some fifteen feet away.

Two more times, she ended on her back, despite casting a warding spell. Her spine signaled that it thought this whole thing sucked, and her hips were in agreement.

This time, Riley rose on her own, straightened her shoulders, ignoring the ache in her head and chest, and focused on the fact that she didn't want to land on the ground again. She put that intention into her spell, mentally building a wall between her and Mort. Maybe that would work, because nothing else was.

The third strike flew toward her like a flaming blue bomb. Then, to her surprise, it shattered against her ward, spreading those blue flames into the night.

Mort smiled, nodding his approval. "Well done. What was different this time?"

"Ah, more visualization," she replied, still surprised.

"Good. Then do it again." The blue on his hands became brighter now, which meant he'd upped the power of his spell.

Oh, crap.

Riley made herself visualize a protective bubble and had the spell up before his reached her. This time, Mort's began digging into her ward as if it had claws, and her bubble abruptly collapsed, knocking her flat on the ground again.

She stared up at the heavens. "Are we dooonne yet?"

"No. Sorry."

Aggravated, Riley struggled to her feet as her temper flared. Before realizing what she was doing, she fired off a spell at him. Mort's near instantaneous ward easily repelled hers.

"No dark-side stuff, grasshopper," he said, waving an index finger in admonishment.

Her anger fell away and she couldn't help but laugh. "You're mixing movie quotes, you know."

Mort grinned. "But you got the message."

Yes, she had. Anger wasn't going to get her anywhere

tonight, but calm, rational planning would. Magic, it appeared, wasn't much different from the rest of her life.

A year ago, she'd been more hotheaded, inclined to anger much faster. The past fifteen months or so had taken their toll, what with the death of her father, her working through the ranks of the Demon Trappers Guild, becoming a master trapper. Beck's steady presence, and that of Mort and her other friends, had helped as well.

The Riley who'd first been handed her trapping license when she turned seventeen had been shaped into the one who stood in this clearing in rural Georgia, casting spells in the dark night.

With a sigh, she raised her magical shields to maximum. This time it was nearly thirty seconds before Mort finally ended his spell, and he never broke through her ward.

Bending over to catch her breath, Riley managed to croak, "Is that what you were hoping for?"

"Yes," he said. Though she couldn't see his face, she could hear the pride in his tone. "Better, much better."

Not from her point of view. Riley's arms twitched and her chest felt like someone had parked Beck's pickup truck on it. But if it kept her and her fiancé alive, let her continue to be a master trapper, then it was worth it. At least it would be once she'd soaked in a tub and taken some aspirin.

"Not bad," a new voice said a moment before she felt his presence.

Oh no.

Riley straightened up to find Lord Ozymandias standing near Mort now. The most powerful summoner on the East Coast—if not the whole country—watched her with faint amusement. Ozy, as she called him, wore his trademark black robe with an oak staff in hand, which always made him look like he'd just stepped out of a Tolkien novel. The first time they'd met, Riley had asked him if he'd bought the staff at a Necromancers"R"Us shop. That was before she knew exactly how powerful this man was. Of course, he'd called her a heartless bitch during that same meeting, so they were probably even.

Tonight his robe's hood was back, revealing his silver hair and the strange glowing sigil on his forehead that seemed to pulsate of its own accord. His eyes were still green with hints of brown, but darker somehow.

"Lord Ozymandias," Riley said, trying to catch her breath. "What brings you to the middle of nowhere?" *Please don't say it's me.*

"You, of course. I wanted to see how Mortimer is progressing with the training."

"And your verdict is?" she asked.

The high lord gave her a nod of approval. "Not bad. I've seen apprentices give up after two blasts. Your stubbornness does you credit."

"My stubbornness will probably get me dead someday," she said, dusting off her pants. "So what am I doing wrong?"

"Nothing that I can see. You're learning how to judge the strength of the magic ranged against you, how to respond. It's all a matter of practice."

She caught Mort's expression and he seemed apologetic. Then she realized exactly why His Lordship was here.

Riley was barely able to get her ward in place before the senior necro's spell struck her. The force of his magic shoved her back six feet, her shoes skidding in the grass. This spell wasn't like Mort's—each necromancer was different—and it constantly changed, adapting as hers desperately tried to find a way to compensate.

Sweat broke out on her forehead and ran down her face. Her head roared and her arms shook as she tried to hold her spell intact. Ozymandias changed his spell's characteristics again and her ward nearly imploded. As the pressure grew, she felt her nose sting, and her breathing grew shallower.

As if on instinct, Riley stopped pushing back, knowing it was futile. Instead, she tried to think of herself as a rock, allowing the powerful spell to roll off her. For a few seconds it actually worked, his gray magic surging over her lighter purple magic, but not penetrating it. There was a sharpness to his spell, like thousands of pinching scorpion claws, each capable of drawing blood and ripping flesh if he so desired. Still, she held on and had just begun to think she had found the way to sustain this resistance for a few seconds more when Ozy called out a single unintelligible word and her ward shattered like a piece of fine crystal.

Riley dropped to her knees, then bent forward, gagging, her nose bleeding and her heart beating so hard she thought she'd suffocate. Her own fractured spell blew through her like a sirocco, finding no release.

"Ground the magic," Mort ordered, his voice tense.

It took a few seconds to realize what he'd said. Then she stretched out her shaking hands and placed them against the ground. Peeling open her aching eyes, she watched as purple magic flowed into the red Georgia clay, highlighting individual blades of grass as it did so.

Gradually Riley's heart rate began to slow as her breathing eased. Finally, when the spell was fully grounded, she dug in her jeans pocket for the tissues she'd stashed there. Pressing them to her bleeding nose, she looked up to find the two necromancers watching her closely. Ozy actually seemed pleased, the creep. When he delicately touched her head, the pounding in her skull diminished.

"You could have given a girl some warning," she said, talking around the tissues. Before he could respond, she added, "I know. No one is going to announce a spell ahead of time. But . . . geez, did you have to nail me like that? I'm just a newbie here."

"You are anything but a newbie, Summoner Blackthorne," Ozymandias said. The senior necromancer looked over at Mort for his verdict. "Your thoughts?"

"She held out longer than I anticipated. The way she began to channel your spell there at the end was intriguing. I've not seen anyone do that before."

"A few are capable of it." Ozy looked at her now. "What were you visualizing?"

"That I was a rock and you were a river. I figured I could just let you slid by and it'd hurt less."

"Huh. Slippery magic. I like that," he said. "I knew you'd come at this differently than the rest of us. You're unique, Summoner Blackthorne."

"Yeah, tell me about it," she mumbled, dabbing at her nose again. Luckily the bleeding had stopped, probably because of Ozy's intervention. "How often are we going to do this torture?"

"As often as it takes until you can handle someone of Mort's level."

She eyed His Lordship. "Not your level?"

"No. The last thing I want is someone who thinks they have as much power as I do. I can only imagine where that would lead."

Of course, they all knew what might happen. In his infinite arrogance, Ozymandias had summoned a high-level demon last year. Instead, he'd gotten a psychotic Archangel who had nearly brought on Armageddon. No, they didn't need anyone else coming close to Ozy's level of magic, at least not anyone who hadn't learned such a sobering lesson.

Mort offered his hand and Riley rose on unsteady feet. "I have orange juice in the car to help combat the dizziness."

She frowned. "I hear the dark side has *cookies*. You guys need to up your game here."

Mort laughed. "I'll remember that for the next time."

"Keep practicing," Ozymandias said. "And now I bid you two good evening." He promptly vanished.

"That was a *sending*? He wasn't even here?" Riley blurted. Mort nodded ruefully. "How much power does that guy have?"

"More than you want to know—trust me."

Thank God he's on our side.

Chapter Two

In contrast to Riley's nocturnal sojourns into rural Georgia, the school's front lobby was bright and cheery. As she saw it, anything would be an improvement as long as there wasn't a necro throwing spells at her.

The last time she'd delivered a presentation at a high school had been right after the first of the year. Beck had just returned to Scotland for his grand master training and she'd found it hard to be upbeat for that school visit. Now there were only a few days left before she was headed to Scotland for her fiancé's investiture, so Riley found herself smiling for the first time in a week.

Though her primary job was to trap Hellspawn and train new trappers, community outreach had become increasingly important, especially in a city where the populace was all too aware of the kind of damage that fiends could wreak. Her superior, Master Harper, would never have done a school talk, because for all his trapping skills, the man just wasn't into being civil. Harper talking to a roomful of teens about demons? That was just asking for trouble.

Which is why when Riley made master demon trapper at the end of last year, Harper had given her one of his incredibly rare smiles and told her this part of the job was now *hers*. That because of her "notoriety"—in particular all her run-ins with Hell and its minions—and her age, she was the ideal candidate to take the message to the civilians. Since there were no less than seventy-eight YouTube videos of her trapping Hellspawn out on the internet, she really couldn't argue that point.

Riley understood the public's fascination with the fiends,

and by extension, the trappers. Sort of. To those outside the Demon Trappers Guild, it probably seemed like a really cool job to take on Lucifer's murderous horde. Heaven vs. Hell. The Grand Game. But it was never that simple. She'd learned that lesson even before she made journeyman trapper.

With the economy finally turning around, a few more schools had reopened. This location had been one of the first, and it looked to be in pretty good shape after years of being shuttered. Sunlight flooded through the windows, and the floors gleamed. The staff looked happy too—no doubt pleased to be teaching in a building designed for education instead of in an abandoned shopping mall or a defunct grocery store.

"Here're your badges," the smiling lady behind the reception desk said, pushing them over the counter. She wore cat-eye glasses with black and red stripes, which should have looked weird but didn't.

"Thanks." As Riley parceled out those badges to her apprentices, three solemn faces studied her. No doubt, they'd already noticed that her makeup was heavier than usual and that she was moving slower than normal, yet so far not one of them had asked why. Bruises were the norm for a trapper, but for once, these weren't caused by any of Lucifer's fiends.

Riley's current group of trainees was a mixed lot: Richard Bonafont was the eldest, in his thirties, and sported a pair of wire-rim glasses, while Kurt Pelligrino was in his twenties and had the muscled bulk of a devoted gym rat. Jaye Lynn, the third apprentice, was slim, red-haired, and about Kurt's age. She was just back from family leave and still had some catching up to do with the other two, who were close to the end of their yearlong training period. The guys would soon be taking their journeyman's exams. Once they passed those, Riley would start training a new group of apprentices.

While they were waiting for the teacher who'd invited them, Riley felt it was time to dispense a few warnings. She waved them away from the reception desk and then asked, "What can go wrong with this talk today?"

"Worst case?" Kurt said. "Some parent goes completely ballistic because we mentioned Hell in front of their darling overly sheltered offspring. Said parent then goes to the school board and throws a major hissy fit."

"Always a possibility."

"Unless said parent has been under a rock for the last couple years," Jaye added, "they'd know there really are demons running around this city."

"Sometimes people live in their own little happy bubble of ignorance," Richard interjected.

"Right up until a Gastro-Fiend tries to eat them."

"That too," Riley said. Jaye's reply had reminded her of the other issue. "Best to keep the black humor to a *minimum*," she cautioned.

Doctors, nurses, cops, paramedics, soldiers, or firefighters, they all had to blow off steam. Demon trapping was no exception, but outsiders didn't understand their macabre sense of humor and thought it disrespectful.

"The last thing I want to do is explain to Master Harper why this visit went off the rails. You know how well that will go. He's a bear on a good day."

"But it would be *you* doing the explaining, not us," Kurt replied with a mischievous grin.

She eyed him. "Trust me, I won't be alone if that happens. You three will get the full Harper bitch session, just like me."

"Oh."

"Master Blackthorne?"

Riley turned to find a woman headed their way wearing navy slacks and a rather cool multi-patterned shirt that had this flowing thing going on. Her hair was in an afro and her skin a light mocha.

"Ms. Marburg?"

"Yes! I am so happy you're here to talk to my students today," the woman gushed. "They're really looking forward to it."

Bet they are. Anything different from the norm had been readily welcomed when Riley was a student. She did a quick introduction of her apprentices and then they were herded toward a classroom at the far end of the hall.

"It's great to see the school being used again," Riley said.

"We're loving it. Last fall I was teaching in a church basement, and now we're back here. We're so backlogged they're holding classes on the weekends now," Ms. Marburg exclaimed.

"That's good news." Riley waited a few steps and then asked, "Anything we shouldn't talk about?"

"No, you should be good," the teacher replied. "I had the students get signed permission slips from their parents to be in class during your talk."

Smart woman. She'd probably learned that lesson the hard way.

As expected, the room was sparse, the few posters and other additions no doubt coming out of Ms. Marburg's own pocket. School districts never received enough money to function, and the teachers tried to pick up the slack.

Riley did a quick head count: twenty-nine kids, all sizes, shapes, and colors—a cross section of Atlanta's citizens.

"Juniors, right?" Riley asked, and Ms. Marburg nodded. It was hard to believe that Riley had been one of those not so long ago.

Moving up to the front of the room, she felt all eyes on her. A couple of the students held up their phones and took pictures. Once she'd been introduced, Riley began her talk like she always did.

"Some people are teachers, some are doctors or lawyers, work at the local convenience store, or do landscaping for a living. Some become cops or firefighters, or stay home to raise their kids. Others join the military to keep us safe." She took a step closer to them now. "Me? I chose to become a demon trapper because my dad was one. I was in awe of what he did, day after day, night after night. He'd come home tired, chewed up, sick, and exhausted. But every time he did his job, someone was safer. And that's why I became a demon trapper."

Riley heard a few muttered "whatever's," which didn't

surprise her. Her fellow teens could be a cynical bunch. After a full four beats, she added, "Okay, let's be honest. You want to know why I do this job?" She grinned. "Because I just love kicking Hell's ass."

"All right!" one kid called out.

Like she'd planned, the group lightened up from there. As the hour passed, her appreciation for her parents rose even further, if that was possible. Before he'd become a master demon trapper, Paul Blackthorne had been a teacher, as had Riley's mom. Riley had always known their jobs had been hard, but dealing with a classroom full of seventeen-year-olds drove the point home. Some were serious, others were silly, and a couple were downright obnoxious. The usual mix for any classroom.

Ironically, Riley was only a year older than these kids, but the difference between her life and theirs was immense. She was an orphan, had crossed paths with the Prince of Hell and a couple Fallen angels, and had prevented Armageddon. All before she'd turned eighteen.

The photographs of the various demons the teacher put up on the screen held the class in awe while Riley patiently explained the differences between the five grades of fiends and how they were trapped. The students especially loved the video of one of the Grade Fives. Geo-Fiends were always impressive, especially when they were generating mini tornadoes and earthquakes, leveling buildings right and left.

The next video was one of her and a couple trappers grounding a Five. As it twisted and fought the magic that sent it back to Hell, the students cheered. It was an awesome video. How anyone had had the guts to get that close to film the action, Riley had no idea.

"That's all CGI, you know, like in the movies," one of the boys called out.

Riley shook her head. "Nope. They're for real."

"I've never seen one."

"If you had, you'd probably be dead," Kurt called out. "I've watched Master Blackthorne ground one of those things, and trust me, they're seriously bad news."

"And they act like cuddly puppies when compared to an Archfiend," Riley said. "Next question?"

"Did you really kill an angel?" a girl asked, her curly brown hair dancing around her shoulders.

"Nope, I didn't." But her fiancé had, and that was why Beck was about to become a grand master.

Riley knew it was time to wrap it up when one of the girls asked for Kurt's phone number—though she was proud when he handled it like a pro, politely refusing without embarrassing the student. Riley hid her smile as various students filed up to the front of the room to get autographs. Her apprentices hadn't expected that.

Once the class ended, they followed the teacher to the school's front entrance.

"That was really great," Ms. Marburg said, beaming.

"It went well," Riley replied, pleased.

Better than a presentation she'd done at a local library a few weeks back. Of course, a Biblio-Fiend had shown up for that one and begun throwing books at the attendees while swearing its head off. She'd warned the head librarian to ward the doors and windows with Holy Water, but sometimes folks just didn't listen. Next time, she'd take care of those precautions personally.

Trailing behind the others, Riley felt an uncomfortable twitch along her spine. When the twitch persisted, she turned and found a tall man standing near a doorway at the end of the adjacent hallway. He was probably forty or a bit older, a teacher perhaps, with pale auburn hair and a slight goatee.

Then his eyes met hers.

Demon. One carefully hiding his true appearance, which meant he was probably a Grade Four—a Mezmer, as the trappers called them. A skilled one, it seemed. Mezmers were masters at worming their way into your head, making you do what they wanted while draining away your life force. Once you were weak enough, they claimed your soul.

How had it gotten inside the building? The school laid down

Holy Water wards on each entrance, which was standard procedure now.

At the moment, Ms. Marburg was chatting with Jaye, while the other two apprentices were discussing their plans for the evening. This was Riley's problem, not theirs.

"Ah, guys, I'm going to hit the restroom. I'll catch up with you," she said, ensuring nothing tipped off her apprentices that something was wrong.

"We'll be at the office," Ms. Marburg called out, and they headed away down the hallway.

Riley turned back and tracked down the demon. To her surprise, it hadn't moved and in fact seemed to be waiting for her in front of a classroom.

"Are you lost?" he asked as she approached.

It was a curious question. "No, are you?"

The hint of a smile appeared. "Some might think so, but I don't."

"You shouldn't be here."

"Because I have no knowledge for these young people?" the fiend replied.

Another curious question.

"Why didn't you hide from me?" she asked. "You had to know I was in the building." Her hand was tucked inside her trapping bag, fingers wrapped around a sphere of Holy Water.

"I felt your presence, but I did not hide because I chose not to. I no longer serve the Dark," it replied.

"The Dark, as in . . . Lucifer?"

Most fiends reacted negatively when they heard the Prince's name. This one didn't even wince.

"I no longer am chained to Hell in any way."

That made her pause. "So you're saying you found a way to break your contract with the Prince?"

A nod.

"Then you thought, 'hey, I'll just become a teacher'?"

The demon chuckled. "Yes. That shouldn't surprise you. You found a way to break your contract and remain a trapper."

"That's not the same, and you know it."

"Isn't it?" it asked, then gestured around. "Here, the students are so filled with light. I have knowledge; they have a thirst to learn. It is a fair trade."

Now she understood. "You're continually pulling life force from them."

The Mezmer looked down at the floor now. "Only in very small quantities. I don't wish to harm them. I find that since I'm no longer one of Hell's own, I need far less." It looked down the hall, past her. "Being in the sunlight and fresh air, hearing laughter, and seeing the love in this world is enough for me."

Riley opened her mouth, then closed it. Was that even possible? A Mezmer could collect small bits of life essence to sustain itself, though they usually just sucked it down like a strawberry shake—and the supplier suffered for that gluttony. Perhaps this one had truly discovered a way to live on much less.

"I understand your skepticism," the demon said, looking back at her. "I will always be what I am, but it is my decision as to how I will live my life. In return for that life force, I give the students wisdom."

Riley blew out a stream of air. *Now what?* She couldn't leave a demon inside a high school, no matter how well mannered it was. It went against everything a trapper stood for.

"I promise I will not hurt them," the Mezmer said. "If I harm them, I will return to the Dark and I will die before that happens."

She frowned. "That's exactly what your kind would say."

"I know, but how many of my kind can cross a holy ward?"

"They can if the Holy Water is fake."

"It isn't. I feel it every day when I walk over it. I will never cease being what I am. I can only stop behaving like one of *his* servants."

Well, since the fiend had mentioned it, there was one way to test that claim. Riley shifted her trapping bag off her shoulder and pulled out her own bottle of Holy Water. Every trapper carried one or two, on top of the various spheres used for capturing Hellspawn.

The Four stepped back, and for a moment, she thought he was going to make a run for it.

"In here," it said, indicating the classroom.

Riley weighed that suggestion. The last thing she needed was for a Mezmer to lose its glamour and create a panic. If it did go on a rampage, she'd have a better chance of trapping it in a confined space.

When they stepped inside the room, she closed the door behind them, hoping she hadn't made a serious mistake. As she turned, the images on the walls caught her eyes immediately—they were all pictures of Mother Nature. A massive waterfall in Venezuela, the Cascade Range, the Sahara Desert, a single island in the center of a sapphire-blue ocean.

"Is this your classroom?"

The demon nodded, which only confused her more. These were not the images she'd think Hellspawn would want to see day in and day out. Or maybe they were, if that fiend had spent an eternity in Hell's bleak and sulfurous halls.

Disconcerted, Riley uncapped the Holy Water—she'd just bought it that morning, so it was freshly blessed—and poured a line on the floor. Stepping back, she left the lid off in case she needed a weapon. The sacred liquid wouldn't stop the thing, but it would burn it, giving her time to pull out her steel pipe.

The demon took a deep breath, murmured something, then walked right over the Holy Water, purposely stepping on it as it passed. Still in its mortal guise, it grimaced, then looked up at her. Its eyes had shifted for a fraction of a second from human to that weird goat-slit thing, then back.

"Hell no longer owns my soul," it said simply.

She blinked. "I've never seen anything like that before." Except she had. "Wait a minute—a Fallen can do that."

"You know I am not one of them."

No, it wasn't. Her experiences with the Fallen had ensured that she'd never be fooled again. "How many of your kind are there?"

"A few hundred in this country, more around the world.

There are not that many of us. Breaking our shackles is uncommon, and it immediately marks us for death."

"Is there some special way you do that?" she asked.

"Yes."

Apparently the Four wasn't going to share that with her. Now she was back to the original dilemma: what to do with the demon. *Teacher*.

Riley recapped the Holy Water and returned it to the pack. "I need to think about this."

The demon's tight posture relaxed a notch. "I understand. But if you tell anyone I am here, it is likely other trappers will come after me. Or those hunters from Rome certainly will. They don't understand us Unbounds."

Unbounds. Now this kind of fiend had a name. And the demon was correct: The Vatican's Demon Hunters had only one way to deal with Hellspawn: kill them. It didn't matter if they were the small ones that stole jewelry or the huge ones—dead was the only way Rome tolerated them.

Den, I wish you were here. Her fiancé would have a lot better idea of how to handle this. In fact, she bet his grand master training had covered this situation. He'd learned all the secret and arcane knowledge about Heaven and Hell while she'd gotten the "here's how to trap a Pyro-Fiend and not get fried" lectures.

Trust your heart. It was her father's voice, and Paul Blackthorne never steered her wrong, even from beyond the grave.

Riley sighed. "Okay, I'm going to act like I don't know you're here, and I'll trust your word that you won't harm these kids. If I find out you are, I will hunt you down and kill you myself. Rome will never get the chance. Do you understand?"

The demon nodded solemnly. "I understand. I know how many Archfiends you have killed, so that is no idle threat." Then its shoulders relaxed even more. "I won't hurt them, I swear. They are the brightness in this world. The future."

There was so much truth in his words.

"Then we'll be fine. Out of curiosity, are you male or female?"

"Male."

"And your name?"

The demon seemed pleased she'd asked. "My old name is no more. My new one is Isra. It means freedom."

That wasn't surprising.

"You changed your name when you broke the bond with Hell."

He nodded. "You may not realize it," Isra said, "but we are the same, Blackthorne's daughter. We have both come out of the pit, and we both seek the Light. We will either triumph or fail, but at least we made the journey."

"The Prince is never going to forget either of us."

"No," Isra said, more solemn. "He will not. However, I will savor every free day I have. You should do the same."

After another long look at the enigmatic demon, Riley left him behind in his colorful classroom, even as her heart and mind warred with each other. She should have done her duty and removed the Mezmer from the building, protected the students.

But as a master trapper, she'd learned that things weren't always black and white. At best, they were a confusing shade of muddied gray. Last December, an Archfiend had sought her revenge because Riley had killed the she-demon's "mate." A mate that a demon wasn't supposed to have, not if the Demon Trappers Guild or the Vatican were to be believed.

Now it appeared that Lucifer wasn't as all-powerful as they'd thought, and that some of his Hellspawn had broken free and quietly integrated themselves into human society. All Riley knew was that for the time being, Isra's secret was safe.

Unless he breaks his word.

Chapter Three

Pluscarden Abbey
Scotland

If someone had told Denver Beck that a poor boy from South Georgia would spend a full week hanging with Benedictine monks at an abbey in northern Scotland, he'd have told them they were drunk or stoned. Or both. Nevertheless, he had done just that at Pluscarden Abbey. Now that he was at the end of his studies as a grand master initiate, this last week was a time to reflect, maybe even say a few prayers of his own.

The abbey had been established in the thirteenth century and became a Benedictine priory in 1453. It'd had its ups and downs, but as best as Beck could tell, these monks had been sending prayers to Heaven for well over five hundred years. It was sobering to realize that was almost twice as long as the United States had been in existence.

Beck had found it easy to fall into the monastic routine. He'd rise at 4:15 when a monk politely tapped on his door, dress, and then make his way down to Vigils at half past to listen to the good friars chant their Latin. He knew a few words now, though not as much as his fiancée, so he followed along as best he could. Even if he didn't understand every word, there was a pure sort of magic in their voices that never ceased to run chills down his spine.

After Vigils, the monks would spend roughly an hour in peaceful contemplation. Beck did the same, but in his own way: He took himself on a walk in the frosty morning air. Sunrise was an hour away, so he had the joy of watching the day begin as he hiked on the vast grounds surrounding the abbey. He found that it was on these walks that his mind and body continued to deal with all that had been thrown at him over the past year. Over the course of this week, he'd come to understand why he'd been given this most daunting task, and why he had to undertake it.

The job of grand master wasn't for everyone. In fact, you had to have killed a Fallen angel to even be considered for the position, and the odds of surviving such a battle were damned slim. If you did survive but were injured, you were sent to Hell where Lucifer did his best to claim your soul for eternity. Some died and their souls were lost.

Others did gain their freedom from Hell, their souls still their own. Of those, a few went insane after witnessing the horrors of the pit. The rare few that made the final cut, and wanted to take on this most special job, were sent to Scotland to train. Even after all the months of study and preparation, it was not a foregone conclusion—the initiate had to make a final decision to take up the Task, as the grand masters called it, or to step away.

In all his wildest dreams, Beck had never believed that he would slay a rogue Fallen, one of Hell's craziest bastards, who'd declared war against Lucifer. Seriously injured, he'd been sent to Hell, and only because of his dead mother's efforts had he found his way back to the land of the living.

He knew that being a grand master was like walking a cosmic tightrope in gale-force winds. It would be his task to balance the Light and the Dark. He'd interact with angels and demons, heads of state, everyday people. He'd have to discover ways to keep Hell in check and to prevent certain antagonistic angels in Heaven from pushing for war—a conflict that would decimate this world.

Sometimes, deep in the night when he lay in his bed, staring at nothing, Beck was sure someone had made a mistake about him. Other times he knew, deep down, that this was his destiny.

As the abbey's day progressed, the monks would continue their prayers, ending with Compline in the evening. Devotion and work, a simple life. There was much to envy here. As Beck saw it, one of his tasks as grand master was to ensure that these holy men had the freedom to live as they chose without interference from anyone, be that Heaven or Hell.

Now, as the sun rose through the trees in the distance and bird song filled the woods, Beck turned back toward the abbey, knowing he'd miss this place. Maybe next year when he returned to Scotland for more training, he could spend time here. Since the monastery had a separate residence for female guests, Riley could even come with him. He hoped she'd find her own kind of peace here just as he had. It troubled him that in the last few months she'd grown more solemn, less full of joy. Weighed down by the responsibilities of a master trapper, and by being Paul Blackthorne's daughter.

Once they were married, he'd try hard to bring laughter back into their lives. God knew they both needed it for the years that lay ahead.

~~*

Once Beck had packed his belongings, said his goodbyes, and caught the train south, he made sure to pay attention to the magnificent scenery. Scotland held a beauty that was hard for him to put into words, always stunning in its own way, whether it was raining, snowing, or brilliantly sunny. On one of the hills in the distance, tiny white dots of sheep moved at random. Farther on, there were snow-capped mountains, rugged in their beauty. Towns and villages passed by, often just a blur through the train window This place had become a second home, and he would miss it.

They'd just gone over a grade crossing where a beer lorry waited patiently for the train to pass when he felt something cold reach out to him. Something far too familiar, and unwelcome. When he looked across the table at the previously empty seat opposite him, he swore under his breath. A quick glance proved that the other passengers in the train car were ignoring the newcomer, or for those more sensitive, unconsciously shifting away from his presence.

"You know, my day was perfect up until now," Beck said, folding his arms over his chest.

Lucifer, the Prince of Hell, smirked. He wore his usual dark clothes, his black hair collar length, midnight-blue eyes sparkling with a blend of both mischief and malice. "Ah, my favorite grand master wannabe."

"What brings you to paradise?" Beck asked, his good mood souring instantly.

"This is Scotland, if you haven't noticed."

"Same thing."

"Cocky as ever, I see. That will change soon. Frankly, I can't wait until you speak that oath."

Beck knew he shouldn't take the bait, but he couldn't resist. "And why is that?"

"Because that gives you more to lose," the Prince replied. "The sum of a human's resistance is easily weighed against how much he or she has to forfeit. I find the right lever, and a soul is easy to claim."

"Some souls, not all."

"Paul Blackthorne wasn't strong enough. Why do you think you will be?"

Beck didn't like hearing his friend's name on this abomination's lips, but he held his temper. The Prince would poke at you until you lost your cool, then maneuver you into doing something you'd best have avoided. When he didn't reply, the Adversary went for another target.

"I have been keeping an eye on Master Blackthorne—the one that is still alive, that is."

"I hear she's doin' well," Beck countered.

"Until today. She made a mistake, one that may cost her dearly."

Beck's fear kicked in, but he tried to cover it. "We all make mistakes, you included. The difference is that most of us learn from them."

The taunting expression in Lucifer's eyes turned flinty. "You skate a fine line, mortal. There is nothing to keep me from killing you at any time I wish."

"I know, but then you'd lose the chance to mess with my head."

"Yours is only one of countless heads I can 'mess with,' as you put it."

"Yes, but how many are gonna be a grand master?"

"True," the Prince conceded. "I'm glad you didn't accept my offer when you were in Hell. When the time comes, your fall from grace will be almost as dramatic as mine. I, for one, will welcome that moment."

"You have nothin' I want, angel."

Lucifer raised an eyebrow. "Not even the identity of your father?" he said slyly.

Before Beck could reply, the Prince of Hell vanished as quietly as he'd first appeared. The few passengers who had felt something wrong began to relax now, resuming their conversations.

You bastard. I bet Heaven threw a party the day you left.

Lucifer knew how to get to him, though. Beck had always wanted to know the name of his father, maybe even meet the man. But no matter what the Prince believed, it was not worth his immortal soul. He returned to enjoying the scenery, knowing that usually the best way to deal with that infernal pest was to ignore it. Still, he made a mental note to check in with Riley. Lucifer often knew things before anyone else did.

Demon Central
Atlanta, Georgia

After the shock of discovering a "free" demon, the rest of Riley's day had seemed mundane—paperwork, more paperwork, then trappings with her apprentices. To her relief, the one in the early evening had forced her to cancel Mort's next lesson. Riley'd made sure not to sound happy about that, but she was. She still had a dull headache from the night before.

This time it'd been Jaye's turn to trap a Three and she'd done it successfully. She'd also acquired a couple deep gouges on her arm from the Three's claws, so Riley made sure she'd been treated with Holy Water and warned her that she'd feel sick for the next couple of days.

"How bad?" Jaye asked, her face registering her worry.

"Because this is your first time at this, it's a light-case-of-the-flu type bad, but only a couple days' worth. Use fresh Holy Water every two or three hours and have your mom keep an eye on you. If the wound becomes infected, call me immediately."

Jaye looked up at her as she leaned against her car, Kurt and Richard hovering nearby. "This kind of thing can kill you," she said gravely.

Riley could hear the resignation in her voice. "Yes, it can if someone doesn't keep an eye on you. In your case, you'll feel icky and then you'll be good." She didn't bother to add that her apprentice would bear the scars for the rest of her life.

The young woman looked over at the two guys. "You had this happen too?" Two nods returned. She'd missed witnessing those injuries because she'd been taking care of her mom. "Well, then I'll just suck it up."

"Best way to face it," Richard replied. "Part of the job."

Jaye sighed. "Can I go home now? I'm not feeling good."

Riley nodded. "You guys go on. I'll take the demon to Fireman Jack. Just make sure someone is watching over our friend here."

"Consider it done," Kurt replied.

Riley turned back to Jaye now. "I'll have the Guild's doc swing by and check on you later tonight. You've never met Carmela, so it's time that happened."

"You'll like her. She's cool," Richard added.

Jaye gave him a dazed look and didn't respond, then headed for her car, cradling her arm.

"I'll let you know how she's doing," Kurt said.

"Thanks," Riley replied.

As her apprentices pulled away in Kurt's car, she looked down at the slavering demon inside the steel-mesh bag. "Boy, do you stink. What do you do, bathe in sulfur?"

In response, the fiend howled at her, all its rank fur rippling to cause the stench to increase exponentially. Holding her breath, Riley dragged the thing to the rear of her car, then deadlifted it into the trunk, trying not to gag in the process. Luckily, she'd been hefting Beck's weights each morning, making this feat possible—only a year earlier, it wouldn't have been.

She could have asked one of the guys to help her, but it felt good to handle her own demons. Plus, she was worried about Jaye. That first wound was always a shock. Now Jaye knew she wasn't invincible, that she could get hurt, and that this was the price you paid for hunting Lucifer's monsters. Some trappers dealt with that okay, but others didn't. Time would tell how it was for Riley's red-haired apprentice.

The Three snarled and clawed at the bag, gnawing on the metal rings as if it could get loose. Riley slammed the trunk with more force than necessary, and then, feeling ornery, she opened it and slammed it again. Inside, the demon howled, long and mournful.

"Shut it, furball. You sliced up one of my people, so you get zip sympathy."

~~*

Once she'd sold the Three, Riley's least favorite time of day had finally rolled around. It was nearing ten when she parked her car in Beck's driveway, an early night by her standards. While she loved spending time with his rabbit, the rest of the evening would be impossibly lonely. It astounded her how quickly she'd become accustomed to having Beck around, sharing a life with him. He'd sit across from her at the breakfast table, razzing her about not being a morning person. Send her text messages during the day. Cuddle with her at night.

Then he wasn't here anymore—off to Scotland because somehow fate had decided this man was to become a grand master. It felt selfish to want him all to herself, but sometimes Riley gave in to that totally self-centered emotion. It was hard to share him with so many when he was as much a part of her life as her next breath.

Riley had vainly tried to fill her free time to stave off that loneliness. Even though she'd graduated from high school and was no longer taking a college course, she still had Latin homework, courtesy of Mort. Then there was spell practice, trapper paperwork, laundry, and housecleaning. Still, without Beck, she was lonely.

After dealing with the alarm, Riley refilled her pack with supplies before placing it by the front door. Toting Rennie out of her cage in the second bedroom, she put the rabbit in the larger playpen in the living room. Riley's shower came next, followed by feeding both herself and Rennie. Then it was couch time for both of them.

In between fawning over Beck's beloved bunny, she checked her e-mail messages. His *were always* read first, even if there was an URGENT BULLETIN from the National Guild. Those people were a lot less of a problem now, but she still distrusted bureaucracy. There was a great deal of irony there, as she was now part of that same bureaucracy.

Beck's e-mail spoke of his train trip back to the manor, how he'd enjoyed most of it. He didn't explain why there was a portion of the trip he hadn't enjoyed, but she knew he'd tell her down the line. In many ways, he was still a very private person, and she respected that.

Riley wrote a quick reply, letting him know about Jaye's injury and that all was good with the house and Rennie. She knew better than to mention Isra in an e-mail—the Vatican had big ears. Once she'd sent the message, the loneliness grew.

With a sigh, she realized she hadn't heard from Kurt so she called him.

"Hey, boss," he said.

"This is a welfare check on Jaye. She settled in with her mom and doing okay?"

"Oh crap, I was supposed to call you. Sorry! Jaye's fine, but she's not at home. She spaced off that her mom was at her aunt's house tonight because of a dialysis appointment in the morning, so I kidnapped our fearless trapper and brought her to my place. The Guild's doc has been here and gone. Now we're watching *Ghostbusters*."

Riley smiled at that image. "Which one?"

"The newer one. She's enjoying it, I think, at least in between chills and trying not to throw up."

Riley remembered that part all too well. "Thank you. My level of worry just dropped to zero."

"No sweat," he said. "Jaye was all for staying on her own, but there was no way that was going to happen. She can be too stubborn sometimes."

"I heard that!" their subject called out in the background.

"You know what to look for if she's getting sicker. The Holy Water I gave her was freshly blessed, so it should do the trick. Call me if you need anything. I mean it."

"I will. Don't worry, boss, we got this covered."

"Oh, and you are off the hook for tomorrow. I'll let Harper know you're keeping an eye on her."

"We'll make it a movie marathon, then. I'll send you updates."

"That's exactly what I want to hear. Later, guy."

After putting Rennie back into her cage, it was close to eleven thirty. Riley had run out of things to do, and that left her the one issue she tried to avoid: Isra the supposedly "free" demon. She'd gone back and forth over whether her decision to leave him at the school had been wise. For a time, she'd thought of dropping the dilemma in either Master Harper's or Grand Master Stewart's laps, but that plan held its own perils. What if they decided Isra had to go? Or what if the Vatican found out and sent someone to kill him? Would that be her ex-boyfriend Simon

Adler, now a lay exorcist, or one of the Demon Hunters?

From what she knew about Rome, it was a good bet they were already aware the Unbounds existed, because there was little those folks didn't know. Nevertheless, the Vatican's stance on demons was ironclad—that they were all destined for destruction. Could Rome accept the idea that one of Lucifer's henchmen gave his boss the middle finger and took off on his own?

"No," she muttered to herself. *Not likely.*

After flip-flopping a dozen times, Riley gave up. She'd done what she thought best at the time, and she would have to live with the consequences. Hopefully those consequences didn't result in any students being harmed.

Making sure the doors were locked, she climbed into bed. Scooping up Beck's pillow, she pulled it to her chest and inhaled his scent, as a hint of his aftershave still lingered. She'd purposely not washed the case after he'd left in December for that very reason.

Two nights from now, she'd be on a plane heading east across the Atlantic, where Beck would hold her close, remind her that life was more than just trapping demons. In his own quiet way, he'd help her navigate all the changes they both faced. First, his investiture as a grand master. Then their marriage.

That would be the most welcome change of all.

~~*

International Guild Manor House
Scotland

Beck quickly learned that his habit of rising with the abbey's monks meant that he would wake at 4:15, even when he didn't have to. He'd always been an early bird—unlike Riley, who would sleep in if he let her be.

So, at 4:16 a.m. Beck found himself staring at the ceiling in his room. Sighing, he rose, dressed, and retrieved the book he'd been reading. He silently made the trek down the three flights of stairs to the main floor, then down another long hallway to the Guild's library. He creaked open the heavy wooden door and found that the massive space was chilly, as expected.

Flicking on a few lights, he decided not to turn on the portable heaters or light the fireplace. Instead, he collected one of the woolen lap robes stacked on a shelf nearby and placed it on the seat of his favorite leather wingback chair. Then he paused, as was his habit, and took in the scene around him. Most people wouldn't bother—it was just an old library after all. He took in the stacks of shelves, both on the main floor and up on the second floor, accessible by a narrow cast-iron stairway. A catwalk ran around the room, the ironwork meticulously maintained. A glance up at the glass dome showed that night still reined outside.

Beck settled into the chair, the lap robe in place to ward against the chill. A click of the Tiffany lamp on the small table next to him and he was ready. With more than the usual solemnity, he opened the book at the aged leather bookmark.

He was now reading at a pace that pleased him. He'd never be as fast as other folks, but still, it was quite an accomplishment for someone who couldn't figure out a menu a year or so before. Much of that change had come because of Riley and her father, neither of whom had ever talked down to him. Instead, they'd patiently instructed him, taking it at his pace. Once that door had been cracked, Beck had shoved it open with a thirst for knowledge that knew no boundaries.

Because it was still an effort to read, he'd found that he retained the knowledge more than others, mostly because he had to concentrate on every word. The book in his lap, a reprint of *All Manners of Demons and Angels*, had been written in the late nineteenth century by a man named Arthur Varnery. Varnery's brother, Edwin, had died at the hands of a Fallen, and to honor that sacrifice, Varnery spent two decades of his life researching and writing about the power struggle between Heaven and Hell. This wasn't the only book on the subject that Beck had read— he'd been assigned a staggering amount of homework over the last seven months—but this one he'd chosen on his own. It'd been a slow read, maybe twenty pages or so a night, partly because the prose was so dense. Beck was currently re-reading the ninth chapter, for it had intrigued him more than the others. One particular phrase had caught his notice because he wasn't quite sure what to make of it:

The madness of angels in highest Heaven, the cunning of demons in darkest Hell. The two are separate, yet twain, for the Light gives and the Light destroys, all in equal measure.

Since it had puzzled him, he'd written it out on a piece of paper and stuck it in his wallet. Once a day or so, he'd pull out the paper, study it, then put it back. Who knew, maybe by the end of his life he'd have a clue what it meant.

It was close to six when the library door creaked open. At this hour, it was probably Grand Master Kepler, the archivist for the International Guild. As Beck's granddaddy would say, Kepler was "older than dirt." In his mid-seventies, he moved at a snail's pace now and had served as a grand master since his early twenties—over fifty years.

But to Beck's surprise, the man who joined him wasn't Kepler, but Trevor MacTavish. Trevor was a lean, muscled sort of man with a ponytail of silver hair and blue eyes. He was Beck's superior, one of the most respected grand masters in the International Guild. This morning, he looked half-awake.

"How soon can ya be packed and ready to leave?" he asked. Trevor's lack of courtesy was unusual, as was the anxiety in his voice.

"Fifteen minutes. Why?"

"We've been *requested* by the Vatican. They have a matter of some concern they wish ta speak ta us about," he said, his strong Scottish brogue overlaying the words.

The Vatican? Did this have something to do with Riley? *No.*

If Rome had an issue with her, as they'd had in the past, they would have contacted her directly. As of yesterday morning, everything had been fine in Atlanta. Still, Lucifer had issued that cryptic warning . . .

"They bother to tell you exactly what this is about?" Beck asked as he headed out of the library with Trevor at his side.

"Ya know them. They're close-mouthed even if ya ask what time it is. In this case, all I was told is that the matter was vitally important and that a *jet* would be waitin' for us at the nearest airport."

Beck came to a halt at that news. "They sent a jet for us?"

"Aye, laddie. That should tell ya somethin' is verra wrong."

Chapter Four

When Beck asked how often a charter jet arrived at a dinky airport in Scotland, Trevor said he'd hadn't heard of it happening before, which is why there was a curious group of gawkers eyeing the plane when they arrived at the airfield. To their dismay, those onlookers received no hint as to who owned the plane, as there was no Vatican City seal on the fuselage.

After a solemn middle-aged man in a black suit checked Beck's and Trevor's passports, he ushered them onboard and ensured their luggage was stowed, all without saying one word. Ten minutes later, they were in the air.

In retrospect, Beck was glad he'd reported Lucifer's recent appearance the moment he'd arrived at the manor, just in case this trip did have something to do with Riley. It probably didn't, but one could never be too careful.

At the news of their nemesis's choice of public transportation, Trevor had just sighed. "The Prince is like some damned annoyin' relative ya can never shake free of. He's always underfoot, at least when it comes ta the pair of ya."

Now, as the jet climbed higher, Beck studied the interior, sure he had to be dreaming. The aircraft had six seats, two in the front that faced each other and four in the back. Their dour escort had taken one of the rear seats—and still had yet to say a word. Beck and his superior had chosen the two seats in the front. He eyed the icons on the armrest with no notion of what all the little buttons meant. He certainly wasn't about to press one without knowing what it did.

Trevor smiled over at him. "Not quite what yer used ta?"

"No. First plane I was on was in the Army, and it sure as hell wasn't like this. Never been in one this small, or this fancy."

"Aye." Trevor showed him how to deploy his table, what the seat adjustments would do, things that like. The grand master had always smoothed the way for Beck, whether it was introducing him to VIPs or helping him function at a dinner party that had too many forks and spoons. This man was one of the people Beck would miss the most when he left for home—not only his superior, but a good friend.

Trevor called to the man in the back, "How long of a flight do we have?"

"Two and a half hours," the black-suited man replied.

So he isn't mute. Could have fooled me.

"We're headed ta Rome, right?" Trevor prodded.

"No, Prague."

When Beck raised an astonished eyebrow at the elder grand master, he received a shrug in response.

"Any way ya can tell us what we're facin'?" Trevor asked.

The man shook his head.

"Well then, that's helpful," the grand master said, his tone tart with annoyance.

Knowing that whatever lay before them probably wouldn't involve much sleep, Beck covered himself in a blanket, laid his seat back, and let his eyes drift shut for a quick combat nap. Sometimes it was best just to shut down until the whole story was laid out at your feet.

Václav Havel Airport
Prague, Czech Republic

Their arrival in Prague was much like their departure from Scotland—uneventful. No lines at immigration and customs because the Vatican knew how to make bureaucratic miracles happen. Their nearly silent escort had been joined by an equally grim-faced driver who drove them deep into the Czech country-side in an unmarked SUV. Like in Scotland, there was snow on the ground and the temperature was hovering just above freezing. He watched with interest as they drove through small villages and past picturesque farms. Curious, Beck dug in his backpack and retrieved a compass, which told him they were headed north.

About ninety minutes later the SUV turned on to a road sheltered on both sides by rows of ash trees and their massive branches bowed over the vehicle, weighed down by crisp, fresh snow. Occasionally some would fall and cover the windshield, though it didn't seem to bother the taciturn driver.

A few miles down, they reached a roadblock manned by the Czechoslovakian military. Beck counted half a dozen soldiers, all armed and bundled up against the cold. There were no smiles, no joking around between compatriots. After their passports had been checked and their IDs verified, the SUV was allowed to drive on. Another four miles or so and they reached yet another checkpoint, this one with a dozen equally somber soldiers, all lined up across the road.

"Whatever's goin' on is really bad news," Beck said under his breath. "They don't haul out the army just for the hell of it."

Trevor nodded. "I agree."

"We will walk from here," their escort announced as he opened his door.

As he climbed out of the SUV, Beck pulled on his backpack. He probably wouldn't be running into any demons out here, but you never knew. Old habits were hard to break, especially when they kept you alive.

He'd figured the air would be crisp and clear, what you'd expect in the countryside. It was crisp all right, but a faint—and familiar—stench hung in the air. One you'd never expect out here.

As they approached the checkpoint, Beck spied a man stepping around the soldiers and heading toward them. Even though this was a good friend, one he'd bonded with in battle,

Beck's nerves went into overdrive.

"I wonder what brings the captain of the Demon Hunters way out here," Trevor said quietly.

They were about to find out.

Captain Elias Salvatore usually had a big smile when he and Beck met up, but not this time. Even more strange, he was not in his uniform, but dressed in a heavy black jacket, slacks, and boots. His dark hair was longer now, skimming the top of the jacket's collar, and he'd shaved his goatee.

"Grand Master MacTavish, Beck," Elias said, stepping forward to shake hands with both in turn. "You made good time."

"Aye," Trevor replied. "So what's this all about?"

"We're not sure," Elias replied. "That's why you're here."

Fear. That's what Beck saw in his friend's eyes, a warrior who had battled Hell's worst. What would it take to scare the leader of the Vatican's Demon Hunters?

As they followed Elias off the road and up a snowy hill dotted with occasional shrubs and hardwood trees, the captain held his silence. Right before they reached the top, he came to a halt, as if reluctant to take any further steps.

Beck sniffed the air, detecting more of that familiar sickening odor. He gave Trevor a glance and the man nodded.

"Brimstone," the Scotsman said. "And smoke, I'd say. A lot of it."

"The stench has dropped considerably," Elias admitted. "It was way worse yesterday."

Which meant the Vatican had been sitting on this scene for at least twenty-four hours, probably hoping they wouldn't have to call in the grand masters. Rome had its pride just as much as any other religious institution.

"Neither I nor my superiors are sure what happened here. We have some ideas, but we need your expertise. Lives depend on your candor."

"As always, ya'll get that honesty," Trevor replied. "Whether ya like the answers or no."

"Understood."

With Elias in the lead, they reached the crown of the hill. He halted again, then gestured toward the valley below where the late morning sun glinted off the bright snow, at least where there still was some. To Beck, it looked as if someone had dumped black, steaming ash in the very center of that valley. The darkness spread outward, devouring the snow like a cancer. In the middle of that blackened area, a few stone buildings still stood, their roofs and windows gone.

A thin haze hung in the air like the smoke over a funeral pyre. The hair on the back of Beck's neck rose.

"Nothin' quite like that smell, is there?" Trevor murmured.

Elias shook his head, his expression mournful now. "This was a town of about twelve hundred people. We have no way of making a proper count of how many died. The bodies were incinerated, as were the majority of the buildings."

"This happen yesterday?" Beck asked.

"Three days ago. At first, the local authorities thought it was some sort of gas leak. It was the brimstone that finally convinced them to contact us."

"Any witnesses?"

"Two, but neither are capable of coherent speech. We're hoping that once the shock wears off we might get an idea of what happened here."

Beck let his gaze range across the destruction.

What the hell is this?

"I'm guessing ya've ruled out a natural disaster," Trevor said.

"Of course," a new voice said. "This is neither natural nor man-made."

Beck turned to find Father Rosetti in his trademark black cassock, but he wasn't the one who'd spoken. Standing next to him was someone *far* higher up on the Vatican's organizational chart. The cardinal's robe was black as well, but with scarlet piping and buttons. He wore a matching skullcap and a wide sash around his middle. His hair was steel gray and trimmed short, and his posture the kind that any drill sergeant would love.

"Father Rosetti," Beck said, nodding in acknowledgement.

"Grand Master Initiate," he replied politely. His attention moved to Beck's superior. "Grand Master MacTavish. Gentlemen, may I present His Eminence, Cardinal Christoph Richter."

One of the big dogs.

"Cardinal," Trevor replied, offering his hand. It was pointedly ignored. After an awkward moment, he lowered it and added, "I read yer report on the increase in demonic possession in Africa. Quite illuminatin'."

Richter frowned, ignoring the compliment. "What do you make of this?"

He had a strong German accent and appeared to be a man of little humor, but then Rosetti had seemed like that once too. At least until he and the trappers had downed a few beers and traded war stories. Beck suspected that would never happen with the cardinal.

"Can I go down there?" he asked, gesturing toward the blackened area.

"You are free to investigate, but don't walk out on that scorched area," Rosetti cautioned. "It appears solid, but it collapses. One of the first responders sustained horrific burns when he fell through."

Damn.

As Beck descended the hill through ankle-deep snow, brushing past blades of tall brown grass, Elias walked beside him. When they reached the bottom, Beck stilled his mind, listening. Nothing stirred. "There's no bird song. Even the air feels wrong."

"I noticed that as well. Usually the wildlife returns after a disaster, though our presence might inhibit them somewhat."

Beck stooped down. When he touched a few blades of dried grass, his fingers tingled and he yanked them back. "What the hell?" He shook out his hand to try to stop the ache. Finally, it lessened. "Any demons here recently?"

"According to the diocese in Prague, there was an increase in Hellspawn but it was months ago. The locals dealt with the problem. It's been pretty quiet ever since."

Beck shifted his pack off his shoulders and retrieved a fast-food napkin from inside. Plucking a few blades of the grass, he dropped them into the napkin and folded it up. After he'd carefully tucked it away in one of his pants pockets, he rose and found Elias watching him intently.

"What are you thinking?" the man asked.

"Nothin' yet. Maybe we can get some sort of readin' off that grass."

"It's not radioactive."

"That's good news, I guess."

As they hiked back up the hill to join the others, Beck asked, "What's with the cardinal? He a hard-ass?"

"Can be. He's pretty much convinced that Lucifer has declared war on us and that this is the result."

Beck shook his head. "I didn't get a sense of the Prince here. Trust me, I know how he feels."

"Probably best you *not* let the cardinal know just how plugged in you are with our enemy."

Beck huffed. "Not plugged in at all. I'm the one who got away and that pisses him off, so he likes to drop by every now and then and needle me. The way I figure it is if he's buggin' me, he's leavin' some other poor bastard alone."

Elias stifled a laugh, no doubt in deference to the situation.

"Any chance someone in this town got on the wrong side of Hell?" Beck asked. "Maybe made a deal with a Fallen and didn't follow through?"

"Possible. But you said it didn't feel like Hell."

"No, I said it didn't feel like the Prince," Beck explained. "Could easily be one of his big boys. Riley has a much better radar about those things than I do."

"Because she gave her soul to one?" Elias asked.

Beck shot him a hard stare. "No, because that same angel trained her how to locate demons—and how to kill them. She has this sixth sense about anythin' from Hell now and can spot one of theirs a mile away. That ability has kept her alive I don't know how many times."

"Understood. You know, you're a lot less volatile than you used to be," Elias said, a note of admiration in his voice. "More measured."

"Comes with bein' a grand master, I guess."

His friend smiled over at him now. "Don't tell my superiors, but I've always been fascinated by how the grand masters walk the line between Light and Dark. I don't know if I could do it."

"There are days I think the same."

They reached the crown of the hill and headed back toward the others. It didn't appear that Trevor and the cardinal had found common ground, Richter looking decidedly uncomfortable.

"If the cardinal isn't good with us grand masters, why were we called in on this?"

"Because the Holy Father insisted that you be."

The pope? Well, hell. "Then let's go tell yer cardinal what I don't know, which is damned near everythin'."

As he'd anticipated, Richter's expression went from somber to disgusted as he listened to Beck's report.

"That is the best you can do?" the cardinal demanded, as if he'd expected the grand masters to clear up this mystery simply by showing up at the scene.

"It's not Hell," Beck repeated.

"Of course it is. Who else would create such destruction?" Richter said, incredulous. "What about you, MacTavish?"

That's Grand Master MacTavish to you, asshole. Instead of voicing his anger, Beck ground his teeth, keeping his temper in check.

"I agree with Beck," Trevor replied. "I don't think it's anythin' ta do with Lucifer. Not his style."

"You'd say that, wouldn't you?"

Beck'd had about enough of this guy. "What would be the point of lyin' about it?"

"It would benefit the Prince to have you misdirect our attention," Richter replied.

"From what?" Trevor demanded, finally losing his own

temper. "Ya don't have a damned clue what happened, or ya wouldn't have summoned us here in the first place."

The cardinal's eyes flashed in response but as he opened his mouth to reply, Beck jumped in. "Look, we can argue about this all day, but people died here and none of us want that to ever happen again. So stop treatin' us like the enemy and tell us what's really goin' on."

There was a sharp intake of breath from Rosetti. Maybe one shouldn't get in a cardinal's face like that, but Beck didn't care. Not when the ashes of the dead were lying only a short distance away.

Cardinal Richter turned his full attention to him now. It looked as if Beck was about to get one helluva dressing down, but instead, the cardinal sighed long and low.

With a quick glance at Trevor, he admitted, "There've been more of these . . . incidents. Our scholars have no notion of what is destroying these towns. It *has* to be Lucifer's doing—there is no other explanation."

"How many others?" Trevor asked.

No reply. So much for a two-way conversation.

"Perhaps the entire town refused the Prince's offer of protection and he destroyed them because of it," Elias suggested.

"Has that ever happened before?" Beck asked.

There were looks among those more learned than he was.

"No, not that *our* records show," Trevor replied. "What about Rome's?"

Cardinal Richter shook his head. "Until we learn exactly what happened here, we have to assume it is of an infernal nature."

"Fair enough," Beck conceded reluctantly. "Now about those other towns—"

The cardinal waved them off. "Clearly you will be of no further value to us." He turned and swept away in a swirl of black, leaving them behind.

"Well, that was helpful," Beck grumbled. He noticed his superior was studying him intently. "Did I go too far?"

"No, lad. Not at all," Trevor replied. "If I ever had any doubts that ya were chosen ta be a grand master—and I've not had any, I might add—challengin' that man would have put those doubts to rest." He looked over at Elias and Rosetti. "So now that Richter's done his posturin', any chance the four of us can talk about this . . . *privately?*"

A quick look passed between the priest and the captain of the demon hunters.

"Let's head back to Prague. There's a restaurant near the airport that might fit our needs perfectly," Rosetti replied.

"As long as there's beer, I'm good," Beck said. He looked back toward where the dead city sat below the hilltop. Maybe he'd have more than one.

Chapter Five

Beck's House
Atlanta, Georgia

"Hey, it's me. Just checking on the patient," Riley said, trying to sound cheery and failing. It was just too early to go there.

Kurt's slightly groggy voice replied, "Jaye's alive, though currently asleep. The fever wasn't as bad as I figured it would be and the claw marks are already beginning to close. She lucked out this time."

"That's what I like to hear. How's she taking this?"

"Soberly, and with great reflection. I remember you warning us that the first serious wound really sends a message," Kurt replied. "Well, she got that message, has processed it, and is moving on."

"Awesome. How soon do you think she'll be ready to trap again?"

"Probably tomorrow."

"I will trust your judgment on that. If she needs another day, no problem. Thanks for keeping an eye on her."

"Not a hassle. She's fun to talk to. Never really realized that when we're trapping—she's so quiet. Get Jaye away from the job and she opens up."

Since Riley'd caught the appreciative looks Kurt had been shooting his fellow apprentice, maybe it was more than that. "If you need anything, let me know."

"Will do. See you tomorrow."

Riley pulled out a carton of orange juice, poured a glass, and then settled in front of the computer. A message from Beck sat at the top of the queue, followed by one from her buddy Peter King.

Beck's was short: The Vatican had asked him and Trevor to help them with some matter, and it was so urgent they'd sent a jet to get them. He knew nothing more than that and would contact her when he had the chance. Told her not to worry if she didn't hear from him for a while.

"The Vatican?" she muttered. That wasn't good news.

At best, the International Guild and the Church had an uneasy relationship. Since the grand masters' mission was to keep the Light and Dark in balance, occasionally they butted heads with the Holy See. Sometimes Rome thought MacTavish and his people were useful; other times they were more antagonistic. A few in Rome still believed that the grand masters worked for Lucifer, which was total B.S.

Riley would always remember Father Rosetti's outright hostility toward Grand Master Stewart and herself when the Demon Hunters had first come to Atlanta. Subsequent events had altered that, but it'd taken the near destruction of the world to do so.

She sent back a quick note to her fiancé, told him she missed him, to be very careful, and that she'd see him soon. What else could she say? On a whim, Riley sent a picture of the wedding cake she'd picked out, even though Beck had left all the planning in her hands. As he'd put it, "We can eat stale cupcakes and I won't care, as long as you and I are hitched." Typical guy.

Peter's e-mail was chatty. His advanced placement tests had granted him sophomore status—his grade point average was off the charts—and he was buried in the latter half of his second semester at Georgia Tech. Because of her responsibilities as a master and his as a student carrying a full course load, their opportunities to hang together had been seriously curtailed. It was one of the things she missed most—spending time with friends who weren't trappers. The job always took a toll, one way or another.

Dashing out a quick response, and regretting she hadn't taken more time on it, Riley headed to work. There were demons to trap and all that jazz. And knowing Mort, he'd find some way to test her warding skills after the meeting tonight. The man was relentless, which was one of the reasons she was still alive.

~~*

It was just after noon when Riley received the text about the Pyro-Fiend. Luckily, she and Richard were already in Woodstock on another trapping run, so they headed toward a restaurant located near Kennesaw State University. For some reason, college students seemed to attract Hellspawn, and no one knew why.

Now, as she stood inside the restaurant, Riley knew this was going to be anything but a simple trapping. "You have got to be kidding me," she muttered, staring up at the fiend.

From behind her, Richard began to chortle.

"It's not funny." That only made him chortle louder.

The crimson demon had managed to crawl its way up onto an exposed ceiling rafter of a popular Mexican restaurant. These kinds of fiends—technically classified as a Grade Two—resembled creepy rubber dolls. This one was about seven or so inches tall, with horns and a forked tail, most peoples' notion of what the Devil might look like. Riley wondered if that was Lucifer's inside joke. This Hellspawn's talent was burning things. A bunch of them had torched the Tabernacle last year while Riley and the rest of the Guild had been inside. Trappers had died, and for that reason alone she hated Pyro-Fiends.

After it'd dropped a few red and orange fireballs on the diners, the restaurant had emptied out like a dorm on the last day of school. Which left Riley, Richard, and Steve, the manager, staring up at the thing.

Of course, the restaurant's patrons were now clustered in front of the floor-to-ceiling windows, noses pressed up against the glass. Heaven forbid they put a safe distance between themselves and Hell's version of a military-grade flamethrower.

"Funny, I do not remember this trapping scenario being covered in the Demon Trappers Manual," Richard said. "Or in any of your lectures, Master Blackthorne." He was clearly enjoying this absurd situation far too much.

Riley gave him the evil eye. "Mostly because it isn't the norm, at least not for this kind of Hellspawn."

"Really?" he said, all innocence.

Yeah, Richard was going to be cleaning the demon cages for the next week—he just didn't know it yet.

Fortunately for them, this was a younger Pyro-Fiend, so its fireballs were more golf-ball sized than like a cantaloupe. They still burned anything they touched, scorching tables and chairs and making big black patches on the concrete floor. The way to stop the fiend was to lob a "snow globe" sphere *above* it. Ideally, the globe would break and generate a nice snowfall, which cooled the demon's fires. Then the trapper just stuffed it in a warded container and the job was done. But a snow globe was impossible because of the firebug's location, which was probably why the dratted thing was high above them.

As she glared at the fiend, it grinned in response. "Yeah, you know what you're doing," she murmured.

Riley briefly considered borrowing a ladder, but discarded the idea. By the time they got it in place and she'd climbed up, the demon would have just scurried to another location. Fortunately, this fiend was nothing like the mature one she and Beck had trapped at Atlantic Station. That one had been a potential killer.

After generating another fireball on its palm, it threw it at the front counter, incinerating a rack of gift cards. Then it high-wire walked along a section of track lighting, all the while cackling like a demented grandmother. The only option they had was to get this thing on the ground.

Riley surveyed the damage so far. "You're going to be closing this restaurant for a few weeks, right?"

Steve nodded. "Oh yeah. The first few fireballs ensured that."

She pointed at the fire extinguisher that he'd been using on the table fires. "What kind is that?"

"Water."

She thought about that for a moment. "You have another one of those?"

Another nod and he headed off to retrieve it.

"What have you got in mind?" Richard asked.

Knowing the demon was listening, she said, "What I have in mind is that I'd love a glass of tea. Can you get me one?"

Richard stared at her like she was nuts, but went to the beverage bar anyway. "Sweet or unsweet?"

He was just yanking her chain now. "I was born in Chicago. That should help you make the proper choice, *Apprentice* Bonafont."

With a bark of laughter, Richard headed for the unsweetened tea dispenser. "You want lemon?"

"Sure, why not?" Riley glowered back up at the Pyro-Fiend now. "Hey, demon! What's up with you? You think you're a bird or something?"

A middle finger came her way, along with another fireball, which she easily ducked. When it slammed against the condiment station, Richard calmly dumped her iced tea on it to extinguish the flames, then went back for more of the beverage.

You had to love a guy who didn't lose his cool.

He returned with her drink at the same time as the manager arrived toting the second extinguisher. Riley took a long sip of the tea, set it aside, and then pointed to the extinguisher. "Give that to my smartass apprentice." She picked up the other one, checked that it was still workable, and then leaned close to the manager. "Can you cut the power to everything inside this restaurant?"

The man blinked, then gave a reluctant nod. "I can. We'll lose whatever's in the freezer, but it was headed for the trash anyway once this thing got in here."

"Okay, good. Cut the power and go outside. Stay out there until this is over. And try to keep those people away from the windows, if you can."

The manager disappeared behind the counter, and after a few seconds, the lights went out. Luckily it was a very sunny day, and with all the windows, they still had plenty of light. With one last look in their direction, Steve hurried out the front door, joining the other gawkers. He immediately set about trying to push them back, but Riley already knew he wasn't going to win that battle.

Beckoning Richard closer, she whispered her plan.

"You think that'll work?" he asked, dubious.

She shrugged. "Unless you want to go climbing up there and grab the thing."

"No, no way," he said, shaking his head vehemently. "I don't like heights."

"What? It's all of maybe fifteen feet off the ground," she teased.

"One foot is too much."

Once Richard had readied his extinguisher, Riley gave the signal and he sent an arc of liquid shooting high into the air. The demon skittered sideways, still cackling, not smart enough to realize what they were up to. Riley sent her stream arcing upward as well, hitting it head on. The demon sputtered, flailing, then moved right back the way it had just come. Richard's stream splattered against it, and the thing howled again, frantically trying to form fireballs.

They didn't have long before both of their extinguishers would empty, so Riley tried to angle her jet of water to coordinate with Richard's. That proved harder than she'd expected, her hand cramping around the handle. Finally, getting increasingly wet, they managed to drive the demon back along the track of lights.

Once their streams merged, the combined power flung the fiend against the front window with a decided *thunk*. As the Pyro swore in fluent Hellspeak, it slowly slid down the glass, making squeaky, squishy noises. Outside, bystanders shrieked and fled.

"Keep the pressure on him!" Riley called out. Trying not to lose her balance, she waded up to the Hellspawn, a bait box open. "Now!"

The instant Richard's stream ended, she grabbed on to the demon and rammed it inside the box, which was lined with dry ice. When she closed it, she made sure that the box was secured tightly and that all the magical charms around the edges were intact. As Riley turned, her right foot went out from under her. Cradling the bait box to her chest, she landed on her butt, hard. Water, and whatever chemicals might be mixed in with it, rolled down her cheek. Outside, a few onlookers pointed and laughed.

Sometimes all you could do was own the moment. So instead of being pissed, Riley smiled and waved, knowing all of this would be on the internet before she even got out the door.

Grinning, Richard offered his hand and pulled her up. "That was awesome!"

"That was sheer luck, and we both know it."

As Riley set the bait box on the nearest table, she could hear the demon mumbling inside, but it was out of luck. The magical charms the witches had created would keep it secured inside, while the dry ice dampened its ability to flame. Once she delivered it to Fireman Jack, it was no longer her problem.

When she made an attempt to shake the water out of her hair, Richard began to snicker. Then laugh.

"Hey, you're no better, dude."

"Tell me about it," he said. "Trappers score!" They slapped wet palms, sending water in all directions.

Ten minutes later, they left the restaurant with their catch still grumbling inside the bait box and gift cards that granted each of them a twenty-five percent discount for their meals over the next year. They'd even gotten a round of applause from the restaurant's patrons—who, sadly, wouldn't be dining here for a few months, at least.

~~*

Riley had given Richard the rest of the afternoon off, and he'd promised to drop by Kurt's to relay the news about the Pyro trapping. She, in turn, had immediately delivered a report to Master Harper in person in case anyone higher up in the restaurant organizational chart bitched about all the water. Harper had only shaken his head at the news, but as she left, she swore she saw a grin on his gnarly old face.

Once she'd showered, Riley drove to Angus Stewart's house. Since Mrs. Ayers, his housekeeper, wasn't home, Riley bypassed the kitchen and headed up to her rooms. There weren't many of her belongings left here now, most having been moved over to Beck's house by this point. Once they married, they'd have a garage sale to deal with the extra bed and some of the other furnishings.

There was one special item still here: her wedding dress.

Currently, it hung in the doorway between her bedroom and the turret room. Riley had moved it here because she didn't want Beck to see it when he returned home. She wasn't overly superstitious, but still, she wanted it to be a surprise.

The Quest for the Gown, as her friend Simi had called it, had been monumental. Simi's bridesmaid dress had been easy to find, but it'd taken them weeks to locate Riley's, especially since she'd refused to buy a new one. They'd gone to a dozen second-hand shops in their spare time, trying to find "the one." Finally, it'd revealed itself, tucked back in the corner of a shop in Chamblee.

The dress was a rich shade of champagne, with a sweetheart neckline, delicate lace appliques, and re-embroidered lace over the satin skirt. It just skimmed the floor and the long lace sleeves helped hide Riley's many scars. She had replaced the existing belt with a slim one of dark blue satin that tied in a bow in the back. It was the dress she'd always dreamed of and when she'd found it in the store, she'd cried. Simi, no doubt relieved that the quest was over, had cried along with her.

Now, as Riley stood in front of the gown, she still found it hard to believe that she was getting married. Her heart accepted it, rejoiced at the union, but her mind was still trying to cope. Part of it was her age; part of it was that she'd found the one man who understood her, who was willing to stand by her for the remainder of her days. Many people were never that fortunate, and she knew she was blessed.

All of Beck's and her friends had been supportive—they understood what she and Den had faced together. But others, like the nosy lady at the hair salon, had felt the need to weigh in with misguided warnings, like how Riley was much too young to marry. How she'd regret it down the line.

"Not a chance," she whispered, reaching out to the dress. Touching the lace made it real, tangible, just like the engagement ring on her left hand. This would be a major step out of her childhood, a bittersweet moment in many ways. Her mother would not be there to fuss with her gown, give her a last-minute hug. Her father would not walk her down the aisle. Though she knew they would be watching over her and Beck, it wasn't quite the same.

Sighing, Riley made her way downstairs and out into the backyard. She'd been in love with Stewart's flower gardens ever since she'd first seen them. Located at the rear of this massive old gem of a house, the tulips were already in bloom, the result of a warmer-than-usual spring. Masses of reds, yellows, and deep purples sat in clusters, waving in the breeze. By their wedding day, even more flowers would be strutting their stuff.

She came to rest near a pair of stone benches at the back of the garden. Here is where Mort would officiate the ceremony. She tried to imagine what it would be like, and failed.

"It better not rain," she muttered. By then, if they were lucky, the annual plague of sickly yellow-green pine pollen would be over.

Riley felt the presence of the witch even before she turned toward the house. Ayden's life energy always appeared bright green to her, and it wasn't any different today as her friend walked through the gardens.

"I was hoping I'd catch up with you," Ayden said. She wasn't dressed in her usual long skirt and blouse, but in a turtleneck and jeans, which meant the magic-infused tattoo on her upper chest and neck wasn't visible. Riley often used that skin art—which apparently changed images of its own volition—as a bellwether of the future. Not today.

Ayden's auburn hair, always a mass of curls, was up in a loose bun. She appeared more rested than earlier in the year, probably because there was less friction between her and a few of her fellow witches. Unfortunately, Riley had been the catalyst for that friction, what with her studies with both the necromancers and Ayden. Finally, her friend had convinced the others that it was to their benefit that Riley learn different kinds of magic. Still, it'd taken a lot of effort to gain that acceptance.

A light breeze ruffling their hair, they drifted to the nearest bench near a bed of brilliant tulips in full bloom. A dragon statue sat in the middle of the flowerbed, an iridescent gazing ball in one of its talons.

"Sorry I didn't get back to you the other day," Riley said as she sat down. "Magical Mort and his boss have been working me over."

Ayden joined her. "Still learning how to ward properly?"

"Yeah. I have a permanent headache now."

Her friend frowned over at her. "That the only reason?"

"No. I'm a bit spooked right now, and I don't know why."

"Wedding worries?"

"No. Not worried about Den's investiture, either. Something else is bugging me, but I don't know what it is."

"Your aura's wonky again," her friend observed.

"Wonky. Such a technical witchy term."

"More like a friend-worried-about-you term. Everything about you is off. You're less mouthy than usual, less upbeat. Something is weighing you down. Figure out what it is and fix it, because it's not doing you any favors."

"Thanks, Mom," Riley replied, with only a touch of sarcasm, because a smart person did not annoy a magic user who had stood up to Archfiends. Her reply earned her one of Ayden's raised eyebrows. On anyone else, it would be just a facial gesture, but not when it came to the witch. "All right, I'll try to figure it out.

So what are you doing here, besides checking on me?"

"Walking the grounds, trying to figure out the best way to lay a ward for the wedding. I have no doubt that Hell would love to crash this party."

Riley shook her head. "I don't think they will, at least not the Prince. He wants Den and me married. Means we have even more to lose, if that's possible."

"That doesn't keep one of his minions from trying to earn points with the boss." The witch hitched a shoulder. "But then, you know them better than I do. If I were your enemy, I'd rain hell down on your special day."

Sadly, Ayden had a point. "You sure know how to make a girl feel good, don't you?"

"Uh huh. Did you decide on a wedding rehearsal?"

"Not having one. Beck and I will meet with Mort before the ceremony and make sure we know what we're supposed to do. We're keeping it simple." Mostly because everything else in their lives was complicated.

"Okay. That makes things easier. Is Master Stewart here? I need to ask him some questions about his property."

"No," Riley said as she rose. The bench had been cold on her butt and she needed to get going. "Angus is in Scotland, visiting his family. He'll be at the investiture."

Ayden remained on the bench, apparently not eager to move. "Beck doing okay with all that?"

"He's having the usual doubts, magnified by the fact that there are only twenty-nine others of his kind in the world."

"Huge leap for a small-town Southern boy," the witch said. "Anyone would feel inadequate."

"He'll do fine," Riley insisted.

"Yes, he will. Him, I'm not worried about."

Riley frowned, getting the message. "So why are you wearing a turtleneck?"

Ayden looked up at her now. "It's cold."

"Not buying that. What's the tattoo showing?"

Her friend's expression flattened. "These weird, sort of white clouds. Nothing else, just clouds. I have no clue what it means."

Neither did she. "Well, I better get going. Will I see you tonight at the meeting?"

"Maybe."

Ah yes, her friend was back to her cryptic self. At least that part of the world was on track. "Oh, don't forget that I have a Magpie that will need to be inside the ward. He'll have one or both of the rings in his little bag. He's manic like that."

"Little demon inside, everything else outside. Got it."

From Ayden's tone, it sounded like the conversation was over. After giving her a quick hug, Riley headed toward her car, still ill at ease. She'd just reached the driveway when her phone rang.

"Blackthorne."

"Riley, it's Simon. You available for an exorcism this afternoon?"

She glanced at the clock on her phone. "Sure. I have a meeting at seven. Will we be done by then?"

"I hope so. This one's at a retirement home. Seems one of the old ladies has taken to hissing at the staff."

"They sure that's not dementia, or something to do with her medications?"

"Not with her flaming red eyes and three-inch claws."

"Ah, there you go. You want to meet there or at Beck's place?"

"At Beck's. I'm downtown right now. I can be there in about ten minutes."

"That works. See you then."

Chapter Six

Václav Havel Airport
Prague, Czech Republic

The restaurant was near the Prague airport, and it was a pizzeria, of all things. When the four of them had settled at a table and ordered their food, Beck noticed that their near-silent escort wasn't present.

"Our bird dog not hungry?" he asked.

"He said he would wait outside," Rosetti said. "He suspects we'll be talking about matters he'd rather not be involved in."

"Coverin' his ass, huh?"

"That's one way of putting it," Elias replied.

They fell silent when the beer was delivered. The restaurant was just beginning to fill up for the lunch hour, so they had purposely located themselves in a back corner to cut down on eavesdroppers.

"What weren't ya willin' ta share in front of the cardinal?" Trevor asked, keeping his voice low.

Rosetti sipped his beer, then set it down. "Another town was destroyed last night, nearly two thousand souls dead, and we have no idea why."

"Where?"

"Spain."

"You do any testin' at that site?" Beck asked.

"Yes," Elias replied. "Sulfur, usual organic compounds. We've talked to experts and they say the amount of energy required to destroy these cities and vaporize their citizens was off the charts."

"Any chance this is terrorism?" Beck asked. "Some sort of newfangled bomb?"

"No. There was no evidence of explosive residue."

Trevor leaned back in his chair, arms crossed over his chest. "All right, ya've laid yer cards on the table. What can the International Guild do for ya?"

From the look that was traded between the priest and the hunter, that was what they'd wanted to hear.

"You can consult your archives and see if there is any evidence that this sort of thing has happened before," Father Rosetti said. "We're running blind right now."

"We can do that. I'll also contact a few experts—discretely, of course—ta see if anyone has heard of such a thing."

"Thank you," the priest replied, relieved. "We are reaching out to sources outside the faith, as well."

Yeah, they're desperate.

"So," Beck began. "Richter is sure this is Hell's doin', but you two aren't. Yer keepin' an open mind. Why is that?"

It was Elias who answered. "The cardinal wants a fallback position if this all goes wrong. The grand masters give him cover if he doesn't manage this crisis correctly."

"Elias and I, we know how you people work," Rosetti added. "We may not agree on doctrine, or on your organization's 'relationship' with Hell, but we know you're good men. That you'll do anything it takes to keep more people from dying."

"Aye, that we will," Trevor said.

"There is another issue involved here." The priest looked over at Beck now. "One that affects you, in particular."

Beck knew where this was headed, and Rosetti didn't disappoint him.

"If neither the Holy See nor the Guild can solve this mystery on our own, we will be forced to ask Riley to visit one of these sites." The man shifted in his chair, uneasy. "Our superiors have seen the video of her alongside the Prince's executioner at the battle that defeated Sartael. The Fallen named Ori had obviously taught her how to fight Hellspawn, and he'd shared his angelfire with her. That sort of . . . intimate knowledge could allow her to discern matters of an ethereal nature that the rest of us might miss."

There was even more of an intimate connection between Ori and Riley than the priest had indicated, and Beck bet Rosetti had worked the rest out on his own. Perhaps Elias as well.

As if to confirm that, the priest added, "I suspect she had carnal relations with him. If that is the case, Grand Master Stewart didn't include that detail in his reports. Sometimes ignorance is best."

Beck gave a terse nod. "How many in Rome have similar suspicions?"

"Besides Elias and myself, a couple others. Richter is not one of them, but he is no fool. Fallen angels are extremely persuasive. Riley would not have been the first mortal to have been compromised, nor will she be the last."

Beck gave Trevor a quick glance. His superior knew the whole story. Riley had insisted on that, wanting no secrets from the grand masters.

"Curiously, out of such a forbidden relationship came good," Elias said. "Riley has her soul, Sartael was defeated, and Ori is dead."

"And Ori's soul is free. Well, at least he's not in Hell." At their puzzled looks, he explained. "Riley convinced Lucifer to let Ori seek the Light because that's all the Fallen wanted. He's in some sort of limbo place now, not in Heaven or in Hell."

Rosetti gave Elias a quick look. "Now that's interesting," he said. "I wonder what the Prince is up to."

"Who knows with that one?"

The server arrived then, bearing two pizzas. Once the woman had left the table, Beck asked, "If Riley does help you, can you promise she'll be treated fairly? That no one in Rome will be lookin' to even any scores?"

Rosetti sighed. "If it were my decision, I would say yes. However, I would not be the only one involved. Some in Rome do not trust her, even now."

"Well, if you can't promise there won't be blowback, then I doubt she'll be jumpin' on any plane to help y'all out."

"Then let's all pray that the last city has fallen and no more will die," the priest replied. He bowed his head, Elias joining him, and said a prayer to bless their food.

Once the prayer was complete, they ate in silence. Beck pulled a piece of pizza onto his plate, even though his appetite had dropped considerably during the course of the conversation. Despite what he'd said, he knew that his fiancée would willingly put her freedom on the line if it meant helping them solve this mystery.

He didn't want to risk her life, or her freedom. But if towns kept being incinerated, he knew it would no longer be his decision.

~~*

Downtown
Atlanta, Georgia

Despite a successful exorcism at the retirement home, Riley's nerves remained on edge, even as she parked her car near the Grounds Zero. She'd still not heard a word from Beck, which was not his style. That could mean he was somewhere he couldn't text her, or in genuine trouble.

Welcome to your new life.

Not that their old one had been all blooming roses and cuddly kittens. This new chapter had her guy facing dangers far beyond that of an ordinary trapper. Of course, he'd never been ordinary at anything, which was why he was about to take the vows to become a grand master.

The pressure was intense—for both of them. Would she be strong enough to handle it? What about when they had children? Her dad hadn't become a demon trapper until she was in the teens, so it'd been somewhat easier that way. Could she juggle pregnancy, teething infants, and trapping while Beck was keeping Heaven and Hell from going to war? Right now it all seemed overwhelming.

At least we're together. Riley couldn't imagine what it would be like to face each day without him at her side.

She'd just reached the stoplight to cross the street to the coffee shop when a booming voice made her jump. "Repent, or Hell will consume you!" the man called out. To make matters worse, he was using a megaphone.

Atlanta seemed to have its share of sidewalk preachers. Some were quiet and respectful, and actually did some good for the community. Others, like this guy, just made Riley grit her teeth. They came out of the woodwork every now and then, not seeming to understand that bellowing rarely made anyone give a damn about their sermons. Especially when they were shouting that everyone was headed for eternal torment. It was not the best sales pitch for their faith.

"You will all perish! You will roast in Hell for your sins! Repent now or forever be Lucifer's slave!" The man seemed to be looking directly at her now. Riley turned away, refusing to get into his face. She'd done that with one preacher a month or so back, and it hadn't gone well. The loudmouth had finally been carted off by the cops because he'd taken to frightening the kids at a local daycare.

Luckily, the stoplight turned to green and she hurried across the intersection, the man's blistering exhortations making her move faster than usual. She wasn't the only one. Since Mr. Hell-and-Brimstone was on a public sidewalk, there wasn't much they could do. Atlanta's Finest would probably try to talk some sense into him, but usually that was a waste of everyone's time.

When Riley entered the Grounds Zero, her stress level dropped by half. Beck still hadn't called or texted, but in this place, there was hot chocolate. Surely, the gods on Mt. Olympus had created that drink solely for her. Especially when it had extra whipped cream and chocolate curls on top.

Her friend Simi was so preoccupied that she didn't notice

Riley until she stood in front of her at the counter. Then, in true Simi fashion, she squealed and gave her a hug, even though they'd just seen each other a couple days before. Simi was on a perpetual high, and her drug of choice was caffeine—the sole reason she worked in a coffee shop.

"Hey, you!" Riley said. "How's it going?"

"All good!"

"Your hair," Riley said, pointing. "It's . . . sedate."

Simi had one setting when it came to hair color: outrageously vibrant. The last time Riley had seen her, it'd been a frosty pink with ruby highlights. Now it was all black with a faint teal blue at the tips. The cut was different too, ending just at her chin.

"You like?" Simi asked as she prepared the hot chocolate. Nice thing about being a regular—all the baristas knew what Riley drank and how she liked it made. She only needed to place an order if the barista was new.

"I love it. It's way cool."

Simi fussed over the drink a bit, then returned with one of the extra-large ceramic mugs. She plopped a cinnamon stick in it, shaved extra chocolate curls on top of the genuine whipped cream, and rang up the purchase.

"I have an interview at the beauty school tomorrow," she said as the total appeared on the register's display. "I wanted to look less manic than usual."

The hair change was a good start, but trying to tame Simi would be like trying to bottle a hurricane. Just one of the reasons Riley liked her so much. "Beauty school, huh?" That was a new thing. "You'll do great. Think of all the experience you've had with your own hair."

"It was Peter's suggestion, actually. The longer I thought about it, the more I liked it. I figured I'd talk with them and see what it's all about."

"Peter? I thought you guys weren't a thing any longer."

"That kinda changed," Simi said with a shy smile. "He's been coming here to do his homework a few times a week, so we're talking more."

"Excellent. You two are right for each other. And good luck tomorrow. Let me know how it goes. I'll be cheering you on."

"I will," Simi said, still smiling. She dropped Riley's change in the tip jar, knowing it was headed there anyway. "You want a refill down the line?"

"Don't know. Depends on how the meeting falls out."

"Good luck playing dictator with the magical folks."

"Thanks." *I'm so going to need it.*

The private meeting room at the Grounds Zero was in the rear of the shop. Someone had spent some effort making it inviting—it had comfy overstuffed chairs, artwork on the walls, and a gas log fireplace that was already lit, giving off inviting warmth. Riley settled into the chair closest to it. At least she could be comfortable while being uncomfortable. As if that made any sense.

The Usual Suspects, as she called them, were representatives of the Summoners Society, the witches, and the Demon Trappers Guild. Mort, and sometimes Lord Ozymandias, stood in for the necromancers. Rada Litinsky, Riley's former neighbor and the most senior witch, was the designated representative for her people. Grand Master Stewart served as the trappers' spokesperson. That left Riley to act as ringmaster because conversations could became heated.

The idea of creating this group hadn't been original, but had come from one of Riley's favorite authors. Not that her life was anything like the fictional heroine Kate Daniels's—Riley just knew a smart idea when she read one. Kate's books were set in a futuristic Atlanta, one that made Riley's seem like naptime in kindergarten. Still, the notion of having all the magical people talk to each other had stuck in her mind. It'd taken some bargaining and cajoling, but eventually the meetings had come to pass. Now it was her job to ensure they remained successful.

Fortunately, Ozymandias, Angus, and Rada got along fairly well. Since the senior witch was out of town, hopefully it'd be Ayden who showed up tonight. She was always even-tempered— unless she encountered rank stupidity, which neither Ozy nor

Mort were capable of. If it wasn't Ayden, it would most likely be Morgaine, who had an axe to grind with both the necros and the trappers. With Angus in Scotland, Master Harper might also attend this session, though, like Ayden, he'd been noncommittal when Riley had asked him about it.

Luckily, the first few meetings had been productive. Everyone had been reasonably polite, and slowly but surely, the ice had thawed between the trappers, the necros, and the witchy folks. There'd been a couple tense moments but nothing that erupted into open warfare, because the most senior folks had attended. Hopefully, tonight would be the same.

The door opened and Mort entered, wearing a pair of black slacks and a stylish red sweater—probably a Christmas present.

"Senior Summoner Alexander," Riley said, smiling up at him.

"Master Blackthorne. Lord Ozymandias sends his regards. He has other commitments tonight so I'm here in his place."

"Ah, more apprentice summoners to fry?"

"Nope. Nothing that fun. Your headache gone yet?"

She groaned. "Barely."

"Then once you're back from Scotland, we'll ramp up the training," he said, settling into one of the high-back chairs, the one with the extra stuffing. He placed a mug of coffee on the small table next to him.

Riley took a long sip of her hot chocolate and sighed as it hit all the right places. "Please tell me it'll get easier."

"You know it will. You are fairly skilled at illusions now, right?"

"Yeah, about eight out of ten attempts."

"Eighty percent isn't bad. Soon it'll be a hundred. When you first started, you were batting zero. Even your levitation skills are improving. You're right on track."

Of all the people who could be teaching her, Mort and Ayden were ideal because they came at magic from different directions, but still somehow complemented each other. She swore they were working together to set up her classes, but she knew they'd never admit it.

Chris Jackson was the next arrival, a wiry man with a ponytail, a great sense of humor, and little tolerance for bureaucratic nonsense. A master demon trapper, he'd had Riley's back from the first day she'd joined the Guild. She always jumped at the chance to trap with him.

"Hey, Jackson. How goes it?" she said. "Filling in for Harper?"

"Yeah. He's got an AA meeting, so he asked me to come to this thing instead."

"That's fine by me. You're a lot more civil."

"That's for damned sure." He chose a seat near Mort and smiled over at the summoner. No worries there—they'd fought together in two big battles last year, so they already trusted each other.

"What are you teaching this girl nowadays?" Jackson asked, a devilish gleam in his eye.

"Warding," Mort said simply. As if it were just that simple.

"Which means he lobs nasty spells and I have to stop them before they flatten me like a bug," Riley said.

"How's that going?" Jackson asked.

The necromancer grinned. "Good. Real good."

Riley smiled at the praise, but that smile began to fade when she felt the witch approaching the room. After Ayden had taught her how to pick up each person's life signatures, some just stuck out more than others. This was one of those.

She took a deep breath a second before the door opened and Morgaine stepped into the room. Making sure she kept a neutral expression, Riley nodded at the newcomer, wondering why her friend wasn't here instead.

"Morgaine. Welcome."

The witch let the door close behind her. She didn't have coffee in hand, but clutched the strap of her leather purse so tight her fingers blanched. Her usually tidy blond hair hung in tangles around her face. She shot a look at Jackson, then at Mort. Riley felt the woman's personal wards ramp up, like she was preparing to cast a spell.

Sensing the threat, Mort straightened in his chair, the tips of his fingers glowed faintly blue.

"We're on neutral ground here, Morgaine," Riley warned. "No spells, you understand?"

"Sorry." To Riley's surprise, the magic vanished as the witch dropped into one of the chairs. All without a snarky comment. This wasn't normal behavior.

Ohhhkay.

"Morgaine, this is Senior Summoner Mortimer Alexander. He's the necromancers' advocate for Atlanta." The witch issued a curt nod, her mouth pursed. Gesturing, Riley said, "And this is Master Chris Jackson from the Demon Trappers Guild."

"Glad to meet you," Jackson said. His expression said he was watching the dynamics in the room with considerable interest.

"Morgaine," Mort said politely.

The woman gave another nod, but didn't respond, her fingers still knotted on the purse's strap.

"We usually open the meeting with any issues or concerns," Riley said. "Kick in anything that's bothering you or your people. That's what this is all about. Sharing information works in our favor, not against it."

Jackson began by recounting a recent encounter between a summoner and a demon trapper. In this case, it was to offer an apology for the trapper's behavior because the man had been an asshole by suggesting that the necros were all sick perverts.

"Harper gave him hell, and then I gave him hell. He knows that if he acts like that again, he's out of the Atlanta Guild." Jackson looked over at Mort now. "Your summoner held his cool, and we appreciate that. Frankly, if I'd been the least bit magical, I would have roasted the guy."

"I probably would have been tempted as well. Thank you for taking care of the situation."

"It's not the first time Hemsey's been a problem. He's new to the area and I'm guessing whoever trained this guy did a piss-poor job of teaching him how to behave like a human being."

Riley nodded. She'd encountered Hemsey on a trapping run and found him a foul-mouthed jerk. They'd traded words and she'd gone out of her way to avoid him since that time.

Jackson looked over at her now. "Maybe when Beck gets back he can give him the 'come to Jesus' speech, since they're closer in age. Hemsey's sure as hell not listening to Harper or me."

"I'll mention it to Den, see what he thinks," she said. Sometimes these new guys just needed to know that the Atlanta Guild wasn't like some of the others across the country. Respect was earned, but never on the backs of others. "You have any issues, Mort?"

Her friend shook his head. "No. It's been quiet. I haven't heard anything about any witch and summoner feuds, which is a blessing. What about you, Morgaine? You heard anything?"

The woman issued a very long sigh and finally set her purse on the floor next to the chair. That, at least, was a start.

"Rada is out of town for a family emergency, and she didn't leave anyone in charge."

That wouldn't bother most witches because they weren't much for organizational structure. As Ayden had once explained, "We do our own thing and try not to be idiots about it. Works most of the time. If not, Rada steps in and slaps wrists."

"What is it that has you worried?" Riley asked.

"Ah, we've had a couple new witches move into town. One of them, Sibyl, is really kind of strange. She's been pestering us about these visions she's having." Morgaine sighed again. "I figured she was just really flaky. Like Luna Lovegood crazy— from the Harry Potter books, you know?"

Riley raised an eyebrow at that. "Okay. What's she saying that's bothering you guys?"

"Well, first she warned Rada that someone in her family was going to be in a very bad traffic accident, and that happened. Then she told Leslie that her job was going to be ending soon. Leslie's employer closed down two days later without any notice."

"She's precognitive," Mort said. Looking over at Riley, he

added, "You see it more in witches than in summoners. They have a more nature-based magic and that seems to aid in the gift."

"Okay, so this Sibyl person," as if that name wasn't a big hint, "is able to see the future. What's spooking you about that?"

"She said," Morgaine began and then hesitated, frowning, "what Sibyl is telling me doesn't make any sense. She keeps going on and on about the death of the world. How it's going to burn away and we'll all be turned to ash. I tried to get her to talk to Ayden or Locasta—maybe they'd understand her better—but she won't. She'll only talk to me and she's driving me crazy."

Jackson shifted in his chair. "How's her see-the-future track record been?"

"Fifty-fifty. My house didn't burn down and Ayden hasn't won the lottery."

"Not yet, at least," Mort said softly. "Our lives are mutable, our paths easily changed by one decision or another. Unplug the iron, don't buy a lottery ticket, and her forecasts don't come true."

"I'm just worried because she keeps calling me, demanding to know why I'm not taking her warnings seriously. Like I know what to do." Morgaine frowned deeper now. "And if that's not weird enough, Sibyl's moved out into this little shack in the woods. Took all her cats with her. She's sure that something's going to happen, and it's freaking her out that no one seems to care."

"So, what can we do for you?" Riley asked, confused as to the group's role in this situation.

"Talk to her. You know stuff other people don't know. Maybe this will make sense to you." Morgaine shook her head. "I didn't want to bother Rada. It's her nephew that got hurt in the car accident and she doesn't need this right now."

Riley didn't really have a choice, even though she thought it wasn't her problem in the first place. For Morgaine to ask for help was unprecedented, so she'd have to make the effort. "I can try to talk to her. Does she know who I am?"

Morgaine sniffed. "*Everybody* knows who you are." That sounded more like the prickly woman Riley knew. The witch dug in her purse, scribbled out a few lines of directions, and then handed the piece of paper to Riley. "Be careful with her. She's wacky, but she's also got a lot of power. If she doesn't trust you, it could get really bad."

"I'll . . . be careful."

"Can you go tonight?"

For a half second, Riley wondered if she was being set up, but then she discarded the idea. Morgaine was not that good of an actress.

"Yes, I can." Because tomorrow night, she'd be headed across the ocean to Scotland, Sibyl's visions or not.

"Thank you. Really, thank you," Morgaine said, relieved. Before Riley could respond, the witch was out the door.

Oh boy.

"And here I thought this meeting was going to be a snore," Jackson said, shaking his head.

"Nothing about us magic users is ever dull, even when we wish it would be," Mort said. Then he eyed Riley. "I'll be coming with you to see this woman."

Since it was rare of Mort to insist on anything, he had to be worried. It would be stupid for her not to accept his help.

"I'm good with that. Who knows, maybe I'll get to practice my warding in real time."

He huffed. "We both should eat supper, get some fuel on board. This Sibyl person sounds unstable, and that might mean a lot of magic being tossed around tonight." The summoner rose out of his chair. "Can you pick me up around seven thirty?"

"Sure." Apparently, she was going to be chauffeur too.

After a nod to Jackson, Mort left them behind.

"Bet you can't wait to get out of town and off to Scotland," the master said as he stood. "I know I'd be counting the hours, the way things are going." He paused at the door. "Send Beck my best, will you? Tell him I'm damned proud of him."

She couldn't stop the smile. "I will. We'll be back soon."

"You better be," he replied. "Don't you dare leave this mess to the rest of us."

Now it was just Riley and the dregs of her hot chocolate. The way her stomach churned, she knew getting a refill wasn't a good idea. As she reached for her phone to check her messages, it pinged. It was Beck.

BACK IN SCOTLAND. LOVE YOU.

Not a word to indicate what had happened between him and the Vatican.

YOU OKAY? she typed.

YES, SEE YOU SOON.

LOVE YOU.

No reply.

Riley tapped her phone against her cheek in thought. Usually when Beck texted, he gave her the countdown to their wedding in days and hours. Not this time. In times past, she would have worried something was going on between them, as a couple, but she knew that wasn't the case.

No, this was because of whatever had happened with the Church. Coupled with the witch's dire warnings and Ayden's strange tattoo . . .

Something was brewing. Something bad.

Chapter Seven

When Riley pulled up on the street behind Mort's house to pick him up, she saw that Ayden stood next to him. She was back in her customary long skirt, with a thick coat on top in deference to the chilly spring weather.

Mort slipped into the backseat, Ayden into the front. "She's going with us," he announced, as if that wasn't obvious.

Before Riley could respond, Ayden added, "Put yourself in Sibyl's shoes and think like a witch for a moment. A paranoid, slightly schizophrenic witch."

Not an easy assignment, but Riley did her best. "Paranoid, huh?" A nod returned. "So if two summoners—even if one is a trapper—showed up on my doorstep, I'm going to freak out. But if those same summoners are accompanied by one of my own, someone I sorta trust, I might not throw spells as quickly."

"That's the plan," Ayden replied. "Sibyl is a loony, but she's often correct with her prognostications, so it's best not to ignore her. Provided she doesn't go ballistic on us—then the gloves are off."

"See, you might get to practice your warding tonight after all," Mort said, sounding way too pleased.

Ayden gave a hoarse chuckle under her breath.

"You know, you two enjoy my agony way too much," Riley said.

"Yup," the witch replied, grinning. "Who else are we going to torture?"

Riley wisely kept her mouth shut.

~~*

Sibyl the witch lived southeast of Atlanta, deep in the country-side. They'd been on the road for almost an hour now, passing both Covington and Social Circle. Then they were off the inter-state and the main roads, headed into the woods on a narrow dirt track. One that really needed grading.

"I hope I didn't make a wrong turn somewhere," Riley muttered, keeping her eyes on the road. You knew you were in rural Georgia when there were no streetlights and no houses, just trees and lots of night.

"We'll find out—" Mort began.

Riley gasped in surprise the moment they crossed the ward, a magical "Do Not Trespass" sign. It was like being doused in ice that had been electrified. Even her companions had held their breath.

"If we try to shield against her wards, she'll consider us a threat," Ayden cautioned. "I think she just means to scare off intruders, not kill them."

"We hope," Mort added.

"I wonder how many more of them there are—wards, that is," Riley replied, moving the car forward again, though slowly.

The answer was two more, each of increasing intensity. By the third, her head buzzed and her heart pounded, and she swore her eyeballs were going to fall out into her lap. Even Mort had clenched his jaw as they'd passed through that last one.

Riley finally parked the car in front of an old two-story house. A single security light illuminated the building, which had a battered, red metal roof and was covered in sun-bleached yellow paint. A black Subaru wagon sat on the other side of the structure. As she looked around, the spiky itch of magic contin-ued to scrape across Riley's skin, sending "go away" messages. If she hadn't been trained in spellcraft, she would never have made it down the driveway.

Even after they exited the car, Riley continued to stare at the house because something was odd there. She closed her eyes, cleared her mind, and then reopened them. There it was, another ward. It pulsed like a quasar, spiraling just about a foot above the ground. Faint arcs of magic looped high in the air until they all converged at the top of the red brick chimney.

"Now that's impressive," Riley said.

"Very," Mort said quietly.

"You want to introduce us?" she asked Ayden.

The witch shook her head. "No, I'm thinking you'll do better than me right now."

Riley sighed. "Well, here goes." She stepped forward. "Hello? Hi!"

"That's a nice start," Mort said, smirking. She shot him a frown, then turned back toward the house.

"My name is Riley Blackthorne. Morgaine said I should talk to you about your visions."

The ward flared, then lowered again, but there was no movement at the door or at any of the windows. Still, high on the roof, something *did* move.

"You see that?" she asked.

"Yup," Ayden replied.

Something clambered down the roof, then the side of the house, where it landed with a rattle of bones. Then it stood upright. It was a skeleton, a tall one with brilliant green eyes. When Riley tried to determine if it was an illusion, she got nowhere. The magic was too strong.

"Hey, Sibyl—"

The ward boomed like thunder as a wave of magic burst out at them. Riley barely had a chance to establish a protective ward of her own before it struck. As it rolled over them, she heard Mort curse—then silence. Blinking her eyes, she was astounded to find her own spell had held. Of course, the others' had as well.

"Well done," Mort said, nodding his approval.

"What he said," Ayden added. "I thought we were going to be scraping you off the ground."

"You weren't going to keep me from getting creamed?"

"Best way to learn is by doing," was the swift reply. Mort

nodded his agreement.

Grumbling under her breath, Riley shook out her limbs to reduce the sting of the magic, then glowered at the house. She took another step forward, patience at an end.

"You know, we came here to help you, and you're being really nasty. I understand if you don't trust me or Summoner Alexander, but Ayden's one of yours." Riley sucked in a breath, still angry. "So either get your butt out here and talk to us, or we're headed back to town, because we all have better things to do than put up with this kind of crap."

Ayden whistled under her breath. "Diplomacy—so not your strong suit."

Riley ignored her, counting down from ten. When she ran out of numbers, she was out of here.

"How dare you breach my wards?" a furious voice demanded. It came from a body that suddenly appeared on the house's front porch, exactly where the skeleton had once been. Which meant Sibyl had been watching them all along.

The woman was over six feet tall and clad in red from head to toe, except for her black boots. The cape and the long dress were tattered, and the face, well, it was right out of a horror movie. One minute, the psychic looked like the Wicked Witch of the West, and then she did this melting-face thing that made Riley shudder.

"Sibyl," Ayden called out. "Knock it off. You're not going to scare them away. Just tell us what's bothering you, will you?"

Apparently, that was the right thing to say, as the illusion dripped away like molten wax. Left behind was a diminutive woman who was probably in her early fifties. She stood all of five feet, clothed in a tidy brown dress with black boots peeking out from under the hem. Her hair was dark with streaks of gray and hung in long curls down her chest. Flanking her were two cats, one black and one white. Both had luminous green eyes, just like their owner.

Riley was smiling before she knew it. "Your cats are very pretty," she said. "Their eyes are gorgeous. They match yours."

The woman blinked, twice, and then her attention went to the necromancer. "I know of you, Mortimer Alexander," she said, her voice light, almost hard to hear. "You appear harmless, but you are very powerful."

Mort shifted uncomfortably. "Ah, thank you, I guess."

Then she was back to staring at Riley. "You are Blackthorne's daughter, the one who fights the demons. You took an angel for a lover."

Riley made a strangled noise at that revelation. *How did you know that?*

Sibyl stepped out further on the porch. Looking up at the dark night sky, she frowned. "They think they know everything, but who cares for them when they hurt? Who mourns for them when they die?"

Riley peered up at the stars, trying to understand. "They?"

"They," the woman repeated, as if their identity was obvious. "You know them well. They have slain whole realms, done as was told to them. Now they are sad, and that sadness will kill us all."

Is she talking about angels, or demons?

"What can we do to prevent the destruction you've predicted?" Ayden asked, seeming less unnerved by her fellow witch's ramblings than either Riley or Mort. Probably because she'd encountered it before.

"You, nothing. Him, nothing. Her . . ." Sibyl turned those bottomless emerald eyes toward Riley now. "Her? Everything."

"What do I need to do?" Riley asked, finding herself annoyed at being stuck in the middle of things . . . again.

"You have it. All of it. Inside you. Here," the woman said, tapping her head, "and here." She tapped her heart. "Listen, feel, care. Never let the Darkness win, for it will destroy everything." Her attention returned to Mort again. "And don't forget to pay your homeowner's insurance. If you do, you'll regret it."

Then Sibyl was gone. Not in a flash of light or anything remotely spectacular. No, she just walked to her door, opened it, let the cats enter, and then closed it behind her. The sign on the portal swung back and forth, and it still read, "Go Away!"

"What was that all about?" Mort asked, his head cocked in complete bewilderment.

"*That* was Sibyl," Ayden said. "One part gifted psychic, three parts total nutter."

They are sad. Head, heart. Never let the Darkness win.

Riley sighed. "Well, that was different. Any clue who 'they' are?"

Both of her friends shook their heads.

"Of course not. Just once, I'd like someone to tell me exactly what to do. You know, 'Go to this place, annoy this person, kill that monster.' But no, all I get is vague warnings."

Her two friends held their silence. It was a smart move.

With yet another tortured sigh, Riley walked back to her car and climbed in. Then waited for the other two to do so as well. They were talking quietly, every now and then throwing a look her way. She resisted the urge to honk the horn because magical folks didn't always have a sense of humor.

Once they were in the car and back on a main road, Mort asked, "So what do you intend to do next?"

"Nothing," Riley said.

"That's certainly a strategy, I guess."

"Sometimes you should just wait until you know you're stuck on a particular path, and then things become clear. Right now, I have no clue. I'm sure the universe will see fit to fix that soon enough. It always does."

"Provided the universe doesn't kill you first," Ayden murmured.

Unfortunately, her friend was right. "There is always that risk. But for now, I'm only going to think about Beck's investiture and getting married. Instead of Sibyl's warning, I'll worry about whether I've ordered enough cake for the reception. Maybe if I ignore this problem, it'll go away."

"Good luck with that," Mort said. "Never worked for me."

"Me neither," Ayden added.

Riley rolled her eyes and kept driving.

~~*

International Guild Manor House
Scotland

Unlike the day before, morning at the manor came late, at least by Beck's standard. Usually he was up by five, went for a run, then ate breakfast and began his studies. This morning, he didn't crawl out of bed until seven, which seemed lazy to his way of thinking. Between the trip to the Czech countryside and the flight back, exhaustion had set in. He should have slept deeply, but a repetitive nightmare had pretty much ruined any chance of a good night's sleep. It was always the same—a sea of people crying out in terror, and then they all died, burnt black in a heartbeat.

This morning, Beck ate breakfast alone, which was also unusual. After tidying up his plate, he headed for Trevor's office, only to find the door closed. Rather than knocking, he respected the man's privacy and continued down the hallway to the library.

It was odd how he now felt so at home surrounded by the written word. It often made him wonder if his father was an educated man of some kind. Since his mother had never told him the man's name before she died, the door to that part of his life was closed. One thing was for sure, he certainly wasn't willing to take Lucifer's offer just to find out.

As Beck saw it, his insatiable craving for knowledge was Paul Blackthorne's most treasured gift. He never took anything at face value now. Again, he paused the moment he entered the library, savoring this room for what it represented—not only for the grand masters, but for him personally.

Even though it was early, Grand Master Jonah Kepler sat at the oak table in the far corner of the room. Stacked in front of him was a mound of books, some quite old.

The scholar looked up and smiled. "Good morning, Denver."

"Sir. How're you this mornin'?"

"As well as can be expected." He gestured at the books.

"Trevor asked if I could check the archives, see if I can determine what is happening with those cities."

Beck looked at the selection. "Would you like some help?"

The man's wrinkled face brightened. "Yes, I would."

"What kinds of things are you lookin' for?" Beck asked, sitting down opposite the grand master.

"Unexplained disasters, in particular. Anything that involves a settlement, a town, or a city with no logical explanation as to what caused its destruction. I'm working on some of the older texts. The stack closest to you is from the early eighteen hundreds. Let me know if something doesn't make any sense."

"Sure thing," Beck said.

Carefully opening the first book, he began to scan the contents, quickly dropping down history's rabbit hole. Even now, he swore he could see Riley's dad smiling at him from Heaven.

~~*

It was past eight that evening before Beck stepped back from his research. He'd paused only for lunch, mainly to ensure that Kepler ate. Often the grand master forgot that there were other things in this world besides books, including food.

Now, in the sitting room near the fire, a glass of whisky in hand, Beck mulled over all he'd read. There'd been no end to the tales of cities having been destroyed over the centuries, and no continent had been spared. India, Indonesia, Pakistan, Japan, China, even Galveston, Texas. All of those had been natural disasters, and bodies had always been left behind. That had not been the case with the town in the Czech Republic, or according to the Vatican, the one in Spain.

Beck had even spent a couple hours researching volcanic eruptions, because they often created a dense cloud of ash that buried whole cities. In the end, he knew this wasn't what had happened with the latest two—there were no volcanoes anywhere near them. When he'd voiced his frustration, Kepler had pointed out that at least they had determined what *hadn't* happened to the two towns. That, he said, was progress. Not in Beck's way of thinking, but he wasn't about to argue.

The door to the sitting room opened and Trevor joined him. Without speaking, he poured himself his own drink and sat in a chair, pensive. No doubt, he was feeling the burden just as much as the rest of them.

"We spent the day goin' through the books and the records," Beck reported. "We're not findin' anythin' that'll help us."

"Jonah said the same. Ya still believe it has nothin' ta do with Hell?"

Beck did another gut check, and the answer hadn't changed.

"It's not them. Doesn't have that sticky tar feel I get when Lucifer or the demons are involved." He took a sip of his whisky, letting it burn down his throat. "What about you?"

"Same feelin'. That opinion will win us no friends in Rome."

"That's for damned sure." Beck paused, inhaling the scent of the peat from the scotch. "Riley'll be here tomorrow. How much can I tell her?"

"As much as ya feel she needs to know. She has our complete trust."

That was reassuring. "I'm gonna be honest here—this whole thing scares the hell out of me. It feels so damned wrong."

"Aye, it does," Trevor replied.

Silence fell between them as they each sipped their drinks.

"Ya gettin' a wee bit worried about the oath yet?" Beck's superior asked.

"Yes." Oh, God, was he.

"Good. That's where yer head should be right now. What about yer weddin'?"

"No worries there. I would have married Riley the day I asked her to be my wife. She's the one who wanted to take it slow."

Trevor gave a nod of understanding. "Big step for a girl that young."

"True, but she's both young and old, if you get my meanin'.

Too old sometimes. She needs to remember that the whole world isn't on her shoulders."

The grand master smiled now. "That's verra good advice, Denver. I'm thinkin' it should apply ta *both* of ya." Trevor drained his drink and rose. "Get some rest, lad. I'll see ya in the mornin'."

"'Night, sir."

The door closed quietly behind him. Glancing at his phone, Beck checked the time and then, on impulse, dialed Riley. He needed to hear her voice.

"Blackthorne." That told him Riley had answered without looking at the display. Her voice held an edge, a tone that indicated she was annoyed by something. Or someone. Luckily, it wasn't him.

"Hey! I've been missin' you," he said. There was a very long pause. "You still there?"

"Yes, sorry. That was just too weird."

"What? That I'm missin' you?"

"No. I was at the Armageddon Lounge earlier today on a trapping run. You just said almost exactly what the Four did, while it was looking just like you."

He shuddered. "Okay, let me start over. Riley, this is yer Backwoods Boy. It's been a helluva couple days. How about you?"

"Same here. I miss you so much right now, Den."

"You'll be here soon. Man, do I have a lot to tell you."

"Anything I can do to help?"

"No, not yet. Once you get here, it'll be better."

There was a silence for a few moments, then noise in the background.

"Look, I'm really sorry, Den, but I've got to go. Simon's here and we have another exorcism. Don't worry, it's not one of the nasty ones."

That's what Riley would say, even though there was no way she could know that until she encountered the fiend.

"I always worry, no matter what kind it is." Beck hated to

let her go, even if it was just on the phone, but she had a job to do. "You go cast out those demons, but remember, no kissin' the ex."

There was a startled gasp. "What? You dog!"

He laughed. "See you soon, Princess."

"I'll be there. Love you. Bye!"

When the call ended, Beck closed his eyes, feeling more alone than he had in a long time. Eventually he opened his eyes, shifted through the images on his phone, and picked the one of Riley he loved the most. She was sitting on their couch, hugging Rennie, but her eyes were looking toward him. She was smiling, about to laugh at something he'd said.

No matter what kind of day he'd had, no matter the fear growing inside of him, those eyes showed him love. Now, as cities died and he had no way to save them, Beck needed that unending love more than ever.

Chapter Eight

Beck's House
Atlanta, Georgia

If there was one person who exemplified how much one's life could change in a year, Simon Adler was it. Once Riley's boyfriend and a demon trapper, now he was the "ex" and worked for the Vatican, exorcising demons. The journey from boyfriend/trapper to the new job had almost killed both him and his deep faith.

Outwardly, he looked much like the Simon she'd first met when he'd been Master Harper's apprentice: bright blond hair, blue eyes, shy smile, and wearing a light blue shirt and black jeans. But if you looked deeper, you saw the physical and emotional scars, like he'd packed a lifetime's worth of torment into just one year. He was still her Simon, though whatever feelings they'd had for each other were gone, destroyed by an Archangel's cunning.

Simon gave her a warm smile as she closed the car door and pulled over her seatbelt.

"How goes it?" he asked as he backed out of the drive.

"Good. You missed a great trapping yesterday. Richard and I had to use fire extinguishers to get a Pyro down from the restaurant's ceiling. There're probably a dozen videos of it on YouTube now."

Simon laughed. "Fire extinguishers?"

"Yup. It was one for the books."

"Anything new from Beck?" he asked as they headed toward

Memorial Drive.

"Yes, there is. The Vatican contacted him and Grand Master MacTavish. Apparently, they needed their input on something and it was so urgent they sent a jet for them. He's back in Scotland now, but he wouldn't tell me what was going on over the phone." She shot her ex a look. "You know anything about all that?"

Simon shook his head. "I called Father Rosetti yesterday but he was out of his office. His assistant was unusually close-mouthed about where he was."

"Huh. Wonder what gives." Riley shrugged. "Well, not our problem."

"At least not yet," Simon replied.

Riley huffed in agreement. Did she dare ask him about the Unbounds? *No.* She trusted Simon, however it was best not to push that trust too far, because some in Rome would love to see her sanctioned for being too chummy with Hell. As if sticking it to Lucifer every chance she got wasn't enough. Apparently, it was all a matter of perspective.

They chatted back and forth about various things—including the fact that Simon was going to be an uncle again—until they reached their destination. When they turned into one of the parking lots, Riley winced. It was the same school she'd visited a few days before. Had Isra violated his promise? Or was this something else?

"What's going on with this one?" she asked, trying not to let her nerves show.

"It's the janitor," Simon replied. "He's been acting strange the last few days, and someone finally figured out he's possessed."

"How'd they figure that out?"

"He kept licking the windows instead of washing them."

"Ugh. But schools use Holy Water wards."

"That was their second clue; the janitor refused to enter the main part of the school. Apparently, they only ward the areas where the students are, not the entire campus."

In a case of déjà vu, they returned to the same front desk that

Riley had visited a couple days before, signed in, and received their passes.

"Back again already?" the lady with the stylish glasses said.

Riley only nodded. Fortunately, she didn't have to explain why before the head of the janitorial department, a beefy guy named Stan, came to collect them. As he led them past the classrooms, and then further back past the workshops, he looked spooked. Mostly he kept fingering something in his hand, probably a talisman of some sort.

"What is this man's name?" Simon asked.

"Lionel Sulic. He's a great guy and a hard worker, though a bit obsessed with cleanliness. But that's okay. That's what we like in a janitor."

"Any problems with him before this?"

"Nope. He's quiet, does his work, and doesn't flirt with the teachers. Makes my job a lot easier."

After passing his office, Stan took them down the hall to a door with a sign that said "Maintenance." He pushed it open and led them most of the way into the room, then stopped. Pointing at another door on the far wall, he said in a lowered voice, "That thing that used to be Lionel is in the supply cupboard. Only comes out at night. I tried talking to it and it just threw stuff at me. Last time, it was a bottle of floor polish. Made a helluva mess."

Riley and Simon traded looks.

"Not a problem. We'll handle it from here," Simon replied in that reassuring tone that even she appreciated. He set the heavy suitcase containing his exorcism supplies on a nearby workbench. "It's best that you wait in your office. Sometimes these exorcisms can get a bit chaotic."

Chaotic. Which was a polite way of saying this could go bad in a heartbeat.

As the head janitor retreated, closing the door behind him, Riley focused on the far door. Nothing screamed serious demonic menace, not like in some of the other exorcisms. The benchmark for that was the one involving two badass fiends and one very scared, demonically possessed five-year-old. It'd taken not only her and Simon but also Beck to overcome the demons. Riley gave thanks daily that the child had survived.

"Heard from Carrina's parents lately?" As she waited for an answer, she put her trapping bag on the bench near Simon's gear and then extracted a bottle of Holy Water.

"Just last week," he said. "She's doing okay. Still has night-mares, but they're less frequent. So far, everything's going good with her." Simon extracted the aspergillum from its slot in the suitcase. "She still says she wants to be an exorcist when she grows up. Though, according to her mom, she calls us 'sorsists' because she can't pronounce the word."

Riley laughed, remembering the child's big eyes and cute little face. "You wait and see. She'll be training demon hunters at the Vatican before she's my age."

"God, I hope not," Simon replied.

It was unlike him to be negative. "This job really getting to you?"

He paused in his preparations. "Some days, yes. I worked with Father Xavier—he's the regional exorcist—last week on a case in Savannah." His blue eyes met Riley's, and she saw profound sorrow. "The woman died. She was twenty-three and five months pregnant. Her heart just couldn't take the strain of the exorcism."

"Oh my God," she said. On impulse, Riley embraced him, knowing how much he was hurting right now. "You did what you could."

"It wasn't good enough," he said, his voice barely above a whisper near her ear. "We lost two lives that day, and her family is devastated." He stepped back from her now, as if he felt he didn't deserve her compassion.

"'We are not God,'" she said quietly. "My dad said that to me when I first started trapping. He warned me that sometimes, no matter what I did, people would get hurt or die. He said the only other choice was to let evil win; then the suffering would be a million-fold."

"I know that, but there are days when I feel so inadequate."

"We're all like that, Simon. Even Beck. If we thought we had this wired, we're wrong."

With a troubled nod, Simon returned to his preparations, still pensive. Having worked with him numerous times, Riley knew exactly what he needed her to do. After assessing the surroundings, she ran a thick line of Holy Water in front of the door through which they'd entered. It was both a blessing and a curse that the room lacked windows. That meant no flying glass, but also no exterior light source if the demon managed to take out the fluorescents overhead.

Surveying the rest of the room, Riley found herself staring at the long workbench, above which was a highly organized pegboard holding various tools—hammers, screwdrivers, chisels, wrenches. Any one of which could easily become a lethal missile if the demon decided to be feisty. Yet another reason to create a protective circle.

To streamline the process, she set the exorcism supplies in the only open space in the middle of the room. These included the aspergillum, her trapping bag, and the metal "prison" that would house the demon once Simon cast it out of its janitor host.

Using a tiny amount of papal Holy Water, they each anointed themselves. Simon always made the sign of the cross on his forehead, while Riley inscribed a heart. Both would serve as armor against the Darkness.

"Ready?" she asked.

A tense nod came her way.

Riley methodically poured a line of the sacred liquid on the floor, leaving open a gap large enough for her to walk through. After another pass to ensure that the liquid was continuous, she traded the bottle for her steel pipe.

This was one of the numerous times during an exorcism when things could go wrong, since they were still basing the level of danger on their estimate of the demon's power. As Simon had once explained, that was like trying to judge the size of an alligator just by seeing the tip of its tail. Stronger demons could cloak their strength, at least until the actual exorcism began.

Riley took a deep breath, focusing her mind and body on whatever waited for them behind that door. With a quick glance at Simon, she tapped the doorknob with a finger, pleased to find it wasn't scorching hot. She'd learned that lesson last January, and it'd taken a week for the burn to heal. After a deep inhalation, she flung open the door and stepped back, pipe ready for an assault of teeth and claws. Instead, high-pitched giggles erupted from the darkened space, followed by the inevitable "Blackthorne's daughter."

Riley edged backward. Once she was inside the circle, Simon sealed it with the Holy Water, and after he uttered a prayer, it immediately flared to life, filling the room with intense light.

"Ouch," the demon said, blinking furiously.

Lionel Sulic was in his mid-thirties, his brown hair askew and his clothes a rumpled mess. He sat on the floor, propped up against the back wall, holding a roll of industrial paper towels in his hands. Still blinking, he tore off a big chunk with his teeth, chewed on the wad a few times, then dramatically spit it into the air. It landed with a plop on the debris-strewn floor. He promptly repeated the action.

"Oh boy," Riley said. "We got a loony."

"Figures," Simon replied, shaking his head. "It's been a while since the last one."

Some demons were dangerous because they packed a load of power; the one that had taken over little Carrina had been like that. Others were weaker but still capable of significant damage, both to the exorcist and the possessed. Then there were the loonies. Riley assumed the Vatican had a more official title for them, but that's what Simon called them and it worked for her.

For whatever reason, some demons just couldn't handle being inside a human's mind, so though the fiend had control over their victim, they lost the capacity for rational thought, at least on a consistent basis. While that lack of sanity made them comical, it also made them highly unpredictable.

With a low sigh, Simon raised the large metal cross, then

cleared his throat.

"Spawn of Hell! Hear me! I am Simon Michael David Adler, child of God, believer in the Risen Lord and seeker of the Light. You are trespassing in this mortal, and it is time for you to depart!"

As always, the power of the words, and of the faith behind them, caused goosebumps to form on Riley's skin.

The demon looked up, spat out another mouthful of paper towels. "Simon the Betrayer. They told me of you." Lionel giggled again, which was so at odds with his goat-slit eyes and his razor-sharp teeth. "Do you know how many windows there are here?"

Simon blinked, confused. "What?"

"Two hundred thirty-three," it said. Then frowned. "No. Thirty-four. I forgot one."

A glance at Simon told her he was struggling not to laugh, which was not what an exorcist should be doing. Maintaining control kept you alive.

"Toilets," the demon said, shaking its head. "There are so many toilets." The roll of paper towels came at them now, unfurling in midair to land a few feet from the Holy Water circle. "All I do is clean them. Over and over and over."

"Better than Hell, right?" Riley said.

That comment brought its attention to her again, as if suddenly registering exactly what they were here to do. Standing on unsteady feet, the demon picked up a can of spray paint.

The janitor's eyes glowed redder now. "Blackthorne's daughter."

"Yeah, that's me. How's about we help you out here? You just leave Lionel behind and we'll get you somewhere where there aren't any windows or toilets to clean. In fact, I can promise that." Because this fiend's next stop after the metal prison would be a quick trip to a local monastery and a hideous death.

"Liar!" Lionel shouted, and slung the paint at her. It bounced off the ward, scattering sparks.

"Demon, I order you to depart this mortal in the name of the

Almighty, the Creator, the Power that cannot be denied," Simon intoned, raising the cross again. He swung the aspergillum, and Holy Water arced toward the fiend.

"No!" the thing thundered as the thick stench of brimstone rolled out of the storage closet, nearly making Riley gag. "I *like* this one. He is simple to control," it said, its voice growing stronger than just a minute before, a lot less crazy. "He is *mine* now."

Simon countered with a stream of Latin, the words pouring forth. No matter how many times Riley heard them, they always sent shivers down her spine.

The fiend twisted in torment. "No! Mine! Mine!" it shouted, and suddenly the contents of the closet flew toward them—paint cans, brooms, buckets, lightbulbs. From their right, a whirlwind pulled the tools from the pegboard and slung them against the sacred ward. Each jarring impact sounded like a gunshot.

Simon's voice rose over the din, never faltering, the Latin growing in volume. When the workbench ripped out of the wall, Riley couldn't help but duck as it slammed into the ward and exploded into dozens of pieces.

"God is my shield and my sword. You have no power here, Hellspawn. Release this soul! I command it in the name of the Almighty, King of Heaven!"

With a high scream, Lionel collapsed to his knees, his head in his hands as he rocked back and forth. Suddenly the metal box at Riley's feet rattled, indicating the demon was no longer inside the man.

That was always the WOW! moment in any exorcism, especially since the box was *inside* the sacred circle.

Simon lowered his arms, his chest heaving. "All glory be to God."

"What he said," Riley murmured. "That wasn't an easy one." She eyed the destruction and then the janitor, who was still on his knees in the closet, staring at them with horror-filled and bloodshot brown eyes.

"They've been getting that way," Simon said. "There've

been more possessions in the last couple of weeks. It's like Hell's working overtime or something."

"Huh." Her encounter with Sibyl came to mind. Were demons the "they" she'd been warned about?

Riley broke the integrity of the ward with the toe of her tennis shoe. "Maybe they have a quota or something. Collect so many souls and you win this fabulous set of steak knives. Or maybe it's a cruise on the River Styx, all expenses paid."

To her surprise, a genuine smile crossed Simon's face. "You have no idea how much I love your sense of humor. It might be sorta dark, but it works. Thank you."

"And you have no idea how much I appreciate your . . ." She struggled for the right word, because it mattered. "Intensity. Your inner strength. You remind me why I do this for a living."

Simon's expression softened. "That means a lot. Thank you."

After another long moment, he looked back at the supply closet. "Lionel? I'm Simon and this is Riley. Welcome back."

The man could only stare at them. As Riley helped him to his feet, she noticed he stank of industrial cleaners and floor polish, but his eyes were normal now.

Then those eyes widened in shock. "Oh my, look at this mess. It'll take forever to clean it up," he said. "This is not good. Not good at all."

"Yup, our janitor is back," she said. "Just don't lick any windows, okay?"

"Why would I do that?" he asked, puzzled. "That's very unsanitary."

"Ah, never mind."

~~*

Simon cheered up as they walked to his car, talking about his newest niece, how he enjoyed hanging with her and the rest of his family. Since he had seven siblings, there always seemed to be someone doing something, whether that was getting married or having a baby.

"Any chance the Vatican will let you stay in Atlanta?" Riley asked.

"Not sure," he said. "Hope so. I like being around the sibs. Though if I do, I *really* need a place of my own."

"Family crowding you?" she asked, smiling over at him as they reached his vehicle.

"It's one of my sisters. She keeps trying to introduce me to NCGs."

"Nice Catholic girls, huh?"

"Yes. She thinks it's time I get married and have kids." He looked over at Riley as he opened the trunk. "I ask you, who in their right mind would want an exorcist for a husband?"

"A demon trapper," she replied without thinking. "Because they would know how it goes."

Simon raised his eyebrow as she realized what she'd said. Flustered, she added, "Not me, of course." She was just digging a deeper hole. "Not that I don't think you'd make a great husband but—" At this point she was stammering, oddly embarrassed.

"I know what you're trying to say." Simon hefted his suitcase into the trunk. "Honestly, I think you and I are better off as friends, though I'm sad it didn't work out the other way."

"Me too," she admitted. "Don't worry, you'll find someone who understands you and your calling."

"God, I hope so. Sometimes it's so very lonely."

Riley had just opened her door to set her trapping bag in the backseat when a panicked shriek split the air. "What the . . . ?"

Simon pointed to the far side of the parking lot as a hairy figure lumbered into view.

"A Three?" Riley said. "What's it doing here?" She grabbed her trapping bag, slamming the car door harder than necessary. Once Simon had his own bag out of the trunk, they took off at a run.

By the time they'd reached the demon, it'd cornered a group of students against the gym's brick wall. There were ten or so kids, both boys and girls. A few of the guys and one girl had put themselves between the fiend and the others. The demon wouldn't care about such heroics—every one of those teens was a fresh meal waiting to be chowed down.

Riley touched Simon's sleeve and motioned for him to circle around from the left. He nodded and headed that way while she went in the opposite direction. They had to do this very carefully, not drive the fiend into the civilians. Hopefully the moment it saw her, it'd come after her. That would allow Simon to herd the others to safety.

As she closed in, she saw a taller figure standing just in front of the boys. *Isra*. He stepped closer to the Three now, and though his lips weren't moving, she knew he was communicating with it, one fiend to another. Holding her position, she judged where Simon was and found he was a little closer to the kids than she was. If they could get into position, they could take the brunt of the demon's attack. All they needed to do was slam it with the Holy Water and the threat would be neutralized.

The Three howled, waving its long, hairy arms in the air, claws ready. It was one of the mature ones, lean and lethal. Isra's eyes caught hers, then went right back to the other demon. She had no doubt he was trying to talk it into leaving, but so far he'd had no success.

The Gastro-Fiend howled again, growing increasingly agitated, no doubt angry that another fiend stood between it and its lunch. If it did attack, what could Isra do without revealing his true form?

There was too much at risk here. "Hey! Furball!" Riley called out, wanting to gain its attention.

The Three whirled, then registered who it was facing. "Blackthorne's daughter!" it snarled.

"Look at you, aren't you smart! And they say you guys are just claws and teeth."

"Chew yourrrr bones!" it shouted, as they always did. It was tipping on its toes to make its run toward her when its bloodred eyes suddenly went wide and its arms lowered. It croaked a single frightened word, one Riley had heard during her time in Hell.

Retriever.

Though it was a bright spring day, the air shifted, like before a tornado, growing increasingly oppressive. Riley's next breath sucked in the sickening stench of brimstone.

"What's going on?" Simon called out.

Before she could reply, the Three took a few steps backward, yowled in terror, then bolted across the grass and into the parking lot in a blind panic.

"What was that all about?" Simon asked as he lowered his steel pipe.

"The end," Isra replied, so quietly Riley almost didn't hear him.

A deafening thunderclap rolled across the sky, causing car alarms to wail in response. In a billowing cloud of smoke and brilliant red fire, something manifested on the grass near the school's sign, the stench of brimstone rolling outward from it like a dense fog.

To Riley's horror, a demon walked out of that cloud. "Oh my God."

The last time she'd seen one of these fiends was in Hell, when she and Ori had stood before the Prince himself. It was at least ten feet tall, its skin a light, muddied tan, with heavy scales running its length like a dragon. Burgeoning muscles rippled along its arms, back, and thighs. Its claws were at least six inches long and wickedly curved to hook and rend flesh. Its teeth were like an Archfiend's, honed like razors. Two fiery crimson eyes burned in hatred.

"What is that thing?" Simon called out.

"One of Lucifer's bounty hunters," Isra said solemnly, both fear and resignation in his voice.

A Retriever. They both knew why it was here.

If Isra was taken back to Hell . . . "Get the others inside, Simon."

"No," Isra said, shaking his head vehemently. "It's more powerful than you can handle."

"I've killed Archfiends," she countered.

"It knows that, and it doesn't care. If we do fight, it will just summon others of its kind. Then everyone in this school will die."

The fiend roared in Hellspeak and Isra stiffened. Then it roared again, pointing at the kids, most of whom were weeping now. It was giving Isra a choice: their lives or his.

"What does it want?" Simon asked.

"Me," Isra said quietly. "If I go with it, it won't kill you. All of you."

"Isra. don't," Riley said, stepping close enough to touch his arm now

The wretched sadness in his eyes made her heart break. He lowered his voice so only she could hear him.

"I've had my time in the Light. I knew it would end someday. We're all on borrowed time. But every second away from Hell was worth the sacrifice." He glanced at the terrified teens, his eyes filling with tears. "At least they will be safe."

"But—"

Before she could stop him, Isra took off at a jog, covering the space between them and the hellish thing faster than she'd expected He stopped in front of it, stared up, and shouted in English, "My life in trade for theirs."

With a cunning smile that revealed those rows of sharpened teeth, the Retriever extended its claws and rammed them into Isra's chest. With a final head-rattling roar, the fiend and its prisoner vanished in a tunnel of fire and smoke.

Riley stared at the open ground as the smoke and brimstone finally cleared. Isra was gone, gone forever. Would he be tortured like Sartael, at least until Lucifer grew bored and slaughtered his captive? She had no doubt that this was what faced the defiant demon, a soul who had dared to challenge the Prince himself. Bowing her head, she closed her eyes to try to stifle the tears, and failed. She was not the only one crying, as sobs issued from the kids behind her. There were adult voices now, and the sound of a siren in the distance.

"He was a teacher?" Simon asked from beside her. She

nodded. "And you knew he was a Four?" She nodded again.

Wiping away the tears, Riley stashed her pipe inside the pack. Though she wanted to leave, she had to speak to the cops and whoever else needed to know what had happened here. But what she'd tell them wouldn't be the real story, because no one would believe that a demon had died to save the lives of mortals.

Chapter Nine

Much later, Simon drove them away from the school, stone silent. Riley wasn't sure if that silence was condemnation or not. Now that she was in the car, away from the teachers, the principal, and the police, her tears wouldn't stop, trickling down her cheeks one by one.

Riley barely noticed as Simon pulled into a small park. When he stopped the car in the lot and turned off the engine, she was out of the vehicle before he could even say a word. In the distance was a picnic table under an oak tree, and she headed for it. Once she'd sat on the weathered bench, Riley placed her hands on her knees, head bowed. The tears finally ended. At her feet, an ant scurried along, intent on its own business. Life moved on even when you grieved.

Isra was gone, a prisoner in Hell. No longer would he guide his students, his eyes alight with the knowledge he craved to share. Someone else would take over, perhaps remove all those beautiful nature photos from his classroom. Why this one demon's loss would haunt her, she had no idea. But somehow, in the very brief time she'd known him, Isra had touched her heart.

Simon quietly took a seat next to her, unease rolling off him.

"Riley . . ." He hesitated. "Tell me what just happened. I have to know."

She owed him the truth.

Riley raised her head and met his eyes. They were filled with concern and confusion. Not surprising, since the Vatican believed every demon, no matter their size, deserved death. Most of the time, they were right.

"I met . . . Isra the other day when I was here to talk to one of the classes. He is . . . was a teacher." *Like my dad. My mom.*

"How could you leave him inside that school knowing he was a Four?" Simon asked, his tone harsher now.

"I left him there because he wasn't like any other demon I've ever met. He said he was an Unbound, that he'd broken away from Lucifer. Isra . . . loved his students. He insisted he would not harm them."

"You know how they lie."

"Except he was telling the truth. I poured a line of Holy Water on the floor and he walked over it. He even *stepped* on it. You know that no demon can do that if the Prince is their master."

Simon stared at her now.

She pushed forward. "That huge demon, I've seen them in Hell. Ori said they're Lucifer's hunters. Sort of like him, except he killed the traitors instead of hauling them back to his master for punishment."

Simon ran a hand over his face, clearly confused. "How do you know this wasn't some sort of head game?"

"Isra said that the Retriever was there for him. It gave him a choice: either surrender or he'd kill all of us."

"And you believed him?"

"Yes."

"Oh God," Simon said, lurching to his feet and pacing now. "You know this isn't going to stay quiet. Someone had to take a video of that whole thing. The other trappers will figure out that you knew the teacher was a demon and didn't do anything about it." He paused, worry filling his face. "Rome will find out what happened here. They will hold you accountable."

"At this point, I don't care. I'm tired of them trying to micro-manage my life because I made one mistake. The truth is, if I trapped Isra the other day, those kids might be dead."

"Or they never would have been in jeopardy in the first place."

He had a point, a valid one. Had she read the whole situation wrong?

"Maybe you're right," she grudgingly admitted. "But I don't regret the decision."

Simon had his back to her now, as if he was at least physically rejecting everything she was saying.

"No matter what," Riley continued, "knowing that demons like Isra exist goes against everything we've been taught. The fiends are no different from us, Simon, at least in some ways. We're a mix of the Light and Dark. Why can't they be too?"

He swung around. "You can't believe we and Hellspawn have anything in common. You know what they do. Have you forgotten about all those who've died? About Carrina?"

Or the pregnant woman he lost last week.

"No, I haven't forgotten Carrina, or the trappers who died in the Tabernacle. Or *my father.*"

Simon grimaced. "Sorry. That wasn't what I should have said."

"No—you, of all people, have a right to ask those questions. But I just watched a demon sacrifice itself to save us. Isra could have tried to escape but he didn't. Now he's in Hell paying for that sacrifice, for that desire to be free."

Her companion sank back down to the bench, as if all the fight had drained out of him.

"At least this time around, Grand Master Stewart won't be on the hook for my decision," she murmured.

"What do you mean?"

"After my . . . *whatever* with Ori, the Vatican made a deal with Angus: He would keep an eye on me, but if I stepped over the line, we'd both pay the price. The price being whatever Rome deemed necessary, including prison or worse. Now that I'm a master, Angus is no longer responsible for my behavior. This is all on me."

It was Simon's turn to stare at the dirt. "What do you intend to do?"

The chance that no one would connect her and Isra was slim, which meant she had to get out in front of this before it all blew up on her—and the Guild. "First thing, you need to file a report with Father Rosetti. Tell him all of it. I'll do the same with Harper and Stewart." *And Beck.*

Simon looked up at her, his blue eyes deeply troubled. "They may call you to Rome. You've given them a reason to do just that."

"They may." She looked up at the sky, tears threatening again. "But no matter what they do, it won't be anything compared to what Isra is facing."

As she walked back to the car, Riley knew that Simon's questions had helped clarify a few things. She felt stronger now, as if her decision had somehow energized her. Demons could be evil, or they could be good. Because of Isra, she would never look at them the same. Even though he was gone, she would let others know of his sacrifice, bear witness to his courage. Maybe that was why they'd met outside his classroom, as if somehow he'd sensed that his freedom was ending and he needed someone to know why his new life had mattered.

When Simon climbed into the car with her, he clicked his safety belt, then looked over at her. "After I take you home, are you headed to Harper's?" She nodded. "Then I'll just drive you there. I want to be with you when you tell him what happened."

That, she hadn't expected. "Why? He's not like he used to be. He might yell and swear a lot, but he's not physically abusive anymore."

"I know, but I want to be there," he said. "Don't argue with me on this, Riley."

She knew that tone from Beck, and it said that trying to change his mind would be futile. "Okay. And thank you. I like that you're watching my back."

He gave a quick nod. "Only returning the favor. You've watched mine often enough."

~~*

Master Harper was behind his desk, as usual, but the look in his eyes told her he'd already heard about the school. Or at least part of the tale.

He gave Simon a nod, then looked back at her. "What the hell happened?"

Riley sank into the nearest chair and let it all out, beginning with her meeting Isra, up through the moment the Retriever took him prisoner. Every word brought back the pain. How she could have grown so attached to Isra so quickly, she didn't know. It made no sense, but little in this world did.

Harper swore under his breath. His eyes went to Simon. "You see the same thing she did? The Four actually surrendered to the other demon?"

"Yes." Simon looked over at her now. "Riley was willing to help him fight it, but he wouldn't let her."

Harper sighed. "Of course she was." He eyed her. "There are some things that even *you* can't kill. Sounds like that big bastard was one of them."

One of the Gastro-Fiends in the service bay set up an unearthly howl, making Riley's skin twitch.

"Go home, get some sleep," the master said. "Then get your ass back here in the morning, first thing." His attention moved to Simon. "You'll need to report this to Rome, right?"

"Yes. I have no choice but to tell Father Rosetti."

"That's all they need," the master said, shaking his head. "At least Rosetti's got an open mind, not like some of those guys. Maybe he can run interference so this doesn't get out of hand."

Or maybe not. "Did you know demons could break free of Lucifer?" Riley asked.

"I've heard about them, but I'd never met one. Figures one of them would find you, Blackthorne. You are a magnet for weird shit."

When Simon began to protest, the master waved him off.

"Go home. We'll do the report for National in the morning. Then we'll just wait until it all hits the fan."

Which it would. How long would it take for the news to percolate up the Vatican's organizational chart? A day? Two? If she was lucky, she'd be in Scotland and in the care of the grand masters before anyone figured out she'd been shielding a Mezmer.

If only Den were here. He'd hold her, talk her through this. Riley didn't think he'd be angry—Beck, of all people, knew that nothing was as it seemed in the Grand Game. If he was angry at her, it'd be because she'd placed herself in danger. But then, that wasn't new.

"Let's get you home," Simon said quietly.

She gave her boss a nod, then followed her ex-boyfriend out the door. Behind her, the Threes set up another mournful howl. To her, it sounded like a death knell.

After Riley had written a very long e-mail to her guy, during which she'd cried yet again, she headed for bed, exhausted. She knew she should eat something, but her stomach wasn't playing nice. She'd just turned off her light when her phone lit up with an incoming call. The display told her it was the man she missed more than anything in this world.

"Hey, Den."

"Ya've had a helluva day," Beck said, then heaved a sigh. "This is gonna earn ya some major blowback, ya know that."

His use of "ya" told her he was as upset as she was. "I know, but I don't regret what I did."

"Didn't figure ya would. Yer better at judgin' Hell's folks than I'll ever be."

Because of Ori. "I seem to attract the ones who like the Light. Go figure."

"Probably cuz of yer name, honey," he replied.

Riley Anora. *Valiant Light.*

"Or I have sucker stamped on my forehead."

"No, I woulda noticed. No matter what, I'll be watchin' yer back. Let me know if anyone from Rome contacts ya."

"Or shows up on the doorstep like they did the last time?"

"That too. But I think Elias would give me a warnin' if that was about to go down. Right now, they've got bigger things to worry about."

It was only now that she registered the exhaustion in his voice. She'd been so self-absorbed, she hadn't realized it was almost two in the morning in Scotland. "Why are you still up?"

"That thing I mentioned the other day? Well, it's getting worse. Once yer here, I'll share it all. I need yer help with it."

"Bad stuff?"

"No, it's way into the fuckin' bad now."

Beck rarely swore like that, which meant this was a very big deal.

"Okay, I'll help you anyway I can."

"Thank ya," he murmured, relieved. "God, I can't wait to have ya in my arms again. I'm not right when yer away from me."

Riley would have sworn she'd used the day's allocation of tears, but her eyes misted anyway. "Same here. There's an emptiness in my heart, this really big hole with your name on it."

"Now yer gettin' all sappy on me, Princess."

"You're the one who started it," she teased.

"Yeah, yeah. I need to get to bed, but I wanted to make sure ya were doin' okay."

"I'm better now. Thanks for calling. You be careful, okay?"

"I will. I love ya. See ya soon."

The tears gave way as the phone's display darkened. With a sniffle, Riley set it on the nightstand. Then, as she settled in for the night, she whispered a prayer for a brave demon, one who had dared to seek his freedom.

~~*

International Guild Manor House
Scotland

Another full day of digging through the manor's extensive archives had only given Beck a dull headache and a sincere appreciation for what Jonah Kepler did daily. Besides conducting research and keeping the library and archives in good order, Kepler catalogued new information, and did it all without a word of complaint.

He looked over at the old man now, who held a book under a desk light to help him read the faint print. Would that be Beck someday? He'd always figured he'd be one of those grand masters who was constantly in the middle of the action. Now he wondered about that. Perhaps when he got older, as his joints grew stiffer and his injuries proved too limiting, he'd be here in this room, searching for some obscure reference to give his fellow grand masters the edge against the Darkness.

It'd be easy to claim that wasn't what Fate had in store for him, but then, he'd never thought he'd learn how to read, let alone be a demon trapper. Or be in Scotland, about to become a grand master. Fate was one truly feisty lady with a wicked sense of humor. It was best not to tempt her further.

He put a leather bookmark in his place, then rose and stretched, feeling a couple vertebrae pop back into place. "I'd like to go for a run, clear my head. That okay?"

Kepler looked up. "That sounds like an excellent idea." He closed his own book. "For me, I think a strong cup of tea would do nicely."

Beck nodded and headed for his room to change into his running clothes. As he passed Trevor's office, he saw that the door was still shut, which it had been for most of the day. He tried not to read anything into that, and failed.

The long drive that led away from the manor was lined with ancient oak trees, and this time of year, they were bare, just stark trunks and branches. In a few months, they'd be full of leaves, green and vibrant. Like they'd been when Beck had first arrived.

I'm gonna miss this place.

Beck's mind began to clear as soon as he picked up his pace on the asphalt. He wore his pack, currently at about fifty pounds, barely noticing it was there now. His pace was in sync with his breathing, limbs, lungs, and heart working in concert. As he ran, feet hitting the pavement, he turned his mind to the research.

Both he and Kepler had begun a list of destroyed cities, writing the cause of the destruction under each one. Some were decimated by conquering armies, others by Mother Nature. When Beck wanted to dig further, Kepler had suggested that he start with maps, of all things. Find out where these cities had been located. Were they near an ocean? Was there a major earthquake, which had generated a tsunami? Was the town near a volcano? What about a large forest? That last question had confused Beck until the scholar explained that a wildfire could have caused that kind of destruction.

So Beck had worked the list, from top to bottom. Some city names he recognized—even *he* knew about Pompeii and Herculaneum. Still, some were new to him, like the city of Helike in Greece, which had been destroyed by an earthquake in the third century before Christ. Or Lisbon, Portugal, decimated by both a massive earthquake and the resulting tsunami in 1755. The list continued into the twentieth century, with San Francisco and Galveston, just to name a few.

In the end, Beck had managed to narrow it down to three places that had been wiped from the face of the earth, for which he could find no explanation of their destruction. Kepler was currently digging into those sites, hoping to discover a commonality.

As he made his way back to the manor, Beck finally hit his stride, clocking in at nearly five miles. Usually he had his head on straight within the first couple miles, but too much was up in the air. Riley's strange encounter with that free demon had spooked him. Not the demon itself, but that Hell had sent a Retriever after it. Why hadn't that thing just grabbed her up while it'd had the chance? Nothing could have stopped it.

The thought chilled him to the bone.

Now he knew that Lucifer's warning on the train had been about Riley's free demon. Which meant the Prince knew where that Four had been but had waited to send the Retriever until

Riley had returned to the school. There had been no reason to do that, other than to ensure she was in hot water with the Vatican.

You bastard. Always stirrin' the pot.

She'd be arriving tomorrow, right in the middle of this mess. At least then, he could keep her safe. Soon he'd be taking his oath, and then after a few days, they'd head back to Atlanta for the wedding.

It all sounded on track, but that was an illusion. There was too much going on that neither of them could control. Deep in his gut, Beck feared that something, or someone, was about to turn their lives upside down.

Chapter Ten

Harper's Office
Atlanta, Georgia

Master Harper only grunted when Riley entered the office the next morning, but she didn't take it personally. They'd never be friends, but at least now they respected each other. Ever since he'd joined Alcoholics Anonymous, Harper had been gaining some needed weight and his anger had subsided. She knew it was a constant battle, but if nothing else, he was one very stubborn man. That trait was exactly what he needed to fight this personal battle.

Riley set her trapping bag by her small desk and parked herself in the creaky chair. After selecting a blank trapping report, she began filling it out in black ink. While the rest of the world was into saving trees, trappers were old school. Though they did use computers—there was one in the office—sometimes close interactions with demons toasted electronics. Cell phones, in particular, which was why Riley always bought cheap ones. Since Master Harper regularly stored Hellspawn in the service bay, he couldn't risk losing all his files to a power surge. Sadly, no system was foolproof—last year, a Geo-Fiend had destroyed his old office, scattering his reports to the four winds.

When Riley reached the part that said DESCRIBE TRAPPING ACTIVITY, she grimaced. Then began writing. It took her over half an hour to finish the report, which included extra pages, to ensure it stated exactly what had happened. Including why she'd made the decision not to capture Isra in the first place. The fact that she was admitting this to the National Guild made her very uneasy. No doubt there'd be some lengthy discussions about this with the board of directors, but she trusted them more than she had last December. A big shakeup had meant the current members were more open to new ideas. And boy, this was one big new idea.

Hey, guess what? There're demons that are good guys. Go figure.

Dropping the pen into a cracked Atlanta Falcons cup with its numerous brethren, she delivered the report to her superior. Harper looked up, took the pages, and began reading. Knowing this would take some time, she went into the service bay, where two Gastro-Fiends were in residence, waiting their turn to be taken to a demon trafficker. From there, they'd be handed over to the Church. In the past, Riley had thought they were prayed over or something. Now she knew that these demons were destined to be killed.

After breaking out the hose, Riley gave them each a long squirt of water, the fiends lapping at the liquid just like dogs. She ignored the usual announcements of her name and various threats. She'd just rolled the hose back up and stored it when she heard Harper call out to her.

Stepping back inside his office, Riley found him frowning. "Is that okay?"

He gave a nod. He tore out the office's copies and jammed the remainder into a FedEx envelope marked for next-day delivery. Which meant it'd be hitting the Guild's office just about the time she was stepping off the plane in Edinburgh. Though the timing would work for her, she regretted that Harper would be the one to field the outraged calls from the Guild's hierarchy.

"What would you have done?" she asked.

He looked up at her, his brow furrowed. "I probably would have hauled that Four out of the school, but I'm not sure. Spent most of last night thinking about that and I still don't know."

"If there are free demons, why hasn't Lucifer hunted them all down? And how do they get free?"

"How does anyone get a second chance?" he asked, his eyes sliding away from her now. "You make the choice, day by day, to stop doing what's wrong. What's killing you."

He wasn't just talking about the demons now.

"That takes an immense amount of courage," she said, hoping he'd get the message.

"Maybe," he muttered. He shoved two trapping orders her way. "Got a Geeker at Grady Hospital and a report of a Pyro near the zoo. You want to take the runs?"

"Sure. You need the apprentices for anything?"

"Nope. Best if they keep out from under my feet today."

Which was his way of saying he really needed some space.

"Will do." She scooped up the trapping orders. "How unhappy is National going to be about what I did with Isra?"

"What do you think?" Harper challenged.

"Master trappers make judgment calls. I made one that day."

"That's the way I saw it. Doesn't mean they're going to like it." From outside came the slam of car doors. "Your kids are here."

Kids. That's what he called them, even though Richard was in his thirties.

"Thanks," she said, then left Harper to his paperwork. Though she appreciated that he was covering her butt, she knew it might prove to be the worst decision of his career.

Her three apprentices looked bright-eyed and ready to tackle the day. Mostly because they had no idea of what had happened at the school the day before.

"What's up this morning?" Kurt asked.

"Lots of fun stuff. Here's a question for you: Which presents more of a public danger, a Geeker at a hospital or a Pyro at the zoo?"

"Pyro. It'll roast all those animals and people will go crazy about that," Kurt replied.

"Hospital," Jaye countered. "A Geeker can get into the computer systems and God knows what kind of damage it could do. Like into the electronics that run the dialysis units or the cardiac monitors."

Of course, she'd be thinking that given her mom's recent illness.

Riley looked over at Richard now. "Which one?"

"Hospital. The Geeker has a better chance of harming a large number of civilians than the Firebug."

"I agree. We're off to Grady."

Richard grinned. "Score one for me."

"Teacher's pet," Kurt razzed. "You're her favorite."

"Last week it was you," Richard replied.

"And the week before that, it was me," Jaye said, "so we're all good."

Yes, you are.

~~*

Edinburgh Airport
Scotland

Looking back, the Geeker had been easy, but Riley's decision to pick up the zoo's Pyro-Fiend and dump it into the dry ice had been a mistake. Not that she or any of her apprentices had been injured, but apparently, the fiend gave off some sort of faint residue. The kind of residue that airport scanners hated.

When she'd walked into the electronic scanner portal and held up her arms so it could verify she was a safe citizen, the machine went nuts. After some strange sort of noises, it promptly shut off, which had caused some panic among the security people. After being patted down twice, wanded three times, and questioned at length, Riley was finally allowed on the airplane. She'd already made a mental note to write a brief article about this issue for the National Guild's magazine, provided she was still a licensed trapper at that point.

After an uneventful flight, she landed in Edinburgh and made her way through customs, then headed for the arrivals area. The last time she'd been in here, necromancers had kidnapped her, hauling her off to a local cemetery. There, they'd summoned a demon, offering her blood as bait. It'd cost all but one of those involved their lives, including the Archfiend.

Riley had expected her fiancé to pick her up, but with whatever was going on with the Vatican, he'd been forced to stay at the manor. This time, she and Beck had taken precautions. She beamed when she spied a familiar face waiting for her, his big smile in place. This was one of her most favorite people on Earth.

"Angus!" she said, hurrying up to him, her suitcase rolling alongside.

Angus Stewart gave her one of his big bear hugs. The grand master was in his sixties, walked with a noticeable limp, and was as Scottish as they came. He'd trained her dad, and in many ways, was as much a father to her and Beck as Paul Blackthorne had been. As armor against Scotland's long, cold winter, he wore a thick woolen sweater, slacks, and a heavy coat. His cane was tucked under his arm.

"Good trip?" he asked as they headed for the nearest exit.

"The best. I slept the whole way."

As expected, Scotland was chilly, with a brisk breeze that cut right through Riley's exposed skin and reminded her that she'd left her gloves in her luggage.

She looked over at Angus, noting his rosy cheeks and the sparkle in his eyes. "How are your grandkids?"

His eyes sparkled even more now. "Rambunctious as always. They're lovin' havin' me around. I'm an easy one ta bribe for sweets."

"Then you're the perfect granddad."

He grinned back. "It's been verra good ta spend time with the family. I'm lookin' forward ta the day I can move home, now that I'll not be worryin' about how things are goin' in Atlanta. Not with the two of ya there."

If anyone deserved time with his kin, it was this man. He'd devoted his life to preserve the balance.

"You make sure to come back to Atlanta at least once a year," she insisted.

"I shall. I want ta see all yer bairns, when ya finally get settled down enough ta have them. Speakin' of which, how goes the weddin' preparations?" Angus asked as they approached a red Vauxhall at the end of a row. He popped open the trunk and tucked her suitcase inside.

"I think I've got everything covered. Mrs. Ayers is still baking like crazy. She's filled the freezer at your place and the spare one in the garage, and is working on mine. We just need to get Beck home and we're all ready." At least she hoped so. She had to be missing something, right?

Once they were settled inside, Angus started the car as she latched her seatbelt. "That dear lady looked ta be in heaven when I left. With all the flour and such flyin' around, I figured it was best ta get out of her way, if ya know what I mean."

"I do. I've gone over a couple of times to help out, but mostly I just buy the baking ingredients and back off."

"Wise lass."

They chatted back and forth amiably until they were on the motorway. So far, they'd avoided one topic in particular.

Just get it over with. "Beck tell you what happened with the Four in Atlanta?"

Angus's jovial attitude withered. "Aye. He called me this mornin'."

"You grand masters know about the Unbounds, right?"

"Aye," he said again. "I'm not surprised Lucifer sent a Retriever for this one. He brooks no traitors in his midst. Ya saw how he purged Hell of his enemies last year."

Part of that purge had occurred during the battle where Beck had been stabbed by a Fallen's fiery sword, a wound that had nearly killed him.

To clear her mind of the still-raw images, Riley stared out the side window at the passing cars as they drove west on the motorway. It was four lanes, divided, and she kept thinking they were on the wrong side of the road. After a couple of days, that would pass. The motorway was clear and dry, but fresh snow must have fallen in the last few days, as it was piled along the sides after the snowplow had passed.

"It's always pretty here," she said.

"Even more so if yer born here," he replied.

Riley gave a long sigh. "I just wish there was something I could do to help Isra, without trading my soul for it."

"Aye, but there isn't."

"I know—that just makes it harder. More than anything, I don't want Simon to get into any trouble with the Vatican."

"I hear ya two work well tagether," Angus said as he switched lanes, the soft *click click* of the turn signal barely audible above the car noise. "Is everythin' good between ya?"

She nodded. "We're more like brother and sister now. I like it that way, and so does he."

"Not all ex-boyfriends would be that friendly."

"No, not at all." Allan, her ex from a few years back, certainly hadn't been. Even now, she wondered how he was doing. Hopefully, Ori scaring the crap out of him had put Allan on a very straight and non-abusive path. If not, he was headed to Hell, for sure.

"Rome is going to get in my face about this."

Angus was quiet for a time as they passed the cutoff to Linlithgow, overtaking a lorry along the way. Riley watched the scenery fly by out the side window. Both fir and deciduous trees lined the road now, some laden with snow.

Finally, he spoke. "Truth is, the Vatican has a lot on their plate right now. I'm not sure if they're gonna bother with ya in the short term, unless it serves some purpose."

"Is that on-the-plate stuff the same Beck's been dealing with?"

He nodded. "How much did he tell ya?"

"Nothing, other than that it's really bad. He said he'd explain it all once I got here."

"Well then, since we have time, I'll tell ya what's goin' on, because when ya two are finally tagether, Rome is *not* gonna be yer first concern."

Riley fought the blush that threatened to warm her cheeks, but it faded when she saw the grim look in the grand master's eyes.

"What's so bad that Beck actually used the 'f' word?"

"Cities are bein' utterly destroyed with fire and brimstone," Angus replied, his voice nearly cracking. "All that's left is ashes. We're talkin' about the deaths of thousands of people. It truly takes yer breath away."

"My God," she said.

"It's three cities now. We lost another one in India just this mornin'. That was over seven thousand souls."

A profound icy shiver coursed up Riley's spine. She remembered the eerie howls of the Threes from the evening before. Had they somehow known what was happening, half a world away? She'd seen pictures of natural disasters, but having everyone turned to ash was unthinkable. Her mind could not conjure up that image, and perhaps that was for the best.

"Beck and MacTavish went to one of these towns?"

"Aye, in the Czech Republic."

"No wonder he's so upset." Riley's hands had started shaking and it took some effort to open her bottle of water. After a long drink, she capped it again. "What's Rome's take on this?"

"They blame Lucifer, of course," the grand master replied. She could hear his frustration. "They've got a one-track mind about Hell. Of course, nine times outta ten, they're right."

She took some time to think it through. "I can see a rogue Fallen, maybe, but the Prince is all about those souls. Why kill a bunch of people he could scare into becoming his servants?"

"Maybe he did get their souls," Angus said, "and then decided ta harvest them all at one time rather than waitin'."

That suggestion was too horrific for words. "No, that would be a fundamental change in his game strategy."

"That's our thought as well."

They drove in silence for a couple miles, each deep in their own thoughts. Finally, Angus seemed to stir out of his musings.

"Ah, here's somethin' nice for a change. Those are the

Kelpies," he said, pointing out the front window. "Aren't they wonderful?"

Riley leaned forward eagerly. She'd heard about the two stainless-steel horse head sculptures, but had never had a chance to see them. They sat on the left side of the motorway, near the water, one with its neck arched into the air.

"Wow, those are *so* cool," she said.

"They were built a few years back at the eastern entrance of the canal. I think they're bloody spectacular, myself."

"I agree. I'll have to come back sometime. I'd love to see them at sunset." Sibyl's seemingly indecipherable warning popped into her head right then. "Did anyone warn that these disasters were coming? You know, like psychics or seers?"

Angus frowned for a moment, shooting her a glance. "Ya know, I'm not sure. Both we and Rome have been scourin' our archives, but perhaps we should be checkin' with the witches as well."

"I talked to one in Atlanta and she said the world was ending."

"And?"

She groaned. You just couldn't get much past this guy. "And she said I had some role to play in keeping that from happening."

He huffed. "Aren't ya the lucky one?"

"Tell me about it." She hesitated, then blurted, "If it is a Fallen . . . who will you guys send to kill it?"

The tensing of Angus's jaw gave her the answer even before he spoke. "Most likely Beck. He's the youngest of us all."

That's what she figured he'd say. There was no way Beck would back down from the challenge. Riley knew that confrontation could only end in two ways—and one of those outcomes meant she'd be alone for the rest of her life.

Chapter Eleven

International Guild Manor House
Scotland

After breakfast, Beck drove to the cottage located on the other side of the loch. He'd stayed there before; the grand masters often used it as a private retreat. Composed of solid stone blocks, with chimneys at each end, it'd been updated somewhere along the line and now had a pair of skylights. Today, in the snow, it looked timeless, like it'd been there for centuries.

Beck had fired up the woodstove to warm the small space, and then headed out for a walk. Hands on his hips, he gazed across the loch to the west. From here, he could almost see where Riley had fought the necromancer last fall. Further down that hill was the manor.

He'd found a solace in this place that was hard to describe. Some might even think he'd been here in a past life. Beck wasn't the kind to believe in all that—living this life was enough of a challenge—but the first time he'd stood outside this cottage and gazed over the loch, he knew he'd been here before. He'd closed his eyes that day and felt the breeze brushing across his kilt, though he'd not been wearing one. He'd smelled a peat fire and heard the pipes in the distance. Felt the weight of a Scottish great sword in his hand.

He'd never told anyone about that, not even Riley. It was one of those private things that you held close and didn't share. Even now, he felt that connection and it stirred his soul in some mysterious way.

It'd been Jonah's suggestion that he and Riley be here the night before the investiture. He'd said that they should have some time alone before their lives changed forever. For all his academic ways, the old man possessed a deeply romantic soul.

Not that the ceremony was a done deal. During the last month or so, both Jonah and Trevor had repeatedly reminded him that he could step back at any time, even during the ceremony, right before he took the vow. That if his heart and mind weren't fully committed, he should step back. No blame would be cast, they'd insisted.

Beck had acknowledged those warnings, but he also suspected that this was what his life had been all about. Well, that and marrying a certain brown-eyed beauty who he loved more each passing day.

He'd just begun his trek back to the cottage when he saw a red car making its way down the gravel track toward the building. He picked up speed, aggravated that he wasn't already there to welcome his fiancée. By the time he'd covered the ground between them, the car had delivered its passenger and started retracing its way back along the road.

Riley came into view now, headed for the cottage. She was bundled up against the cold, her backpack on one shoulder, suitcase in hand. She placed the luggage on the stones just outside the front door and was about to knock when Beck called out her name. She turned toward him, blinking in the bright sunlight.

Chucking off her backpack, she took off at a run across the snowscape, her hair flowing behind her, brownish red in the sunlight. When they drew close, she launched herself at him. As Beck's arms encircled her, he buried his face in that hair, reigniting the memory of her scent. This was *his* woman, and there was no other in the world who could come close to her. Their first kiss should have melted the snow at their feet. The second probably did. It was only after that one, and the need for air, that they stepped back to study each other.

"God, you're beautiful," he said, brushing back a lock of hair that had fallen into her eyes. It shimmered in the sunlight, dark in some places, auburn in others. Her cheeks were rosy, as were her lips. She seemed older somehow, though it'd only been a few months since they'd last seen each other.

Riley didn't reply, just hugged him again. He could feel her trembling and he knew he was doing the same. Finally, she released him, stepped back, and took one of his hands in hers, glove to glove.

"Please tell me this is the last time we'll be away from each other for so long," she said.

He saw the pleading in her eyes, but he couldn't lie. "I hope so, but I can't make that promise. You know why."

Riley nodded sadly. "We'll do our best, then."

"We always do." He placed a kiss on her cheek. "Come on, let's get you inside and warmed up. It's damned cold out here."

As they walked, he saw her stealing glances at him. Did he appear any different to her? Older? Smarter? Or was he the same as when he left Atlanta in December?

When they reached the cottage, he opened the door, set her luggage and backpack inside, then stepped back outside.

"You going to welcome me to Scotland like you did last time?" she asked, her eyes full of longing now.

"What do you think, Princess?" he said.

Beck swung her up in his arms, stepped over the threshold, and kicked the door shut.

~~*

Riley woke in the solidly muscled arms of her fiancé in a small, yet comfortable bed. She rolled over onto her back and tugged the duvet up to cover herself. Above them, the aged ceiling beams reflected the last rays of sunlight in shimmering patterns that streamed through the windows. The potbellied stove, which was positioned in front of one of the fireplaces, poured out a steady heat, along with the earthy smell of peat.

"Any way we could just stay here by this loch, watching the sun rise and set, and never see another demon again?" Riley murmured.

Beck rolled over onto his back as well. "We'd have to get really good at trappin' and raisin' our own food. Because it doesn't sound like you intend to make many trips to the grocery store."

She gave him a mock frown.

"I know what you mean," he said. "There's a kind of peace here that gets inside of you. It's why this cottage belongs to the International Guild. It's one of their retreats. They've got a few of them around the world."

"I'd buy it from them in a heartbeat. Well, I would if I had any money."

"Makes two of us."

Riley sat up, tucking the bedcovers around her again, and studied the interior of the building more closely. At the far end of the cottage, a pair of stuffed chairs sat in front of the wood stove, an end table with a bronze lamp in between them. The kitchen had a small refrigerator, gas stove, and microwave, as well as a rectangular table covered with a green tablecloth, which matched the curtains. Two wooden chairs were tucked under the table. On the other side of the kitchen was the bathroom, also very small.

"Rennie would love this place. So many things to chew," she said, searching around for her clothes. To her chagrin, they appeared to be scattered from the door to the bed.

The instant her feet touched the cold slate floor, she regretted it. She groped for first one sock, then the other, pulling them on. On the other side of the bed, Beck was doing the same, though not hopping from one foot to another. He was used to this now.

While she got herself in decent shape, he pulled food from the refrigerator, then made her a sandwich and heated some chicken noodle soup. Figuring she should do something useful, she tossed more peat into the stove, then walked to the large window that overlooked the loch.

"It's snowing." It was just light flakes, but as she watched, they grew heavier. It only made the scenery more gorgeous.

"Supposed to be about four inches or so. That's just a dustin' for these folks."

Riley turned toward him now, hearing something else in his voice, an edge of worry. She knew it had nothing to do with them as a couple, so maybe it was what he was facing tomorrow. "You ready to take your vow?"

Beck paused in his soup stirring, his back to her. "Yes. And no."

She joined him at the stove, took the spoon from him, and shooed him away.

"Gettin' bossy the older you get," he said.

"You're just figuring that out?" He smirked at her. "What part of the 'no' are you willing to talk about?"

Beck took one of the kitchen chairs, turned it around, and sat, straddling it. He rested his arms on the back. "It's one helluva thing I'd be agreein' to do."

"Yes, it is. You'd be responsible—well you and a few others—for keeping the balance between Heaven and Hell. That's a huge job."

"We try, at least. Not sure how much good we do," he admitted.

"What spooks you the most?" she asked, leaning against the counter.

"Not bein' good enough for the job."

"Okay, that's a valid concern. What could you do to make yourself better prepared? More studying?"

He shrugged. "I don't know. I think I could study for the next ten years and never been good enough."

Riley smiled, understanding now. "Which means you'll do fine. You know your weaknesses and your strengths. That's about all you can do, grand master or not."

He cocked his head. "How'd you get so wise, Princess?"

"Not wise, just older." Behind her, the soup began to boil, and she stirred it a few more times before pouring it into earthenware bowls. "What happens if you decide not to become a grand master? You'd be taking all that knowledge with you when you leave."

"They got that covered. It's some sort of magical thing. Jonah would do it. I'd remember a few things but not much. That way their secrets remain safe."

"Huh. I wondered how they'd handle that."

"Better'n lopping off my head," he said. "That's how they used to do it, until they decided a spell was more practical."

"No kidding."

Once all the food was on the table, they settled in. Beck had a beer at his elbow and Riley had hot tea.

"Angus tell ya about why we went to Prague?" he asked in between bites of his sandwich.

She nodded. "You know, of all the things I figured you might be facing, this wasn't it."

"Yeah. I've spent the last few days with Jonah, goin' through the archives, tryin' to find somethin' that matches what I saw at that site in the Czech Republic. So far, no luck."

"What about the Vatican?"

"They're doin' exactly what we are, but they're not sharin' anythin' right now."

"If they're convinced it's the Prince, they may not," she replied.

He shook his head in dismay. "That's what worries me."

"What was it like?"

"I can't really describe it, and I've seen death so many times before. These folks never stood a chance. From what we can tell, one minute they were alive, and then everything burned, them included."

"My God. How do you fight something like that?"

He shook his head, his eyes riveted on his hands now.

Riley finished her soup, collected the dishes, and set them in the sink to wash, taking solace in the mundane actions.

"Tomorrow mornin'," Beck began, his tone so serious she turned to him, "tomorrow mornin', at dawn, I'd like to watch the sunrise with ya. Will ya do that with me?"

If he was using "ya" instead of "you," Riley knew there was only one answer she could give. "Of course I will."

~~*

When Beck nudged her awake at quarter to six, it was still dark. Fortunately, he'd remembered that it would take some time for Riley to get dressed and stumble out the door. There was also blessed silence, as her fiancé had quickly learned that talking to her first thing in the morning was a waste of time, if not life threatening.

The instant Riley stepped outside, the shock of the cold air made her cough, slapping her awake. "Whoa!"

"Not bad, actually. It was way colder a few weeks ago."

She groaned, her breath forming a thick cloud as they hiked through the snow. It had that crisp sound, crunching under their boots. Winter in the Highlands was certainly not for wimps.

"You actually go running at this unholy hour?"

"Yup. It's real quiet, so I can think things through."

Though some might believe Beck incapable of that kind of deep introspection, they were just buying into his good-old-boy persona, the one that made him seem like a pushover. Instead, he had an instinctual sense of people and their motives, honed by an abusive mother and a hellish childhood.

When Beck took her gloved hand as they walked into the slowly retreating twilight, Riley sensed that whatever he intended was too solemn for idle chatter, so she held her silence.

It'd been a huge deal for her when she'd taken the oath as a master trapper—so important that she'd wept openly in front of the entire Guild. Only a few of the trappers had smirked at that; most knew that had been her way of paying tribute to her dead father.

What Beck faced was many levels above that. So much so, she couldn't even imagine the amount of pressure he was feeling. He'd hinted at it the night before, but now it had to be weighing on him, body and soul. Which meant that today, of all days, she had to be by his side, reminding him he'd been *tested* and *chosen* for this great honor. That he was equal to it, despite his many doubts.

Beck guided them to a location near the waterline, which was dotted with smooth rocks. None of them were big enough to sit on, so they remained standing. Some sort of animal tracks skirted the waterline. A fox, perhaps?

He stripped off his gloves, stuffing them in his pockets, and gestured for her to do the same. The chilly air immediately nipped at her fingers. In the distance, the sun began to appear over the hills, painting rose tones on the fresh snow.

Beck cleared his throat. "Back in the day, there used to be this . . . marriage ceremony they'd do here in Scotland."

His eyes were on her now as he reached into his pocket and pulled out a strip of green cloth with white and gold embroidery on it. "Today I'm goin' to take a vow to spend my life keepin' the world safe. It would mean so much to me if my wife watched me take that oath."

Something had pushed him to do this, something Riley did not understand, but she knew that questioning him would only weaken the gesture. This wouldn't be a legal marriage, but that didn't matter. The man she loved wanted to claim her as his wife, here and now. The bond between them would be as strong as any law could offer. *Stronger.*

"I'm liking this old Scottish tradition," she said.

Relief played over his face, as if he'd thought she might deny them this moment. With some effort, they managed to tie the cloth around their entwined hands.

Beck smiled now, his warm brown eyes radiating his love. Taking a deep breath, he looked over the loch. The sun rising over the water caught the side of his face, highlighting his square jaw, his inner strength.

He turned back toward her. "From this time forward, I claim you as my wife, Riley Anora Blackthorne. There is no other, and there will be no other. I will always love you and protect you, even with my life."

Riley felt the light sting of tears. She took a few seconds to gather her words, to ensure they honored his.

"From this time forward, you are my husband, Denver Beck,

the man who will stand by me, love me, and fight by my side. I love you more than anything in this world, and I will protect you with my life, in this world and all worlds to come."

They kissed. When she opened her eyes, she saw a sheen of tears in his. Seeming embarrassed, he looked away after he removed the strip of cloth and tucked it into a pocket.

Beck tugged on his gloves, still blinking away the tears. "Well, *Mrs. Beck,* how's about we go back to the cottage and start our marriage the proper way?"

He was always pushing that name change button. "Sure, *Mr. Blackthorne,* that'd be fine," she said.

"You are so damned stubborn."

"Me?" she said, as they hiked to the crown of the hill. "This from Mr. *My Way or the Highway?*"

"Mouthy, too. Never noticed that before," he said, grinning. "Oh well, can't have a perfect wife, I guess. Just have to do with the one I got."

Riley managed to scoop up a batch of snow and form it into a snowball before taking off at a run. Something told her to duck, and his missile went sailing over her.

"Hey, no fair!" he said, hurrying to create another snowball. "You can't use those Jedi magic tricks on me."

"Wanna bet?" she said, then nailed her new spouse dead center in the chest.

Riley knew she'd never make it to the cottage before he caught up with her. But with Beck, losing was just as much fun as winning.

Chapter Twelve

Beck and Riley had reluctantly packed up their belongings just after lunch, and left the cottage behind. He'd tried to lighten the sad moment by claiming this had been their first honeymoon, and that they should do this each year on their wedding anniversary. Even as he made that suggestion, he knew the demands of their jobs would make it hard to keep. Still, in the time they'd spent in that small house, they'd grown even closer. He didn't understand what it meant, but he knew Riley felt it as well. Sometimes the most important things in one's life were impossible to explain.

When they'd arrived back at the manor, Angus was in Trevor's office, the door closed yet again. Riley had promptly retreated to the room next to his to take a nap. He'd expected that, since he'd rousted her out before dawn. Knowing he wouldn't see her for an hour or so, Beck went in search of Jonah to find out if there had been any new revelations.

The elder grand master looked up from his current book and smiled, sending a few of his wrinkles in new directions.

"Thanks for suggestin' we go to the cottage. We watched the sun rise this mornin'. It was . . . special," Beck said.

"You do what you had planned?" Jonah asked.

Beck nodded. "She's my wife now, at least by old Scottish tradition."

"Good," the old man said. "You're as much man and wife now as any law can bestow. That's what matters."

"We'll make it all legal soon enough." Beck pulled out a chair and sat, then peered at the book Jonah had in front of him. Given the state of the binding, it was a very old one, which was why the archivist wore cotton gloves so as not to damage the fragile pages. "Find anythin'?"

"I'm not sure. This is a transcription from the original Aramaic into Latin about a city that was destroyed during the reign of a minor king in Chaldea. It speaks of a voice that comes in the night, telling the inhabitants of that city that their time is at an end. Only those outside the city survived, which is why we have a record of the event."

Jonah frowned, put his cotton-gloved hand on the manuscript, and followed along for a couple lines with his finger. "It says that there was an unrelenting rain of fire and brimstone. Once all were consumed, a spinning column of flames rose into the heavens and only ashes were left behind." He paused, looking up at Beck again. "Of course, we're trying to visualize this horror through the eyes of witnesses who lived five or six centuries before the birth of Jesus."

"I've seen videos of firestorms. They're wicked things, with minds of their own. It could account for what I saw north of Prague."

"Like Dresden, then."

Beck quirked an eyebrow, not knowing what Jonah was talking about.

The grand master noticed the expression. "The bombing of Dresden, Germany, was during the Second World War, in 1945. The reason I remember it so clearly is that my father was in one of the British bombers. He never spoke of what happened, but it marked him for life. My mother said that the man who'd climbed into the plane that day never came home. It broke him, and he committed suicide when I was five."

"Sweet Jesus."

Jonah nodded solemnly. "The British and the Americans bombed the city. After the first attack, they returned three hours later so they could hit the rescue crews. The resulting firestorm sucked all the oxygen out of the air and people suffocated no matter where they were."

"How many died?" Beck asked.

"They estimate twenty to thirty thousand. When you described what you saw in the Czech Republic, I thought of Dresden. Or, in the case of this ancient city," he said, tapping the book, "it could have been a methane explosion. There are deposits in that area, which is now Iraq and eastern Syria. If one of those natural gas deposits somehow began to leak, perhaps in multiple locations, an explosion could have easily leveled a city."

"But what about the voice-in-the-night thing?"

Jonah shrugged. "Who knows what they thought happened? So much of that history was oral and embellished with each telling, until it finally was written down."

"So we're really no further ahead than we were a few days ago?" Beck said. He'd so hoped there'd be some "that's it!" moment

"Well, we do know the blades of grass you brought back from the Czech Republic are infused with sulfur. It matches samples taken at the other locations."

That really wasn't progress. "Hell sure has a thing about brimstone. I can still smell the stink of it from when I was down there."

"Me as well." The old man's eyes went distant, as if sorting through his memories. When he spoke, his voice was thick with emotion. "It was my grandfather who showed me the way out of Hell. He was a hard man, rarely laughed, a coal miner. He scared me when I was a child, he was so gruff. I never fully trusted him until that moment, but something told me that if I didn't, I was done for." Jonah stared at the fire in the hearth now. "Every morning, I whisper a prayer that he's free, no longer in Lucifer's chains. He certainly earned that freedom."

Beck looked down at the table, rubbing a finger across the wood. "It was my mama. I didn't trust her either. Until then."

"Even those who have hurt us the most may become our allies," Jonah replied softly. He rose stiffly, an indication of his advanced age. "One of the blessings of being an old fellow is the right to wander off for a nap whenever I choose. I'm going to do just that. I want to be especially bright for tonight."

Tonight. When Beck's life would change yet again.

Jonah laid a thin hand on his shoulder. "I remember well all the doubts that tumbled through my head the day of my investiture. Your fears are not unique, Denver, but your abilities are. I know you don't believe me, but you are here because you were meant to be. Trust in that, if nothing more."

"Thank you," Beck said, a lump in his throat.

He watched as Jonah walked slowly out of the library, the man's final words rattling around in his head. Once the door closed, Beck rose and went to the section of the library dedicated to the lives of the grand masters. Kneeling, he chose a biography at random, then headed for his favorite chair, the one near the hearth. Once settled, he cracked open the book. This one was about the life of Hiram Joseph Halevi, who was born in 1801 in Jerusalem and died in Amsterdam in 1887. A Jew—because being a grand master wasn't a matter of religion, but of commitment.

There was a spidery inscription on the front page, written in now-faded black ink.

"'The man who never knows fear, never values life,'" Beck read aloud.

He closed his eyes and whispered into the quiet room. "If this isn't right, tell me now. Don't let me mess this up, because too many are countin' on me. Too many people can die. I'd rather be a nobody than fail them."

No voice came from the heavens, no warnings on the wings of angels, just profound silence and the constant heat coming from the hearth. When Beck opened his eyes, he found he'd shut the book. Perhaps that was all Halevi needed to tell him.

It was time for his vow.

~~*

Fifteen minutes before the ceremony was to begin, Riley tapped on the door between Beck's and her interconnected rooms.

Usually they left it ajar, but this afternoon he hadn't opened it, and she'd respected his privacy.

"Come in," he called out.

She entered to find her fiancé still fussing with his kilt, the one he'd worn last October, the red and black tartan. On his bed lay all the extra bits: the sporran, the flashes, and the *sgian dubh.*

"You need some help?" she asked.

Beck gave a nod, unusually solemn.

Taking the cue, Riley handed him the sporran and then helped him drape it around his waist. As he fastened it, she knelt and inserted a flash in the top of each of his knee socks. Finally, the small knife went into the right one. It was like preparing a knight for battle.

When Riley rose, she found him watching her intently. He held out his arms and she walked into them. He didn't say a word, but placed a kiss on her forehead. It wasn't a quick peck, more a reverent acknowledgment of the incredible bond between them.

"Thank you, wife," he said, his voice rough.

"You're welcome, husband." Riley laid her hand on his freshly shaved cheek. "No matter what you decide tonight, I am proud of you. Nothing will ever change that."

He blinked. "It helps knowin' yer by my side, no matter what." He flicked one of her earrings. "These look familiar."

"They're my favorite pair," she replied, mostly because he'd bought them for her. She was also wearing the dress he'd given her, as well as the demon claw necklace. Each of those were her way of honoring him.

"Well, let's get this done."

After they'd exited his room, she took Beck's hand and squeezed it as they walked down the hall toward the staircase, his skin cool to the touch. The wooden floors creaked under their feet, and there was the scent of furniture polish in the air. Various paintings were positioned on the stone walls along the hallway, most of them hunting scenes. Beck's thousand-yard stare told her he wasn't registering any of this.

He'd made it partway down the first flight of stairs when he came to an abrupt halt. When he looked over at her, the panic in his eyes was unmistakable.

"What the hell is Sadie Beck's bastard doin' here?" he asked in a whisper.

Riley walked down a couple steps, turned, and gazed back up at him. His hands were fisted at his sides, his breathing labored. He was an incredible man, with a will of steel, but the chains of his past often weighed him down.

"That's a good question," she replied. His eyes dropped to hers now, as if she was going to confirm his every doubt.

No, I'm not. Riley gestured toward the portraits that lined the wall along the staircase, all grand masters who'd come before him.

"I've been studying these people ever since you came here." She pointed at one painting, an East Indian man with pure white hair and a grave expression.

"Did you know that he was an untouchable, at the bottom of the caste system in India? Or how about this one?" she said, pointing at another portrait. "She came from Mexico. Poor, one of eight kids, with barely an education." Riley walked down another flight of stairs, Beck on her heels.

She stopped in front of another painting, that of a young black man. "Then there's this guy. Nathan Johnson grew up as one of ten children on a farm in South Carolina. His dad was a sharecropper and their family was dirt poor, as they say. Nathan could read and write, but he had nothing else to his name. Until that summer day in 1904 when he managed to kill a Fallen. It'd attacked a priest in Charleston, and though he wasn't Catholic, Nathan stepped in to protect him because he said it was the right thing to do."

Riley gazed up at the man she loved. His mouth was a thin line, his jaw clenched. "I'd say that Sadie Beck's son is in good company here. Grand masters aren't born, Den, they're chosen. It doesn't matter what you were in your past, all that matters is that you are here now."

Beck blinked a few times. "Sharecropper's kid, huh?" She

nodded. He stepped down to stand next to her. Reaching cut, he touched her chin. "I'm not sure about that chosen thing. I'm here because of you. I heard yer voice when I was in Hell, beggin' me to come back. You never gave up on me."

"And I never will."

Holding hands, they continued their descent, past even more portraits of men and women of all races and religions. Once on the ground floor, Beck led her to a separate hallway and a small chapel located on the backside of the manor. As they approached, she noticed that the pocket doors to that room were closed. Standing directly in front of them were Grand Masters Stewart, MacTavish, and Kepler.

"Master Blackthorne," MacTavish said.

"Good evening, grand masters," she replied.

After a quick kiss on her cheek, Beck went to join them. Seeing them together—three of them in kilts and Kepler in a crisp black suit—was like stepping back in time.

You belong here, Den. You're one of them, no matter how unsure you are.

With a nod toward her, MacTavish opened one of the pocket doors and the four of them entered, the door sliding closed behind them. Beck had warned her that there'd be a private meeting before the ceremony, for the grand masters only, and not to be concerned.

Before Riley had the opportunity to fidget, there was the sound of footsteps in the hallway as an earnest man in a cassock approached. For a few heartbeats, her chest tightened.

Was Father Rosetti here for her? *No.* Beck had invited him and Elias Salvatore for the investiture. At least she hoped that was why he was here.

Once she'd recovered, Riley made sure to smile, hoping to cover her momentary panic. "Father Rosetti. It's good to see you again. Den will be so pleased you're here tonight."

"I wouldn't miss it," the priest replied as he stopped next to her. "It is such an important occasion, both for him and the grand masters."

"Yes, it is. Funny how things have changed between the Vatican and these guys," she said, angling her head toward the chapel.

"A change brought on by you, in many ways," the priest replied.

"In some ways, but not all."

He nodded his agreement, studying the twin closed doors. "Are we permitted to see the actual ceremony?"

"Yes. They have a private meeting with the initiate beforehand. Probably hush-hush grand master stuff," she replied. "Secret handshakes and all that."

A rare grin appeared on Rosetti's face. "We do a lot of that in Rome, too. Is he nervous?"

"*Very.* Lots of doubts."

"As there should be. Anyone who takes on this task and doesn't have doubts is a fool."

"It's not a job I'd want. How do you balance good and evil? Sometimes evil people do things that turn out good. And vice versa. How do you make a judgment call when that's the case?"

"I'm not so sure on the evil-doing-good thing, but I agree in principle. Trying to decipher if someone's actions are because of Hell's influence, or otherwise, is very difficult. Make the wrong one and people may die. A child who might have been a great leader could perish. Or a mass murderer could go free."

"You do the same, in your own way," she observed, realizing they were talking about more than just hypothetical situations.

He looked over at her now. "As do you. It is not a pleasant burden, but it is the one we've been given."

Sometimes we even get it right.

More footsteps headed in their direction.

"Elias!" she said. "I was hoping you could be here."

The roguishly handsome captain of the Vatican's Demon Hunters joined them, giving Riley a tight hug. "How is our bride-to-be?"

She rolled her eyes. "If I'd known all the fussy stuff involved, I'd have just eloped. I doubt Beck would have minded at all. As long as there's barbecue and beer afterward, he's happy."

Elias laughed. "Your friends would miss that special moment, though," he said.

"Any chance either of you will make the ceremony?" She'd sent them invitations.

The pair traded looks.

"I'm not sure. It all depends on . . ." Elias said.

Rosetti nodded his agreement. "We'll try to be there."

"Fair enough." Especially with what Rome was facing now. "I know you'll be with us in spirit."

"Indeed."

Riley turned back toward the chapel. What was taking so long? How was Beck doing? Had he given in to his fears and decided not to take the oath?

"God will guide him," Father Rosetti said, as if reading her mind.

"I hope so."

To her relief, the pocket doors slid open then, one by one.

"It's time," Angus said, his voice unusually quiet.

As Riley stepped through that doorway, she swore she felt the faint tingle of magic. Some sort of ward, perhaps? She had expected a traditional chapel, maybe with an altar, a few candles here and there, and various religious symbols on the walls. That was not the case here.

The interior was stone like the rest of the manor, both the walls and the floors. The room itself was rectangular, and when you entered, you faced the longest side. It was surprisingly devoid of furniture, only seven chairs, four on the left and three on the right. They were made of solid oak, with high backs—no cheap folding ones here.

Beck and MacTavish stood nearby, talking intently, while Kepler had already taken a seat. Her fiancé turned the instant she entered the room. He gave a quick nod and then returned to his conversation. At any other time, she might have felt slighted, but not tonight.

Angus politely gestured to the three chairs to their right,

indicating that they should sit there.

As they settled in, Rosetti said, "This is a watershed event for us. To my knowledge, no one from the Holy See has ever attended an investiture."

That pleased her. "I'm sure a certain infernal individual isn't the least bit happy you're here." Riley absolutely refused to use his name in this place. "He'd prefer we fight each other rather than work together."

"Very true."

She eyed the priest now. "Does that mean there's some sort of truce in place right now? Because when I first met you two, things were not good between the grand masters and Rome."

"A truce makes it sound like a temporary cessation of conflict," Rosetti replied. "Détente is probably a better word. Our relationship with the grand masters is often dictated by the guidance of the Holy Father. The current pope had no objections to our attendance here today." He hesitated. "I must admit, I too had misconceptions of how the grand masters go about their work."

"Those misconceptions went both ways," Riley admitted.

"Sadly, yes."

As they waited for the ceremony to begin, she found her breathing was too shallow, so she tried to calm her nerves by studying her surroundings. As with most rooms in the manor, the chapel was chilly, oddly without a fireplace or woodstove to provide heat.

On the wall to her left, a set of six wooden doors had been folded back to reveal a large stained-glass window. With a start, she realized it was the one in MacTavish's office, behind his desk. Riley hadn't realized that room backed up against this one, since every time she'd been in the office, the doors had been closed.

As was always the case, the stained-glass artwork was fully lit to show Luficer's Fall in vivid detail. A reminder that anyone could plummet from grace given the right temptation.

"Remarkable, isn't it?" Elias said, studying the stained glass.

"Sure didn't go like he'd planned."

"Nothing ever does when you're working against Heaven's will," Elias said.

Sometimes it didn't even go well when you *were* doing exactly what they wanted.

Her eyes tracked to the opposite wall from the Fall; five narrow, clear glass arches filled the space. The center one was taller than the others, creating yet another arch. Pure light poured through them. Next to her, Elias and the priest were murmuring in Italian, their attention riveted on those arches, awe in their expressions.

Riley frowned. *How do they do that?* It was dark outside and it didn't look like they had any special lighting.

The longer she studied it, she knew she'd seen that kind of brilliant white light before, at the cemetery when Heaven's army had dropped out from the sky. A quick glance at the stained-glass window then back at the arches.

Then it hit her: This small chapel had Hell on its left, Heaven on its right. The grand masters stood in the middle, the fulcrum upon which the two were balanced.

"'Hail holy light, offspring of Heav'n first-born . . .'" Riley murmured.

"You know your Milton well," Rosetti said.

All too well.

With a grave expression, Grand Master Kepler rose and carefully ascended the two steps to the dais. Behind him, from floor to ceiling, was a stone wall full of niches, each demarked with a brass plaque. The inscriptions were too small for Riley to read. Inside each of those niches was a votive candle, almost all of which were lit with a blue twinkling light. However, a group in the very center was white. She wondered at their significance.

Kepler positioned himself behind a low padded bench, the kind used for kneeling while in prayer. Near that was a table upon which sat a chalice, a sheathed sword, and a white linen cloth.

As the grand master arranged the items on the table to his

liking, her fiancé's attention remained riveted on the wall of votives, his hands resting on his thighs, his fingers flat against the kilt's fabric.

Closing her eyes, Riley prayed, for both Beck and herself.

Chapter Thirteen

Beck had been told that each votive candle represented a grand master, and that those with a blue flame were no longer with them. Those still alive had a bright white one. Except one votive, which had no flame at all.

Mine.

Once Beck took his oath, gave his life to this cause, the candle would light on its own. According to Angus—and Beck wasn't sure if he believed this—the candle changed color in the event of his death. That was often the first indication of the loss of one of their own.

Those who'd renounced their vows, or had sided with Hell, were no longer on this wall. This was only for those grand masters who had remained true to the calling.

His palms were sweaty now, his heart hammering, every breath tight. This was what he'd been working toward all these months, perhaps for all his life. Could he take the next step? Dare he take the next step?

Beck swore he felt a loving hand on his shoulder, and he knew it was Paul's. It wasn't the first time it had happened, but this time it nearly brought tears.

Grand Master Kepler cleared his throat. "This is a solemn occasion. There are only twenty-nine of us in the world at this moment. Perhaps soon, there will be one more."

He looked down at Beck now, his expression one of deepest affection. "Denver Beck, are you willing to stand before us and be judged?"

Beck rose, his knees more unsteady than he'd like. He

glanced toward the wall with the five arches and the Light, then back at the old man.

"Yes, I am." Behind him, he swore he could hear Angus sigh in relief.

"Do any in this room have concerns that this man will be unable to fulfill his duties as a grand master?"

Beck's heartrate picked up again, knowing there were so many reasons why he shouldn't be here. Even before he could begin to count them out in his mind, he realized the room was silent.

"There are no objections, then," Kepler continued. "Does anyone wish to speak as to why this young man *should* become one of us?"

To Beck's surprise, the captain of the Demon Hunters rose.

"I am Elias Salvatore, and I met Denver Beck a little over a year ago. Even though the situation was difficult for both of us, I found him to be a trustworthy and honorable man." Elias paused. "I can attest to his valor during our battle with the rogue Fallen, his courage when my men and I were trapped on a roof with undead demons. I will always remember his humor, even when things were at their darkest. You will find no better choice for a grand master."

Elias resumed his seat as Beck stared, astonished at the man's testimony.

Angus rose next. "I second all Captain Salvatore said. I've come ta love this lad like a son, because he is the true embodiment of one of my dearest friends, Paul Blackthorne. Paul, may he rest in peace, saw this young man's potential before anyone else, and made sure that I realized it as well. We're here taday not only because of this lad's tenacity and courage, but because of another man's wisdom. Paul was right—this lad is more than worthy ta become one of us."

As Angus resumed his seat, it was Trevor's turn. "Denver and I have spoken on many an evenin', after he'd completed his day's studies. We have shared not only some fine whisky but also his life story.

"It is said that 'what's past is prologue.' So it is with Denver Beck. His harsh childhood made him strong, where others would have been broken. He has been tempted by the Prince himself, and turned away from that seductive path. He has stood his ground with a Fallen and triumphed."

Trevor's eyes went to the Vatican's men now. "The One who created us gave us free will. Our task, as grand masters, is ta ensure that all have a chance ta make those personal choices, be they for good or ill. I truly believe Denver is worthy ta join us in our quest ta balance the Light against the Dark."

"Anyone else?" Kepler said.

Riley rose now, wiped away her tears with a tissue, then cleared her throat.

"It may be said I'm biased—I am engaged to this guy, after all." There were chuckles at this. "But I've known Den since I was a kid. Okay, maybe that wasn't that long ago, though it feels like it. We've argued and fought over the years, but no matter how angry I was at him, I knew he was there for me. For anyone who needed protection."

She looked over at him now, and her gaze was like a loving caress. "I've watched him feed the homeless, stand up to arrogant politicians, fight Hell itself. Someday, when a new grand master is walking up that stairway, they'll see his portrait. Then someone will say, 'That was Denver Beck. He was true to the calling. He never wavered, and he never forgot that love is the most powerful weapon in the universe."

Riley blinked back more tears, then dropped into her chair, as if all her strength had gone into her testimony. Beck rubbed at his own eyes and his fingers came away wet. The love and support he felt was overwhelming. Kepler gave him a few moments to regain his composure, then gestured for him to come forward.

Beck took his place on the kneeler. As he knelt, he was mindful of the kilt. It wouldn't go over well if he flashed the room. That thought nearly made him laugh. When he raised his eyes, he saw the twinkle in Kepler's eyes; the man had divined his thoughts. The scholar picked up the chalice and indicated that Beck should hold out his hands, palms up. He did so, not pleased at the faint tremble.

"Because temptation is one of our greatest dangers, we test our oath takers to ensure that they are untainted." He carefully allowed a few drops of the liquid to land in Beck's left palm, then his right. The Holy Water tingled, but unlike Riley, no crown appeared. That suited him just fine. As instructed, Beck raised his hands, turning them so the palms would be visible to the others.

"He is not of the Darkness," Angus said solemnly. "May it always be so."

As he lowered his arms, Kepler put aside the cup, then drew the sword, setting the scabbard aside. Beck stared at the blade, then realized what it was: the sword Angus had thrown to him during the battle, the one he'd used to slay Sartael. Suddenly he was back in that moment, hearing the shouts, the screams, feeling the agony burn through his shoulder where the Archangel had stabbed him. Knowing he was going to die. Knowing if he did, Riley would be next.

Kepler's dark eyes watched him now. "Denver Beck, child of Sadelia and of a man only known to God, do you willingly accept the tasks set before you as a grand master? Are you willing to sacrifice your life to protect the innocent, to stand against the Darkness, to share the Light, to weigh and judge, and to accept the consequences of those decisions? Do you vow that your service will always come first, beyond all things?"

Beck took a long breath. This was it. If he took the oath, he was saying that being a grand master was more important than everything else in his life, even Riley. His heart ached anew.

The silence stretched out, but neither Kepler nor any of the others prodded him for his answer. Once again, his eyes strayed to the image of Lucifer, recalling all the times he'd faced him, the souls of the damned trapped in Hell's walls, pleading for release. His own mother, who he had thought never loved him, yet she'd guided him back to life.

He turned his head toward the opposite wall, the one with

that Light. If Sadie Beck could defy Lucifer in his own pit, then her son would take this oath, to honor her.

He looked back up at Kepler. "Yes, I am willin'," he said in a firm voice. This time he heard Riley sigh in relief.

"Then repeat your vows."

Beck cleared his throat, which had suddenly grown tight.

"I, Denver Beck, do swear before this assembly, and before the hosts of Heaven *and* Hell, that I accept the noble task set before me. I will strive to keep this world whole, to keep it safe. I will do this until my dyin' breath. I make this oath on the bones of those who have come before me, and the souls of those who will follow."

Kepler lightly tapped him on his right shoulder with the flat of blade, then the left, then finally on the top of his head, all the while chanting in Latin. Beck knew the meaning of the words, as he'd been studying the oath for the last week.

Honor, vigilance, duty, and compassion.

A tall order for a simple country boy.

Kepler set the sword aside, picked up the chalice again, and inscribed a mark on Beck's forehead, one known only to the grand masters. He felt the liquid burn into him, though it would leave no visible scar. That didn't matter—he'd always feel that mark inside his soul.

It was as if his eyes were being opened for the first time. Colors became truer, the shadows deeper. The meaning of the Light poured through him, as did the true nature of the Dark. He finally comprehended the task that lay before him.

Oh my God.

Beck blinked up at the grand master in frank astonishment. The old man nodded his understanding. Then a kindly smile came his way.

"Denver Beck, you have taken your vows and chosen our path. Welcome to the International Guild, Grand Master. We are very honored that you have chosen to join us."

That, he hadn't expected. "Thank . . . thank you."

"And now, let us all share a few moments of silence."

Heads bowed as each found their own way of giving thanks. Beck wasn't very religious—he accepted that. Nevertheless, he was grateful for what he'd been given, and he gave thanks for the woman he loved, and who loved him. For his close friends, even those no longer alive.

I am blessed.

When he opened his eyes, he found the votive candle that signified his time as a grand master was lit with a bright white flame. Kepler hadn't done it, of that much he was sure.

His eyes tracked to the old man, and he received a smile.

"Grand Master Denver Beck, you may rise now."

Beck did just that, then shook Kepler's hand. "Thanks for everythin', Jonah."

"You're welcome, young man."

Beck had barely gotten down the stairs when he received a bone-jarring thump on the back from Angus, as well as a booming, "Congratulations, lad!" Trevor just winked and headed out the door, no doubt to organize the whisky for the party afterward.

It was when Beck turned to look at Riley that he almost lost it. She was crying, despite the huge smile on her face.

"Ah, Princess, don't do that," he said.

She walked into his arms, and he kissed the top of her head. "I love you, Grand Master Beck," she whispered. "Even if I am always going to be second in your life."

"A really, really close second," Beck said. When she looked up at him, he gently wiped tears off her cheeks. "Bought yerself some of that stay-put makeup, didn't you?"

She laughed. "Is it working?"

"Sure is. But honestly, I wouldn't care either way. Yer always beautiful to me."

Once they parted, he shook hands with both Rosetti and Elias.

"Thank you for bein' here tonight. I really appreciate it," he said.

"We were honored to witness this moment." Elias's eyes moved to the window to their right. "I see things a little more clearly now."

"I hoped you would."

"May God walk with you every second of your life," Rosetti said, then made the sign of the cross.

"Thank you. I'm definitely goin' to need it." Beck gestured toward the doors that led to the hallway. "Now that all the serious stuff is over, it's time to celebrate."

"Any chance of some whisky?" Elias asked.

"Might be. MacTavish said something about havin' a bottle that's more than twice my age."

"How old are you?" Rosetti asked.

"Twenty-four."

He watched the two men do the math. A couple seconds later, he was alone in the room as they hustled down the hallway. Turning back toward the wall with the candles, Beck zeroed in on his, the weight settling on his shoulders like a heavy cape.

"Well, now I've done it," he muttered.

He closed the pocket doors behind him and headed down the hall, in search of his fiancée. With each step, he swore he could hear the footsteps of all the others who had come before him.

~~*

"Whoa, they went all out," Beck said, his hand resting lightly on Riley's lower back. The low hum of voices greeted them as they entered the dining room. The long table had been pushed up against a wall and covered with food. An open bar sat in one corner and the fireplaces were lit. Riley guessed there were about thirty people in attendance.

"They don't get a new one of you guys that often, so they better celebrate," she said.

"Promise to help me up the stairs if I get drunk?"

"Sure," she replied, though she knew that wouldn't be the case. There were too many important movers and shakers in this room for Beck to go wild.

"Let me make sure that Elias and Rosetti have found that old

Scotch and then I'll be right back. Don't get yerself kidnapped, okay?"

She groaned. Leave it to her fiancé to remind her of the last time she'd been in the manor. "Any summoners here?"

"Might be one or two," he said. After a quick peck on her cheek, he headed into the room.

Riley wandered closer to one of the fireplaces as the heat was always welcome. It was also a good location to admire the weaponry on the wall. She particularly admired the swords, carefully arrayed in the shape of a fan. It was a good bet every one of them was battle ready.

"Impressive," she said.

"Like those, do ya?" MacTavish said, joining her. Not surprisingly, he had a glass of whisky in his hand.

"I do like swords. They're very effective against Archfiends."

"Aye. Did ya recognize the blade during the ceremony?" She shook her head. "It's the one Denver used to kill the Archangel. Angus brought it over with him."

"Really? Wow. I wondered why he was staring at it. By the time Beck was lopping off Sartael's head I couldn't see anything. I got a little too close to the Fallen's sword, and my eyes didn't appreciate that."

Her attention wandered to the crowd. A couple she recognized, but the rest were a mystery. "Who are these people?"

"Well, ya've got a few members of Parliament, representatives of various religious institutions, freethinkers, the usual mix. Let's collect our new grand master and I'll introduce the two of ya around."

As promised, MacTavish did the honors, walking her and Beck from group to group. First, he'd introduce Grand Master Beck, with noticeable pride. Then it was her turn.

"And this is Master Demon Trapper Riley Blackthorne, who is also an apprentice summoner," he'd say, equally pleased.

Over the course of the evening, they met a rabbi from Baltimore who was attending a conference on immigration in Glasgow, a kind, middle-aged man with serious eyes. Then there were the Scottish, Swedish, and German diplomats, each effusive in their own way. And a *bhikkunī*, a Buddhist nun, from Taiwan. Her shaved head was strikingly beautiful, as were her chocolate-brown robes. She spoke with a low, measured voice that reminded Riley of listening to a gentle rainfall on a spring day.

By the time they'd made the rounds, Riley had gained a wider appreciation of the reach—and the power—of the International Guild.

Now Den's a part of all this.

After a brief pass down the buffet to pick up some carrots and some stuffed shrimp, she returned to talk to Archdruid Scrimshaw. The druid's emerald gown was shot through with little stripes of silver and gold, and her red hair was just as flaming bright as it had been when they'd met during Riley's last trip to Scotland.

"You're looking much better than last October," Scrimshaw said, sipping some sort of fruity cocktail. "Not being enchanted helps, no doubt."

"That's for sure."

"Your aura is much purer than it was the last time," the archdruid replied. She angled her head toward Beck, who was sharing a story with an Asian gentleman. "It's in sync with the new grand master's." She smiled. "Good choice, by the way."

"Yes, it was. I got lucky."

"You both did," was the swift reply. "You're a summoner, on top of being a demon trapper. Does that present any problems?"

"It does. Sometimes it's really difficult," she admitted. "It took a while, but I finally got most of the trappers to trust that I'm not going to turn them into newts, or something worse."

"Bet you're tempted sometimes," the druid said, waggling an eyebrow.

"Sooo tempted." *Especially a couple of those guys.*

Beck's laughter from across the room made her smile. This was *his* night, and she was so happy he was enjoying it.

"Love is magic in its own way," Scrimshaw said. "Savor

every moment of it. I'll be sure to offer up the proper blessings for both of you."

"Thank you. We'd appreciate that." Riley hesitated, then decided to head in a different direction. "We have a psychic in Atlanta who's warning us that something very bad is going to happen. End-of-the-whole-world sort of bad. Have you sensed anything like that?"

Scrimshaw's expression changed in an instant. "Yes, but none of us can figure out what's causing it. I was going to speak to Grand Master MacTavish after the reception. Perhaps he knows what's going on."

"Good idea." Whether the grand master would share everything he knew was another issue.

After a few more minutes, the archdruid drifted away to talk to a couple from Finland, leaving Riley on her own. As was her habit, she took a mental snapshot of the moment. This photo included the old manor house's wood-paneled room, a blazing fire in both hearths, drinks flowing, and laughter. The sight of her fiancé taking his rightful place in the world.

As if he knew she was thinking of him, Beck raised his glass of whisky to her, and winked. For just a few seconds, everyone else faded into the background. She studied him as only his lover, and wife, could. His blond hair, more tamed than usual, curled at the collar of his Prince Charlie jacket. It made him look rugged, like he'd stepped out of another century. Those deep brown eyes were filled with joy, alight from within. He stood at ease in that kilt, owning the room. Owning her.

As the rest of the world slowly came back into focus, she blew him a kiss, so proud she was afraid her heart would burst.

~~*

The well-aged scotch had proved worth the wait, though even as Beck accepted the heartfelt congratulations, the weight of his new job had already begun to settle on his shoulders, its presence undeniable now. Something had changed the instant he'd taken the vow and his forehead had been inscribed, something deep within him. Angus had warned him to expect that, but he hadn't figured it'd be so profound.

Now, on his own for the first time in over an hour, he tried to sort through his impressions, to determine what was wrong. Why he felt so uneasy.

Angus joined him. "Let me guess, right now yer tryin' ta shut down all the buzzin' in yer head. Not only because yer a grand master, but because somethin' else is nudgin' ya too."

Beck frowned at him. "You feel it? That something's wrong?"

Angus nodded. "All of us do. The balance is off in some way. I felt it a while back, but it was subtle. Now it's anythin' but."

"It has somethin' to do with what I saw in that town north of Prague," Beck replied, keeping his voice low. "Don't know how I know that, but I just do."

"That was Trevor's impression as well. We'll find out soon enough if it's somethin' we have ta confront. Perhaps it'll all settle down on its own."

"Not likely."

Angus shook his head. "Good lord, yer as much a cynic as I am, lad, and yer only in yer twenties. I canna imagine what yer gonna be like when yer my age."

Though he tried, Beck couldn't contain his snort. "I can just guess what you were like when you were twenty-four."

"Best ya don't ever hear those tales." His friend and mentor gave him a light slap on his back. "Come on, lad, there's more whisky ta drink." He looked over to where Riley stood with a group of politicians. "And I'd say it's time ta rescue yer lassie."

"Now there's one job I don't mind at all."

Chapter Fourteen

Breakfast the next morning was quiet because Beck was the only one up. He'd risen early, as usual, placed a kiss on the forehead of the beautiful angel asleep in his bed, and left Riley behind. Even as he trudged down the stairs, he knew he should be smiling. His life was great—he had his woman by his side and Sadie's son was a grand master. Folks respected him. All of that was a damned miracle.

It had been the nightmare that had stolen his happiness. He'd dreamed he'd been kneeling in front of the smoky remains of a large city and all its people. Riley was next to him. When she reached out to touch the ground, she disintegrated in front of his eyes, turned to ash in a heartbeat. As he'd jolted awake from the nightmare, bathed in sweat, his heart hammering, he'd touched her arm to reassure himself she was still alive. Instinctively, she'd curled closer to him, giving him that reassurance even in her sleep.

Now, alone in the small dining room off the kitchen, Beck found himself staring at the food on his plate, his appetite absent. Nevertheless, he forced himself to eat and had just finished his coffee when Angus and Trevor joined him.

"Yer up early," his mentor said.

"He's always that way," Trevor said, picking up a plate from the sideboard and studying the food choices. "Usually, he's run five miles by the time he shows up at the table. Makes me feel like a damned invalid."

"Ah, ta be young again," Angus said, bringing a cup of coffee to the table.

Beck felt the tension in the air, despite the good-natured banter. "What's happened?" he asked.

Both grand masters looked at him now.

"Yer too damned perceptive, ya know that?" Angus muttered.

Trevor waited to answer until he'd taken his seat. "We lost another town overnight. In China. The only reason we know about it is because a survivor managed ta get the news out before the government could supress it."

"How many died?" Beck asked, his mind pulling him back into his nightmare.

"Fifteen thousand or so. From the initial reports, it appears ta be the same as the others."

"God, when will it end?" Beck murmured.

"Aye," Angus said, frowning. His hands gripped his coffee cup with such an intensity that Beck was sure it would shatter. "The survivor claims she heard a voice shout somethin' but didn't understand the words. She said there was this strange mist and if ya came anywhere near it, ya died. The woman fled ta the hills, then turned ta watch the city be consumed in fire."

"That matches the other cities, as best as we can tell," Trevor said.

What the hell were they up against? "Does the Vatican know?"

Before he could reply, the door to the kitchen swung open, revealing Elias and Father Rosetti, their grim faces supplying the answer to Beck's question.

"You heard the news?" the priest asked.

"Aye," Trevor replied. "May God rest their souls."

Rosetti gave Elias a quick glance. Something passed between them, and the hair on the back of Beck's neck rose.

"I just spoke to my superiors," Rosetti said. "In . . . light of the news, they have . . . ordered us to escort Riley to Rome. They are hoping she can help determine the cause of these catastrophes."

"She has nothin' to do with this," Beck replied. "Ya know that."

"What we know is that the death toll is rising and she has

certain special . . . insights. We are," Rosetti paused, "we're desperate at this point. We have to know what is causing these mass killings."

That was a rare admission of Rome's powerlessness, at least in this situation.

Before Beck could reply, Angus cut in. "What if she refuses ta go with ya?"

"We were told that Riley Blackthorne *must* accompany us to Rome no matter what it takes. That if you refuse to allow her to accompany us, there will be repercussions."

"It's still her decision," Beck spat.

"I'm afraid it's not," Angus said, shaking his head wearily. "Riley agreed ta play by Rome's rules, whatever those might be. She really has no choice, lad." His eyes went back toward the two men. "I'll accompany her, as her representative."

Elias was already shaking his head. "We were told no one else but Riley."

Beck rose. "Well, ya might not be allowin' Grand Master Stewart to go with her, but ya'll not turn me down. As her fiancé, I have a right to be there."

"She's eighteen. She's legally an adult by Italian law," Rosetti replied.

"Still, he does have a right to be there," Elias argued. "That he's also a grand master may prevent damaging the progress we've made between us and the International Guild."

Rosetti ground his teeth, thinking that through. Much as Beck would have liked to shout and argue, he held his breath. Now was not the time to bully someone who clearly wasn't happy with the orders he'd been given.

"You know we can't protect her," Elias continued, "no matter how much we'd like to think we can. Once we're inside those walls, Cardinal Richter can order us to be on our way, and Riley will be on her own. With Beck there, she'll have someone watching her back."

"A grand master will ensure that Riley's rights are not abridged," Trevor said quietly. "Not unless Richter wants one helluva battle with us. Considering the situation, he's got ta be smarter than that."

The priest's frown grew deeper. He muttered something in Italian, probably a curse. "Fine, Beck can come with us. I will somehow *fail* to inform the cardinal of that fact." He glanced at Elias. "I'll take responsibility for this."

"No, we'll share it, because I heartily agree with the decision. Riley must be treated fairly. We need her as an ally, not an enemy."

If everyone could just remember that, it'd be great.

As if on cue, all of them turned toward Beck. He knew what they wanted.

He pushed his chair back. "I'll wake her up and give her the news. How soon do we leave?"

"In half an hour," the priest replied.

~~*

Beck stood in the doorway to his room, gazing at the young woman he loved. Riley was still asleep, curled up like a sleepy kitten, her hair spread over the pillow. With a groan, he sat on the bed, put his hand on her shoulder, and gave her a little shake.

"Waaa?" she murmured. "What time is it?"

"A little after seven."

"And you're waking me up . . . why?" she asked, her eyes slowly coming open.

He opened his mouth to answer, but found he didn't have the words.

Riley blinked, studying his face as she raised her head. "What's happened?"

"Father Rosetti has been ordered to bring ya to the Vatican."

She blinked again. "Is this because of Isra?"

"No, they want yer help."

"Help with what? Lucifer's shoe size? How demons can dance on the head of a pin?"

This was the Riley he loved.

She pulled herself up to a sitting position, tucking the bedclothes around her. "What do they think I can do?"

"They want ya to tell them which of Hell's baddies is pullin' this shit."

"Another city's gone, right?" He nodded. She shook her head in despair. "How soon are we leaving?"

"In about twenty-five minutes."

"Of course." She let her body fall back onto the bed, worry filling her eyes. "Please tell me you're coming with me."

"Of course I am. Rosetti and Elias are riskin' their jobs to make that happen, so don't blame them for this. They're caught in the middle, just like we are."

Riley huffed, then waved a hand. "Give me some space. I need to pack."

Her reaction puzzled him. "Yer not as upset as I'd figured."

She sat up again, frowning, hair curling around her shoulders. "I've been waiting for this to happen. I'll do what I can to help them, but if they think they're going to keep me there for more than a day or so, they're wrong. I'm getting married, and *nobody* is going to keep me from that."

Beck quirked a smile. "There ya go. I'll be back in a bit to help ya with your suitcase."

The moment he shut the door, he heard a lengthy stream of Hellspeak swear words. Hopefully Riley'd get all that out of her system, because that's the last thing she should be doing inside the walls of the Holy City.

~~*

As Riley walked down the three flights to the ground floor, she didn't hurry. She really needed more time to gather her courage. Beck hadn't said it, but they both knew there might be more going on with Rome. The cities' destruction *was* a valid excuse to get her within the Vatican's walls.

If she could help them, that would be great, but would they let her go free once she'd done her part? Or would they conveniently decide to grill her about Isra, how she'd left a fiend free to harm innocents, violating one of the fundamental rules of demon trapping?

It was a risk she had to take.

As she went down, step by step, she studied the faces of the grand masters, drawing strength from each one. She halted in front of an empty space, the one where Beck's portrait would be hung. It was to have been started this morning, but the Vatican's retrieval order had put an end to that.

Part of her was deeply frightened, though she tried not to show it. These people played for keeps, especially when it came to the Grand Game between Heaven and Hell. Who knew what they would do to her?

It'll be okay, her father's soft voice whispered in her head.

"Thanks, Dad." For right now, she'd choose to believe that—because the alternative was to freak out.

She found Angus and MacTavish waiting at the front door, their expressions telegraphing their concern.

"Lass . . ." Angus began.

"It'll be okay." *My dad said so, and I trust him.*

"Beck will let us know what's goin' on," MacTavish said. "If we need ta raise a stink, we will. Yer not goin' inta this alone."

"I know, and I appreciate that. Thank you."

After giving Riley a hug, Angus opened the front door and she stepped outside into the snowy landscape. The twin lions that flanked the front stairs were mounded with snow now, as if they were hibernating for the winter. At the foot of the newly cleared stairs sat a black SUV, one of the Guild's employees in the driver's seat.

Her fiancé and Rome's two representatives watched her descend. Both Elias and the priest had shuttered expressions, which told her how serious this whole thing would be.

She gave all of them a nod, channeling that resolve she'd tapped into on the long walk down the stairs, then waited as Beck opened the rear door. There was no need to talk. This was Rome's chess move. Soon, it would be time for hers.

~~*

Like the last time Riley had visited Scotland, this trip had been filled with firsts: her impromptu handfasting at the loch, Beck's investiture, her first sip of whisky almost three times older than her. Now it was her first time on a corporate jet.

Once they were in the air, Beck—after ensuring that she was comfortable—tilted his seat and went to sleep. On some level, it irritated her that he could just shut down like that. Maybe someday he could teach her how to do that, because it looked like a good strategy when you were facing a battle.

And that's exactly what this whole trip might become, though of course it'd all be very solemn and proper, Vatican style. She understood their dilemma: They were dealing with decimated cities across the globe and had no clue as to who, or what, was causing that carnage. In times of crisis, people looked to their leaders, both secular and religious. The Vatican had drawn a big fat zero, so much so that they'd felt the need to drag her to Rome to help them sort this out. That spoke of absolute desperation.

Or extreme cunning. They could be using this situation to lure her to Rome in order to settle the matter of Blackthorne's daughter, once and for all.

Nevertheless, if this was all about the cities, Riley didn't really know what she could do to help them. Sure, she was good at sussing out demons and angels from ordinary people, and she had even killed three Archfiends on her own. But unless she somehow was in a town right before it was destroyed, there would be no way to know who was behind this.

Were these deaths a ploy to set the grand masters and Rome at each other's throats again? Destroy that détente that Rosetti had spoken of? It sounded just like something Lucifer would do. Riley was aware that the Church was deeply concerned she'd go "dark," as they called it. With her demon-killing abilities— courtesy of Ori—and her magical talent, she could do a lot of damage.

At risk was her soul. If she surrendered it, Lucifer might

use her to co-opt Beck. The International Guild would have no choice but to kill one or both of them. From Hell's perspective, that would be a total win-win.

As spooked as she was, Riley suspected that the grand masters were even more nervous. Beck had been placed in an incredibly sensitive position, stuck between her and the Holy See. Even for a seasoned grand master, that would have been difficult. For one not yet twelve hours old . . .

With a muted sigh, Riley turned toward the window. They were above the cloud layer now, the sunlight unimpeded. In the distance, she saw another jet, headed in the opposite direction. She leaned back in her seat. So many questions, few answers. It was then that she noticed Father Rosetti watching her closely.

"Have faith," he said softly. Next to him, Elias gave her a reassuring nod.

"I'll try."

With one last look at Beck, she adjusted her seat back, pulled up the blanket, and closed down her mind. She was going to trust that her dad had a glimpse into the future. After all, he was in Heaven, and that had to count for something.

~~*

Vatican City State
Rome, Italy

Riley had always wanted to visit Italy, and now she was here. The circumstances weren't ideal, but she might as well make the best of it. As they drove along, every now and then Beck would point out something of interest as scooters and small cars zoomed past them. Space was at a premium here, and the narrow streets only reinforced that spatial economy. Despite the Vatican's license plates, Rome's citizens ignored the limo. No big deal for them, apparently.

It was only once they were off the highway and into the heart of the city that Riley finally got a sense of Rome and its antiquity. The buildings ranged from modern to centuries old. Many were multistory, with balconies sporting a pair of chairs, maybe a small table—suggesting that the occupants liked to watch their neighbors come and go.

Palm trees, blooming flowers, so many people on foot. The fountains they passed made Riley stare in wonder at mythological beings amid the flowing water, surrounded by tourists with their ever-present cameras. Thick old walls loomed here and there, a reminder that this place had been inhabited for twenty-five hundred years.

"How many people are there in Rome?" she asked.

"Just under three million, at least within the city," Elias replied. He seemed pleased that she'd asked this question—and not about what awaited her within the Holy City.

"And the Vatican?"

"A little over eight hundred."

"Huh." Riley knew small towns in Georgia that had bigger populations than that.

Beck took hold of her hand where it sat on the seat between them and gave it a reassuring squeeze.

"Look at you, a grand master one day, and in Rome the next," she said, teasing.

His frown told her he didn't think it was funny. Truth was, neither did she. Maybe it was time to address the elephant in the car.

"What's this Cardinal Richter like?" she asked, eyeing the two men across from her. She could have asked Beck, but sometimes the direct approach was best.

Elias blew out a stream of air, then glanced at Rosetti as if for guidance. For a man who faced Hellspawn without flinching, this hesitation was unusual—and told her just how powerful the prelate must be.

"Cardinal Richter holds rather rigid views on certain topics," Rosetti replied, his words carefully measured.

"That's a nice way of sayin' he's got a stick up his ass," Beck said, his voice lowered so the driver wouldn't hear him.

"He is rigid, but not unbendable," Rosetti replied. "There are those within the Church who are unwavering in their views, even when presented with new information that counters those positions."

"Okay," Riley said. "He's a tough case, but he will change his opinion if the argument is sound." She looked over at Beck now. "Better than some we've met."

Beck nodded in agreement.

"However, Cardinal Richter is more hardline than many of us. He sees good and evil as strictly black and white," the priest added.

"Easier than seeing all the shades of gray," she replied.

Rosetti nodded. "He's not fond of the grand masters or the demon trappers. He prefers that the only interactions with Hell be made by the Vatican's hunters, because he knows where their loyalties lie."

In other words, Elias and his crew. Which made her wonder why Captain Salvatore was here and not off in some other part of the world, turning demons into corpses. Now was probably not the best time to ask about that.

"What's the best way to approach His Eminence?" she asked instead.

"With complete honesty," Rosetti replied. "He may not like your answers, but that's the best way to gain his respect."

"Is it just him we'll be meeting?"

The priest shifted in his seat, his tell that he was uneasy. "Three or four others might be there besides His Eminence."

This might be an inquisition after all.

"Since I'm trusting you that I'm going to be treated fairly, I want these people to see what happens when I put papal Holy Water on my left palm. They have to understand that I'm not with Lucifer right up front." Seeing that crown flame to life should solve the "is she or isn't she?" question. Or at least she hoped it would.

"That can be arranged," Rosetti replied.

"Thank you." That was as far as she could take this right at present—the rest was just going to have to play out down the line. It wasn't like she could just bail out of the car and make a run for it, though that idea was tempting.

They were passing a bakery now and she could smell the fresh bread and pastries. It was nearly two in the afternoon, Italian time, and though they'd had meat, cheese, and bread on the plane, she was still hungry.

"When do we meet with the cardinal?" she asked, hoping it was as soon as they arrived.

"Tonight at seven," Rosetti replied. "I requested that you have time to settle in your rooms, have a meal, perhaps rest. That way you can be at your best for the meeting."

This man was doing everything he could to help her, and he deserved her gratitude.

"Thank you. I know we didn't hit it off right when we first met, but I appreciate everything you do." Her eyes moved to Elias now. "You too."

They both nodded. All four of them had come a long distance since the day Riley had sat across the table from Rome's representatives. No matter what, she did not want to see that trust destroyed.

A few minutes later, the limo turned down a narrow road, bordered on one side by a high wall. After a short distance, they pulled up to an archway and stopped. Two guards checked Riley and Beck's documents, verifying their identities. Once that was accomplished, the car was waved inside.

"Welcome to Vatican City," Elias said. "You've just entered the world's smallest country." A country that was the heart of the Roman Catholic Church.

"We don't have our own airport, but we do have a heliport," he continued. "Also, a pharmacy and a radio station, just about everything a small country would need."

The vehicle finally came to a halt in a large courtyard, bordered on each side by an old stone building. The structure was only four stories, and a few of the windows were open, no doubt to let in the fresh spring air. Riley could easily imagine the men scurrying about in their cassocks throughout the centuries, intent on their duties.

Both Elias and the priest exited the vehicle as soon as it stopped. Before Riley could open her door, Beck took hold of her arm.

"We'll get through this. I'm not gonna let them hurt ya. Ya have to trust me."

She leaned over and gave him a kiss on the cheek. "I do. Though this scares me, I feel I'm here for a reason and I don't think it's all Rome's doing."

He tried to give her a reassuring smile. "Okay then, Mrs. Beck, let's show 'em how it's done."

They were met by a man who was probably in his late fifties. His dark hair was carefully trimmed, his black suit immaculate, and a plain silver band indicated he was married. He kept his expression cautiously neutral. After giving Beck a quick glance, the man returned to his conversation with Father Rosetti. Since that was in Italian, Riley only caught a few words here and there.

"Tryin' to figure out what to do with me?" Beck asked Elias, his voice lowered so as not to interrupt.

"Yes. They're arranging another room," the hunter replied. "If you'll excuse me, I need to do a few things now that I'm back home. It was good to see both of you again." He held out his hand and Beck shook it. "Congratulations, Grand Master."

"Thank you."

"Always a pleasure, Master Blackthorne," he said.

Since he was being formal, Riley did the same. "It was good to see you again, Captain Salvatore."

He gave a nod, then walked across the courtyard.

Once he was out of earshot, Riley asked, "Shouldn't he be out snuffing demons?"

"I asked him about that and he said he's on leave from the team."

"Any idea why?"

Beck shook his head. "Pretty closemouthed about it all."

"Huh."

The conversation between the priest and the other gentleman came to an end, and Rosetti turned toward them. "This is Mr. Albero. He will serve as your host during your stay. He has prepared a room for you, Master Blackthorne. He'll arrange another one for you, Grand Master Beck."

"Thank you. We appreciate that," she said.

"I'll take my leave, then," the priest said. "Hopefully, I'll be able to attend the meeting this evening."

Able to, or allowed to? Riley had a feeling that it was more the latter. "Thank you, Father Rosetti."

"Go with God, both of you," he said, then walked away in the same direction as Elias had gone.

Beck stepped up, offering his hand. "Mr. Albero, I'm pleased to meet you."

It was just the kind of thing her dad would have done, that personal touch.

The man seemed taken aback for a moment, but then he shook Beck's hand. "Welcome to the Vatican, Grand Master," he said, his voice full of rich overtones. Riley wondered why he'd been picked to babysit them, and if he resented that assignment.

"Mr. Albero," she said, mindful that she was a representative of the National Demon Trappers Guild and the Summoners Society. Probably the only one this man would ever meet.

"Miss Blackthorne. If you will please follow me."

She resisted the urge to point out that she was *Master* Blackthorne—there was no reason to ruffle feathers so soon. There'd be plenty of time for that later.

They followed him through a door, Albero carrying her suitcase. To her surprise, Riley found the interior of the building unremarkable—white walls, tile floors, mullioned windows. It reminded her of an old school, well constructed and utilitarian. They passed another man, who gave their escort a nod and then studied her and Beck with open curiosity.

Albero led them to a staircase and they ascended two floors, then followed him down a hallway. He finally stopped in front of a door, produced a key, and unlocked it. It pushed open with a creak to reveal a cozy space. The room was furnished simply: a bed, an old wooden desk, a chair, and a wardrobe. Sort of like the Vatican's version of a single-occupant dorm room.

"The bathroom is through that door," Albero said, pointing.

"This is great. Thank you," Riley said as he handed off the key.

"I shall make arrangements for your room, Grand Master," Albero said. "It will be just there." He gestured across the hall. "Please wait here while I retrieve the key. It is not wise to wander around unescorted."

"We'll stay put," her fiancé replied. "Thank you."

As the man headed down the hallway, Beck stepped into her room.

"Reminds me of your room at the manor, except the view isn't as grand," she said.

"Hopefully, I have my own bathroom. If not, I might have to use yer shower," he said, grinning.

"They're not going to allow any premarital anything here, you know that."

"I know. Told you we shoulda gotten married last December."

Riley laid her suitcase on the luggage rack. Once she had the lock off and the suitcase opened, she groaned. She'd packed in such a hurry that everything was wrinkled. Hopefully they had an iron around here somewhere.

"Riley?"

She looked over at Beck, who was sitting on the end of her bed now. She knew what he wanted to know, because they were on the same wavelength.

"I'm not freaking, at least not out loud. I'm going to face whatever they throw at me. If I can help them keep people from dying, then it's all good." She dropped a pair of jeans back into her suitcase. Who was she kidding? "Okay, I'm lying. I'm spooked. Can't help but be. This is the freaking Vatican. They've never trusted me, from the moment I started trapping demons."

Beck nodded, then beckoned her over to sit by him on the

bed. When she did, his arm went around her waist and he pulled her tight up against him.

"Well, they didn't take our passports or our phones. So far, they're bein' real civil. Maybe this isn't as big a deal as we think."

When Riley gave him a "you're talking B.S." look, he sighed in agreement. "Yeah, I know."

A couple knocks indicated that Albero had returned. Beck moved to the door and opened it.

"I have the key to your room, Grand Master. Supper trays will be delivered this evening at five. I shall come for you at quarter to six to give you a tour before the meeting at seven. In the meantime, rest from your journey."

"*Grazie*," Riley said.

As Beck adjourned to his room, Riley went back to her suitcase, laying her clothes out on the bed one piece at a time. Trying to smooth out the wrinkles in her best shirt, she found her hands trembling.

"I'm here for a reason," she whispered. "I'm here because I'm supposed to be."

If she was wrong, then God help them all.

Chapter Fifteen

As promised, their meals had been delivered at five, and after they'd eaten, Albero had arrived to take them on the tour. So far, that had consisted of a lot of walking. Beck hoped Riley's shoes were comfortable. His certainly weren't.

Now that he was a representative of the International Guild, Beck had dressed with care. He'd chosen his favorite blue shirt, a black suitcoat, and black slacks, but no tie. Riley had gone for the same somber look, in the black dress she'd worn at her father's and Sadie's funerals. She'd pulled her hair up into a loose bun, and the demon claw necklace was on full display. When Beck had first noticed it, he'd given her a thumbs-up.

The walking continued down long corridors with offices located on either side. Occasionally there'd be a painting or statue along the way to add some class, but for the most part, it wasn't what he'd expected.

They followed Albero for at least ten minutes, passing people every now and then. Some would speak to their guide, greeting him; others went by in silence. The Vatican's inhabitants mirrored its global reach—men and women of all races and ages. Priests and nuns, men in dark suits, women in conservative dresses. Trevor had warned Beck that it was easy to get overwhelmed by the grandeur of this place. So far, all they'd seen was a lot of Vatican worker bees.

It wasn't until they stepped outside that Beck had a clue where they might be headed. The sun was beginning to set, casting rose-gold light on the basilica in the distance.

"*Piazza San Pietro.* St. Peter's Square," Albero said.

"Wow," Riley murmured, her eyes wide.

"The colonnade," he continued, pointing to the dual semicircles of high stonework around them, statues arrayed along the tops, "was designed by Bernini and finished in 1667." He paused to let them take in the scene. "There are one hundred and forty saints in total. The basilica itself was completed nearly four hundred years ago, in 1626, during the pontificate of Pope Urban the Eighth."

"It's *huge,*" Riley said, doing a slow three-sixty. "I saw pictures of this place when the new pope was chosen, but *this* is incredible."

"Yes, it is. The papal apartments are just there," Albero said, pointing to the right at a four-story white building. "The Swiss Guard barracks is near there as well."

Though he was just as awed as Riley, Beck held his silence. He suspected that there was more going on here besides the "let me show you our pretty church" tour.

His hunch was validated when Albero led them through the square and into the basilica itself. Especially when the guards made no attempt to stop them even though it was after closing time.

"I am sorry we don't have more time, for it is quite marvelous," Albero said.

Beck gave his fiancée a quick look. Did she realize what was going on here? What better way to intimidate them than a carefully calculated display of the power of the Holy See. A reminder that once Riley and he were inside these walls, they were subject to the Vatican's laws. This tactic was exactly what Beck would have done, and he wondered who'd orchestrated it.

Probably the cardinal.

Once he'd sorted all that out in his head, Beck turned his attention to the interior of the building.

"Sweet Jesus," he murmured, staring up at the ceiling so far above them. Though he'd watched numerous videos about this place, seeing it in person was completely different.

"Michelangelo's Pietà," Riley said, stopping to gaze at the

statue on their right. "The man was such a genius."

Albero nodded. "Mary holding the body of Jesus after the Crucifixion. It's one of our most evocative pieces."

"Yes, it is." She walked closer to study it. "The pain of such a loss . . . And he caught it all in stone."

The further they walked, the more the space above them opened, as if it were a gateway to the higher realms.

Riley moved ahead of them, silently taking it all in.

"The basilica does not trouble her," Albero said, puzzled.

"No reason it should," Beck replied. *Not with Heaven's mark on her.*

For some reason, Albero had thought his fiancée wasn't on the side of the angels. The only way he'd believe that was if it'd come from one of his superiors. That didn't sit well with Beck.

They continued to wander through the cavernous space, stopping to admire various works of art, until they stood in front of what Albero said was the papal altar, directly over the tomb of St. Peter.

The sensations were all-encompassing now, leaving no doubt in Riley's mind that she was supposed to be here. Part of it was the majesty of the place—you couldn't help but be in jaw-dropping astonishment, no matter your beliefs.

There was a presence here, and it filled her with peace and lifted her spirits. It was exactly what she needed, because she'd been feeling increasingly overwhelmed. "Too much, too quickly" is how Mort had summed it up for her. Here, she felt as if she wasn't alone, that all her burdens, though difficult, were manageable.

Heaven's crew was up to something.

Gazing up at the stained-glass window above the altar, she whispered, "Please help me find out who's killing all these people. Then help me figure out how to stop them. This can't keep happening."

And since she *was* in the center of Catholic Christendom, what better place to ask for a blessing for a certain angel?

"In the cemetery where my parents are buried," Riley said, still whispering, "there's a gargoyle on their mausoleum. It's the one that's facing east, toward the sunrise each morning." From behind her, she heard faint footsteps as someone crossed the vast open space, headed for an exit.

"Ori was one of yours, until he trusted the wrong person. He paid with his life to save others, to save me and Beck. He's free from Hell now. Please find a way to send his soul the Light he loves so much? He has paid for his mistake and he deserves mercy."

Riley murmured a nearly silent "amen," then turned away, hoping someone had heard that prayer. Her eyes met Beck's as he stood next to their guide. He didn't say a word, but she suspected he knew what she'd just done. And he approved.

She would have headed back the way they'd come, but instead something drew her around the altar, then further into the basilica. In a niche to her right, she found the painting.

As she stared at the artwork, Albero and Beck joined her.

"This is the Archangel Michael's altar," their escort explained. "The painting depicts him slaying the Devil."

Riley scrutinized the image and couldn't stop the frown. The painter, for whatever reason, had given Michael a soft, feminine face, though his arms revealed defined musculature. Like the real Archangel, his hair was blond. That was one of the things that had startled her when she'd first met the supreme commander of Heaven's army, how close his hair color was to Simon's. At least the artist got that right.

"No, that's not really him," she said, turning toward their guide. "The Archangel Michael's face is very male, and he's arrogant, like everyone he meets is beneath him. Oh, and his sword is a lot bigger, and on fire."

Albero blinked. "How would you know all that?"

"I met him once. We bargained, and mankind got lucky." She turned back to the painting, then shook her head. "Nice try, but that's so not him. This guy, I might even like. The real Michael—not happening."

As she walked away, she heard Albero ask, "Is she jesting with me?"

"No, she's not. I saw him too," Beck replied. "The paintin' is pretty and all, but it's not even close. The real Archangel would scare the livin' daylights right out of you. He's a total hardass."

Shocked, their escort fell silent for the rest of the tour.

~~*

Riley had hoped that she and Beck would be sitting down with the cardinal in his office, talking through the problem. That wasn't even close.

The room Albero had taken them to was about thirty by thirty, a nondescript space with white walls, tan curtains and a bronze crucifix on one wall. A long and intricately carved ebony table sat in the front of the room, behind which were four black chairs. A similar number of notepads, pens, and glasses of water were aligned in front of each chair with mathematical precision. A second table sat opposite this, probably ten or more feet away. Behind it were two chairs, most likely for her and Beck. There were also a few chairs for an audience, should one be allowed.

The remainder of the space was stark, the only bright spot an aged tapestry that hung between two tall mullioned windows, located right behind that ebony table. Curiously, the textile's image was of King Solomon seated on his throne. At his feet were an infant in swaddling clothes and two women pleading for custody of the child. It fit the room, somehow, though Riley didn't know why.

Albero pointed them toward that second table. "Please be seated. His Eminence will be here shortly." His message delivered, he left by a side door, no doubt to tell the cardinal they'd arrived.

"That was one fancy church," Beck said as they settled into the chairs.

Riley nodded. "So many gorgeous pieces of art. I'd like to take more time and look around. Maybe we'll get a chance later, once the cardinal realizes I really can't help him that much."

Beck eyed her now. "You know why we got the tour?"

"Besides being good hosts?" she said.

"Besides that."

"It was their 'don't think of crossing us' speech, without all the shouting and hand waving. Pity it didn't work."

He laughed. "Yup."

"They seem to forget our history, that we met Michael and that I talked him and the Prince out of going to war. That we've both been to Hell and still have our souls. These people have tremendous global power, but right now, they need us more than we need them."

Beck's grin appeared. "Got it in one, Master Blackthorne." He leaned over and dropped a kiss on her cheek. "Still, don't let them rattle you, no matter what."

She squeezed his hand in solidarity. "We'll be okay."

The far door opened and Albero reentered, and without saying a word took his place behind them. A minute or two later, a tall, solemn man in black entered.

"That's Cardinal Richter," Beck whispered.

Riley could have guessed that by the scarlet accents on his black cassock, though she really wasn't that savvy about the latest Vatican fashions. Richter wore a skullcap, a wide sash called a fascia, and a pectoral cross on his chest. Two other men entered the room, both clad somewhat similarly to the cardinal. All of them appeared to be in their late fifties, or maybe early sixties.

Three cardinals? That wasn't a good sign.

Once they'd taken their places at the table—Richter in the very center—his eyes rose to meet hers and it felt like she was being judged even before this meeting had begun. Richter held himself rigidly, as if bending in any manner was a sin. But in those eyes, she saw the apprehension. Maybe even a hint of fear.

Albero conducted the introductions. "His Eminence, Cardinal Christoph Richter," he said, gesturing toward the man in the center. "The Most Reverend Jesus Alvarez," who was on

Richter's left, and to his right, "The Most Reverend Franklin Prager."

"Bishops," Beck muttered quietly. She gave a quick nod, relieved, though she wasn't exactly sure why.

Albero gestured toward them now. "Master Riley Blackthorne and Grand Master Denver Beck."

"Is there some reason a *grand master* is present at this meeting?" Bishop Alvarez asked. His accent suggested Latin American origins.

"Riley is my fiancée," Beck replied. "And the International Guild felt one of their own should be here today because of," he paused to hunt for the right words, "the seriousness of the situation."

"Ah," the bishop replied, nodding.

The far door opened and Father Rosetti entered, followed by a familiar face. Clad in a navy suit and tie, Simon Adler gave the room's occupants a quick sweep, and then his eyes settled on Riley. He delivered a faint nod of acknowledgement, then followed Rosetti to the chairs behind her and Beck.

What's he doing here?

For a moment, Riley felt betrayed, then immediately knew that was wrong. Simon would never betray her again. But why was he here in Rome?

Oblivious to her inner dialog, the cardinal began. "We have requested your presence today, Miss Blackthorne, to inquire into certain matters regarding your time as a demon trapper. In particular, we have questions as to certain actions you have taken."

The "requested your presence" part was bending the truth, and it appeared they were going to ask her about Isra. It was time to establish a few ground rules.

"I prefer to be addressed as Master Blackthorne, Your Eminence." *I paid in blood for that honor.*

Richter raised an eyebrow, then flipped a page in the file in front of him. "Master Blackthorne, then."

"Pardon, Your Eminence. Master Blackthorne requested that

she be tested with Holy Water before this meeting continues," Father Rosetti said.

There was a long silence as Richter's eyes bore into the priest. "Then do so."

It was Simon who moved to her side now, setting a small metal box on the table in front of her. He opened the container, pulled out a clear glass vial of papal Holy Water, then turned his back on the front table.

When Riley looked up at him, he smiled. That one gesture made this whole moment bearable.

"This was blessed by His Holiness just this afternoon," he said so all could hear him. Which made her wonder if he'd ever met the pope.

Simon deftly let one drop of the sacred liquid fall onto the mark on her right palm and stepped back so others could see the results. As the liquid burned into her skin, Riley gasped. This was so much stronger than the other times she'd had this done. Perhaps because it was fresher, or because she was inside these walls.

When the burning began to subside, she held up her palm so others could see the result—or in this case the lack of one, since Hell's mark was not present. "My soul is my own."

Simon repeated the application on her left palm. This time the pain was intense, the crown pulsing with her rapid heartbeat. To her shock, it blazed upward in a brilliant white light, dancing above her palm.

"Not somethin' ya see every day," Beck said, his way of taking a jab at the men seated behind the front table.

Slowly the effect ended, but Riley swore she could still feel the Holy Water racing through her veins. Was that even possible?

"Thank you, Simon," she said, as he packed up the Holy Water and returned to his chair.

Riley turned her attention to the trio in the front of the room. Richter's expression had grown hard to read, while the bishops just stared at her.

"While you are not overtly in liege to the Prince, you may

still be aiding his cause nonetheless," Richter said.

So there it was: Your soul is yours, but we're pretty certain you're cheering for the wrong team.

"I'm not here to talk about my immortal soul, not when people are dying," she shot back.

"Before we discuss such a sensitive matter, we must be assured of your status with Hell."

"You just saw that I don't have one."

Richter didn't respond right away, taking his time pulling a page out of his file. "And yet, some of your actions reflect a certain . . . closeness to the Prince and his servants that tells us a different story." He glanced down at the paper. "Your first transgression was allowing a Fallen named Ori to become your paramour."

Oh no.

Riley tried not to grimace, and failed. The revelation was embarrassing in a roomful of men, but it was doubly so since Simon was here. As her face warmed, she swore she heard his sigh from behind her.

"Do you deny you had carnal relations with a Fallen?" Richter asked.

"No, I don't. We spent one night together." A bittersweet time full of joy, then betrayal and tears. "I was angry and jealous, and it was a stupid move. I believed what he told me." She remembered that night so well. "Strangely enough, not all of it was lies. Ori *did* want to keep me safe, which is why he ended up in trouble with Lucifer. He may have followed the Prince into exile, but he knew he'd made a mistake. He craved the Light like you and I need oxygen."

"Not likely," was the tart reply.

"No, it's true. I'm hoping that one of these days Heaven will take him back."

"Again, not likely." Richter continued. "You are currently studying magic with a necromancer."

"Yes, and a witch as well." They already knew all this, so why were they tromping over familiar ground?

"That association places your soul in danger," the cardinal pressed.

"I don't believe it does. The witch and the summoner are good people. They fought against Sartael's demons and risked their lives to save Atlanta."

"C.S. Lewis said it best," Bishop Prager cut in. "'Indeed the safest road to Hell is the gradual one—the gentle slope, soft underfoot, without sudden turnings, without milestones, without signposts.'"

"With all due respect to Mr. Lewis, I didn't gradually *slope* into Hell. I was dropped into it feet first." She leaned forward on the table. "You guys have *no* idea what it's like to stand in front of Lucifer with hundreds of demons breathing down your back, every one of them wanting to tear you apart and eat your flesh. Until you've been there, you'll never know what it's like to hear the screams of the damned. Trust me, it makes one big impression."

"We have only your word that you made this journey," Prager said, his eyes narrowed.

"Why would I lie about that? What good would it do for me?"

Beck stirred. "She's not lyin'. I was there when Riley returned from Hell. She stank of brimstone, and the terror in her eyes is somethin' I never want to see again."

There was a quiet conversation between the three prelates.

"We shall accept that you have experienced Hell," Richter said. "Would you return there for any reason?"

That was a trap, a perfectly crafted one. She opted for the truth. "I would go back."

"What?" Beck blurted, gaping at her like she'd lost her mind.

Riley looked him straight in the eyes. "I would go back for someone I loved. If it came down to me or them, I'd go. But I'd try to get both of us out of there. I know I'd lose, but I'd fight for that person, no matter what." She paused. "I'd fight for you."

"Same here," he said.

There was silence in the room now, the kind she couldn't

read. Richter studied her intently, even as Alvarez leaned over and whispered in his ear. The cardinal gave him a sharp look, then went back to his notes.

"We have received reports that you allowed a Hypno-Fiend to remain in a school, where it could have harmed the students. That you sided with this Hellspawn instead of trapping it."

Simon groaned. Riley very much doubted his report had said anything about "siding with this Hellspawn," but that's the way the cardinal wished to spin it.

"The Mezmer was an Unbound, able to walk across Holy Water."

"An illusion."

"No, it wasn't. And because I have trained with a summoner, I can say that." Riley drew a deep breath, gaining time to order her thoughts. The fact that they were laying out all her sins was suspicious, and it made her even more cautious. "The Holy Water was blessed the night before I met the demon. Isra could cross it, which meant he was what he claimed to be: a demon who'd broken Lucifer's chains."

"That is *not* possible," Richter said, shaking his head.

"I wouldn't have thought it was either, but I saw the proof. When the Retriever came to the school, Isra refused to let me fight it. He did not want his students harmed. Instead, he walked up to that huge-assed demon and surrendered."

"Hellspawn serve only the Prince," Bishop Prager insisted. "They have no morals. They are of the Darkness."

"This one wasn't. By surrendering, Isra faced eternal torture. I saw what that meant when I was down there. Sartael was in chains that never stopped moving. He couldn't sleep, couldn't eat. They cut into his skin every second of every day. *Forever.* That's only one of Lucifer's many torments." The thought of Isra in those chains made her heart ache.

"Perhaps he has already had this demon executed," Prager said.

"Not his style," Beck cut in. "He's all about keepin' his power. He'll make an example out of this one so the others don't get any bright ideas."

Riley nodded. "Exactly. After Sartael's mutiny, Lucifer purged Hell. Any form of rebellion makes him livid, and even more paranoid."

"Demons are not redeemable," Richter insisted.

"Why not?"

"They cannot be. They are made of the Darkness."

At her hesitation, Beck shot her a concerned look. Did she dare go there?

"And where did that Darkness come from?" Riley asked. "Who created it in the first place?"

"What do you mean?" the cardinal asked.

"In Sunday school I was taught that God created everything. He certainly created the angels, one of which is Lucifer. Except Lucifer gets it in his head that he's bigger than his boss, and then is thrown out of Heaven. He takes along a bunch of his buddies and sets up his own little kingdom in Hell."

The cardinal's face registered his displeasure at her rather glib overview of celestial history.

"Because the Prince doesn't have his own soldiers, he creates demons. But where does he get the power of creation?"

Alvarez blinked, while Prager just frowned.

"I'm sure you're going to tell us," Richter replied acidly.

She leaned forward in her chair. "Lucifer, for all his cunning, is just an angel, God's flunky. Now I know that sounds like I'm minimizing his threat, and I'm not. He's incredibly evil, a nasty piece of work." She sucked in a deep breath, hoping she wasn't making a mistake.

"But . . . he's still alive only because he's *allowed* to exist. If I were God, I would have killed him out a long time ago. However, if I've learned anything in the last year, Heaven's actions don't always make sense. At least in the short run, like my lifespan. Over millennia? Yes. It's a very long game for them."

"And?" Richter said, his tone telling her he was reaching the end of his patience.

"My guess is that Lucifer is still alive because we mortals

need choices, that free will everyone keeps crowing about. We can walk toward the Light or embrace the Darkness. Or both, sometimes." She'd been there herself.

"That doesn't make sense," Alvarez argued.

"Actually, it does," Riley said. "Adam and Eve were fine in the garden; then God tells them not to eat from one particular tree. Why did He do that? Would they have even noticed that tree if not for Him? No, that was the first test of free will. God set them up—follow His laws, or take a taste of the forbidden. We all know how that turned out."

"Your point?" the cardinal demanded, glowering.

Riley circled back to her original argument. "My point is, Lucifer can only create demons because he is allowed that power *by God.* That means some portion of those demons have a connection to Heaven."

Richter stared at her now. "I never thought I'd hear a demon trapper say such a thing."

"I'll agree, it's a really weird idea, and I know firsthand how evil Hellspawn can truly be. But if a demon has any bit of Light inside them, why can't he or she want to be free of the Prince?" She paused. "Why can't they want to do good instead of evil? Because if we mortals have been given that choice, why not them? Why is it just about us?"

Alvarez muttered something in Spanish under his breath. It didn't sound like agreement.

"That is outlandish," Prager said.

"Perhaps. Still, I saw something in that Four's eyes that told me he didn't want to be Lucifer's any longer. Isra sacrificed himself to save those kids. Isn't that what you guys are always talking about? Sacrifice?"

"Not for those in Lucifer's army," Richter said primly.

"My dad's soul was the Prince's once, but he sacrificed himself to save us from Sartael. He paid his debt, and he's with my mom in Heaven now. If it could happen to him, why not a demon?"

There was another quiet, but tense, conversation between all the clerics, held at just a low enough level that Riley couldn't pick out one word.

Father Rosetti gently touched her shoulder and she nearly jumped. She turned around, wondering what he thought of all this.

"Interesting theological premise. It probably won't pass muster, but I enjoyed hearing it anyway."

At least she'd amused one of the Vatican's folks. "The idea certainly surprised me when I first figured out what was going on."

Simon didn't comment, his face pensive.

Riley turned back to the front, her sense of unease growing. This recap of her sins was wasting time. She was just about to suggest that they move on when the men ended their conversation.

Richter was the face she zeroed in on, and she knew she hadn't made her case.

"We have discussed your positions regarding Heaven and Hell and find them unorthodox, if not bordering on blasphemy. Because of those positions, we do not feel you will be of any further assistance to us."

Beside her, Beck uttered a muffled swear word. Riley was about to argue with the decision when he laid a hand on her arm. "Don't bother."

Riley ground her teeth instead.

"We'll make arrangements so you may depart in the morning," Richter said, gathering up his notes.

"What are you going to do about the cities?"

The cardinal stared a hole into her, the seconds ticking down. "What we've always done—pray," he said, then left the room, the bishops in tow.

Rosetti sighed deeply as he walked in front of their table, his eyes on the far door. "I'm sorry they weren't willing to listen."

"Not your fault. They asked the hard questions and they weren't ready to hear the answers."

"That is often the case."

Simon crouched down next to her chair. How was he going to react to the news about her and Ori?

"Don't worry, I certainly won't throw the first stone," he said. "I'm not that much of a hypocrite."

"Thanks," she replied, relieved.

"I've always divided everything into Good versus Evil, which is why it was so easy for Sartael to play with my head," he admitted. "I'm not sure if I accept that demons can be good, but I saw that Four give himself up to protect those students. If he could do that, why couldn't he fight against Lucifer, not for power, but for freedom?"

"I like the notion," Beck said. "Mostly because it's the Prince's worst nightmare."

"Yes, it is." Simon stood. "I need to get going. I have a meeting with some of the students in the latest exorcism class." He glanced over at Rosetti. "Someone wants me to tell them *exactly* what it's like."

Riley whistled. "That oughta be fun."

"We'll see how many are still in the class when I get done." He bent down and gave Riley a quick embrace, then shook Beck's hand. "I'll see you at the wedding."

As the priest and Simon left, there was a gentle clearing of a throat behind them. She'd forgotten Albero was still here.

"Would you like to return to your room?" he asked, rising from his chair.

Riley needed time alone to sort through everything that had happened tonight. "Do you have a garden here? Somewhere quiet?"

"Yes, we do. It is very restful. I will see that you are escorted there."

"While yer doin' that, I need to call Scotland," Beck said. "Trevor needs to know what happened tonight."

Riley shook her head in frustration. "I don't know what else I could have told them. I wouldn't lie about Isra."

"I know. You did what you had to do."

Then why do I feel like I failed?

Chapter Sixteen

Beck's call to Trevor took longer than he'd expected, mostly because the senior grand master wanted every single detail. After he'd had laid out Riley's argument regarding the Unbound demons, there was a lengthy silence on the other end of the line. It grew so noticeable that Beck checked the cell phone's display, just in case he'd been cut off.

Trevor finally spoke. "Ya have ta respect a lassie who's willin' to stand up ta a cardinal while inside those walls. Especially one like Richter."

"What I don't understand is why we're rehashin' stuff they've known for months. Well, except for the Isra thing. Why not get on with it?"

"They're not known for movin' fast. Usually they don't need ta. What's goin' on has shaken the foundations of the Church. My guess is that they were ensurin' Riley was completely above board before they asked for her help."

"Yeah, well, she didn't pass muster. I'm not too upset about that, to be honest."

"Aye. Let me know when yer boardin' the plane. I'll make sure someone is at the airport ta pick ya up."

"Thanks, I will."

"'Night, lad. Stay strong."

"We got no other choice."

~~*

After delivering Beck to his room, Albero had arranged for

Riley to be driven to the Vatican Gardens, a sizable green space on the western side of the enclave. Curiously, she'd rated a young Swiss Guard as her escort this time. His uniform was the dead opposite of camo, with wide stripes of blue, red, orange, and yellow, which made him look like a garishly plumed bird. Despite that, the way he held himself and the focused intensity with which he watched over her said she was in safe hands. The Vatican might not know what to do with Blackthorne's daughter, but they certainly wouldn't allow any harm to befall her. At least, not unless it was their plan to inflict that harm.

After wandering around for a time, keenly aware that the guard was about thirty or so feet behind her, Riley finally chose a stone bench. It sat near a series of sculptured hedges, which filled the night air with a woodsy scent. The temperature was dropping, and she regretted not bringing a coat or sweater.

Closing her eyes, she laid her hands in her lap. Perhaps this quiet place could help calm all the chattering inside her mind. It was both distracting and annoying, as well as a promise that she wouldn't sleep well tonight if she didn't shut it down.

When just sitting quietly didn't do the trick, Riley turned to a meditation technique Ayden had taught her. This one required her to create a brilliant sphere of golden light and have it float lightly in front of her. She'd usually vary the size of the sphere, or the density of it, efforts that made her focus her thoughts and shut down the mental noise.

But doing magic here, thumbing her nose at the Church? No, this was their patch of ground, their rules. Instead, Riley visualized that glowing sphere inside her head and let it float around, clearing out the confusing thoughts. As she did, her heartrate dropped and her mind began to clear.

She went further into the meditation now, allowing the peace to engulf her. In this state, she thought she could feel the planet's rotation, the movement of the winds and the oceans. When she'd said something about that to Ayden, her friend had given her a raised eyebrow and a "go figure."

Once her mind felt less chaotic, she replayed the meeting,

word by word, expression by expression. Richter had been just as worried at the end of the meeting as in the beginning. That he didn't trust her to help them didn't make much sense. She'd assisted Simon in conducting exorcisms—had proven to be a valuable ally during those encounters.

No, she'd crossed the line with Isra, and there was no way they were going to accept that. Riley sighed in frustration. At least it hadn't been a totally wasted trip—she and Beck had gotten to visit Rome and see the basilica. That was worth something.

Now, as she sat in this garden, hearing the faint street sounds outside the Vatican's walls, she knew something was fundamentally wrong. Beck had said as much, and only now did she feel the same.

On impulse, she tested the edges of that wrongness, and to her surprise, it pushed back. It wasn't Darkness, like Hell, or Light, like Heaven's angels. Something in between. As she pushed harder, trying to understand whatever this was, the wrongness vanished like a sea fog in a strong breeze.

Only a few heartbeats later, her breath tightened, each inhalation growing more labored. A panic attack. Riley hadn't had one of those in months, not since Ayden had taught her how to head them off before they went too far. But this time, nothing she did seemed to help. Her body began to tremble and she bent over at the waist, sucking in each breath with increasing difficulty. Each inhalation caused a harsh wheezing sound. Her vision tunneled. She tried to move, to call out to the guard, but was unable to form words.

Just as she was about to black out, the tightness in her chest was gone, as if it'd never been there in the first place. Surprised, Riley sat up, took a deep breath, and found no restriction. The roaring in her ears was gone as well. With each subsequent breath, her heartbeat decreased to normal.

"What the heck was that?" she murmured. In such a deep and relaxed state, it should have been impossible to trigger a reaction.

Riley remained on the bench for a few minutes more, as

the sweat on her forehead chilled in the night air. The attack had come after she'd explored that sensation of wrongness. Whatever it was had poked back. Shaking her head in confusion, she rose and wound her way past the flowerbeds until she found the guard standing patiently where she'd last seen him.

"*Grazie,*" she said.

He nodded, and when they reached the car, he drove her back to the building where she and Beck were staying. As she'd anticipated, Albero waited for her by a side door—how he knew when she'd be arriving wasn't apparent. After exchanging a few words with her guard, he followed Riley to her room.

"Did you enjoy the gardens?" He sounded genuinely interested.

"Yes. I found peace there." *At least until I couldn't breathe.*

After reminding her that breakfast would be delivered at seven in the morning, Albero left her at her door. She texted Beck as she entered her room so he knew she was back. He joined her a few minutes later, just after she'd brushed her teeth and gotten into her nightclothes.

As she opened the door, he looked her over with concern. "Early night?" She nodded. "Jet lag kickin' yer butt?"

"That and whatever's going on here. Too many questions, not enough answers. That always tires me out." She climbed into the bed, deciding not to tell him what had happened in the garden. He had enough worries right now.

"Would you stay with me until I fall asleep?" she asked.

"Sure."

They curled up in bed together, him fully clothed except for his shoes, which he'd kicked off. Riley snuggled against his chest, inhaling the reassuring scent that was her fiancé.

"So, tell me more about this weddin' we're havin'," he said in her ear. He did this every now and then. At first, she couldn't figure out why he was having her repeat the same information, but then she realized it was his way of reassuring himself that it was really going to happen.

As she explained how Angus's back garden would be set

up, where he'd stand, where she'd be, the types of flowers that would be blooming, she could feel him relax. And in the act of telling him all this, she relaxed as well.

Now, as she drifted off to sleep, she felt him place a gentle kiss on the top of her head. Some people tossed around the words *soul mate* far too easily. In their case, she knew it was true. Two hearts joined together, forged in the flames of love and adversity, no matter what Heaven or Hell threw at them.

Forever.

~~*

The knocking on Beck's door pulled him out of a strange dream, one that'd had him lost in Okefenokee Swamp, surrounded by floating skeletons that kept trying to bite him. As he fumbled his way into his pants, he glanced at the clock on the wall, thinking he'd overslept. The clock proved him wrong—it was nearing five thirty in the morning.

Albero was just raising his hand to knock again when Beck swung the door open. The man blurted, "You must wake Master Blackthorne and have her dress. You are both to leave as soon as possible."

"Now? I thought we were goin' later this morning," Beck said, his brain clearing slower than he liked.

"I was not told your destination, only that you were to be made ready and to leave your luggage here."

Which meant they weren't headed back to the manor. He knew he wasn't going to get anything else out of this man, so he gave in. "Okay, I'll get her up."

Albero, who always moved so sedately, scurried off.

Beck closed the door. "Ah, hell," he muttered, suspecting what had happened while they slept. "God, I hope I'm wrong."

To his surprise, Riley managed to wake up, dress, and be out her door in under fifteen minutes. Her hair was combed, but she'd skipped the makeup. Deep circles sat under her eyes, which told him she hadn't slept any better than he had.

"Promise me there will be hot tea and something to eat," she said as they followed Albero out of the building.

"Hopefully. Depends on where we're headed."

She peered over at him. "You think another town's been destroyed?"

"Don't know, but I bet so."

A car waited for them in the courtyard, and from there, they were driven further into Vatican City. Riley gnawed on her bottom lip, staring out the side window. Beck took hold of her hand, which was trembling. Something about her had changed since she'd been in the garden the night before.

"You okay?"

Riley shrugged. "Bad dreams."

"Same here." She looked over at him now. "Lots of dead people."

"I . . . had a panic attack while I was in the garden," she said, though her voice told him she'd been reluctant to admit it. "I haven't had one for a few months. It ended so quickly, not like usual. I went from not being able to breathe to being just fine."

She'd been out there fighting for every breath while he'd been on the phone to Trevor? "Why didn't you tell me that last night?" he demanded.

"Didn't want you to worry. Probably all the stress," she replied, but she sounded unsure.

"Yeah, stress." Or maybe something else. Frowning, Beck turned away from her until his temper cooled.

Gotta trust her judgment.

Even when it scared the hell out of him.

From what Riley could tell, they were still within Vatican City, heading west. To her relief, the trip was short. The car pulled up to a helipad where a white helicopter waited for them, lights on, pilot already in the cockpit. In the thin morning light, Riley made out the words *Repubblica Italiana* on the side.

"Is this the pope's helicopter?" she asked.

"Yes, it is," Albero replied, then climbed out of the car. He opened Riley's door. Two men stood near the helicopter, both in black: Richter and Rosetti.

The cardinal beckoned to them. "Let us go now," he said, then climbed into the copter. Beck took hold of Riley's hand as they reached Father Rosetti.

"Is this a repeat of our last trip?" he asked.

The father nodded solemnly. "This city was here, in our own country. Cardinal Richter wishes us to view the site."

Why had he changed his mind? Or maybe it hadn't been his decision to include Riley on this journey. Either way, it didn't matter now. As her mind tried to come to grips with the destination, and what they might see there, her stomach reminded her that there hadn't been any breakfast. She tried to ignore it. Given the circumstances, that was a minor concern.

Beck must have heard her stomach growl, so he dug in his backpack and handed over a bottle of water and a protein bar.

"You rock, you know that?" He smiled. "You have some for you, or should we share?"

"Already ate."

She wondered if that was true or not, because it'd be just like him to give up his own food. "Ever been in a helicopter before?"

"Yeah, in the Army. Of course, this one's a lot fancier than that one."

This copter *was* fancy, with padded seats and all the bells and whistles.

It must be nice to be the pope.

Beck's expression flattened. "One of those times was when I was bein' flown out of the country after the IED hit us."

The cardinal's eyes tracked to Beck, then to her, as if weighing what he'd overheard. Riley broke contact and stared out the window, trying not to conjure up a picture of what the inside of that Army copter had looked like.

She failed, and the image filled her head: Beck on a stretcher, bloody leg covered in bandages, suffering in silence, torn by guilt because he hadn't managed to save his fellow soldiers. The thick smell of blood, the cries of the other wounded. The sheer horror of that journey.

Sometimes it was easy to forget that he'd been to war—unless she saw his scars. Occasionally he'd wake from a nightmare, screaming for a medic to help his buddies. She'd hold him, talking quietly to help him shake off the night terrors. Eventually he'd stop shaking and go back to sleep. He always returned the favor when one of her own nightmares came to call.

The helicopter rose slowly now, noisier than she'd anticipated as the blades began to pick up speed. From their new lofty vantage point, St. Peter's Square and the basilica were backlit by the rising sun. At one of the entrances to the enclave, a line of vehicles awaited their turn through the security checkpoint.

As they headed north, the city stirred to life beneath them. Cars moved on the street and people walked to work, despite the early hour. And yet, somewhere in their country, another city had died, its citizens no longer able to greet the dawn.

"Father Rosetti?" He turned toward her. "How many towns has it been now?"

Rosetti gave the cardinal a look, which earned him a nod. "Five."

"All destroyed the same way?" Rosetti nodded. "Witnesses?"

"Very few. Most of them are incoherent wrecks who barely make sense."

"Do these places have anything in common?"

"Not that we can determine."

"Which countries?"

"The Czech Republic, Spain, India, China, and now Italy."

"But nothin' in North or South America?" Beck asked.

"No."

"I thought I was of no further value in this investigation," Riley cut in, angry now. It was unlikely they could have prevented these deaths, but the losses rankled. If she'd expected Richter to flinch, she would have been disappointed.

Ignoring her comment, he insisted, "We must know what kind of Hellspawn is destroying these towns."

Wait for it . . .

"And then you will destroy it."

Riiight. "Why not the Demon Hunters? That's their job."

"You'll have their assistance, but you seem to have extraordinary luck when it comes to killing Hellspawn."

"Luck" acquired by Ori hauling her out of bed night after night, teaching her how to track and kill these things. Expertise paid for by scars that would never disappear, both on her body and inside her mind.

"Yeah, luck," she muttered.

"If you destroy this demon, we will be reassured that you are not in league with Lucifer," the cardinal added. "If not, our concerns as to your loyalties will be validated."

This was stupid. They didn't even know what was killing these people, and Richter had already drawn a line in the sand, at least when it came to her. She ground her teeth, trying not to snap back at him. The cardinal was backed into a tight corner, one that he and the entire Vatican shared. This time they had *no* maneuvering room, because the disaster was on their home turf.

If their prayers failed and people kept dying, the Church would look powerless when their faithful needed them the most. The Demon Hunters were very good at their job, but something that could level cities was likely beyond their abilities. There was a genuine possibility that Hell would win this round, and to the Vatican, that was unthinkable.

Riley knew how this would go: If she didn't solve their problem, the Holy See would claim she was working for Lucifer. She shot a quick glance toward Beck, and his deep frown indicated he was just as pissed as she was.

"Why the change of heart?" she asked.

The silence was like a dead zone. Finally, the cardinal huffed in disapproval. "The situation is too dire not to use your skills, despite our uncertainties."

"You want me to help you, I'm fine with that. But if you just want someone to be your sock puppet, I'm not going there—do you understand?"

Apparently Richter did, as his expression grew chillier. "No matter what you do, our initial concerns remain. We will be watching your every move," he replied.

"Of course you will."

Because no matter what she did, her decision to give her soul to Ori to save peoples' lives would haunt her for the rest of her days.

Chapter Seventeen

Province of Grosseto
Italy

The arrival of the papal helicopter would usually generate considerable media interest, except they'd landed in an open field where their only audience was a herd of curious cows. Three cars waited for them—two were their police escort, the final one their transportation.

Once they were all loaded up in yet another SUV, the atmosphere inside wasn't any better than in the copter. Not that Beck blamed Riley for that. In fact, he'd had a hard time keeping his mouth shut when she'd been working over Richter, but this was her battle. A battle he shared, but not as the stronger partner bailing out a weaker one. He and Riley were equals and Rome needed to accept that, or she'd tear into them just like she did an Archfiend.

At least his gut had been right about the Vatican's motives: They were in a bind, and they knew it. In many ways, the grand masters were as well. It was only a matter of time before some bright reporter pulled all the pieces together and realized the catastrophes were not from natural causes. In fact, he was surprised it hadn't happened already. Perhaps it had, and Rome had found a way to muzzle that news. Eventually the spotlight would turn on Rome and the International Guild because they were supposed to keep the world's citizens safe.

What kind of demon destroys cities? A Geo-Fiend could do a lot of damage, but not like he'd seen north of Prague. Beck'd even checked the Guild archives and hadn't found any of the known demons that matched that kind of power, at least ones that were found on the mortal plane. He had no doubt that there were a bunch of them down in Hell.

Was this a Hellfiend they'd never seen before? And if so, just how was Riley supposed to kill it? Often the only edge you had against the things is that you knew their strengths and weaknesses. A new one, fresh out of Hell? You'd be dead before you knew it. And if it was a Fallen . . .

No matter what, she's not facin' this alone.

He did a quick check on his fiancée and found that her temper had cooled and she was back in control, like she hadn't just gotten in a cardinal's face. It was times like this that he saw the changes in Paul's daughter. She still had her flighty moments—hell, he did too—but that ever-deepening reservoir of calm she displayed reminded him of the soldiers he'd served with in Afghanistan. The ones who were battle hardened, had witnessed too much death and destruction to ever go back to the way they were.

It hurt to know the woman he loved had taken on so much pain, so much loss. But at the same time, he was damned proud of Riley for not buckling under the weight of what Heaven and Hell had thrown at her.

God, I'm a lucky man.

The tension in the car hadn't eased one notch, so Beck decided it was time to step up to the plate.

"Father Rosetti," he began. The man turned to look at him over the back of the seat. "I have heard that you received a very special medal from the pope. Congratulations."

"How did you learn of that?" the priest asked, surprised.

"We grand masters have our ways of findin' out things," he said, smiling.

"I feel very honored," Rosetti said humbly.

"What medal is it?" Riley asked.

"The Benemerenti," Beck said, pronouncing the word with great care. It'd taken him a while to get it right.

"It's awarded for exceptional service to the Holy See," the cardinal added, not looking in their direction. "Well deserved."

"Thank you, Your Eminence," the priest replied.

"Congratulations," Riley said. "Are you still going to split your time between the Demon Hunters and training the lay exorcists?"

"No, the hunters will have a new priest to watch over them. I'll be working solely with the exorcists."

"Good," Beck replied. "Riley and I are *really* impressed with Simon's work. He's solid, no matter the strength of demon he's facin'." He noted that Richter continued to stare forward but was listening to every word. "Your training shows."

"Mr. Adler has proven to be very dedicated," Rosetti replied.

"It's certainly a difficult job. I know I don't ever want to see some demon inside a five-year-old kid again. That still gives me nightmares."

The cardinal turned toward them now. "Do you like doing the exorcisms?" he asked, his eyes on Riley.

"I do." She grew pensive. "It's really different from trapping fiends. Simon says I make things easier for him. Seems I have a way of riling up Hellspawn, making them mad. When they get angry, they make mistakes."

Works on cardinals too.

The car turned down another highway, and now, Beck could smell the rank odor of brimstone.

"Hell's calling card," the cardinal murmured.

Beck gave his fiancée a look, and she hitched a shoulder. It was time to find out who or what was killing these people. And stop it.

It took some time to get through the roadblocks, despite the police escort. Fortunately, the SUV had tinted windows, as a jostling herd of photographers waited for them by a makeshift police barricade. Once they were through that gauntlet, Riley heaved a sigh of relief.

"We have tried our best, but slowly the news organizations

are sensing a pattern," Rosetti admitted. "We decided it may be for the best that they know what happened, at least in Italy."

"Once you have determined what type of Hellspawn this is, we will announce that to the press," the cardinal said. "We wish that you be present for that, as well."

"Me?" That was a big change from "we don't trust you."

Beck gingerly cleared his throat. "Yer kinda well known, ah, worldwide."

"The YouTube videos?" she asked.

"Yeah. You've got a fan club or two out there. Can't say I blame 'em."

He was trying to make light of all this, but it only seemed to add more pressure. At what point did it become too much, and she just snapped like a dry twig?

The vehicle came to a halt, and the moment Riley stepped out of the car, she nearly gagged, the stench of brimstone was so strong. Beck had his hand over his mouth and nose, at least until one of the police officers handed them surgical masks. It helped, but did nothing for their eyes, which filled with tears from the sulfur. In the distance rose a cloud of gray steam, curling up in thick tendrils into the morning sky.

After Rosetti had spoken to a man who looked to be in charge, they set off in a single line down a two-lane asphalt road. Up a short hill, then down the road to where the grass and the trees—and everything else—abruptly ended.

Riley's mouth dropped open in shock underneath her mask.

Hell. She'd seen this kind of thing when Ori had taken her to meet his boss, except inside the ashy pit had been the dead, writhing and crying for help. Here, there were no structures, trees, or people, only a vast, black, ashy pit of annihilation.

"Dear God," she murmured. Next to her, Rosetti crossed himself.

A man behind them said a word she understood all too well: *Armageddon.* Even before she knew she was moving, Riley headed toward the blackened area. She only vaguely registered that Beck was walking alongside her.

As they drew closer, he said, "Don't walk out into that. It's ashes, but ya can sink deep into it and get burned."

She halted, shaking her head. "Do you hear that?"

"Ya mean the buzzin' sound?"

It wasn't buzzing to her. Instead, it was as if a rare violin hadn't been tuned properly, every note glaringly off key in some way. Riley gritted her teeth.

The scene reminded her of one she'd seen on the nightly news: a Japanese town buried deep in volcanic ash. Except that ash had been gray, and the buildings and cars and dead were still in place, entombed. The closer she came to the Black, as she'd come to think of it, the stronger the impressions. They hammered at her, wave after wave, but she couldn't comprehend their meaning, they were so jumbled. Shaking her head to try to clear it failed.

"Careful," Beck said as she edged forward.

"I will be." She frowned, then looked back to see if Rosetti and Richter had followed them. They had. The cardinal's eyes watched her intently from above his mask.

"Do you hear that noise?" she asked them. Both of the Vatican's men nodded. "Was it like this in the Czech Republic?"

"No," Rosetti replied. "At least, I didn't hear anything."

"Me neither," Beck replied.

What was different about this location?

"Is there any way to tell if this ashy area is perfectly round, or if it's jagged?"

Rosetti put the question to the man who'd escorted them to the spot and gained a quick reply in Italian. "It's uneven. It follows the city's boundaries exactly."

"Huh," she murmured.

"What're ya thinkin'?" Beck asked as the two clerics moved closer.

"I was wondering if this was caused by magic. Like if someone set a circle, then cast a spell *inside* that circle to cause this destruction."

"But the spellcaster would be killed, wouldn't they?" Beck

argued.

"Not if they were outside of it. It'd be just the opposite of how you'd usually use a sacred circle, but it might be doable if you had it conform to the city limits."

"It'd take a lot of power."

"Yeah, but we both know spellcasters who could do it, if they were crazy enough. Luckily they're not."

"Why all the brimstone, then?" Beck asked.

"Maybe to blame this on Hell?" she replied. "No, I don't think that's the case. I don't get the sense of any residual magic."

"Ya'll figure it out," he replied quietly, touching her elbow.

She gave him a thin smile, his support deeply appreciated. They both knew she was so far out on a limb that even the birds had abandoned her.

The Black kept pulling at her, so Riley moved forward until the toes of her shoes were nearly touching the debris. Unless it was her imagination, the pile almost seemed to pulse, like it had a heartbeat. Now that she was close enough, the stench of sulfur was infused with other scents: burnt wood, flesh, and bones. Riley swallowed repeatedly to keep her gag reflex in check.

"Jesus," Beck said. "I can't imagine what it was like to die like this."

Her eyes kept flooding in protest, and wiping them didn't seem to do much good. Backing up a bit, she squatted down, hoping desperately for some clue as to the force that had wiped this city from the earth. As she did, some of her tears fell onto the ashes, vanishing in an instant.

Come on. Give me something. I can't stop this if I don't know what's going on.

As if in response, the ashes closest to her feet shifted. For a second, she thought it had been her imagination, but those same ashes started to rise rapidly, forming into a cone. Before she could move away, they took the shape of a hand.

"What the hell is that?" Beck said.

The hand hung in the air for only a fraction of a second, even with her face, and then its index finger swiftly touched her forehead. Riley fell back in shock, landing in Beck's arms, and he quickly pulled her away across the grass.

"What happened there?" the cardinal demanded.

She was about to tell him she had no idea, but her lips couldn't remember how to form words. Instead, her eyes searched across the vast stretch of black, but now it was a modern city, filled with people, buildings, cars. Kids on bikes and parents with strollers. Couples holding hands. A bride and her groom descended the steps of a centuries-old church, smiling as people threw flowers and called out their congratulations.

In a single blink, they were gone, suffocated in a curtain of white mist. Then the fire came, raining down, incinerating everything and everyone. The many souls cried for help, screamed their prayers. Something had snuffed them out as easily as she might an ant under her shoe, turning their lives, their very bodies, into dust.

"Riley? You okay?" Beck called out. His arms were around her, holding her close.

More images roared through her mind now, each one more intense than the last. She stood on a hilltop above an ancient city. It was night, but somehow she could make out the tall stone buildings, some with rows of pillars, like a palace. Carved images were everywhere and people hurried along broad streets, some with baskets on their heads. Smoke from cooking fires and the smell of roasted meats hung in the air.

A voice rang out, one that cut through the darkness like a shard of lightning. It spoke in a tongue she didn't understand, a language ancient even when the universe was created. She'd heard it before, on a battlefield.

The sharp smell of fresh blood filled her nose as a thin, white mist descended from the sky. For a moment, it looked pretty, falling in rivulets, like streams of pure lace. When it reached the sandy ground, it pooled, then crept along, seeking any openings. It slithered under doors and into open windows, passing like a plague in the night. The prayers grew louder now, and *this* language she recognized. Then came the cries, the shouts, the screams of terror.

It's killing them.

As they died, Riley found herself struggling to breathe, as if she was there with them, crawling on her hands and knees in the sand, desperately begging for air.

In her mind, that ashy hand grabbed on to hers, pulling her along with it, through the white mist, through the skies, through time itself. Words formed in her head now, searing like they were composed of molten silver, burning with an intensity that seemed to scorch her from within.

I am Death, the Destroyer. In me, there is no life.

I struck them down, from the babe in the womb to the oldest of the old, as was commanded. I slaughtered them all and sang of it as if it was a great honor. Now I slay them to honor what I have become, what I shall always be.

I am Death, the Destroyer. In me, there is no life.

"Riley!" Beck yelled, shaking her now.

Her eyes snapped open, bathed in tears. "Dead. They're all dead."

Then the ashy darkness seized her.

Beck lifted her, rising, adjusting her in his arms. "Gotta get her away from this sulfur. She's havin' trouble breathin'."

As he hiked up the hill, panic pushing his pace, his mind processed what he'd just witnessed—a black, ashy hand had come out of the wreckage and touched his fiancée. He would have thought he was hallucinating if Riley hadn't reacted so badly.

Hanging limp in his arms, each of her breaths generated a high-pitched wheeze.

"Dyin' on me is not happenin', ya hear?" he barked. "Ya just keep breathin' and we'll get through this." Her lack of response, along with those breaths, caused his panic to multiply.

Behind him, he heard Rosetti on his phone, so that by the time they reached the copter, there was a man in a uniform waiting for them. He'd placed a blanket on the ground and had what looked to be a medical kit open. Beck laid Riley on the blanket and then dropped to his knees at her side, one of her pale hands clasped in his. As he curled his fingers around hers, he saw that her nailbeds were blue. Her lips were the same when they removed her surgical mask. As Rosetti relayed what had happened, the man examined Riley.

"Silvio usually travels with the Holy Father in case there is any medical emergency," Rosetti explained.

"Understood. I was in the Army and treated the wounded. Just tell me what to do," Beck said.

With a nod, Silvio handed him a mask and an oxygen canister. While Beck positioned the mask on Riley's face, slipping the strap over her head, and then adjusted the oxygen flow, the medic inserted an IV. "Does she suffer from asthma?" Silvio asked as he taped down the IV site. One of the police officers stood just behind him, holding the liter bag of fluid so it flowed properly.

"No," Beck replied. "Not allergic to anythin', at least not that I know of. She does get panic attacks, but this isn't one of those.

"Then I will administer epinephrine to help open her airway."

Beck nodded, familiar with the medication. There'd been a soldier in his unit who'd gotten bitten by some damn bug or another and had stopped breathing. While Beck had performed CPR, the medic had rammed a needle full of epinephrine into the guy and brought him back from the brink. From that time on, the soldier had been called Bad Bug by his buddies.

Silvio gave the shot as Riley's breathing had still not eased. Then he leaned closer, listening to each side of her chest with a stethoscope. After a few more minutes, he repeated the task. With a satisfied nod, he leaned back, removing the earpieces. "The tightness is easing."

"Thank God," Beck said. Out of the corner of his eye, he saw Rosetti make the sign of the cross. To his surprise, Richter did the same. "Shouldn't she be wakin' up?"

"Yes. That concerns me." The medic looked up at Rosetti

now. "She must be examined by a physician as soon as possible."

The priest nodded. "Is it safe to transport her?"

"Yes."

With Beck's help, they loaded Riley inside the helicopter, then Silvo sat in the seat next to her so he could continue her care. While they prepared for the trip, Rosetti spoke to the pilot in rapid-fire Italian. With a quick nod, the man immediately began working through his pre-flight checklist.

"The cardinal and I will be remaining here," the priest announced. "I've instructed the pilot to take you directly to the Vatican, and he will let them know you have a patient on board. Do not worry, our medical facilities are excellent."

"Thank you," Beck said, right before the side door closed.

He could tell she was better already: Each deep breath told him that. Still, minutes later, as the helicopter rose from the ground, Beck said a prayer for the woman he loved.

Chapter Eighteen

Vatican City State
Rome, Italy

When Riley woke, her first impression was that someone had parked a grand piano on her chest. Fortunately, with each subsequent deep breath, the sensation began to fade.

"Hey there, Princess," Beck said. "About time ya woke up." To anyone else, he would have sounded calm, but she knew him too well. At least this time he wasn't going to chew her out for trapping a Grade Three demon on her own.

It took Riley a while to realize that they were in her room at the Vatican. She certainly didn't remember anything of the journey back, which meant she'd been unconscious. That explained the worry in Beck's eyes.

As if reading her mind, Beck added, "Ya had trouble breathin' and passed out. Their doc thinks it was a reaction to the sulfur," he said. He let go of her hand. "I need to let Albero know yer awake. The man is freakin' out about as bad as I was."

Riley heard the door open and close. No, Beck didn't freak out that easily, so this must have been a lot worse than she'd realized. As she closed her eyes again, a few memories began to creep back. None of them were welcome.

Beck returned, sat in the chair near the bed, and reclaimed her right hand, stroking it reassuringly. "He's gonna send up some food."

"Sounds good." Right now, she needed normal—not the throat-tightening dread she'd experienced this morning.

"Funny how ya didn't have a problem with the brimstone when ya came back from Hell that time," he added.

Riley eyed him but didn't reply. She hadn't thought of that. After taking a deep breath, and relishing just how good that felt, she rubbed her forehead where the finger had touched her. All the while, Beck kept staring at her.

"How long was I out?"

"About seven hours. Ya woke up once when the doctor was checkin' ya over, told us to stop messin' with ya, then went back to sleep. Doc said not to worry, that ya were just exhausted from havin' so much trouble breathin'."

But you worried anyway. She would have done the same.

Riley remembered none of that conversation, but the length of time in bed explained why a trip to the bathroom was desperately needed. Once she explained where she was headed, Beck made sure she was steady on her feet, then backed off.

When she exited the bathroom, her fiancé stood by the window, staring out at the courtyard below. He appeared deep in thought—so much so, he didn't realize she'd returned until she'd leaned back against the headboard and tucked the bedclothes around her. Folding her hands in her lap, Riley tried to find the right way to tell him what she'd experienced.

Before she could figure out what to say, Beck turned toward her, sighing. "What happened out there?"

"Tell me what you saw."

"Well," he began, then hesitated, running a hand through his hair uneasily, "I saw a bunch of ashes rise up in the air and become a hand. It touched ya and then things got bad."

The expression in his eyes pleaded with her to tell him he wasn't crazy.

"Yes, it touched my forehead and then . . . I saw things inside my mind."

"What kinds of things?"

"That city? I watched them all die, Den. Every single death."

"Jesus." He paused, then asked, "What killed 'em?"

"There was this white mist and it choked them to death.

Then fire rained down, burning everything, everyone. The ashes are all that's left."

He dropped into the chair as if he had no more will to stand. "I don't think the others saw what we did."

"I'm not sure if that's a good thing or not," she admitted. It was sure going to make it harder to convince the Vatican of what they were up against.

"Ya know what's doin' this, don't ya?" She nodded. "Demon?" She shook her head. "Angel?"

"Yes."

"A Fallen then," Beck murmured, then shook his head in dismay. "It'll be up to me to try to kill it."

"No, it's not a Fallen, Den. And I don't think you *can* kill it." Not if what she suspected was true. "Promise you won't volunteer to do that."

His eyes weren't meeting hers now.

"Den? You must promise me. If I'm right, I don't think any of us can stop this creature."

"Sometimes," he began, his voice thick, "ya take on a mission ya know is gonna fail. That way people can see yer tryin'.'"

She jerked her hand away from his. "No! You'll throw your life away. I don't want to spend the rest of my days a widow, you hear me?"

His eyes finally rose. "I hear ya. But sometimes ya just don't have a choice."

"This isn't a regular angel, not like Ori or Michael or Martha. It said its name is Death."

He acted as if he hadn't heard her, getting to his feet, his face set. "I'll go see if I can speed up that food a bit."

A swift kiss landed on her cheek, and then he was out the door. She rubbed that spot, and then her hand drifted to her forehead again, remembering the finger that had touched her this morning. Fingers made of the bodies of the dead.

Riley dropped her own hand back on the covers. She had to find a way to explain to Richter and his people what they faced, and keep Beck safe.

A tingle began on her left palm, then flared like it was on fire, making her yelp in surprise. Probably a not-so-subtle reminder that she still owed Heaven.

"This is *my* deal with you, not Den's. Keep him out of it, and I'll do anything you ask." *Anything.*

~~*

The following morning they were back in the same meeting room, but this time there were more men on the other side of the table. As before, Cardinal Richter sat in the center, so he was still the most senior of the clerics. In addition to Bishops Prager and Alvarez, three others had joined the party. From Albero's introductions, Riley now rated two more bishops and an archbishop.

Lucky me.

No doubt, what she was about to tell them would funnel right up to the pope. She could only imagine how well that was going to go, especially if they thought she was lying. To help her explain, on the table in front of her was a Catholic Bible, in English, with the appropriate pages bookmarked, and next to it sat a candlestick and a tall white taper, which was already lit.

As Riley waited for the clerics to settle into their chairs, she tried hard to channel some smidgen of inner tranquility. It didn't work, not when she was about to deliver faith-challenging news to one of the most powerful religious organizations on the planet.

She gave Beck a sidelong look. This morning, right before Albero had come to collect them, she'd told him what she'd seen after the hand had touched her forehead. His mouth had dropped open and his eyes had gone wide. When he'd finally absorbed the news, he'd stared at nothing for some time, then bowed his head in shock.

"We're fucked," he'd said, uncharacteristically blunt.

It was when he'd raised his eyes and Riley looked into them that she saw exactly how frightened he was.

"Maybe. Maybe not," she'd replied.

The general shuffling at the front of the room ceased as Richter brought the meeting to order.

"I am told you feel well enough to attend this morning. Is that correct, Master Blackthorne?"

"Yes."

"Your collapse yesterday was because of the sulfur?"

"I don't think so. The sulfur certainly didn't help, but that wasn't the root cause."

"I see." Yet he didn't ask the expected question.

Bishop Prager jumped in. "What kind of demon are we facing?"

"It's not a demon."

It was as if she'd just introduced a skunk into the room. Agitated muttering grew into raised voices, demanding to know what she meant by such a thing. Only when Richter raised his hand did the noise end.

"Explain," he ordered.

"The being that is destroying those towns is not one of Lucifer's."

"Then what is it?"

Riley took a deep breath, knowing this might be a step too far for these men, but the truth had to be revealed.

"It is an angel, but not a Fallen." She let that rattle around in their heads for a few seconds. "I wish it were a demon," she said, surprised at how strong her voice sounded. "But it's an angel, and it's one of," she paused, pointing upward, "theirs."

"You're saying it's from Heaven?" Alvarez demanded in astonishment.

"That's impossible! Why would God destroy our cities?" Prager spouted.

"Perhaps she is hiding Lucifer's plans by lying like this," one of the other bishops added. She'd already forgotten his name, because none of that was important right now.

"You have proof?" Richter asked.

Riley nodded. With a firm hand, she flipped open the Bible to one of the bookmarks and traced down the text until she found the appropriate passage.

"Genesis Nineteen One: 'When the two angels reached Sodom in the evening, Lot was sitting at the gate of Sodom. As soon as Lot saw them, he stood up to greet them, and bowed to the ground.'"

Alvarez tried to interrupt, but she cut him off. "And the angels tell Lot, 'We are about to destroy this place, for the outcry reaching the LORD against those here is so great that the LORD has sent us to destroy it.'" She traced her finger down further. "'Then *Yahweh* rained down on Sodom and Gomorrah brimstone and fire of his own sending. He overthrew those cities and the whole plain, with all the people living in the cities and everything that grew there.'"

She looked up into eyes that spoke of frank disbelief. "Fire and brimstone. Sound familiar? That's what's happening to these cities. It's no demon—it's one of God's own."

"Ridiculous," the archbishop said. "This is an outrageous fairytale."

"Y'all consider the Bible a fairytale?" Beck asked, his voice low, though it carried to every corner of the room. All eyes turned to him now, none friendly. "Because if that's what Riley sensed, that's what it is."

"I refuse to believe this," Alvarez replied.

Richter ignored him. "Why would Heaven destroy these places?"

"What I sensed was hard to comprehend, at least by a mortal. I felt . . . so much. Disillusionment, sadness, a feeling of being lost somehow." Riley paused, trying to frame her thoughts. "I heard the angel's voice in my head. It showed the cities it had destroyed, both in the present and the past."

"You see, it is one of the Fallen," Prager said. "They are masters at playing with our minds."

"I know what a Fallen feels like when they're inside my head. This was *not* one of them."

"Then which Divine is it? Certainly not Michael or any of the Archangels."

"No. This angel has one purpose only, to do God's will."

"All of them follow His will," the bishop argued.

"Yes, but this angel metes out death on God's command."

Richter blinked, his eyes widening in comprehension. "*Lieber Gott,*" he murmured.

He understands.

"I witnessed the deaths of those people, every single one of them, from the youngest to the oldest. I felt the moment of their last choking breath, then the incineration of their bodies. And if that wasn't enough, I was shown the deaths of countless others over the millennia. Of cities bathed in fire, fields covered in rotting corpses before the flames consumed them. Villages crying out for mercy and receiving none."

"You have an unlimited imagination," Alvarez said acidly.

"Do I?" she replied, raising an eyebrow.

Riley flipped to another section of the Bible, one further back. "What I saw through this angel's eyes is what is written in the Book of Exodus, chapters eleven and twelve: 'Then the LORD spoke to Moses: One more plague I will bring upon Pharaoh and upon Egypt. After that he will let you depart.'"

She moved further down the page.

"'And so at midnight the LORD struck down every firstborn in the land of Egypt, from the firstborn of Pharaoh sitting on his throne to the firstborn of the prisoner in the dungeon, as well as all the firstborn of the animals. Pharaoh arose in the night, he and all his servants and all the Egyptians; and there was loud wailing throughout Egypt, for there was not a house without its dead.'"

Riley looked up from the text.

"The angel is the Destroyer, God's personal executioner. It has slain millions in His name, not only the firstborn babies of Egypt."

Stunned silence met her. One of the bishops opened his mouth to argue, then let it close again.

Richter recovered more quickly than the rest. "You certainly don't believe God is ordering it to slay these people."

Riley looked down at the scrap of paper Beck had dug out of his wallet, where it lay near the Bible. He'd been carrying it for some time, he'd said, because he didn't understand it. Now they both did.

"In the mid-nineteenth century, a man named Arthur Varnery wrote the following: 'The madness of angels in highest heaven, the cunning of demons in darkest Hell. The two are separate, yet twain, for the Light gives and the Light destroys, all in equal measure.'"

Riley held her right palm toward the burning candle. "At this distance, the fire doesn't hurt me." She moved her hand closer, feeling the increasing heat, the sting. "But if I am too close to the flame, I'll be burned. It's like that with Heaven's Light. Too close, for too long, and it burns."

She pulled her hand away, blowing on the throbbing skin.

"When they talk about people averting their eyes in the Bible, that's not hyperbole—the Light is that strong. I stood between Michael and Lucifer, talking them out of Armageddon, and I felt that raw power. It burned right through me. I'm still alive only because my exposure was *very* short."

Riley took a very deep breath, praying these men would understand. "The Destroyer has been doing God's will since the day it was created. It has blindly gone about its tasks, nation after nation, tribe after tribe, family after family. Babies, the unborn, it didn't matter. If it was told they should die, they died. It carried out its duties as only a devout servant can. And it was praised in Heaven for doing so."

She sucked in another deep breath. "But for every one of those souls who perished, it heard their cries, witnessed their last breath. And now, all of those deaths, even in the lowest households of Egypt, have driven it insane."

Riley blew out the candle, and the smoke rising upward reminded her of the cities that were no more.

"This angel of death has been so close to that Light for untold time, and it's burnt out. It suffers from immense guilt, because even executioners have souls. It's finally gone rogue."

The men at the front of the room continued to stare at her. Some had their mouths set in grim lines; one, the archbishop, had his hands intertwined as if in prayer. She'd just told them that Heaven was their enemy. Or at least, one of Heaven's angels.

Riley carefully closed the Bible, letting it rest in her hands, her finger rubbing over the fine leather. She made sure to soften her voice now. "It's my guess that the Destroyer is no longer taking its orders from Heaven. It's killing on its own, because it knows no other way to exist."

"But surely, if that were the case, God would end its life," one of the bishops countered.

"Would He? Or is this another one of those tests of His? Maybe we're supposed to learn something from this, but I have no idea what that might be."

As every eye watched her, Riley rose and walked up to stand in front of Cardinal Richter, placing the holy book on the table in front of him. "You asked me to tell you what you're facing. I've done that."

"You are certain?"

She flipped over her left hand to display the crown. "I am certain."

"This has to end," he said. "People cannot keep dying."

"I know that. But your city killer is an angel, and not a Fallen. Which means it's not in my skill set, or that of the grand masters."

She nudged the book forward until it touched the tips of Richter's fingers. "This is the Church's problem. Unless you can convince God to destroy this thing, it's just going to keep on killing until there is no one left. This angel, Your Eminence, is a slow-motion Apocalypse."

Riley didn't wait for a reply. As she headed down the hallway toward the stairs to her room, she was aware that no one was following her; Beck had stayed behind.

Don't martyr yourself. Because that's exactly what his death would be. Even MacTavish had echoed that sentiment when Beck had called him with the sobe news.

Mr. Albero finally caught up with her near the door to her room. "Master Blackthorne?" he called out, hurrying toward her.

She stopped, key in hand, that hand shaking. "Yes?"

"Is there anything you need?" he asked, halting a few feet away.

"Only to go home," she said.

He nodded his understanding, then headed back the way he'd come, moving much faster than usual. Who knew? Maybe the kind clerk would make that a reality.

~~*

When the whole-body tremors struck Riley the moment she shut the door behind her, made it to the chair and dropped into it. Curving her arms around her sides, she hugged herself tight, as if somehow that would ward away the future they faced.

When she was a kid, she'd been afraid of the monsters that she was sure lived in the dark. Her mother or father would reassure her, remind her that no harm would come if they were there to protect her. She'd always gone to sleep safe in their love, unaware that that feeling of security wouldn't last forever. After her parents died, the dark was still there, and so were the monsters.

The shakes finally lessened. Not knowing how long Beck would be, or if Albero could pull off a miracle and get them out of here, she rose and began to pack. It was busywork, and she threw herself into it. Because of that, the task went quickly. She was just about to zip the suitcase shut when there was a knock at her door.

After she opened it, Beck entered, his eyes pointedly not meeting hers.

"When can we leave?" she asked.

He shrugged, then dropped onto the end of the bed with a weary sigh.

Her heart clenched. "You told them you'd try to kill it, didn't you?"

"No, I didn't. Why do I feel like a coward for that?"

Riley sat next to him, taking one of his hands in hers. It was cool to the touch, and she could feel his muscles tense under her fingers. "You barely killed Sartael and almost died in the process. This angel isn't anything like him. It's like comparing a flintlock rifle to a nuclear warhead."

"I know, but I still feel like a coward. It didn't help that they tried to guilt me about it." He pulled her into his arms, his lips touching her temple. "I'm damned proud of you. Took a lot of courage for you to tell them the truth."

"At least they believed me. I was afraid they wouldn't."

"You weren't the only one." He hesitated. "I'll go pack. I don't figure we're goin' anywhere, but we'll act like we are."

As the door closed behind him, Riley flopped back onto the bed. She knew what the Church's next move would be: using her freedom as a bargaining chip with Beck. She could almost hear Cardinal Richter as if he were in the room with her. "We'll allow Master Blackthorne to return home if you do this one little favor for us, Grand Master," he'd say. "If you refuse to aid us, then we will be forced to dig deeper into her ongoing relationship with Hell. No doubt, that investigation would take considerable time."

For the Vatican, time was not measured in days or weeks, but in decades and centuries. She knew her fiancé—he'd agree to the offer in a bid to keep her safe, trading his life for her freedom. Then he would die and the darkness would win, again.

~~*

About an hour later, Rosetti tapped on Beck's door, causing him to set aside his book. When he opened it, the priest stepped inside. Once it closed behind him, he announced, "You are free to return to Scotland."

Beck blinked. "I'm surprised. I figured Richter would want me to commit angel-cide."

"The Holy Father has weighed the matter and prayed for guidance, and his orders are for you and your fiancée to return home."

"Huh. You think he knows something we don't?"

"I would count on that."

"Well, I suppose he's more plugged in than any of us," Beck allowed.

Rosetti gave a wan smile. "At the very least. Cardinal Richter is not pleased, of course. However, I am." He stuck out his hand and they shook. "Go with God, Grand Master Beck."

"You too, Father Rosetti. I appreciate all yer support over the last year."

"As I do yours."

As the door closed behind the man, Beck wondered if maybe someday that man would be the pope himself.

"Be damned good at it," he murmured.

~~*

Beck had gone downstairs with the luggage, which left Riley on her own. As she took one last look at the room to ensure she'd left nothing behind, she still couldn't believe they were being allowed to leave. Especially since he'd said that the order had come from the pope himself.

As she walked into the hallway and let the door shut behind her, the sound of muted voices caught her notice. There were two men further down the hallway in close conversation. One was Father Rosetti. The other was older and . . . clothed all in white.

They turned at the sound of the closing door. Father Rosetti leaned closer to his companion and gestured toward her, and the pope nodded his understanding. After studying her for a moment, he made the sign of the cross. His soft-spoken benediction reached her ears, though he was some distance away. When it ended, she gave a respectful nod in return, surprised that he would take time to offer such a blessing.

As Rosetti and the pontiff continued down the corridor, resuming their conversation, Riley slowly translated the Latin.

Remember that you are not alone, for this path you walk has been readied for you far longer than your short lifespan. May God grant you wisdom and courage, for your fate is our fate. In the name of the Father, of the Son, and of the Holy Spirit. Amen.

Riley stood motionless for another minute or so, allowing that blessing to become part of her. Then, with a long sigh, she walked toward the exit. Their time in Rome may be at an end, but she knew that Beck's and her part in all this was just beginning.

Chapter Nineteen

Oakland Cemetery
Atlanta, Georgia

It was dawn when the sharp crack of stone made Martha look up from where she'd been puttering around the old Jewish section of Oakland Cemetery, tidying up the graves of departed Hirshes, Koplins, and Pinskys. Another crack came, and then an anguished cry rent the air. Now she knew exactly where it'd come from.

In the blink of an eye, she appeared near the Blackthorne mausoleum, her senses on alert. The sun had risen just enough for it to spotlight the structure's pitched roof and its sentinels, the gargoyles.

The fifth one was gone.

Alarmed at what this might mean, the angel stalked around the side of the building in time to hear yet another low moan. She found the source of those sounds in a heap on the cold ground about ten feet from the mausoleum.

"What nonsense is this?" she muttered, her hands on her hips.

The newcomer was nude, which wasn't a big deal to her kind. Still, she noticed that he'd managed to strategically place one of his wings to shield his privates. That degree of modesty came with too many years of living among the mortals—their prudishness rubbed off on you.

The Fallen's confused dark eyes stared up her. His mouth opened and closed, unable to form words. She couldn't even imagine what was going on inside his head.

Her eyes shifted up to where Ori's gargoyle had once sat. The sun had just skimmed past it, illuminating more of the mausoleum's roofline now. The stone sculpture that had housed him was scattered in pieces around the angel. Some of those shards had cut his skin, causing blue blood to trickle into the grass.

"Rahmiel," he said, barely above a whisper.

It was the first time he'd ever used her real name, and it felt like a portent. Was this the Prince's doing or . . . Martha looked up into the sky for guidance and received complete silence.

"Huh." Scratching her chin, she sighed and moved closer, then sat on the ground near him. "Tell me, is this a good thing or a bad thing?"

Ori's eyes had finally cleared. He pulled himself into a sitting position, that wing still carefully placed. After some thought, he whispered, "I . . . don't . . . know." His voice was rough, as if it hadn't been used for a long time. Which it hadn't.

Martha eyed his wings, noting that the gray that usually outlined the tops of them was gone, leaving them pure white. Like hers, and the wings of all those who inhabited the upper realm. Despite that change, she didn't sense he was one of theirs, not like she did with the others. And yet, there was no foul taint that encompassed someone touched by the Prince's hand.

"Huh," she repeated, still flummoxed.

The necromancers could summon a reanimated corpse.

Only her boss could truly raise the dead.

"How long has it been?" Ori asked. It appeared her fellow angel's mental fog had begun to clear.

"A little over a year," she said. "Riley Anora Blackthorne is now a master trapper, and she is to be wed to the one whom you taught how to kill us."

"I see," he responded quietly. His troubled eyes rose to hers again. "Why am I here?"

She hitched a shoulder. Like the Archangel Michael, or any of the others, would bother to tell her.

Ori gained his feet and stretched his wings like he'd just risen from a long nap. He shook them, dislodging a few feathers, which floated to the ground. Clothing had also appeared—black T-shirt, black jeans, black jacket.

"I was at peace," he said, his voice louder now. Growing angry.

"I would argue with that," she said, rising as well. "You were at rest. Clearly, whatever you're supposed to do isn't done yet."

Martha waited for his reaction as she dusted the grass and dirt off her clothes. She'd have to tidy up the remains of the gargoyle, ensure that none of the flowers had been damaged by the angel's fall.

"I was at peace," Ori insisted, though his tone said otherwise. "Now I'm . . ."

"Back in the Grand Game," she said. At least, that's what the mortals called it. She and the other Divines had their own terms for that eternal give and take between Heaven and Hell.

Ori opened his mouth to argue with her assessment, then snapped it shut. With a curt nod, he stalked away, his wings vanishing as he departed down the path toward the bell tower.

Martha looked upward again. "Is this because of—?"

A crack of thunder cut her off.

"Just asking," she grumbled.

Her natural inquisitiveness, especially the habit of asking uncomfortable questions of a certain overly proud Archangel, was why she was now the celestial guardian of this cemetery. Some of her kind had felt it was a demotion of sorts. She'd never seen it that way.

No, not many got a ringside seat as the Grand Game played out in front of them.

~~*

Ori's disorientation had manifested itself in aimless wandering. He'd retraced his steps through Atlanta until he found himself at the exact spot where he'd died. It didn't look any different, though there was new concrete nearby, no doubt to cover the gaping hole Lucifer had created when he'd dragged one of the traitors back to Hell during the purge.

Here, Ori's death had severed the bond between him and Blackthorne's only child. Her soul had been set free. Somehow, he knew that this fact remained unchanged, that his sudden "rebirth" had not touched her, at least not in those terms.

"Why am I here?" he murmured. None of the people walking near him could hear him, and he was certain that if they had, they wouldn't know the answer. Ironically, that was one of the questions often rattling around in the mortals' heads. A query that he used to take full advantage of, allowing him to move one step closer to claiming their soul.

Not anymore. Lucifer had released his hold on him, so Ori was no longer one of the Prince's servants. Yet he didn't feel as if he belonged in Heaven, either. He felt . . . unmoored.

A pair of young women walked by, one of them giving him the eye. She smiled at him and winked, clearly interested in what she saw. He smiled back before realizing what he was doing. Old habits die hard, even for Fallen angels.

Ori hadn't lied to Rahmiel, the one the mortals called Martha. Well, not entirely. He *had* been at peace, savoring the morning light from his perch on top of the mausoleum. The awareness of his surroundings had fled in only a matter of days, and yet he always knew when the sun's rays hit his prison. Yet he sensed nothing else, unaware of the passage of time or the events around him.

Now he was alive, *again.* Some might rejoice at that second chance, but Ori did not. All the temptations that had cost him so dearly were still out there. It would be so easy to talk some unsuspecting mortal into giving up his or her soul. As easy as taking a breath.

He walked away from where he'd died now, though he had no destination in mind. That he'd been called back to life by the Creator wouldn't sit well with the Chief of the Fallen. If he wasn't careful, didn't guard every step, he could find himself in

Hell, suffering from Lucifer's wrath. Because if he'd learned one thing over the countless millennia, it was that the Prince held a grudge.

He paused now, ignoring those who walked around him without realizing they were close to an angel. He closed his eyes, hunting, and then found Riley Anora Blackthorne in the country the mortals called Italy. She was with the man who would be her husband. The one who had become a grand master.

Even as he tried to get a sense of her life now, something pricked at the corners of his mind. Something ancient and familiar, laced with a fanatical purpose. Slowly, the shocking realization set in.

Now he understood why he'd been rousted from the grave.

~~*

International Guild Manor House
Scotland

Riley stared out the side window as she and Beck were driven back to the manor. She'd readily agreed with his suggestion that they stay at the cottage tonight. While she'd been dropped off near the loch, Beck had begun to pack up his belongings for the flight home tomorrow. He also needed to carve out a time to sit for his formal portrait, something that had to be done before they returned home.

Oddly ill at ease, despite the fact that she loved this place, Riley started a fire in the stove to warm up the cottage. Then, as if driven out of that warmth, she went out to sit on a rock in the snow to watch the sun cast gold beams on the loch. For one disconcerting moment, the scene around her turned to blackened ashes, but then, with the blink of an eye, it went back to pure white snow.

"Why are you letting this happen?" she whispered. "What's the point of all these deaths? What do you want us to do?"

If it was just a matter of being less wicked, then why allow the angel to destroy a whole town? Because all that did was make people fearful and angry—more likely to turn away from the Light than toward it.

"Help me understand. There has to be a way to stop this." *Without losing the man I love.*

Riley blinked away tears as the water in front of her turned darker gold. In the distance, she swore she could hear a bagpipe, low and mournful. Its haunting notes cracked open her emotions, finally allowing them to spill out like sand from a damaged bucket. The first tear rolled down her cheek, chilly in the twilight air. Then another and another. Finally, she was openly sobbing, hugging herself and rocking back and forth in agony.

"I can't do this anymore," she cried.

It'd been too much, too quickly. The death of her mother, then her father. Being loved and then betrayed by both Ori and Simon. The lethal cunning of Sartael and the Prince. The deaths, the battles. The choices.

Oh God, the choices. Riley had tried to make the right ones and then paid the price, over and over. Now she was teetering on the edge of that abyss again.

"I'm not strong enough," she pleaded. She was only eighteen. Most people her age were just testing the waters, learning who they were, what they wanted in life.

She'd had no chance to come to grips with herself, her strengths and weaknesses. She'd been shoved into this role, half-formed and yet expected to lead.

No one ever thinks they're strong enough. But you are. You always have been.

Riley gaped in astonishment. It was her mother's voice in her head now, soft and reassuring.

"But I don't know what to do. If we fight this thing, we'll die—"

Or you'll win. Trust your heart, Riley. Because everything happens for a reason. Everything.

Her mother's voice faded out and with it, Riley's tears. Her mom had always told her how much she was loved, how she'd make mistakes but that was what being human was all about. Now, from beyond the grave, Miriam Blackthorne had reinforced that message.

The last of the sun slowly bowed out behind the distant hills. The piper's last note hung in the air, then faded away, heralding another day gone.

"Thanks, Mom," Riley said. As she stood, a light breeze touched her hair, like her mother had always done. "I miss you too."

~~*

As Riley approached the cottage, she saw that more lights were on, which meant Beck had arrived. She found him on the couch, his boots off, feet up, and eyes distant.

"Den?"

He looked over at her and smiled, the connection between them instantaneous. That smile was what drew her in every time. A bit of bad boy, all good man.

"You doin' okay?" he asked as she removed her own boots and heavy outer clothes, stashing them in their proper places.

"Better. Just puzzled. And very overwhelmed."

He gave a jerky nod and now she noticed the sheen in his eyes. He hadn't been crying, but he was feeling the same emotions nonetheless.

"I brought some supper up from the manor. It's in the oven, staying warm." Which explained the enticing scent of roasted chicken she'd noticed when she'd first entered the cottage.

Food sounded good, but not right now. Riley walked over to stand in front of him and offered a hand. Beck rose, no doubt seeing the troubled look in her eyes. He drew her into his arms.

"If you go after this thing, we do it *together.*"

She felt him tense under her fingers. "Riley, that's—"

"The only way it's going to be," she said, not looking at him now. If she did, she'd start to cry again. "Because if you die, I die right along with you."

"No," he whispered, touching her hair.

"*Promise me,*" Riley insisted. She could have put a magical push behind that command, but she didn't. This had to be his decision.

He ground his teeth, then let his jaw relax. "Ah, hell. I promise. But it goes both ways—ya don't go after this thing on yer own."

She raised her head from his shoulder. "I won't. I wouldn't do that to you."

That seemed to mollify him. "Well, no matter what we face, we're stronger together. Always have been."

"Always will be."

The touch of his lips to hers filled her with an unexpected peace.

When the kiss ended, he whispered, "Our last night in Scotland."

That made this moment even more poignant. "I love you. I always will."

"Then show me," he whispered. "Because time is growin' precious, even for us."

~~*

Beck's House
Atlanta, Georgia

Their house had weathered their absence quite well. A little stuffy, but a good airing out would fix that. While Riley pulled clothes out of their suitcases and dropped them into the washer, Beck retrieved his rabbit from the neighbor's. That task usually took some time because Mrs. Merton liked to catch up on their lives. Since she was always good about watching both the house and Rennie, he never rushed his visits. In fact, he looked forward to them.

Once the washer was running, Riley called Angus. He'd returned to Atlanta the day after Beck's investiture, since no one had been sure exactly how long Riley and her fiancé would be Rome's guests.

"We're home," she said, closely followed by a huge yawn.

"Good ta hear it. I still canna wrap my mind around Heaven bein' the cause of all this destruction."

"Neither can I."

A long sigh came down the line. "I sent an e-mail ta Beck with the details on the two meetin's he's got first thing tomorrow. Can ya make sure he sees that?"

"Sure." *Meetings*. The newest grand master was going to be thrilled about those.

"Oh, and Harper's been missin' ya, not that he said so in plain English, mind ya."

That made her smile. "The apprentices doing okay?"

"They are, but he's got some concerns about the lass, Jaye."

"What's going on?"

"Best ta ask him. He was his usual bitchy self taday, so I didn't press him on the subject."

Some things never changed. "I will. Thanks, Angus."

"I ken that it's hard ta think of good things right now, but soon ya'll be married."

"I wish it was tomorrow."

"It'll come soon enough. Now go ta bed. Ya sound knackered. Send my regards ta Beck."

"I will. Bye, Angus."

When the call ended, she sent a quick text to tell Harper the same news and was stunned when he replied immediately.

NEED TO TALK TO YOU FIRST THING TOMORROW.

"Ohhhkay." That didn't sound good. With a groan, she acknowledged the text and set the phone aside.

Still no Beck, which meant Mrs. Merton probably had new pictures of her grandkids to share. With a yawn, Riley wrote a sticky note and tacked it on the bathroom mirror so her fiancé would read his e-mail. It sounded as if things weren't right in Atlanta, either.

Chapter Twenty

To Beck's astonishment, Riley was up before him. At six in the morning. He stared at her as she leaned against the kitchen counter, clad in jeans and a navy T-shirt. "You sick or somethin'?"

"Nope. My brain says it's eleven, not the crack of dawn," Riley replied as she poured hot water in a mug. When she gave the contents a stir, he realized it was hot chocolate. An empty cereal bowl sat nearby, as well as an orange rind.

"Long as yer okay, I'm goin' for a run. What's yer day look like?"

"Harper wants to talk to me first thing. Something to do with one of my apprentices. And Mort sent me a text reminding me that we need to do more warding practice."

"Bet you can't wait," he replied. Bending over, Beck re-laced one of his shoes, then straightened up. "Wanna join me for a run?" he teased, already knowing the answer.

"Ha! Like I'm that crazy. I'll stick with the weights this morning."

"Weights?" he asked, confused. She nodded in between sips of hot chocolate. "So who are you and what happened to my delicate little Princess?"

Riley shot him an expression that told him he wasn't as amusing as he thought. "I've been working out since you left in December."

"Any particular reason, other than just gettin' stronger?"

"My left shoulder was too stiff from all the scars. Lifting weights loosens it up. Cheaper than going to a physical therapist."

That made sense. "Is it workin'?"

"Yes, I can lift it above my head now," she said, demonstrating. "At the first of the year, I had trouble doing even that. Hard to thump Hellspawn on their furry little heads otherwise."

Now he knew why she'd seemed more toned than in December. He grinned, tapping her nose with his finger. "Yer amazin'."

"Not really. It's just that sometimes I feel forty rather than eighteen. That sucks, so I'm trying not to go there."

"Yeah, I hear you. I'll be back in a bit. You gonna be here?"

"Don't know. Figured I'd make a run by the cemetery and visit the folks' graves before I go to Harper's."

"Okay, then I'll see you tonight."

Popping up on her toes, she gave him a kiss and then retreated to the bedroom.

"Liftin' weights, huh?" he murmured to himself. "Anythin' that keeps you alive, I'm all for it."

Out of the corner of his eye, Beck saw a small blur race across the kitchen counter, the pint-sized Klepto-Fiend who insisted on living with them.

"Yeah, I saw you. That weddin' ring better be where I left it, you hear me?"

An irritating demonic snicker came from behind the loaf of bread, suggesting that his warning was too late. No doubt the ring was stashed in the Magpie's little bag along with all his other loot.

"You do realize I'm a grand master now, right?"

Another snicker, this one bordering on a laugh.

"Keep it up and I'll ward every damned door and window."

A blur retraced its steps across the counter and in its wake was a ring. Beck smiled until he picked it up, only to realize it wasn't the one he'd bought for Riley.

"Hey!"

Another round of laughter, then there was nothing but silence.

"Damned demons."

~~*

Riley took a deep breath and savored the morning air as she trudged from the parking lot into Atlanta's most famous boneyard. Scotland might still be in the throes of winter, but Oakland Cemetery was courting spring like a besotted lover. Crocuses and hyacinths bloomed in enticing colors, and trees were already showing their leaves. Birds flitted here and there, animated and noisy in their hunt for nesting materials and food.

That activity and beauty seemed to clear the cobwebs from her brain and make things a little less gray. Riley had been struggling with that grayness, as she called it, since she'd seen the dead city in Italy. Her near breakdown at the loch hadn't helped. She usually wasn't so emotionally labile, but recently everything seemed to hit harder than usual.

What continued to haunt her was the carnage the angel had caused, both now and in the past. It was so unfathomable. She'd read that passage in Exodus when she was a kid, even attended a friend's Passover Seder in grade school. It just hadn't registered exactly how devastating such an event—the deaths of hundreds of thousands of citizens—would have been to a nation.

The pharaoh made a compelling bad guy, the ideal villain, refusing to set the Israelites free despite an ever-increasing run of horrific plagues. But Heaven had a role in that tragedy as well, for God had "hardened" the ruler's heart, which had ultimately led to the slaughter of the firstborn. The Destroyer had been the one to deliver the killing blow.

Now, even more depressed by thorny theological issues that scholars had debated for centuries, Riley frowned her way up the path into the cemetery. As she neared the gatehouse, she spied a familiar figure on the small structure's steps, apparently waiting for her. Martha wasn't knitting, but just staring off into the distance, her hands clenched in her lap.

She knows about the Destroyer. I bet they all do.

In Hell, a rogue Fallen would rally followers to overthrow Lucifer. Could it be like that in Heaven?

"No," Martha replied, plucking the question directly from Riley's mind.

She sat next to the angel, or next to an older woman in orthopedic shoes and dowdy clothes, if you didn't know who she really was.

"Why isn't God stopping this angel from killing people?" Riley asked.

Martha shrugged. "I asked that very question of Michael the other day and he ignored me. I don't think he knows, either."

It almost sounded as if she and the Archangel Michael were buddies, though Riley suspected that wasn't the case. Michael was too much of a jerk to have many friends.

"You'd be right about that," this angel said, reading her thoughts again.

Riley stared at her companion. "That's . . . honest. Usually you're very careful about what you say to me."

"True, but things are changing," was the swift reply.

"You folks going to do something about this? Or are you just going to watch us die, one town at a time?"

Martha looked toward her now, her frown slowly vanishing. "Something has already been done."

Riley's hope surged. "The Destroyer's dead?" That hope crashed with a single headshake. "Then what do you mean?"

"The prayer you made at the church caught the right ears."

The only church she'd been in recently was St. Peter's Basilica. She'd stood in front of the saint's tomb and asked that Heaven give her some help with the city killer.

"No, the other part of your prayer," Martha said. "About the one who fell."

Ori. Surely she couldn't mean . . .

No matter how rude it was, Riley was up and running now, leaving Martha behind without a word of farewell. Down the path, then hard left, soles slapping on the asphalt as she raced past the bell tower, her hands pumping to increase her speed. Her swift approach startled a squirrel, which bolted into the bushes in a blind panic.

When she skidded to a stop in front of her family's mausoleum, her heart pounding and her lungs gasping for air, she stared up at the roof. And began to count.

1 . . . 2 . . . 3 . . . 4 . . .

Four gargoyles, not five. The one that sat facing east, toward the sun, was gone.

"Oh my God, he's back in Heaven!" she cried.

"No, he's not," Martha replied. She stood near Riley now, though she hadn't bothered with the running part. "He's been freed from his stone prison for the time being. The Fallen is alive once more."

Riley blinked rapidly to curtail the tears that came without warning. It was better than she'd hoped: Ori was alive. "Will he be allowed to return to Heaven someday?"

"That, I do not know. Not all will welcome him back, if that's the case."

"Why not? He made a mistake. He admits it."

"Some envy him his time of freedom."

"Freedom? You have any idea what Hell is like?" Riley quickly realized that wasn't likely. "No, you probably don't. Ori hated Hell and never stopped craving the Light, even though he was Lucifer's executioner."

Martha gazed up at the empty spot on the mausoleum. "This time, he'll be doing that same job, except for us."

"He can stop the Destroyer?" Riley blurted.

The angel's face saddened.

Now Riley understood. "Heaven called him back from the grave and gave him a suicide mission because he's expendable."

"Some might say that. Others might see this as a chance for him to redeem himself."

"But—"

Martha vanished, not bothering to say goodbye.

Shaking her head, Riley gazed up at the empty spot on the roof where the Prince had imprisoned Ori over a year ago.

"Glad you're free. Please don't get yourself dead again, okay?"

From a nearby tree, a squirrel began chittering at her, as if she was a dangerous intruder. Riley walked to her parents' graves, spending time there in hopes of finding courage.

Finally, she retraced her steps to her car.

Ori was alive, which meant at least one good thing had resulted from her trip to Rome.

~~*

The individual sitting on Beck's front steps was the last person he'd ever think he'd see again. In fact, he'd rather counted on that. For a dead Fallen, Ori looked to be in good shape, still wearing those black clothes and black leather jacket. His dark hair was tinged with silver at the temples, and those eyes were more haunted than ever.

"Angel," Beck said as he came to a halt at the bottom of the stairs. He wanted to ensure that this was the real thing, not some higher-level demon messing with his head. "Yer alive again, huh? Some reason yer on my property?"

Ori raised an eyebrow. "I thought you grand masters were always hospitable. Or is that only the Scottish ones?"

This was the real deal. Beck's gaze flickered toward the house. "Riley know yer not on top of the Blackthorne mausoleum, collectin' bird shit?"

"She just discovered that my former 'home' is no more."

Bet that was a shock.

"Which team are you workin' for now? Because if ya've gone back to the Prince, I'll be fetchin' my sword."

"I'm not Lucifer's plaything any longer," Ori said in a dark tone. "I have a new master, one who is equally adept at pulling my strings. Better at it, it might even be said."

That still didn't mean he wasn't in the Prince's entourage, his leash held by another Fallen. "That new master in Hell?"

Ori shook his head and pointed an index finger toward the sky.

"They took you back?" Beck asked, surprised.

"Your astonishment mirrored mine when I found myself alive. I was still trying to get my head around this when suddenly I'm hauled in front of a certain self-righteous Archangel." He huffed in annoyance now.

"I'm not *taken back*, as you put it. Instead, I have been informed that I have a task. If I perform that task well, I will be considered for reinstatement in the Heavenly Host. If not, I'm back to being a roost for those birds you spoke of."

"They want you to kill the Destroyer."

Ori nodded.

"And the chances of that are?"

"Not likely," the angel admitted. "Which, I suspect, is why I was ordered to do it. If I succeed, fine. If I die, no big loss."

"That arrogant Archangel happen to be Michael?" A nod returned. "You two aren't best buds, are you?"

"No," Ori said, putting a world full of meaning in that one word.

"If yer thinkin' Riley is gonna help you . . ."

"I don't believe that would be your choice," the angel replied.

"The hell it isn't," Beck said, moving up two steps now. "She doesn't know how to kill angels. You do."

"And so do you."

There it was: the lure. The unspoken "this is how you keep the woman you love alive." It was a damned tempting one.

"I kill Fallen, not the ones from Heaven, so unless yer tellin' me this thing has sided with Lucifer, it *isn't* my problem. Or Riley's."

Ori's expression saddened. "Unfortunately, I fear it will be."

"Meanin'?"

"Sometimes events overrun us and we have no other choice."

Which was eerily similar to what Beck had told his fiancée in Scotland.

Ori rose now, gave him one last pitying look, then vanished as if he'd never been on the steps to begin with.

"Ah, hell. Not again."

~~*

When Riley arrived at Master Harper's place, he was in his usual spot: behind his desk, a cup of coffee at hand. As the most senior trapper in the city, he was the one who got stuck with most of the paperwork. That usually consisted of forms from the city of Atlanta, the state, and the federal government, all of which needed to be filled out and returned by certain deadlines. From the times she'd collected his mail, Riley knew that those forms arrived daily.

Riley was rather hoping that when Harper finally handed in his trapping license and retired, all this mindless minutia would fall on one of the other masters, like Jackson maybe. She also suspected that this was wishful thinking, because it was likely to all land in her lap. Once again, she'd be following in her dad's footsteps.

Harper appeared more tired than usual, the scar on his face pulled tight. He'd probably missed her help while she was gone, but he'd never admit it.

"Blackthorne," he said, his tone as dry as ever.

"Master Harper." She wandered into the kitchen, warmed up a cup of water in the microwave, and dropped a teabag into it. When she returned, she found him folding up a multi-page form and jamming it into an oversized manila envelope.

"Which one is that?"

"Last month's trapping recap for National. I swear there're more pieces to it each time."

She nodded, pulled a chair in front of his desk, and worked on dunking the teabag to bring the brew up to the proper level of caffeine.

"They're still arguing about what to do with you because of the Four at the school."

"Okay." That was the best she could hope for.

"Stewart told me what happened in Rome," Harper said. He had leaned back in his office chair, his "Same shit, different day" mug in hand. She'd bought it for him last Christmas and it seemed to be his favorite.

"I got to see St. Peter's Basilica, was blessed by the pope, and made a lot of senior clergymen very upset."

"So, pretty much the usual for you, then."

Riley grinned. "At least Beck's a grand master now."

"He'll be good at that."

She cocked her head. "Thought you didn't like him that much."

"Beck's okay," Harper said. "Mouthy, but then that's probably why you two hitched up."

She saw a faint hint of amusement in his eyes now. It was welcomed.

"No doubt." Now that the tea was done, she jettisoned the teabag into the wastebasket and then returned to her seat. "You have any questions about what happened over there?"

"Yeah. What the hell is going on? We have enough problems with Lucifer and his demonic bastards, and now we got a rogue angel from the other address? You know, I didn't sign up for this kind of bullshit."

He'd summed up the problem perfectly. "Neither did I." She thought of Ori now. "Maybe Heaven will get that sorted out."

"Yeah, right." Harper leaned forward, placing the cup on his desk. "Got a problem closer to home. One of your apprentices is acting hinky."

"Jaye?"

A nod. "When she's in here, her eyes aren't meeting mine, which makes me wonder if some demon's playing with her head or something. I asked the other two and they don't know what's going on. Check it out, will you?"

"Will do. Anything else?"

Harper unearthed four trapping orders and pushed them across the table.

"Glad to see you missed me."

He raised an eyebrow. "The demons did, at least."

She smiled. "Good to be home, even if you are a grouch."

"Uh huh."

Riley'd just rinsed out her cup when her three amigos arrived. Kurt and Richard were joking back and forth, but Jaye wasn't joining in. If anything, she seemed distracted.

"Hail, O Illustrious Master," Kurt said, then laughed. "How was bonny Scotland?"

"Great." These three had no idea what had happened in Rome, and she wasn't about to share that information. "Beck's all grand mastered, and the snow was pretty." She handed the trapping orders to Kurt, as he was the closest. "You three doing okay?"

The two guys nodded immediately, but Jaye didn't. Instead, she just stared at Riley.

"Something's up, right?" The girl nodded. "You want to share here or somewhere else?"

Jaye shot a nervous glance toward Harper, then angled her head outside.

"Okay, let's go do our jobs," Riley said, leading them out of the office.

From Jaye's expression, she didn't figure it'd take too long before the girl spilled whatever was bothering her. Her guess was right. They'd no more than reached Riley's car when she saw Kurt give Jaye a nudge.

"Hey, talk to us. Whatever's going on, we're here for you, okay?" he said.

Jaye nodded, but still looked upset.

"Is it your mom? Is she sick again?" Riley asked gently.

"No, but something's wrong. She's been complaining about these two home healthcare people who come to see her. Says they don't feel right to her."

"Don't feel right how?"

"She said they make her nervous."

"Are they abusing her or something?" Richard asked.

"No, it's just that when they're in the house, she says it feels hard to think, and then she's really tired after they leave. I don't know what's going on and it's making me nervous."

"Did you request someone else come see her?"

Jaye nodded. "I was told these were the two handling our area and unless there was a specific complaint, Mom's stuck with them."

Riley frowned. "Is she home now?" Jaye nodded. "When is the next time these caseworkers are supposed to visit?"

"This morning at ten."

It was just after nine now. "Okay. How's about we drop by on the way to the first trapping."

Kurt frowned. "What do you think's going on?"

"Not sure."

Riley had her suspicions and the best way to rule them out was to be there when the pair visited. She put her arm around Jaye's shoulders.

"Don't worry, we'll make sure your mom is okay. Can't have you worrying about her when you're learning how to keep the world safe."

Jaye laughed raggedly. "Is that really how you see this job?"

Riley sidestepped the question—the answer was too complicated at the moment. "Why didn't you tell Master Harper about this?"

"I don't know. He always looks like he's going to rip off my head."

"That's his default setting. You guys ever have any hassles and I'm not around, talk to Harper. He can be snarly, but he'll watch your back. Okay?"

Three nods came her way. "All right, let's go see what's up with your mom."

Chapter Twenty-One

As they approached Jaye's home, Riley asked, "Do you ward the house?"

"No," she replied. "Should I?"

"Yeah, I would." Even though Riley didn't at her home because of the Klepto-Fiend that lived with them. She glanced over at the guys, knowing it was time for them to take the next step. "You two as well. You're far enough in the biz that some Hellspawn might think you'd make a tasty target."

"I feel so special," Kurt replied, placing a hand over his heart.

"I already ward my place," Richard said. "Call me paranoid."

No, just wiser. He was older than the other two and knew that if life could find a way to kick you in the gut, it would.

This wasn't the first time Riley had visited Jaye's mom over the course of the woman's illness. Trisha was in her early fifties, and it was good to see she'd added some weight to her still too-slender frame. Still, Riley could see the ravages of the kidney disease. Even more alarming, her eyes were dull now, unlike the last visit—even though Jaye had said her mom's dialysis was going well.

Though the house was small, it was tidy and nicely decorated. There were pictures of Jaye and her brothers on a wall near the fireplace, as well as other family photos. But there was something else here as well, and Riley felt it as clearly as a change in the weather. If anything, her senses had become even more acute since her encounter with the ashes in Italy.

Jaye's eyes kept darting between her mom and Riley, her worry evident.

"Tell me about these care workers. What are they like?" Riley asked.

"They feel wrong," Trisha said. "I don't know how to explain it. I didn't like them from the moment they came through the door. I'm always so tired after they leave. It wasn't like that with the other woman who took care of me before I started dialysis."

"Okay, then let's find out whether or not this is a demonic problem."

Fifteen minutes later, the house was completely warded with Holy Water and Jaye's mom was headed to a friend's house until Riley issued a verdict.

"You sure about this?" Richard asked as they waited.

Riley shrugged. "We'll find out soon enough."

"Hey, we won't laugh if you're wrong. At least not for very long."

"Yeah, thanks."

There was the slam of car doors. Jaye, who'd taken a location near the front window, said, "It's them."

"Okay, let's find out if my hunch is right."

Kurt and Richard headed for the back door, while Riley and Jaye played front-door greeters. The instant they stepped outside and walked a few feet toward the newcomers, Riley knew she was right. To anyone else, this pair would look like middle-aged nurses' aides in crisp white uniforms, though both wore too much makeup. To her, their vibes were strong, like the stench of rancid, smoky grease.

Which made her instantly furious. She couldn't do a thing about the rogue angel, but these monstrosities were hers to deal with. They were strong, and one of them might even be near the transition to an Archfiend.

Jaye took a deep breath. "Are they . . . ?

"Yes, they are."

"Oh my God."

The two supposed healthcare workers stopped dead in their tracks, both staring at Riley. The stench of brimstone began to rise around them, something they'd usually mask. They'd figured out who she was and what she could do.

"How's Trisha doing today?" one of them asked, its eyes tracking down to the door's threshold. Those same eyes narrowed. Nothing says "welcome home" like Holy Water.

"Fine. Mom's . . ." Jaye began.

Riley shot her a quick glance.

Crap. One of the Mezmers had gotten inside Jaye's head, probably whispering all sorts of promises, like "I'll make sure your mother never gets sick again."

In a single, practiced move, Riley had her sword out of her backpack. "You're done here."

"Blackthorne's daughter," one of them hissed, its illusion still holding.

First Kurt appeared and then Richard, one from each side of the house. Both had Babel spheres in hand.

"Do it," Riley said.

One of the spheres struck the closest demon, and its illusion drained away to reveal a tall Grade Four, far more advanced than what they usually faced. This was the one closest to becoming an Arch-Fiend. No doubt, the life force it'd taken off Jaye's mother had helped in that transition.

To Riley's disappointment, Kurt's Babel sphere went wide. She sighed. Clearly, it was time for more target practice.

"Sorry!" he called out.

Richard lobbed another sphere and it struck the smaller demon, making it squeal. Its illusion promptly vanished, giving them a glimpse of a short, hairless thing that would probably have haunted Riley's nightmares if there weren't worse things doing that already. It began staggering around, scratching at its hide like it had fleas. If she was lucky, her apprentices would deal with the lesser demon, and that would leave her only one Four to worry about.

Time for the Blackthorne touch.

She zeroed in on the taller of the two Hellspawn, the stronger one.

"You know, I've met so many of your kind, but pulling

energy out of sick and dying people? That's way beyond evil. I bet even Lucifer thinks you're total scum."

The demon hissed back now. "Blackthorne's daughter. Whore of Heaven."

Whore of Heaven? That was a new one. Good thing Beck wasn't here.

"Kurt?" No reply. She shot him a quick glance to find that he was staring into space, a dreamy look on his face. Richard, at least, was still in the game. He gave her a nod, signaling his readiness.

"Now," she said.

She moved closer to the stronger Hellspawn, only to have it hiss again, then turn on its heels and take off at a run.

"What?" she said. "Come back here!"

"Got it!" Richard yelled. He had wrestled the smaller demon into one of their makeshift bait-box prisons. This guy was going to be one helluva trapper someday.

"Kurt?" He blinked and slowly came out of his stupor. "Watch that thing," she said, pointing to the box, "and try to wake up Jaye. Richard, let's go."

With her apprentice at her side, Riley sprinted after their foe, down the street and across the front yard of a two-story brick home, trapping bags banging against their backs.

"Why did it run?" he called out as they followed their quarry.

"No clue," she said. It'd been strong enough to cause them serious trouble, but instead it'd happily thrown its fellow Hellspawn under the bus and taken off. Maybe her reputation in Hell was more badass than she thought.

The Four easily leapt over a chain-link fence and into a landscaped backyard. As it took off for the rear fence, a small barking streak came racing off the porch. The demon turned, eyed the dog barreling toward it, and sneered. Its claws extended, looking to scoop and impale the furious four-legged bullet.

"No!" Riley cried, scaling the fence and landing with an awkward thump on the other side. Richard followed her over, but with more grace. Once he'd regained his feet, he sent his steel pipe end-over-end through the air, slamming into the demon's shoulder. It screamed, rearing back in pain, its red eyes blazing in fury. Then it turned that fury back toward the puppy, as it was the closest prey.

Too far away to save the dog's life, Riley began to murmur under her breath, forming a spell on the fly. She felt the power build inside the incantation, her anger feeding it. When she cast the spell, it took the form of a fiery purple arrow rocketing through the air toward its target.

The spell struck the Hellspawn mid-chest, burying itself deep inside. A second later, there was nothing left. Well, nothing but bloody bits of demon splattering everywhere, chunks flying in all directions. Some struck Riley before they dropped to the ground.

She blinked. Then blinked again. That was a spell on steroids.

"Well, that's one way of doing it," Richard said, brushing slimy pieces of Mezmer off his jacket and face. His wide grin said he'd found the outcome totally righteous.

Fortunately, the little dog was unharmed, and it continued to growl and bark, the efforts vibrating its body. It danced around one of the bigger demon pieces, then snagged on to it and dragged it over toward them.

Like a proud lion, it laid that grisly portion in front of Riley, then danced around some more, yapping shrilly. Now that it was closer, she saw it wasn't a puppy, but one of those miniature Doberman pinschers, the kind of beast that didn't know they weren't full-sized and sported all the attitude of their bigger brothers. He appeared to be wearing a black mask that covered his eyes and forehead. With that kind of marking, he was probably named Raider or Bandit.

Even as Riley smiled at the dog's antics, the spell's backlash backhanded her. She landed on her butt, so tired she was afraid of passing out.

"Riley?" Richard's voice came from far off.

Groggily she felt something tug on her jacket—it was the Min Pin gnawing on the fabric. His immense bat-like ears stood straight up like antennae, and he wore a thin black collar with metal studs.

Even as her head throbbed and her very bones ached, Riley broke down in laughter. "Hey, look at you, mighty demon hunter!"

Richard joined her, reaching out to pet the little guy. "Dude, you are fearless." He gave her a sidelong look. "You okay?" She nodded. "That was seriously strong magic, wasn't it?"

"Yeah. And I swear, I had no idea I could do that."

"Huh." He glanced at the remains of the Four scattered all over the yard. "When we first starting training with you, you told us that unless you could deliver either a live demon or the corpse of one, it's hard to collect the bounty. How's this going to work?"

He flicked a bloody piece of Mezmer corpse off her sleeve for emphasis.

"It's not going to be easy. Which is why you're going back to Jaye's to get some trash bags."

His eyes widened. "We're bagging all this up?"

Riley looked toward the house now. "We better, or this dog's owner is going to be seriously pissed. Especially when this stuff starts to rot." With a sigh, Richard rose to his feet. "That was a strong Four and it didn't get in your head. That's a really good thing."

"I heard it. I ignored it."

"How?"

"Remember that day at the college when those computer monitors showed us what Hell was like?" he asked.

"Yeah." Fire, brimstone, lots of ugly fiends, with the Prince himself all decked out like a warlord.

"Well, all I have to do is think of that. Seems to work most of the time."

She gave him a thumbs-up and went back to scratching the puppy, who'd decided her lap was a cozy place. Riley tried to ignore the black blood on her fingers and the foul stench of exploded Four that filled the yard. Hopefully it wouldn't ruin the grass.

How did I kill that thing?

Only one way to find out. She fished out her phone and dialed a number from memory.

"Riley? How's it going?" Mort asked, his usual jovial self.

"It's been . . . interesting. Are you going to be free tonight?"

"Sure. Something up?"

Her eyes swept over the yard and the glistening pieces of Mezmer. "Yeah, you could say that."

~~*

Though he was still trying to get his head back in Atlanta's time zone, Beck's new job had begun the moment he'd checked in with Angus. Not everything a grand master did was exciting or earthshaking. In fact, most of it wasn't that way. Still, Beck rated meetings right up there with standing thigh-deep in a river full of piranha while being pecked to death by crows.

His first meeting was at City Hall, with the mayor's office. He'd never been fond of politicians—they were too good at looking out for themselves and conveniently forgetting everyone else. He'd grudgingly admit a few were decent, but most were great at glad-handing and bullshit, with no follow-through.

After being introduced as Master Beck, and then politely correcting his title to include the word "Grand" in front of it, he'd put on his patient, "I'm a good ol' boy" face and answered their questions as best he could. No, everything was fine demon-wise, and there had been no increase in the number of Hellspawn in the city. Of course, this report was courtesy of Angus, since Beck had not been in the country for the last few months.

All the excitement of learning new things, the pride that came with becoming a grand master, had been tamped down by the realization that this was his life going forward. Meetings, then more meetings. Talking to people who had no clue about Heaven and Hell's Grand Game, who would probably lose their shit if they were told the truth. And Beck, being who he was now, and given what he knew, couldn't tell them.

He'd been waiting for one particular question and it came near the end of the meeting, from a less talkative councilmember. The guy looked like he'd been saving this one up for last.

"What is this about a demon killing one of our teachers?" the man asked.

Damn. He'd already talked to Angus about this, and the only choice was to lie. He most certainly couldn't admit that the teacher had been a fiend, one who could walk right over a Holy Water ward. People would freak at that news.

He ordered his thoughts before replying. "There was a problem in one of the schools. Though there was a trapper onsite, the teacher chose to sacrifice himself to the demon, rather than let the kids get hurt."

"That is what we heard. But why was a fiend anywhere near a school?"

"Because we can't ward the entire city?" he replied.

The frowns Beck received in return told him that wasn't an acceptable answer.

"We have to ensure our children's safety," another councilmember chimed in.

"Then the best you can do is ward yer own homes, school buildin's, and places where they play. Unless yer willin' to handle the extra expense of wardin' the entire school grounds."

The circle of frowns told him that wasn't the case.

"This is not what we want to hear," the mayor said.

"I know, but it's the reality. Until the day Lucifer stops targeting this city, there'll always be a risk. The trappers do the best they can. They've died to keep you folks safe. Last year proved that often enough."

It was a dirty move on his part, but as Trevor had often said, there were many ways to get people to back off, and guilt worked as well as any.

By the time the meeting had ended, Beck had developed a headache. To his relief, the second meeting had been cancelled due to a water leak. He smiled at that, counting his blessings as he drove toward Angus's. He owed his fellow grand master a report on how it had gone at the mayor's office, and then had to deliver the news about his encounter with a certain angel this morning.

Once he was in the Scotsman's driveway, he sent a text to Riley.

AT STEWART'S. HOW'S IT GOING?

He got the reply just as he'd walked through the kitchen door.

MESSY. I CAST A PROTECTION SPELL AND BLEW A FOUR TO BITS.

Beck let the door close slowly behind him, rereading the message in case he'd gotten it wrong. Frowning, he typed, THAT EVER HAPPEN BEFORE?

NO. WILL TALK TO MORT TONOC. MIGHT BE LATE. I'LL PICK UP DINNER. FRIED CHICKEN OKAY?

THAT WORKS. LOVE YOU.

He returned the love, then clipped his phone back to his belt. *Damn, she's getting solid at the magic stuff.* He wasn't exactly sure if that was a good thing or not.

As he pondered on his fiancée's latest bit of news, Beck trudged through the kitchen. An inviting plate of oatmeal cookies sat on the counter near the stove, so he claimed two, and a pair of napkins, and headed to the back of the massive house.

Beck found his mentor in his office, staring at a laptop. Next to it was a stack of paperwork. *That'll be mine someday.* He certainly wasn't looking forward to that.

Though Beck was considered part of this man's family, he still knocked on the doorjamb and waited for the wave to enter. Sitting in the chair in front of the desk, he placed a cookie on a napkin within the older man's reach.

Angus looked up, smiling. "Have fun at the meetin's?"

"Lots of hot air at the first, but then, that's politicians for you. They were worried about how it was a teacher could get carried off by a demon." Beck recounted how he'd spun the tale.

"Hopefully that'll settle them down," Angus replied. "The last damned thing they need ta hear is that this teacher was

Hellspawn."

"Amen." Beck smiled now. "The second meetin' was cancelled."

"Damn," Angus muttered. "That means I'll probably get stuck with it."

"You will not hear me mournin' about that," Beck said, grinning.

"Figured." Angus scooped up the cookie and polished it off in three bites.

"After my run this mornin', I had a visit from an angel."

"Oh?" Angus said, his attention captured.

"Ori's been called from the grave, and Heaven's got their leash on him this time."

His friend's face registered his astonishment. "Lucifer's former executioner is back on Heaven's payroll?"

"Yup. He's as alive as you and me. Though I think it's more of a trial-basis thing."

"Hmm. Heaven doesn't do resurrections unless they have a verra good reason." Angus paused for only a moment. "Ah, he's after the city killer."

Beck nodded. "They're danglin' the forgiveness carrot in front of him if he pulls it off."

Angus gave him a long look. "Why do I think there's more ta it than that?"

"Ori's hopin' for a little help. From me and Riley."

The Scotsman leaned forward, his elbows on the desk and fingers tented. "Riley ken that?"

"She knows he's alive, not that he's hopin' she'll toss her life away, along with mine."

"Shite."

"That pretty much sums it up," Beck replied. "Honestly, I don't know if Ori can kill it, even if we do help him." With a sigh, he rose. "I bet that's why the Vatican let us go. Rosetti seemed to think the pope knows something that the rest of us don't."

"That *would* explain it."

"Sorry to take off, but I've got to meet a few trappers. I'll be back after that, if you need me."

Angus nodded. "Aye, I do. Send the others my regards."

"I will." Beck paused in the doorway. "When you kill a Fallen and get hurt, you go to Hell for punishment. What happens if it's one of Heaven's angels?"

Angus didn't answer right away. "No precedent for that. I suspect the punishment wouldn't be any different, except there might not be a way out. At least not for those who've been there before."

Like his fiancée and him. "I was afraid you were gonna say that."

Chapter Twenty-Two

Once Riley and Richard had washed up and changed clothes at Harper's, they entertained the elder master with the tale of cosmic demon destruction. They got a laugh out of him, which to Riley was almost as stunning as what led to that laugh.

The rest of the day was spent on the other runs, and now it was close to five as they hauled the fruits of their day's labors to her favorite demon trafficker, Fireman Jack.

Jack was in a good mood as usual, at least until he saw the three supersized trash bags. He flicked one of his barber pole suspenders in thought. "What kind was it?"

"Four," Riley said.

"You carve it into sushi?"

Knowing that Jack's assistant might be listening to this conversation, she shook her head. "No, had a little accident is all."

Behind her, she could hear Kurt's snort, coupled with Jaye's stifled laughter. Only Richard kept a poker face, and she knew that was barely holding.

"Is there enough to know it was a Mezmer?" Jack asked.

"If you want to glue all the pieces back together. The claws and feet should help with the ID. As I see it, we saved the Church some time."

"You're a lot more bloodthirsty than you were a year ago."

"I've got a lot more scars than back then."

Jack nodded his understanding. "Then come on upstairs— we'll get the paperwork and payment settled."

The apprentices hadn't been in Jack's office before, though

Riley had several times. Not surprisingly, his wall populated by paintings and pictures of historic fires caught their notice. But then, his office was in an old fire station, so what else would they be?

"Wow, these are cool," Kurt said, checking them out with a wide smile.

"About every major city has had some conflagration," Jack explained. "Seems right that they should be here, in this building."

Riley kept the smile to herself as the demon trafficker verified her paperwork, filled in the lines that he was required to complete, and, after her signature, handed over the cash for the demons.

"So is that new grand master of yours too good to visit a mere demon trafficker?" he asked, amused.

"Probably. You know how stuck-up Beck is," she said.

Jack laughed. "When did you guys get back to Atlanta?"

"Last night."

"Ah, that explains why you look half-asleep, and why Den hasn't dropped by."

"That'd be it. He was off early to a meeting at City Hall. I far prefer trapping demons."

"Better him than you," Jack replied. "Hey, not too long before you become Mrs. Beck, is it?"

Everybody asked that question. "No, it isn't, but I'm keeping my last name. I'd hate to confuse the newspapers the next time they print my latest screw-up." Or confuse the demons. She'd been "Blackthorne's daughter" to those things since she first started trapping.

Jack scooted back in his chair, propping his feet up on the desk. "You guys taking a honeymoon?"

"Beck has a buddy with a cabin in North Georgia, so we're going there for a few days. Can't be gone too long, not after I was just in Scotland."

"At least you're getting some time on your own. I'm really looking forward to this coming Saturday."

"So are we."

"And in the future, please don't bring me any more trash bags full of Hellspawn. The Church is really going to give me crap about that."

"I'll do my best," she said, though exactly how that would happen was anyone's guess.

~~*

Mort's nephew Alex didn't meet her at the door to his uncle's place like he usually did. Instead, it was a woman, and because this was the home of a necromancer, this lady was dead. Only a slightly gray cast to her skin would tip you off that she was on the wrong side of the grave, because Mort was an incredibly talented necromancer.

He was also a conscientious one. He'd have made arrangements with her family so she could serve as his housekeeper for however long she could handle the job. With his expert after-death care, that usually came out to about a year. For that service, the family received excellent compensation, and at the end of that term, Mort arranged a tasteful reburial, covering all the expenses. From what Riley had seen, he always chose families that desperately needed the cash. Riley might not like the idea, but she knew he would treat the woman humanely. That was better than some of the necros.

"Hi, I'm Riley. I'm here to see Mort."

"He said you would be arriving. I'm Letitia," the woman replied. When she'd been among the living, Letitia had probably been in her late fifties and quite statuesque, the opposite of her new boss.

"Nice to meet you."

Letitia studied her for a moment. "You know what I am?"

"Yes."

"And that doesn't bother you?"

"Nope. Not really," Riley replied.

Her answer seemed to make Mort's newest employee happy.

Letitia seemed sharp for a reanimate. Riley's dad had been that way, but needed frequent naps to maintain that level of intelligence. She also took her job seriously and insisted on escorting Riley to the owner of the house, even though Riley'd been here many times.

Walking down the hallway, she sensed another presence and groaned. Lord Ozymandias. He seemed to be spending more time with his fellow necro.

As she entered the room, Riley steeled herself.

"Senior Summoner Alexander," she said, then turned to the other man. "Lord Ozymandias."

"Summoner Blackthorne," His Lordship replied, an unreadable expression in place. He wasn't in his robes, and the strange sigil on his head was muted. It was almost like this was the real guy, not the one he portrayed in public.

To Riley's relief, there was a cheery fire in the fireplace, a fireplace that hadn't been there the last time she'd visited. She concentrated and saw the blank wall. "Nice illusion."

Mort smiled. "You're getting a lot better at spotting those."

She chose the only available chair. "I'm guessing you've involved *him*," Riley said, angling her head toward the senior summoner, "because what I did this afternoon isn't normal."

Mort's mouth twitched, holding back a smile. "Yes, though what you did isn't quite as unusual as you would think."

"Indeed," Ozymandias said as he settled back in his chair, crossing his arms over his chest. "Tell us exactly what happened."

Riley took a deep breath and gave her report. Unfortunately, trying to read either summoner's expression while she did so proved futile. These two would be daunting poker players.

"Is what I did wacked?" she asked.

"A few questions first," Mort replied. "What were you feeling when you cast the spell? Was it fear for yourself?"

"No, it was a strong Four, but I've taken down stronger demons."

"The apprentice who was with you—were you afraid for him?"

"Not really. The fiend couldn't get a foothold in Richard's head, and he's smart enough to know when to back off if things go bad."

"What was your major concern when you cast the spell?" Ozy asked.

"The dog. The thing was about to rip it apart."

The two men traded looks.

"You were afraid the dog would be killed," Mort said.

"Killed and probably eaten," Riley said, shaking her head. "If the demon had just fought me or Richard, that would've been fine, but it went after something that couldn't protect itself."

Mort nodded as if she'd just confirmed something. "That's why your spell was so strong. Your emotions augmented the magic."

"Emotions?"

"We all have our hot buttons. I'm particularly sensitive to bullies because I was harassed all through school." Mort huffed. "Even after I became a summoner."

"Bet they don't do that now," Ozy said, an eyebrow quirked. If he'd been anyone else, he would've been grinning.

"No, not as much," Mort replied. He turned back to Riley. "You appear to have a couple hot buttons. One is your intolerance of irresponsible authority and the other is your fear of innocent people being harmed. You will sacrifice yourself to save anyone you deem a noncombatant. Your anger at what the demon was about to do—in this case, murder and devour a harmless pet— pushed your spell far beyond its normal parameters."

"Okay," Riley murmured. "How do I *not* do that? What keeps me from blowing someone to atoms?"

"Nothing," Mort said, "only your control of the magic."

"But I've never done it before. Why now?"

"You're learning how to channel your spells more effectively," Ozy said. "For some, this is a normal stage—at least for those of us who have a strong will. Now that you know you're capable of such a thing, it's up to us to teach you how to calibrate your spells in those particular situations."

"You two do this?" Both nodded. "And if I do want to kill something?"

"Then you're all set," Ozy replied dryly.

She winced. "Why do I think this control thing is going to require a buttload more magic practice and another family-sized bottle of aspirin?"

The wide grin that formed on Mort's face confirmed her suspicions.

"Great. Just great."

"Tomorrow night, out in the woods," Ozymandias said. "We'll keep annoying you until you snap."

She eyed him. "Going to use the 'sacrifice the kitten' trick again? Remember, the one you tried on me when you were trying to get to my father's body?"

"Maybe this time I'll use a real one rather than an illusion."

He was jesting. At least, she hoped he was. "I doubt it," she said. She'd seen cat hair on his black clothes, and that told her there was a feline in his life somewhere.

"Tomorrow night," Ozy repeated. "At eight. You know the location. Bring along that grand master of yours. You'll be far too exhausted to drive home."

That sounded like a dismissal, so she rose, gave Mort a nod, and left the house. Trudging back to her car, she could just imagine what Beck would think about hanging with the magic slingers. Still, if she pitched it right, convinced him it was a way to keep them both safe, he'd go for it. It was kinda cool that she knew how to steer him in the right direction. It was very likely he was using the same technique on her.

The only good thing about all the upheaval in her life? She wasn't freaking about the wedding. Simi had warned her that if she became a bridezilla—and who had thought up that term?—there would be an intervention, and not one that Riley would like.

Fortunately, that hadn't been needed. She'd decided to panic the night before the wedding, but no sooner. Because by that time, there was nothing she could do if anything wasn't going right. Now, if the rest of the universe would be as mellow, they might just pull this off.

~~*

Riley's intention to scoot home and spend time with Beck had been short-circuited by a text from a dear friend. A friend she hadn't seen in almost a month, which was embarrassing on so many levels.

Peter King was waiting for her in her favorite booth at the Grounds Zero, a cup of coffee at his elbow. He was an avid collector of T-shirts and the one today said, "Here, Hold My Beer!" He rose and gave her a lengthy hug, then ruffled her hair just to annoy her.

"Someone probably just took a video of that and will be posting it later," Riley said as she slid into the booth opposite him. "My fiancé is the jealous type."

Peter grinned. "You know, I can see the headlines now: 'World Famous Demon Trapper Ditches Fiancé for Handsome Nerd.'"

Riley let loose a laugh. "I've missed you, my friend."

"Same here."

Peter's hair was still the same length, but a little bit darker now, and there was a hint of a goatee. Despite his hefty academic load, he looked good. Happy.

"Been watching your exploits on YouTube," he said, pulling his coffee cup closer. "You've been busy."

There was so much he didn't know, so much she needed to share. "Ah, there's more going on than just that."

With a quick look around to ensure no one was close enough to overhear her, she leaned over the table. Lowering her voice, she brought her best friend up to speed. By the time she finished, Peter's face was ashen. He took a few gulps of air to steady himself, then heaved a sigh.

"Killer angel, huh?" Riley nodded. "I really don't know why I bother with online gaming. It seems all the scary crap is for real nowadays." She gave a grunt of assent. "Any chance of this thing coming here?"

"Nothing is keeping it from doing just that."

"Of course," he muttered. "What are your chances of stopping the thing if it comes here?"

"Little to none."

"Okay, situation normal, then." Peter grew serious. "Well, no matter what, my best friend is getting married on Saturday."

"Peter—"

His eyes remained riveted on hers. "I repeat, my best friend *is getting married* on Saturday. A best friend who is more like a sister to me, because all I have is brothers and they're driving me crazy. Right now, everything but her wedding is secondary in my world."

Sister? He'd never told her that before. "Okay, you're my honorary brother, but if your sis says to get the hell out of town, you do it."

He stared at her, probably because she didn't swear that often, and then frowned in thought. "If this angel was an online game, it'd say it's glitching," Peter said, falling back on gamer terminology. "Fix the glitch and then it's all good."

Clearly, he wasn't getting in tune with reality here, so she gave up. "Saturday it is."

He squeezed her hand. "You've got this. I know you do."

Riley wasn't convinced. If something happened in Atlanta, would she have the guts to stay and fight the thing? Why wouldn't she just grab Beck and the bunny and make a run for it? Who would fault her?

It's not who I am.

Long ago, a frightened young girl had made a stand against the Darkness, to honor her dead father's memory. Now that commitment was as much a part of her as the blood in her veins. Her fiancé was no different.

Peter must have seen something on her face, because he leaned across the table and gave her a hug, even though he came perilously close to upsetting his coffee. "Well, I'm off to see

Simi and then I'm heading home. Do me a favor—unglitch this thing."

Peter's mention of his ex-girlfriend caught Riley's notice. "How are you two doing? Simi and you?"

He beamed. "Good. Really good. We worked out our problems and we're solid now."

Solid? How had she not known that? But then, just how good of a friend had Riley been, at least recently? She was so focused on being a master trapper and a summoner, and all the stuff for the wedding, that, stupidly, she'd let some of her friendships drift. Peter being one of those.

Studying him now, she remembered when he'd been an odd little kid who'd told her silly jokes and seemed to know everything that was on the internet. Now he was a young man, whip-smart and full of promise. A friend who had stood by her, no matter what.

"We'll do everything we can, Peter, but there are no guarantees."

"There never were, Riley. You know that as well as anyone." He rose from the booth. "Tell Beck I'm thinking of him."

As he walked out of the coffee shop, she vowed to be a better friend, because sometimes there was no tomorrow.

~~*

After making sure Rennie had been fed, watered, and sufficiently fussed with, Beck had opened a beer, settled in, and brooded. He'd been at it for an hour—though still on the same beer—trying to get a handle on what was headed their way.

Four more days until the weddin'.

It felt selfish to ask for that time, what with all those people dying. It was just that he and Riley had put their lives on the line so many times—he just wanted something for himself. In this case, to hear his fiancée say, "I do."

His gut, which was rarely wrong, told him that wasn't a sure bet.

Beck heard the car pull into the drive, but didn't move from his position on the couch. Eventually, the key turned in the lock and the door opened to reveal the young woman he loved. Unfortunately, Riley looked as tired as he felt, moving slower than usual. Since, by their internal clocks, it was somewhere near one thirty in the morning, that wasn't unexpected.

"Sorry," she said when she saw him. "I stopped to talk to Peter and then I got called out for a trapping. One of the guys hurt his ankle during the run, and they needed backup."

"Which trapper?"

"McGuire."

Beck snorted. "The asshole give you any grief?" McGuire had been in Riley's face ever since she'd become a trapper. In fact, he'd been the one to call down the National Guild on them late last year. That move had almost cost Riley her trapping license.

"No, he was actually civil," Riley said, shutting the door behind her. "He was in too much pain to be an ass. Color me surprised."

"Catch the demon?"

"Yup," she said, head in the entryway closet, methodically refilling her trapping bag. It was a habit you acquired from the moment you became an apprentice—a demon trapper always restocked their bag before doing anything else. That way, if a run came in the middle of the night, you weren't fumbling around half-asleep. Beck hadn't followed that rule once and had earned a couple scars for his oversight.

Once the closet door was shut, Riley looked over at him.

"You look wiped," he said.

"I feel it."

She removed her shoes and joined him on the couch, curling up next to him with an afghan tucked around her.

"Today has been strange," she said. "Like, 'boy do I have some news for you' strange."

"Would some of that be an angel whose name begins with 'o' and ends in 'i'? The one that's no longer on top of yer family's mausoleum?"

She raised her head and stared at him. "Yes. But how did you know that?"

"He was sittin' on our front porch steps when I came back from my run this mornin'. Smug as ever. Well, maybe not *quite* as smug." No, something about Ori had changed since his death.

Riley leaned back, frowning. "When I talked to Martha this morning, she said my prayers had been answered. Since one of those was about Ori, I did a quick gargoyle count and found he was gone."

"And?" Because there was definitely an "and" after that sentence.

She laid her head back down on his chest. "It looks like Heaven brought him back to life to kill the Destroyer."

"That's what Ori said. He also didn't act like his chances of doin' that were great." Beck hesitated, unsure if he should tell her the rest.

Riley raised her head again. "What are you leaving out?"

Damn. She was just too quick, even half-asleep from jetlag. "I know you made me promise—"

"Ori guilted you into helping him, didn't he?" Riley demanded, pushing out of his arms. "You think you owe him because he told you how to kill Sartael."

It was far more complex than that.

"I owe that . . . feathered bastard because he taught *you* how to fight demons, how to be so badass you've killed three Archfiends all on yer own. I owe him because yer still alive."

Riley's eyes widened.

"And yeah, he did tell me how to take down Sartael."

"He's guilting you. He's *really* good at that, Den," she said, quieter now. "Don't ever forget he's a Fallen."

"I won't. I know I promised not to go after this thing, but I see now that there's more to this than just some crazy-assed angel. Heaven didn't bring Ori back from the dead just because they were bored." He shook his head in resignation. "One thing you learn as a grand master is that some of these events have been in motion for a *very* long time."

"What do you mean?"

"Don't you find it odd that it's us three in the middle of all this?" He held up a finger. "Lucifer's former executioner." He held up a second finger. "A grand master." Finally a third finger rose. "And Paul Blackthorne's daughter. I swear we've been set up all along."

Her brow furrowed. "You really think that?"

"Yeah, I do," he said. "I know that if I don't stand by Ori when the time comes, I'm gonna lose everything." He took one long, deep breath, desperate for her to understand just how much she was at the center of his life. His future. "All I have in this world is because of you. You were the one who never doubted that I could be whatever I wanted. As I see it, I have to do this or I'm not worthy of your love."

Riley looked away, toward the window, though it was pitch black outside. "Looks like grand masters are really good with the guilt too."

"Don't mean to do that to you, but it's important that you understand where I'm comin' from."

Her eyes returned to his. "You did the same for me—you never doubted that I could be whatever I wanted to be. You might not have liked doing that, but you were there for me."

"Just watchin' yer six," he said.

"It was more than that. I was a kid, scared, just trying to find some meaning in my dad's death. You stood by me, kept me from getting myself killed because I was too stubborn to listen. You made sure I knew that there was more in life than just demons."

"Then you know why I must do this," he replied solemnly. "And why I'll do everythin' I can to keep you out of it."

The fear in her eyes was so stark it almost made him back down. Tentative at first, Riley moved back to him, leaning against his chest. He put his arms around her, never wanting to let go.

For several minutes, she was quiet, not giving him an answer. As time passed, his heartrate increased, as did his worry. Then she unearthed her left hand from under the afghan, holding it up so he could see her palm and the vivid black crown.

"The fact that this is still here tells me I'll be standing with you two." She looked up at him now. "Ori told you that, didn't he?"

"He hinted at that. I ignored it."

Riley slid her hand back under the cover, leaning back against him. "I wish it were that simple."

A few minutes later, she'd fallen asleep in his arms, soft and safe, like he always wanted her to be.

If only it could be that way forever.

Chapter Twenty-Three

It was past dark when Beck pulled the truck up to the open stretch of ground where Riley was to meet the summoners. Mort's car was already there, but it sat empty. About fifty feet away, in a grassy field, two small bobbing lights hovered above the ground. Beck guessed those were the necro version of flashlights.

He hadn't liked the idea of bringing Riley all the way out here—she was still exhausted and hadn't bounced back from the jetlag as quickly as before.

"What's goin' on tonight?" he asked, trying to keep his aggravation in check.

"They're going to teach me not to lose my cool and blow stuff to bits."

"How do they do that?"

"No clue, but I suspect it's not going to be easy. Well, at least not for me."

Turning off the truck's engine, he frowned. "If you get hurt doin' this, I will bust someone's ass, you understand? Doesn't matter if they're a summoner or not."

She laughed, then leaned over and planted a kiss on his cheek. "You are awesome, Backwoods Boy. You know that?"

"What I am is tired, cranky, and not in the mood for any magical bullshit." *Not after another day of meetin's.*

"Then you better wait in the truck."

"No way," he said, opening his door.

There wasn't much he could do against a necro, unless he could get close enough to throw a few punches. Since this was their friend Mort, and no other than Lord Ozymandias, getting

physical was off the table. Instead, he'd have to resort to glowering with his arms crossed over his chest to remind them that he
wouldn't be pleased if Riley was harmed in any way. Hopefully,
that was all it would take.

Riley gave her fiancé a wary look—Beck was more on edge than
normal, and she knew Ori's sudden reappearance was to blame.
She'd vacillated between being thrilled at that news and angry
that Heaven was treating the angel like a pawn. He'd had enough
of that with the Prince.

Tall grass brushed against her jeans as she walked toward the
summoners. Around them, the night sounds were muted—even
nature respected the power of magic. In the distance, she heard
the hoots of an owl as well as its movement in the branches. Trees
surrounded them, some fully budded. There was no breeze, just
the chilly air, darker than usual, the new moon only a few days
away.

As they approached the bobbing lights, Mort came into view.
He was in his black robe, cheery as usual.

"Riley," he said. He raised an eyebrow at Beck, who she
knew was right behind her. "Good to see you, Grand Master."

"Thanks," he replied curtly.

Mort gave her a puzzled look and she rolled her eyes, mostly
because she knew Beck couldn't see her do it. Lord Ozymandias
came out of the darkness now, wearing his standard inky black
robe, the sigil on his forehead dimmer than usual. If not, it'd
have worked rather well as a headlamp.

She'd asked Mort what that sigil meant, and he'd neatly
sidestepped the question. Someday, when everything else settled
down, she'd find out, because she bet there was a really good
reason as to why the most senior summoner on the East Coast
had that on his forehead, especially when none of the other
necros did.

Ozymandias studied her companion's sour expression. "I see
you have concerns, Grand Master. What you need to know is
that to get her properly angry, which will significantly enhance

her magic, requires some unpleasantness on our part."

"As long as she's not hurt, I'm fine with it," was the gruff reply.

"Well, since you put it that way . . ."

A second later, dozens of tree roots shot up from the earth, encasing Beck like a woody set of chains. He twisted, shouting in indignation.

Ozy looked over at Riley.

"All you're doing is pissing him off," she said.

"No concern for your fiancé's safety?"

"Not the kind that would make me try to blast you to pieces. I know you won't hurt him."

"Why do you make that assumption?"

Through all of this, Beck had continued to shout his outrage, but at present, those shouts were muffled by a large leaf that had gently placed itself over his mouth.

"Chill, will you?" Riley told him. The man she loved glared back at her, his eyes promising payback.

Riley turned her attention to the two necromancers. "I make that assumption because the only time you've been intentionally cruel was when your back was against the wall with Sartael. You won't intentionally hurt Den because you don't need the grand masters on your case."

Ozy reluctantly nodded. "Then I'll have to change the scenario, because it's the only way you're going to learn."

The bonds holding Beck disappeared, though his glower remained.

Twenty feet or so to his left, a little girl appeared, walking out of the darkness.

"Riley!" she said, smiling and holding out her arms to be picked up.

"Carrina?" This was an illusion, but it was an excellent one. Anyone who wasn't a magic user would have been fooled. "That's not going to work," she began.

A Gastro-Fiend appeared behind the child in a heartbeat, its fangs dripping saliva in anticipation of a meal. With a howl, it began to run toward its helpless prey.

Riley reacted instantly, the spell cast and the demon blown apart even before she took her next breath. Except this time, there was no debris, just a shower of . . . bright pink confetti?

"Nice touch," Mort said, grinning.

"It helps to liven things up," Ozy replied.

Carrina's form wavered for a moment, then vanished, while Beck stared, his mouth open.

Heart pounding, head thumping, Riley glared at His Lordship. "You knew I'd fall for that."

"I'm not the only one. The higher-level demons will instinctively target your weaknesses." He glanced over at a frowning Beck. "Now that one of your hot buttons can protect himself, they'll find other means to break you."

"He's right, Riley," Mort said, his tone softer than his superior's. "What would you have done if this was the actual child and the demon gave you a choice of her life or your soul?"

She closed her eyes, knowing the answer. "How did you know about Carrina?"

"I didn't," Ozymandias replied. "The spell I cast let your mind fill in the details."

"Oh."

"To achieve our goal, for the next hour or so I'm going to make you very, very angry," he explained, though curiously he didn't sound pleased about that notion. "You're going to learn how to react so that you can match the strength of your spell with the appropriate level of threat, rather than just blowing everything up."

"But it's fun to blow stuff up," she said.

A true smile came to Ozy's face now. "Don't I know it."

Riley laughed, enjoying the moment—because this next hour was just going to be brutal. She gave a quick glance at Beck, hoping he was on board.

"This oughta be fun," he said, grinning, his surliness gone.

She took a deep breath. "Okay, Ozy, do your worst."

Mort groaned. "I really wish you hadn't said that."

~~*

Beck had moved out of the field of fire, parking himself at the base of a tree. It proved a wise move. He already had a healthy respect for what the magical folks could do, but tonight just upped that respect yet another notch.

Throughout each and every scenario that the two necros threw at Riley, he could tell they were doing their very best not to hurt her. Instead, they were toughening her up, teaching her how to handle her power wisely. It was a pity more folks didn't have that kind of training.

Now, as he watched, the high lord began to weave a spell, magic swirling around him like a swarm of hummingbirds. The illusion formed about fifteen or so feet away, and it was an Archfiend, its leathery wings outstretched, multiple eyes blazing dark crimson. The hands at the ends of its wings raked wickedly sharp claws through the air. Beck had seen this one before—it was the armored she-demon Riley had killed last winter.

"Blackthorne's daughter!" it shouted as a flaming sword formed in its right hand. Then it sent its multiple eyes toward Beck and smiled, a truly hideous sight.

Beck felt the threat, because this illusion was just too realistic. Ozy had even gotten the peculiar brimstone stench of the creature correct. Before Beck realized it, he'd pulled his sword from his trapping bag and gotten into a fighting stance. When he noticed Mort's bemused smile, he shrugged.

With a slash of its wings, the Archfiend rose into the air, its blade crackling with flames. As it dove toward her, Riley whispered something under her breath and the spell flew upward toward the fiend. The single purple arrow struck the fiend in the middle of its chest, sinking deep into the armor. The instant it hit, the illusion vanished with a resounding pop.

"Cool," Beck said, setting his sword down by his trapping bag.

"Crap," Riley muttered in return, slumping to her knees in exhaustion. "I shouldn't have blown it up."

"How do you usually deal with an Archfiend?" Lord Ozymandias asked.

"I have to kill them. Trapping them is too risky."

Riley had no more than uttered those words when her face screwed up in thought. Then she nodded wearily. "You made sure I wasn't automatically defaulting to 'stun it' mode every time I cast a protection spell."

"Exactly right." Ozy's staff appeared out of nowhere and he leaned on it, as if he was also weary. "You will have to make that judgment call in a fraction of a second. Like being a magical cop. Do you handcuff them, or do you shoot them?"

Mort looked at his superior, then back at her. "What he's not saying is that making a mistake will give you nightmares for the rest of your life."

Ozymandias nodded solemnly and headed toward Mort's car, his posture telling Beck that the subject was closed.

"Get some rest. You did really well," Mort said, then followed his superior. Their car pulled out long before Riley regained her feet.

When Beck started to tell her how awesome she'd been, she waved him off. "Just take me home."

As Beck drove the truck toward Atlanta, Riley slept in the front seat next to him. He knew it was hard for her to straddle these two worlds—summoner and demon trapper—and tonight was ample proof of that. Despite that, she'd learned what she'd needed to learn, kept her sense of humor, even when one of her spells backfired and threw her high into the air. Luckily, Mort had been paying attention and she'd landed gently. Still, the power of the spell had rebounded on her, and she'd spent the next few minutes dealing with a nosebleed. Now he knew why she'd worn black.

Riley was still asleep when he pulled into the driveway. He debated waking her then decided not to, at least not yet. Entering the house, he dealt with the alarm and then went back for her, fully prepared to carry Riley inside if she didn't wake. When she did finally rouse, he wasn't surprised to see her staggering out of the truck like she'd slugged a six pack.

"Yer so out of it," he said, smiling.

She blinked up at him. "Be careful, Backwoods Boy. I know how to do some kickass spellcasting now."

"You might, but not tonight."

"That's the truth."

By the time she made it inside, Riley was barely moving. He got the door closed and locked, then guided her down the hallway walking behind her with his hands on her shoulders.

"I need a shower," she said.

"Tomorrow morning. You'll fall asleep and thump yer head, the way yer movin'."

"Okay."

The fact she hadn't argued with him told him her battery was nearing empty. He set her on the edge of the bed and helped her undress, then tucked her in.

"'Night, Summoner Blackthorne."

Riley gave him a goofy grin and then closed her eyes. She was asleep even before he leaned over to place a kiss on her forehead.

~~*

Beck's morning run did nothing to get him in the "zone." Instead, with each increasing mile, he found himself fretting about almost everything. He thought of adding more distance, trying to exhaust himself, but suspected that wouldn't work. Part of that worry would vanish on Saturday, once he put a ring on Riley's finger. But the rogue death angel issue was out of his control, and that worried him even more.

Once again, Riley's angel waited for him on his front porch. In fact, Beck had been expecting that. Ori's posture was just as tense, his dark eyes troubled. Beck joined his visitor on the steps, sitting next to him and staring out at the street. Cars were going by now, people hauling their kids to school, headed to work. Another day in Georgia's capital.

There was prolonged silence, as if neither of them knew what to say.

It was the angel who took the first step. "You still hate me for seducing Riley."

Dammit, he went there. So far, Beck had managed to keep his anger tamped down, because he'd finally accepted that it was a matter of pride. The last time Ori had been here, he'd been too surprised to broach the subject. Now, Beck could let this escalate, finally bury his fist in this Fallen's face for what he'd done to Riley, or . . .

"You angels eat real food?" he managed to choke out.

The look of surprise he received said his visitor hadn't expected that question. "This one does."

"Okay, then let's get you some breakfast. Riley is probably still sleepin' and it's best not to wake her. She can be growly in the morning."

A trace of a smile appeared. "You're a lucky man, Denver Beck."

"I know. And as much as I'd like to hate you, I can't. My stubbornness drove her right into your arms, so if I'd been less of a dick, you wouldn't ever have had that night with her." To his surprise, Ori nodded in agreement. "And, you taught her how to fight demons. If you hadn't, she'd be dead."

"I think we've all paid for that one night's mistakes."

"That's for damned sure." Since they were being candid, Beck asked the question that had bugged him ever since that final battle. "How is it that a nobody demon trapper like me could kill Sartael, and Lucifer's executioner couldn't?"

If he'd expected the query to upset his visitor, he'd have been wrong.

"I wasn't allowed to," Ori replied. "When I was brought back to the living, I asked that question myself."

"And?"

"Sartael was strong because he was the demi-lord of a number of demons, and could draw life force from them. But I was the Prince's *personal* weapon. I should have been able to kill the traitor, but whenever I went up against him, I was never at my top skill. I didn't realize it until after the battle in the cemetery."

The angel was dragging out the answer. "Who was messin' with you?"

"Michael."

"The Archangel? Why'd he do it?"

"He is not fond of me."

Beck huffed, knowing there was more to that answer than the angel was offering. "Got in his face, huh?" He received the nod he'd expected. "So you knew you were probably gonna die when we fought Sartael that second time?"

"Yes. That's why I told you how to kill him," the angel replied. "It was the best way to keep Riley safe."

"Damn," Beck murmured. "If you hadn't, I wouldn't be a grand master. I wouldn't even be alive."

His visitor nodded. "Which made me wonder why Michael would go to such lengths, even though he detests me." Ori leaned forward, placing his elbows on his knees. "The three of us have been set on our individual paths, but those paths have interwoven in ways I cannot fathom."

"I said almost the same thing to Riley last night. Don't know about you, but I'm damned tired of that kind of thing."

Ori snorted. "Try living like that for a few millennia."

Beck shook his head. "I couldn't even imagine." He watched a jogger run past, her long hair swinging behind her head like a pendulum. "So, you good with bacon, eggs, pancakes, and coffee?"

"You're cooking this feast?" The angel's wry tone said he considered that a minor miracle.

"Of course," Beck replied, trying not to be offended. "Like I said, wakin' my fiancée up too early is just askin' to have yer ass handed to you. Wonderful woman, but she is *not* good company first thing in the mornin'.""

Ori nodded in sympathy. "I remember how upset she was whenever I summoned her to the cemetery at dawn."

"Yer damned lucky she didn't take a sledgehammer to yer statue and chip you into tiny pieces."

The angel actually laughed.

Once they were inside the house, Beck did a quick check on Riley, who was cocooned in the blankets, oblivious. He closed the bedroom door and set about making his celestial guest some breakfast.

First time for everythin'.

Chapter Twenty-Four

Riley woke to the smell of bacon, the olfactory equivalent of a blaring alarm clock. Hearing Beck puttering around the kitchen, she zombie-walked to the shower in her bedclothes. Even the hot water didn't clear the cobwebs. It was only after she'd dried her hair and dressed that she realized Beck was talking to someone, probably on the phone. She'd just made it to the kitchen when a familiar voice filled her mind.

Riley Anora Blackthorne.

She stopped dead in her tracks, staring in shock at the figure sitting at the kitchen table, watching her intently. Ori's midnight-black hair still reached his shoulders, but shots of silver resided at his temples now. His eyes were as dark as ever, but seemed to be more guarded, if that was possible.

Instinct made her probe for an illusion but she didn't find one. "You really are alive." For a second, she thought she might cry.

Ori gave her one of his cautious nods, the sort that told her things weren't as cheery as they seemed. "At least for the time being." He took a deep inhalation. "Your fiancé was kind enough to invite me to breakfast. I accepted, because hospitality rates highly among my kind."

His kind in Heaven. Hell couldn't care less about hospitality unless the recipient was screaming in agony.

Riley moved to the table and drew out the extra chair Beck had placed there, trying to adjust to this new reality. The last time she'd seen Ori, he'd been bleeding to death. She'd wept over him, then traded the favor Lucifer owed her so he could die in peace, rather than be called back into the Prince's service.

"I . . . didn't think I'd ever see you again."

Now that was the understatement of the century.

The angel's smile was gentle, a reminder of their past. "I certainly didn't expect this, either." After a lengthy pause, he added, "You are . . . happy?" It was as if Beck wasn't in the same room with them.

"I am." Her eyes went in search of her fiancé, who was pointedly ignoring their reunion as he retrieved a plate from the oven. "Very happy."

"You are getting married?" Ori asked.

"This Saturday."

Beck broke their tenuous connection when he set the plate in front of her, then gave her shoulder a tender squeeze. "Orange juice or hot chocolate?"

"OJ. Thanks."

Her first lover and the man she'd spend the rest of her life with, in the same room, sharing a meal.

Talk about awkward.

Riley scrutinized their expressions, their posture, but saw no outward tension, no barely contained aggression. If anything, it seemed they'd finally accepted one another.

That's a miracle.

The faint uptick of Ori's mouth told her he'd heard that thought and agreed.

A glance down at her plate made Riley smile, a reminder of why Beck was the man she loved—every portion was precisely Riley sized. When they'd first started living together, it'd been hard for him to understand that she couldn't pack away as much food as he did. He'd finally figured out how much she could eat and had adjusted accordingly. It was just one of the many little things that made her adore him.

When she looked up, Ori was watching her again. Beck was doing the same.

"I'm not liking the silence here," she said.

"Just waitin' for our guest to drop whatever news he has,

because I'm bettin' that's why he's here," Beck said as he returned to his chair. "It sure isn't because of my cookin' skills."

Ori leaned back in his chair, eliciting a faint creak from the wood. "It took me some time to get my bearings. One just doesn't go from full-on dead to breathing again without some adjustment." He reached out and tapped the handle of his coffee cup. "Once I could think straight, I visited each of the cities the angel has destroyed. Unfortunately, my efforts to track the Destroyer have been futile."

"I'd think you angels would be able to find each other pretty easily," Beck said.

"Not really. You're seeing us as all the same, but we are as diverse in personality and skills as each of you mortals." Ori fell silent for a moment, as if ordering his thoughts. "Some of us, for lack of a better word, are simple. Those simpler angels were created for a specific task."

"Unlike you and the Archangel Michael and some of the others."

"Exactly." Ori's eyes rose from his cup now. "The simpler ones go about those tasks without realizing the bigger picture. The Destroyer is one of those less adaptable angels. It has its job, and that's it."

"You call it an 'it,' not a he or a she," Beck said.

"That's because it does not have a sex. It merely exists as an extension of the Creator's will."

"So how do we stop it?"

Ori shook his head. "I don't know. I spent some time with the rare few survivors in each of these cities. Most are so traumatized they can't even tell me their name. But I can see inside their minds, and each of them showed me that there was little warning before the Destroyer arrived in their cities."

"We still have no idea where it will go next," Beck said, his tone gruffer now.

Ori did not reply. Instead, he gazed at Riley, as if waiting for her to understand something left unsaid.

"It might come here," she said. Even as she spoke the words, she knew they were as true as prophecy, and sadly the angel at their table did not contradict her. "It might come here because of me. The moment my tears touched the ashes in Italy, I felt a connection. Maybe that connection goes both ways."

"It is possible," Ori said, earning a glower from Beck across the table. "Or it was always meant to be this way. Mortals think in terms of your life span, seventy or eighty years. Heaven and Hell's timelines span millennia." He looked over at Beck now. "I have no doubt that this is why the grand masters are so successful; they think further out than most."

"Sometimes, but we still have our blind spots."

"Sadly, that's not just a mortal weakness."

"I think I was in touch with it even before I went to that city in Italy," Riley said. At Beck's puzzled look, she explained what she'd felt right before her panic attack in the Vatican's gardens.

His breathing sped up, usually the first sign that Beck was growing angry. His eyes snapped to Ori, then back to her. "Ya didn't think to tell me that? Like, before we hauled ya to that ash pit and ya damned near stopped breathin?" Beck growled.

Riley frowned in response. "I didn't figure there'd be a problem."

"Next time, tell me everythin'," was the terse response.

"Then you would have insisted I stay behind, and we wouldn't have known what we're facing. There're risks I'm willing to take, Beck. That was one of them."

The silence from the other side of the table made her glance over.

"Explain to me how the ashes touched you," Ori said, sounding almost as upset as Beck.

"They just kind of grew upward and formed into a hand. It touched my forehead."

"Then she damned near died," Beck grumbled, still angry.

"Besides the breathing issue, what else happened when you were touched?"

Riley explained the vision, how it'd led her to determine the cause of all these deaths. "I felt a rigid sense of purpose, as if nothing else mattered. That fits with your description of a simple, task-oriented angel."

"Simple or complex, we are nothing more than servants. We exist only to fulfill the Creator's will."

His dark tone struck her. "Do you hate being an angel?"

Ori took a long time before answering, his hands clenched around his coffee cup. It was hard to imagine this guy had been created by Heaven, then tempered in Hell's eternal fires.

He set the cup on the table, his eyes meeting hers. "No, I don't hate being an angel. I don't comprehend Heaven's strategies any more than I understood the Prince's. I serve because it's what I was made to do." He sighed heavily. "There are times I envy you mortals. You have so much more freedom than divine beings, even than Michael himself."

"Might be one of the reasons he's not fond of us," Beck suggested.

"That is very likely," Ori replied.

Riley's mind jumped to Isra. "Are there free angels?" she asked, propping her elbows on the table. "Ones who are not allied with either Heaven or Hell?"

Ori cut a glance over at her fiancé, but didn't answer. From his carefully neutral expression, she guessed he wasn't allowed to share that information.

"Are there free angels?" Beck jumped in. "Our archives say there are. Like the free demons, they serve as their own masters."

Her eyes went back to Ori, but she didn't dare ask if that's what he hoped for when this was all over. "So . . . you guys *can* free yourselves," she murmured, certain things becoming clearer now. "That's what the Destroyer's done. It's gotten free, but instead of settling down and living a quiet life, it's continued to kill, because that's what it was made to do. But this time *it* decides who lives and dies." She eyed the other angel now. "Am I right on that?"

"Yes. There are some things I'm allowed to say, and so many I am not. However, if you reach a conclusion on your own, I may be at liberty to let you know if you are correct."

"Bet you love that little rule."

A smirk filled his face, making him look almost human.

"Your return to Heaven is based on whether you stop the Destroyer, right?" He nodded. "Okay, then how can we help you do that?"

"I don't know. I honestly don't," he said. "We'll know when the time comes."

"And if you die, where will you go? Heaven or Hell?"

"Again, I do not know." Abruptly, Ori rose and pushed his chair back to the table. "Thank you for your hospitality, both of you."

"How soon do you think this is gonna happen?" Beck asked.

"Soon. Be ready, for we will get little warning."

Beck took hold of Riley's hand, rubbing his thumb over it. "All or nothin'?" he asked.

"The only way to go," she replied.

The angel issued a grim smile, the kind that told you he was a formidable ally. "All or nothing it is."

He gave them one final look and then exited the house, quietly closing the door behind him just like a mortal guest.

"That's a meal for the books," Beck said, shaking his head in wonder. "A grand master, a master trapper, and an angel. All of us have been to Hell, all of us got free."

She gave him a long look. "You know, I think you're right—this was all planned, probably from the moment I became a trapper. Or you moved to Atlanta."

Beck shook his head. "Further back than that, I'd bet. This could have begun the day Ori left Heaven with the Prince." He winked at her. "Remember, it's not always about us, Princess."

"Uh huh." Picking up a single slice of bacon, she munched on it, though it had no taste now. Knowing the pancake would be no better, she ignored what little remained. Since Beck had cooked breakfast, Riley began loading the dishwasher.

"We're getting married in two days," he announced, his eyes tracking her every movement. As if she didn't have that clock counting down in her head, as well.

Riley blinked. "Crap, I forgot to pick up something from the witches. I'll have to do that this morning."

"The only thing that matters is that yer there."

Beck came to her now, wrapping his arms around her. Leaning her head against his chest, she heard his steady heartbeat against her ear. She savored the rise and fall of his chest, his muscled arms around her, hugging her tight.

"Two days, and yer mine forever," he whispered.

I already am, Den. I already am.

~~*

Breakfast with the angel had messed up Riley's schedule, though she wouldn't have missed that for anything. The fact that Ori was alive was still mind blowing, though she wondered how his former boss in Hell was going to take the news.

Since she was already late, Riley texted Harper to let him know she was delayed, then made a quick trip to the Terminus Market in Centennial Park. Ayden had laid back a set of four quartz crystals at the Bell, Book, and Broomstick, which would anchor the corners of the protective circle she'd cast for the wedding. It seemed she was going all out to ensure the safety of the guests.

Once the purchase was paid for and the crystals safely tucked inside her trapping bag, Riley hiked out of the market toward where she'd parked her car. Unfortunately, it'd begun to spit rain, so she turned up her coat collar and hurried past the other tents.

"Please, no rain on Saturday," she pleaded. She'd obsessively checked the weather reports, and right now, there was a fifty-fifty chance that they'd be getting married in Angus's ballroom instead of the garden. When she'd grumbled about that, she hadn't received any sympathy. It was the South and it was spring. The weather was whatever it wanted to be.

Once Riley was across the street, she didn't head directly for her car, but veered toward the trappers' shrine at the remains of the Tabernacle. She always stopped to pay her respects to the dead, to ensure they knew that they were not forgotten. The night the building had fallen would never leave her—her dead father, fresh from his grave, calling out his warning to her and the other trappers. Being overrun by demons who surged right across the line of Holy Water. The Pyro-Fiends dropping fireballs from above, spreading flames in their wake. The screams of the injured and dying as they either burned or were ripped apart by demons. Then there was the Geo-Fiend who had tried to kill her even after she fled the horror inside the building. It'd been Ori who saved her that night.

Now, the once proud church-turned-concert-venue was a shrine to the fallen trappers. There'd been one in place since the morning of the tragedy, the flowers and little cards with prayers laid among the wreckage, even as the body bags had stretched out in one long line.

After months of legal wrangling, someone had bought the site to keep it out of the hands of developers, and a permanent memorial had been built. Curiously, the new owner had chosen an archway for the design, constructed from the bricks of the fallen building. Riley liked that imagery, as if the dead had walked from this world into the next. The fallen trappers' names were carved on the interior of the arch and Riley trailed her fingers over those now, as high as she could reach, remembering each man and how he'd died.

"This monument turned out better than I thought it would."

Riley swiveled to find Lord Ozymandias standing behind her. The near crack in the senior summoner's voice was unusual enough to catch her notice. His expression was somber as his eyes slowly traversed the names on the arch, resting on each one for a time.

It'd taken someone with considerable pull to fend off the developers, with significant resources to buy this plot of ground and pay for the shrine. That same someone had endowed college funds for the deceased trappers' children and ensured that the widows didn't go hungry.

Riley was annoyed that she hadn't made the connection before today.

"You did this, didn't you?" she said.

Ozymandias's eyes returned to her. "Yes. Very few know that, and I'd prefer to keep it that way."

"Then it'll be our secret," she said. She gazed back up at the arch. "This is the way they should be remembered, not in the body bags."

"That's what I thought."

"Why did you do it?" she asked, gesturing toward the arch.

"The demons were here that night because of my rampant ego, my quest for knowledge no matter who it hurt. I can't bring these men back from the dead, but I can ensure that this city will never forget their sacrifices or their bravery." He paused, swallowing hard. "I am relieved there aren't more names on this arch. Yours and Beck's, in particular."

"Thank you. This means a lot to me."

Ozymandias looked away for a second, regaining control, then turned back. It was only then Riley realized that he wasn't in his jet-black robe and the sigil on his forehead was curiously missing. Glamour had hidden it. To anyone else who couldn't see through the spell, he looked normal, in slacks, a pressed shirt, and black suitcoat.

She gestured at his clothes. "This is a new look for you. Everyday person. I think it weirds me out more than the robe."

Ozy didn't laugh, but the expression on his face said he really wanted to. That expression quickly faded. "Grand Master Stewart told me what's happening with this insane angel of death. He contacted the witches as well."

"I was hoping he'd do that. Any chance we can use magic against this thing?"

"We can try, but if we can destroy it, what will Heaven do? Shrug and move on? Or will there be something worse sent down to punish us for killing one of their own?"

It was hard to imagine what could be worse, but he did have a point. "Any ideas from the witches?"

"No. Apparently one of them has been raving her head off with warnings."

"That'd be Sibyl. She's kinda crazy." An overwhelming sense of sorrow blanketed her now. Was it because of this place, or was it something else? "If this thing comes here, Beck and I have no idea how to stop it." *Neither does Ori.*

"Did you know how to prevent Armageddon?" His Lordship asked.

The question jarred her. "No. I just got lucky. I really don't think anyone but the Archangel Michael was jonesing for war."

"And yet you figured that out on your own because you're very perceptive. Maybe this situation isn't so much a matter of your skills as a trapper, or with magic, but one of empathy."

Riley had just begun to think that through when a familiar chill rolled through her. She shifted her trapping bag on her shoulder. "Oh crap, him again."

Ozymandias didn't reply, but turned to stare at a figure walking toward them. A figure in all black. "That's—" he began.

"Yeah, that's the Prince. I wondered when His Infernalness would show up."

Beside her, His Lordships's robe appeared, as did the symbol on his forehead and a staff in his hand. He was in full necromancer mode now.

Lucifer stopped about six or so feet from them. Today, Hell's tyrant looked like any other Atlantan, though minus a coat. His midnight-black hair was still longer than collar length. Like Ori, he had silver strands mixed in.

His eyes narrowed as he studied her companion. "A summoner. A powerful one, at that. Ah yes, I remember now. You were Sartael's pet."

Ozymandias's expression grew stony, his fingers tightening on the staff.

"We all make mistakes. Mine was bigger than most," the necromancer replied. "But never on the same level as yours."

This would only escalate if she didn't intervene. "Some reason you're here?"

Lucifer's eyes shifted to her. "I hear you made some heads spin in Rome."

She didn't fall for the bait.

"The angel of death can be stopped," Lucifer continued, his delivery as nonchalant as if he were commenting on the weather.

Here we go.

"Do you realize that you're still really predictable? Your temptations have three distinct parts: the Tease, the Offer, and then the Dire Consequences if I ignore that offer." Lucifer's brows furrowed. "So go on, give me the spiel. The clock is running."

The frown deepened. "This angel can be stopped and I can tell you how. I can ensure that no more cities are destroyed, and you and that troublesome grand master of yours will get married. You'll have children and grandchildren. You'll live until you're very old, because I can ensure that."

"How?" she asked.

"Riley . . ." Ozymandias warned.

"Doesn't hurt to ask," she said.

"You can't expect me to give up that kind of knowledge for free," the Prince replied.

"Actually, I *do* expect the answer for free," Riley said. Just being near this fiend made her skin crawl. "Because if the thing does come here, all the hard work you've put into this city was for nothing. Beck and I will be dead and you won't get our souls. You will lose big time."

Lucifer's eyes darkened, his jaw tight, his arms crossed over his chest now. "Perhaps your deaths are exactly what I want, if your souls are pledged to me."

"Nope, not buying it. This angel is your *worst* nightmare," Riley retorted. "You might pick up a few souls here and there, but in the long run, you'll lose. This isn't good business, at least for you."

"It will come here. It will destroy this city."

She could tell by his tone that, for once, Lucifer wasn't lying.

"If it does, I'll do what I can. If I die, I die. But my soul will be mine."

"Then I'll see both of you in Hell," the Prince said, his voice harsher now. "For when you die, you'll pay the price for trying to kill a Divine. Except I won't protect you. You'll belong to whichever demon wants you. You know what that means."

She did, all too well.

"Or maybe Beck and I and . . . Ori will be able to kill this thing."

Lucifer gave a snort. "You expect a dead Fallen to help you? You are delusional."

Riley couldn't hold back the self-satisfied smirk. "You sure?"

Lucifer abruptly jerked his head to the east, toward Oakland Cemetery, no doubt searching for that one special gargoyle on top of her family's mausoleum. Riley knew the instant he realized Ori was gone. The resulting stream of Hellspeak curses was impressive—but then, he'd invented the language.

As always, Hell's boss quickly regained control, and he made one last offer. "Give me your soul and Isra will be released."

Isra. Riley closed her eyes, feeling the tears that could so easily form. She might be headed for Hell anyway. Why not free the demon along the way?

Because this is the Prince of Lies. The anger that overtook her at that moment was so profound it shook her to the core.

Steeling herself, she glowered over at him, putting as much contempt into her words as possible. "No! Not today, not tomorrow. I would love to see Isra free again, but I will never forget every evil thing you've done to those I love. For the rest of my days, I'm your enemy, Lucifer, *never* your servant. And if you think I'm dangerous now, give me a few years."

He glowered back. "Then your world will die. Your lover, your friends, their families, all of them *will die.*"

Her heart clenched. "Then that's the way it's going to be," she said.

"Fool!" Lucifer snarled, and then he abruptly vanished. Fortunately, the few bystanders didn't even seem to notice he'd been there in the first place.

The shakes set in, like they always did, and she knew there was no way to stop them.

"Well done," Ozy said, still at her side. She'd forgotten he was there. "You made a difficult choice."

The lives of millions versus her own. The decision sounded selfish, but she knew the Prince, knew he would find a way to screw her over and let all those people die anyway.

"He'll go after Beck too. Always does. He never quits." She hesitated. "But if I've learned anything over the last year, it's that there are always worse things than death. Hell being one of them."

Ozy's face paled and he turned slowly, staring south.

"What's wrong?" she asked.

The answer was a shaft of lightning that speared down from the Heavens, sizzling and smoking until it reached the ground. The instant the lightning impacted, white sheets of mist began to drift down along its former path. A voice boomed through the sky now, older than the world, speaking words that began with the birth of the universe.

Riley didn't understand them, but she knew their meaning, felt the terror lodge in her chest—her city was about to die.

"No!!"

"Take my hand. I can get us there quicker," Ozy said. When she hesitated, he shouted, "Take it now!"

She grasped his hand, felt the slap of powerful magic, and then her world went black.

Chapter Twenty-Five

Beck was in Demon Central, having just bitched out a journey-man trapper named Hemsey. He'd heard from various sources that this guy was an asshole, and those reports hadn't even come close to the real thing. At first, he thought his warnings were doing some good, but then Hemsey had offered some inventive curses about Beck's sexual preferences.

Rather than beating the crap out of him, which he would have done before he became a grand master, Beck just nodded and told Hemsey that his license was history, that by the end of the day he'd no longer be in the Guild. That'd earned him a torrent of swear words and another middle finger. It'd taken all of Beck's control not to return the gesture.

He'd just headed back toward his truck when a lightning strike came out of the clear sky, followed closely by an ear-rattling thunderclap. Looking to the west, in the direction of the strike, Beck's gut clenched at the sight of the misty curtain.

"Sweet Jesus in Heaven," he cried, then took off at a run. He had to find some way to get to where that mist was, because that's where Riley would be. If it was their day to die, he wanted to be by her side.

~~*

Ozymandias's hand gripped hers so tightly it made her fingers numb. The utter darkness eventually gave way to pale stars and bizarre dragon-like beasts winging in the air near them. Shivering from the cold, Riley abruptly landed on her feet in a parking lot, staggering a few steps to keep from falling.

Shaking her head to clear it, she bent over until she could regain her breath. "What . . . was . . . that?"

A choked voice came from somewhere behind her. "Magical taxi," Ozymandias replied. "Not recommended . . . unless an emergency."

The way her head kept spinning, she agreed. Ayden had once said this man could walk between the worlds, and Riley suspected that's what had just happened. It took more than a few swallows to convince her stomach that losing breakfast wasn't required.

Eventually able to raise her head, she eyed the surroundings, then realized they were west of Demon Central in an area of the city called the Gulch. It consisted of a big, open section of parking lot, bordered on the east by a parking ramp and on the west by the railroad tracks, Centennial Olympic Park Drive, and the new stadium.

Today there were fewer cars here. Since death was pouring out of the sky near the south edge of the lot, that was great news. Unfortunately, that put it dangerously close to the traffic on Martin Luther King Jr. Drive. Once it reached the ground, the unearthly fog began to spread, slowly advancing across the pavement, inch by inch. As far as she could tell, it had no scent, at least not one discernable over the engine oil and rubber tire potpourri.

Riley lurched to her feet and her head spun again, her equilibrium off. The desire to curl up on the ground was so powerful she had to force herself to remain upright. A glance at Ozymandias showed he'd made it to his feet as well, leaning heavily on his staff, and the sigil on his forehead maybe a third of its usual brightness. Whatever kind of spell he'd used, it'd been a powerful one if it could jump two people from the Tabernacle to here in a matter of seconds.

As she'd feared, there were more onlookers now; some on the top deck of the parking garage were taking photos. Somewhere nearby, a police siren wailed. The Destroyer's mist didn't care what the mortals did, continuing to spread across a few of the parked cars, creeping inside them even though their windows were closed. Fortunately, it moved slowly, which might give her some time to figure out how to stop it.

Because this location was bound to attract even more of an audience—CNN was only a short distance away—it was only a matter of time before everyone in the metro area, and the world, knew something funky was going on here. If they tied it to the other cities, there'd be unholy panic as Atlanta's citizens tried to escape. You just couldn't evacuate hundreds of thousands of people on already bumper-to-bumper highways.

To Riley's relief, flashing lights now sat at both ends of the overpass to the west, cutting off the through traffic. In the middle of that road, with a prime view, was a news truck, its antenna mast already deployed and sending video to the main studio.

So far, there was no Ori or Beck, but at least she wasn't alone.

"How do we stop this stuff?" she said, peering over at the senior necromancer.

Ozymandias stood a little straighter now, looking less weary. "We have to contain it. What we do with it after that, who knows?"

Riley'd come to the same conclusion. "Me or you?"

"You. I will reinforce your magic as needed."

Which told her just how exhausted he was.

As Riley began to work the spell out in her mind, the distinctive flap of wings broke her concentration. She and her companion turned as one to watch a figure in silver armor descend from the sky.

Ori's wings were all white now, and despite the armor, his arms were bare, with cryptic blue runes pulsing just underneath the skin. Even in a city as accustomed to weird stuff as Atlanta was, his arrival caused gasps from the onlookers.

Yeah, that's a real angel, and this time he's not working for the bad guys.

He landed and carefully folded his wings, arms crossed over

his chest. "Riley," he said, nodding toward her. "Necromancer."

"Fallen," Ozymandias replied without rancor.

"If that cloud reaches any mortal, they are dead," Ori warned.

Mortal. Like her and Lord Ozymandias. "Not just the first-born?"

"Every one of you."

Not what she wanted to hear. "What are we supposed to do with that stuff?"

"You're the summoners, you work it out," the angel said crisply.

"And just what will you be doing?"

"Trying not to die . . . *again.*"

Even before Ori finished his sentence, a bolt of lightning slammed into the earth some fifty feet behind them, followed quickly by a boiling mass of clouds laced with fire. The rancid stench of brimstone heralded the enormous figures who stalked out of that cloud.

Retrievers. Three of them.

"Oh hell!" she cried.

These fiends were exactly like the one at the school, nearly ten feet tall with that odd scaling pattern to their skin and claws made for rending. For once, three sets of fiery eyes ignored her. Instead, they zeroed in on the angel.

"The Prince is a sore loser," Ori said. A white-hot flaming sword formed in his right hand and his armor seemed to glow now. "A *very* sore loser."

Turning, he walked a few paces ahead, then spread his wings. Shouting something in the tongue of the Divines, he took off toward the trio at a trot. Leaving her and the necro to handle the death-dealing mist. She wasn't quite sure who got the worse deal.

"What kind of demons are those?" Ozymandias asked as swirls of protective magic formed around him.

"Retrievers. They're Hell's bounty hunters," she said.

It took every ounce of will to turn her back on Ori now, to let fate run its course. Even in the short time that she'd been distracted, the mist had moved even further into the parking lot, relentless in its efforts to suffocate the city.

"A containment spell, huh?" Riley muttered. She'd worked on those with Mort, but they'd never been a high priority. Mostly, she'd set a spell to keep a few ants in one corner of Mort's house. The ants, of course, were illusionary because no self-respecting necromancer would allow insects in his house. At least not her teacher.

"Visualize whatever works best for you," Ozymandias advised. "That will increase the spell's power."

From behind them came the sounds of battle, punctuated by the ferocious howls of outraged demons.

"Focus," she whispered. She could do nothing for Ori, but she could save thousands of lives. "Just focus."

If only it were that simple.

~~*

One of the advantages of being a local "hero" and having your face all over the newspapers and the internet was that Beck could race up to an Atlanta cop, show his new grand master's license, and demand to be taken to wherever that mist was. With lights and siren. That had happened, which would have been very cool if not for what that mist meant for the city.

It continued to spread even as Beck sprinted across The Gulch's pavement. As he'd expected, Riley was already here, and she had company, the magical kind. Since she appeared to be weaving some sort of complex spell, aimed at the mist, Beck knew not to break her concentration.

Instead, it was the Retrievers' deep bass howls that sent him in a new direction, toward the north end of the lot where they were fighting one lone angel. These kinds of Hellspawn were easily on par with Archfiends, just as powerful and just as blood-thirsty. From what he'd learned, they never stopped hunting until their prey was either dead or a prisoner in Hell. It wasn't professional pride that made them that tenacious, but a desire for survival—Lucifer made an example out of any Retriever that failed to do its duty, in the most excruciating ways possible. Since they were ignoring Riley and Ozymandias, that meant the angel was their target. That didn't surprise Beck in the least.

Despite the fact that there were three of them, their battle wasn't going well. One fiend was covered in black blood and favoring its left arm; another had a massive gash in a tree-trunk-sized thigh. The third had part of its skull caved in.

Ori moved so fast it was hard to keep track of him, using a combination of aerial and ground fighting tactics. That seemed to confuse the demons, who were probably used to their victims being lower-level Hellspawn.

Beck pulled his short sword from his trapping bag, then lowered the bag to the ground with a sigh. Holy Water wasn't going to stop these things, but neither was his puny-assed blade. Unfortunately, it wasn't practical to tote his claymore around the city. If he lived through this, maybe he'd find a way to solve that problem.

As he drew close to the Retriever with the damaged leg, he quickly realized that this thing's reach was much longer than his sword. Since it was easily half again as tall as him, it did have to reach down to engage him. Still, its claws were perfect for spearing unprotected flesh. At least the angel had armor.

"It would help," Ori said, ducking to miss a swipe of his opponent's claws, "if you'd actually fight that thing."

"Easy for you to say. You gotta a fiery sword and I have a toothpick," he replied, working to get within fighting range.

"Excuses, excuses," was the muffled response.

Ori had taken to the air at that moment, lunging upward to avoid a full-on attack by two of the demons, one from the front, the other from the back.

Beck kept dancing around, waiting for an opening, which seemed to annoy the monstrosity in front of him. A quick glance over his shoulder didn't give him good news—the mist was still advancing. In fact, it looked like it was planning on trapping Riley and the necro in the middle of it.

Filled with worry for his favorite trapper, he turned his attention back to the Retriever, which was sizing him up just as he was it. The gaping thigh wound told him exactly how to fight this thing. If he could inflict more damage to that leg, eventually it'd be on the ground. Once that happened, Beck had a chance to kill it.

He began a series of hit-and-run stabs, most of which missed the leg, though some sliced it up even deeper. By now, the Retriever was barely standing, blood draining down onto the pavement in torrents.

"You are not our enemy. Leave us and we will spare you," the thing offered.

"I'm calling bullshit on that one," Beck replied, moving forward and then immediately having to retreat when the fiend reached out to grab him.

The dying shriek of a demon filled the air as Ori took down one of his attackers. No sooner had that one turned to ashes on the pavement when two more arrived, fresh, uninjured, and keen to earn Lucifer's praise. The angel was wounded as well, rents in his wings that dripped blue blood. His strikes were not as solid as before. If they didn't kill these demons soon, Ori was headed to Hell and Beck would probably be joining him for the journey.

With a rebel yell, Beck charged forward, then shifted to the side at the last minute. Executing a drop and roll, he got himself behind his opponent. Scrambling to his feet, he adjusted his position and swept back his sword to deliver the blow.

The demon had just begun to turn toward him when Beck sliced through the back of its injured thigh, as high as he could reach. The thickness of the creature's hide almost saved it, but with Beck's whole-body weight working against the edge of the blade, it sheered through the Retriever's skin and bit deep. So deep that the demon toppled to one knee, bellowing in rage.

Now that the damned thing wasn't so tall, Beck scrambled up onto its back. Even as the demon struggled to regain its feet, Beck raised his sword and rammed the point down into the softer flesh at the back of the neck. The blade bit deep, so deep that

Beck found himself hanging from it as the demon flailed, trying desperately to dislodge the source of its pain. Claws dug at him, just missing his throat but scoring his shoulder.

Knowing he had no choice but to let loose of the blade, Beck fell away, hitting the pavement hard. As he clamored to his feet, he could feel the throb of the wound, blood running down his arm and coating his left hand. The damned thing had clawed him right where Sartael's blade had struck home.

Sweat running down his face, his arm aching, he watched as the Retriever slowly sank to the ground, blood pouring in streams from that injured thigh. It was dying and it knew it, and the hate in its eyes was almost as powerful as its master's. Beck was already moving toward it, keen on retrieving his sword when it died. Seconds later, the demon became ash, taking Beck's short sword with it to its grave.

"What the hell?" That had never happened before.

Ori grunted in pain as another demon died, his sword considerably less fiery than before. That only left one of the original three, and it was growing steadily weaker. The two new replacements hung back, letting that injured one wear Ori down. It was a smart strategy.

Beck took in the odds and knew they sucked, especially since he was without a sword. What was Lucifer's plan here? Was his hatred of Ori so intense that he'd ignore what Heaven had unleashed in this city? Or . . . had the angel of death sided with Hell?

No. It just didn't feel right. But somehow, keeping Ori occupied played into Lucifer's plans.

Ya bastard. Just once, he'd like someone watching his and Riley's backs.

As Beck turned to make the run to his trapping bag to collect his remaining weapon—his knife—something appeared at his feet in a shimmer of light. Something long and pointed.

"What the . . . ?"

He stared in stunned amazement at the claymore. The instant he bent to retrieve it, he knew it was the one he'd used to kill

Sartael. The one Angus had brought back from his investiture ceremony in Scotland. How it'd made the journey from Beck's bedroom wall to here didn't matter. He had a weapon now.

"Thank you!" he shouted to whoever had made that happen, and he jogged over to join forces with the angel.

"Decided to make yourself useful?" Ori asked, his chest heaving from exertion as blood ran down his face and matted in his hair.

"Damned straight," Beck replied.

With a bloodthirsty grin, he set his sights on the nearest Retriever, one of the newcomers. It was time to send a message that the Prince of Hell would never forget.

It was a difficult spell, hard to formulate correctly, especially since what Riley wanted to contain kept moving on her. As she worked through the parameters of the incantation, the waterfall of mist from the sky slowed to a trickle, then finally halted. That bit of good news didn't seem to matter, as it had multiplied in volume as it spread across the earth. It had also begun to surround her and Ozymandias. There was still a way to escape, but that gap would be closing very quickly.

Riley was only a few breaths away from a full-blown panic attack. Even now, she could feel her lungs tightening.

Make whatever you fear something you can laugh at.

That had been Mort's advice whenever she found herself locking up in some truly frightening situation. It didn't happen as much with the demons anymore, but this new threat was an off-the-charts nightmare. What truly frightened her was that this fog wasn't a person, something solid she could fight.

Wait a minute . . .

Even though the idea was wacky, she rebuilt her spell on the fly, then cast it. It was pure illusion, with as much power as she could channel. The first figure appeared just outside the misty pool. Because it was easier to visualize someone she knew, she had chosen one of Beck's neighbors. Mr. Kim was a kind, older Asian gentleman who had this obsession with leaves. The moment one fell on his lawn, he fired up his leaf blower—usually right when Riley had the incredibly rare opportunity to take an afternoon nap.

Which is exactly what he did in Riley's spell. Mr. Kim started his blower and attacked the mist just like it was a sea of oak leaves. At first it didn't work, so Riley closed her eyes and tweaked the spell. She was only vaguely aware of the battle behind her, the cries of the demons, the sound of breaking glass and bending metal as one of the cars was used as a weapon.

"Focus," she murmured, and her mind zeroed back in on the illusionary Mr. Kim. As he passed back and forth, the leaf blower making a racket, the mist began to retreat, blowing back on itself just like it was made of leaves. Gritting her teeth at the effort, feeling the sweat pop out on her forehead, Riley carefully layered more power into the spell. Mr. Kim #2 appeared. To her relief, he worked in tandem with #1.

But it still wasn't enough. She'd need so many more Kims to corral this stuff, which kept crawling closer and closer. To her surprise, another Kim appeared at that moment, followed quickly by five more in rapid succession, then five more. Soon an even dozen of her illusionary neighbors tackled the mist from all angles. Riley was so shocked, she almost lost control of her own spell.

Standing next to her, Lord Ozymandias positively glowed with magic, his eyes shut, one hand uplifted. As the multiple Kims drove the mist into a smaller, yet denser pool, it began to rise into the air in a thick column, swirling in a slow circle.

"Destroy it," His Lordship ordered.

Riley knew exactly what to do with it. She carefully ended her first spell, her illusions disappearing, and then crafted one to shape the mist into something she could defeat: an Archfiend. No sooner had it been created—all misty-white wings, glowing sword, loincloth, and multiple fiery red eyes—than a frightened little girl clutching a calico kitten appeared in front of it.

Ozy, you rock.

Without hesitation, she blasted the monster with all the magic she had. The "demon" blazed for a moment, turning smoky black, the mist roiling like a billion writhing ghosts, and then it vanished with a resounding boom. The little girl and tiny cat faded from view.

Riley blinked in astonishment—the mist was simply gone. No wisps anywhere. They'd just earned themselves a reprieve.

Sagging to her knees, her energy gone, she took a few deep breaths, so tired she thought she'd pass out. Ozymandias wasn't in any better shape, leaning even more heavily on his staff. The sigil on his forehead was so faint it was barely noticeable.

"We did it," she said, her throat dry and her heart pounding. She wiped at her nose, pleased to see it wasn't bleeding.

"You did it. I helped," he replied, his voice unusually weak.

Riley forced herself back to her feet, her head still spinning. Turning to check how Ori fared, she saw her fiancé decapitate a Retriever with one mighty stroke. Once the head came free, it rolled across the ground and bumped the toe of Ori's shoe right before it turned to ash.

"Show off," the angel called out.

"That's how we do it in Georgia," Beck replied, breathing heavily. "Damn, those are big mothers."

"At least now there are fewer of the accursed things."

Riley's eyes skipped over the piles of ash, counting. Five Retrievers were dead. "Good job."

Beck must have heard her, as he turned and then smiled. She could tell the instant he realized the mist was gone.

"Hot damn, Princess! Look at you!" he shouted, then took off at a sprint toward her, sword in hand. As he drew closer, she could see the blood on his chest, the claw marks on his shoulder. It was a miracle he was still alive.

She was in his arms a few second later. Actually, only one arm, as he made sure his blade came nowhere near her. Beck hugged her tightly, smelling of blood and sweat—and worry.

"Well done, Summoner Blackthorne," Lord Ozymandias

said wearily. "And now I need to rest." Without waiting for a reply, he simply moved a few steps away, then vanished.

"How does he do that?" Beck asked.

"No clue. And I don't want to learn how." Not after that trip from the Tabernacle.

Ori had joined them now. Instead of a smug, "we saved the day" expression, his was unusually solemn. He kept studying the area where the mist had been. The ground where it had touched was darker now, the pavement cracking in wide streaks, gradually turning to powder.

"This was too easy," he announced.

"Easy?" Riley countered, annoyed that he'd make that claim. "Really? Did you see what we had to do to stop that stuff?"

"This was too easy," he repeated.

"But we—"

A low-pitched rumble filled the air, one that made the hair on the nape of Riley's neck rise. In the sky above them, where the mist had first appeared, was a spinning column of fire.

"Move!" Ori shouted.

They sprinted north, Beck's hand on Riley's elbow as that pillar touched down behind them, the force of its rotation swirling dirt around its base. When they finally stopped running, the three of them turned and stared at the manifestation in front of them.

"It's the Destroyer, right?" Riley asked, praying the answer was "no."

Ori nodded. "It's probably wondering why the city isn't a graveyard yet. It'll want to know why."

One of those reasons would be Riley.

The fiery tornado quickly evaporated like it'd never existed, and in its place stood a figure clothed in a pure white robe. It stood about seven feet tall. No face was visible, for its head was draped in a shroud. A slight breeze shifted that shroud, but it made no other movement.

It reminded Riley of the "angel" in the Edinburgh graveyard, the one that had turned out to be an Archfiend. Her senses told her this wasn't demonic, though she wished it was. She knew how to deal with one of those evils.

Behind them, the congratulatory cheers of the onlookers had died down, replaced by profound silence. A quick glance revealed hundreds more people now. Though they were being kept back by the cops, they still lined the nearby roads and were filling the parking deck for a view of Atlanta's latest "wonder." A wonder that was here to finish what it'd started.

"So now what?" Beck asked, his patience at an end. He was tired, bloodied, and pissed.

"Now we wait," Ori said.

Beck grunted. To keep from losing his temper, he took hold of Riley's hand, startling her when he did so. A gentle smile came his way, despite her weariness. How could this one woman mean so much to him, be the center of his world? How had she broken down his defenses so thoroughly that even touching her hand meant everything to him?

He wished for so much now. The chance to marry her. That someday they might have children. To watch his wife grow round with his baby, then to hold that newly birthed son or daughter in his arms. He knew he'd cry when that happened, even if he tried not to. They already had the names picked out: Paul Arthur if it was a boy, Emily Rose if it was a girl.

But all that was nothing but dreams as long as this white-robed son of a bitch was in their town. Beck reluctantly let go of her hand.

"Enough of this. It's time we let this thing know who it's up against." Riley's grin told him she'd been thinking the same thing. "You with us, angel?" he asked.

Ori gave a nod. "It seems your impatience is communicable."

"Then let's show this crazy-assed creature some true Southern hospitality," Beck said, moving forward.

Chapter Twenty-Six

He made his stand about twenty feet out, took a very deep breath, and then let loose. "Hey! I'm Grand Master Denver Beck. I've already killed one angel in my lifetime, and I can probably make that two. If ya back off, go home, and quit this bullshit, then it's all good. If not, ya got one helluva fight comin'. Ya hear?"

Ori shook his head in amazement. "You're actually marrying this man?"

Riley nodded. "We're a matched set. Trust me on that."

"*DEATH.*"

The word reverberated around them and then flowed through Riley's body, almost as if she'd said it herself. Once that reverberation ended, the white shroud gradually slipped off the angel, pooling on the ground at its feet. The figure immediately began to shift, revealing wings that opened to a span that equaled Ori's, perhaps fifteen or more feet, wingtip to wingtip. The exterior feathers were white, the ones on the inside of the wing blood red.

As it lifted its face, it revealed its crystalline blue eyes, the last thing multitudes had seen right before they'd died. Its face was unnaturally pale, and as the hood fell back, straight white-gold hair appeared. This creature was older than the universe, and from what Riley could tell, it had no particular gender. Death didn't play favorites.

It ignored Beck, its attention going to Ori, eyes narrowing.

"*You are Fallen. You are of the Prince.*"

She could hear it in her mind as clearly as if it had spoken out loud. From Beck's reaction, he could as well.

"I am no longer Hell's slave," Ori replied, steel in his voice.

That seemed to puzzle the other Divine. "*How?*"

"After I died, Riley Anora Blackthorne," he said, gesturing toward her, "prayed for my soul to be released from the Prince's chains, and that plea was granted. Heaven breathed life into me and now I am here."

As if not comprehending how that could be, the Destroyer moved its focus to her fiancé now. "*Mortal,*" it said, making it sound like a curse. With one word, it stripped away all of Beck's accomplishments like he was meaningless. Riley ground her teeth, but held her silence. If there was any way they could convince this thing to stop killing cities, their pride was a cheap price to pay.

Finally, its gaze came her way. She felt the depth of its regard, its attempt to root around in her mind. She gave it a firm shove away, and that made it blink.

"*Blackthorne's daughter.*"

Only demons called her that, and yet this was not Hellspawn.

"*Ha mashhit,*" she said. That was its name in Hebrew, and if anyone knew the destructive power of this thing, it was the Jews.

Its eyes narrowed further.

"*You were of Hell. Now you are not.*"

It must have sensed Heaven's mark on her palm. "I have paid for my mistakes."

"Why are ya here?" Beck asked.

"*To bring justice. To punish the wicked. As I have always done.*"

Like its eyes, its voice was stunningly devoid of emotion. Could any creature be a stone-cold executioner and also have a heart? Ori did.

"I am different," Ori said, reading her mind. "I questioned and argued when the need arose. This one accepted all it was told."

The Destroyer glowered at its fellow angel. "*You were made to serve. You broke your oath.*"

"Yes, I did. Just as you have."

"*I do what must be done.*"

"Is yer boss tellin' ya to kill people?" Beck demanded. No reply. "Then yer not doin' right, are ya?"

Again, no reply.

"Why Atlanta?" Riley asked. "There are no more wicked people here than in any other city on this earth."

"This is Lucifer's city. He rules here. All must perish."

Riley's temper stirred and she took a few steps closer. "This is *not* Lucifer's city. He's barely holding on here because we won't let him win." It was then that she felt the power emanating off this thing, felt it seeping into her skin. "Who told you that lie?"

The longer she stared into those eyes, the more her bones felt like they were melting from the inside. She remembered this from the cemetery, when she'd stood between the armies of Heaven and Hell. She didn't dare stay close to this Divine for too long or she'd die.

"I am not blind. I am not like you mortals."

"You're worse than us," she snapped. "You've violated Heaven's laws. You're no better than the Prince."

"I do what must be done."

This angel was so different from Ori, or Martha, or any of the others she'd met. It was like a computer prototype, capable of a few tasks, but unable to learn new ones. She wondered if God had made it that way on purpose.

"Yes," Ori said, once again hearing her thoughts. "To be an executioner, it is best if you don't feel emotions so keenly. This one is only a tool of the Divine Wrath."

But something had made it cease following orders. A desire to be more than just a tool, perhaps?

"I shall never stop. I bring no mercy. I bring only death."

There was a faint tremble in the angel's voice now, a minute crack in its composure. A nearly immortal creature made of Light, once close to the throne of God, then given a holy task: divine retribution. Sure, this angel was only a weapon and someone else was aiming it at its victims, but that slight quaver in its voice told Riley that the Destroyer *had* felt every single death. Despite its emotionless eyes, its flat affect, it did have a conscience, and the guilt was eating it alive.

"If you try to destroy this city, we will kill you," Ori warned.

The angel's eyes blazed brighter. "*I cannot die. I am death itself.*"

"All things perish, even us."

"*Why do you stand with the mortals?*"

"Because they are worthy of my protection," Ori replied.

"*They are an abomination.*"

"Sometimes," Ori replied. "They can be as evil and hateful and wicked as any Hellspawn. Yet they can also be as loving and forgiving, heroic and compassionate, as any in Heaven." He sighed heavily. "They utterly confuse me, but the more time I spend with them, the more I like them. They are truly the Creator's children."

"*They refuse to obey the commandments.*"

"Is their disobedience equal to the death of a city? While that degree of retribution might have worked millennia ago, it doesn't now. The mortals have changed, just as we have."

"You have no idea what it is like to be a mortal," Riley said. "You send your mist down and kill us, then incinerate our bones and our homes. But you never get your hands bloody. Well, this time you will. We will probably die here, but we will make you bleed, make you know what it's like to fear for your life. Because until you do, you will not realize the evil you commit."

The expression in the Destroyer's eyes changed. That shift wasn't sudden, but gradual, like it had examined its heart and not liked what it'd found there. It lowered its head, no longer meeting their gaze.

Beck looked over at her and shrugged. Ori gestured for her to step back, closer to them. She could hear the crowd now, a susurrus of voices carried on the morning breeze. Some were singing; others chanting. Still, the Destroyer did not move.

Finally, its head rose and its eyes opened. "*I shall feel this blood you speak of and know what it is to fear.*"

That was as much of a challenge as they were likely to

receive.

Riley pulled her short sword free of its scabbard, tossing the latter out of the way. She'd slain an Archfiend with this weapon, and though it didn't flame like the angelic blades, it was special to her.

"All or nothin'," Beck said. His grim expression said he expected to die today. He looked over at her now. "One way or another, we'll be together when this is over."

"All or nothing," she replied, taking one last look at the man she loved. Her worries about the wedding—whether there'd be enough food, the myriad logistics of the reception—were unimportant now. What mattered was that she was here, with him.

A crisp snap of flames heralded the reappearance of Ori's sword. Angelfire licked along the edges of the long blade. He gestured toward hers but she shook her head. "No. This is fine." She didn't want him sharing any of his power with her. He'd need it to kill this Divine.

"Remember what I taught you, Valiant Light," he said.

He glared up at his fellow angel and called out something in their ancient language. A final warning, perhaps. In response, a sword appeared in the Destroyer's hand, just as fiery as the one Ori wielded.

"Another day, another monster," Beck muttered, then dashed toward their enemy, Riley by his side.

Only their angel reached the Destroyer.

Beck and his fiancée found themselves walled off from the battle by a curtain of ash, as if only a fellow Divine was worthy of a fight to the death. The ashes didn't look dangerous and they were thin enough to see through. But when you tried to penetrate them, your skin felt like it was peeling off your bones.

"What the hell is that stuff?" he said, lurching away and slapping at his face like it was covered in mosquitoes.

Riley's blotchy red face told him she was suffering as badly as he was.

"I don't know, but it's gotta go," she said. Closing her eyes, she began to whisper something under her breath. Beck took the hint and stepped back.

When her spell struck the ashes, they dropped to the ground in a long line.

"Well done," he said, grinning.

Riley gave a brief bow, smiling with pride. They'd only managed to take a few steps forward when the ashes began to move again. Instead of a wall, they formed into a pair of angelic warriors, in armor and with swords, though luckily minus the wings. All of that was made of those ashes.

"Sorry!" Riley said, backing up. "I could try it again."

"No!" With their luck, they'd end up with more of these things. "We do it the hard way. Watch my six, will ya, Princess?"

"Always," she said, and then they squared off with their ashy opponents.

They quickly learned that these warriors were designed to keep them away from the angels' battle, as they only fought when he and Riley tried to get to their companion. That didn't set well with Beck. As he parried a thrust, then hacked at his opponent's sword arm, he caught a glimpse of his fiancée retreating from her attacker. His inattention almost got his throat cut, so he got his head back into the game. He just had to trust that she could keep herself alive.

Besides the whole blocking gambit, fighting something made of ash was difficult. A sword cut didn't seem to hurt it—it just reformed around the slash. It didn't bleed; it didn't need to breathe. In short, these damned things were unstoppable.

Riley had come to the same conclusion with her own ash warrior. The moment she stepped back, it didn't follow her, just waited for her to approach again. Beck joined her, breathing heavily.

"What do we do with these things? Ya can't kill 'em," he complained.

She crouched down, trying to loosen up her cramping thigh muscles. Right now she'd kill for a drink of water.

Water.

She rose, handing Beck her sword. "I'm going to try one more spell."

"Are ya sure that's wise?" he said. "The last one was a bust."

Riley decided to ignore that. Closing her eyes, she thought about how to deliver the effect she wanted. Once she was sure she had a grip on the incantation, she opened her eyes and shot it out the end of her fingers. To most, her spell would be invisible, but she saw it as hundreds of small arrows. As she'd intended, they defied gravity and curved upward to hover over each of the ash angels. Then they cut loose.

The twin rain showers soaked the area beneath them. At first, the angels tried to move out of the way, but the spells followed them. Drenched, they began to melt, just as ashes would in a rainstorm, until they were no more than two dark puddles on the pavement. With a wave of her hand, Riley opened holes in the concrete, sucked in the water and muck, and closed them tightly.

Beck's kiss came out of nowhere, followed by a gleeful hoot of joy. It was cut short by Ori's cry of pain. Riley claimed her sword and they raced into the battle.

Ori's hope that he and the other angel were evenly matched had come true, but because of that, neither of them was winning. The Destroyer was not a fighter, and it made amateur mistakes, but its elemental power always seemed to save it when Ori managed to deliver what should have been a killing blow.

One thing was for sure—whoever had been limiting Ori's fighting ability in previous battles was no longer doing so with this one. That was a blessing. Whether that would prove enough was another matter.

Now, as he folded his wings, wincing at the bright shard of agony from a severed wing tendon, he scrutinized his opponent. The Destroyer's neutral expression was gone, and in its place was resignation, as if it knew that today might be its last.

"*Do you fear death?*" it asked.

Did he? When he'd been Lucifer's executioner, he'd longed

for it. Now?

"I do not fear it. Nor do I seek it," Ori said. He'd been given a second chance, and he did not want to waste it, though his arms felt leaden and his numerous wounds dripped his lifeblood onto the ground.

"*The mortals come.*"

"Maybe now we can end this."

The Destroyer raised its sword, hopefully for the last time.

As Beck and Riley charged toward the angels, Beck's plan to strike a wing went wrong immediately. When he finally got into a position to swing his sword, that same wing smacked him like he was a fly, sending him end-over-end across the parking lot. Spitting to get the dust out of his mouth and blinking to clear his eyes, he swore as he stumbled to his knees.

How in the hell is it doin' that?

Riley rolled across the lot right behind him, like she was a piece of lint.

"So that's the way it's gonna be, huh?" he said, shaking his head as he reclaimed his sword. It was like trying to kill a big freaking bird. Beck charged right back toward their enemy. Because no matter what, he wasn't going to let some celestial serial killer win.

Every time he got anywhere near the thing, it whomped him. He had bruises all over his body now, and his left knee was aching as bad as his left shoulder. At least his sword arm was good. Unfortunately, Riley didn't look to be in any better condition.

"Why is it playing with us?" she demanded, her hair tangled and her eyes blazing.

Just as he was about to make yet another futile run at the thing—and he was afraid it might be his last—something shot out of the sky, arcing downward toward their enemy. Whatever it was split down the middle, each branch striking a wing. The Destroyer screamed and writhed, struggling to break free as the stench of burning feathers and flesh filled the air. Beck began to retch. Riley slapped a hand over her nose in horror, gagging as well.

When the assault ended, the wings were gone, the wounds cauterized by the fire. It'd been a surgical strike, as the angel's robe was untouched.

"My God," Beck said. Had Heaven evened the odds, or was that Hell's doing? Did it matter?

The Destroyer wavered on its feet, the blue in its eyes nearly black now, smoke rising from where its wings had once been. It tightened its grip on its sword, murder in its eyes.

Beck and Riley closed ranks around Ori. They were all wounded in some way, dirt and blood ground into their clothes.

"Maybe I should have taken Lucifer's offer," Riley joked.

"And listen to that loudmouth for eternity?" Beck said. "No way."

She laughed, and then her humor vanished. "I love you."

"Right back at ya."

As their enemy moved closer, sword blazing, Beck found himself humming an old Scottish tune, the one Angus had taught him. The one his friend had sung that day in the cemetery when he'd been sure he was going to die.

It was three against one as they engaged the wounded killer. When Riley had to lurch back to avoid a slash that probably would have disemboweled her, Beck rammed his sword into their foe's side. He felt it slide home, but when he moved to drag the sword upward to inflict the most damage, he found himself sailing through the air again. The landing was awkward, immensely painful. For a second, he thought his back was broken. Dazed, he heard Riley cry his name.

Above him was the Destroyer, fiery sword poised to cut him in half. He couldn't move fast enough to save himself. As the sword began to fall, Beck wondered how soon someone in Scotland would notice that his candle had gone dark.

Chapter Twenty-Seven

"No!" Riley charged, slicing deep, bringing blood to the Destroyer's sword arm and chest. It whirled on her, slamming the pommel of its sword into her right arm. Ori heard the bone snap as she screamed and fell at Beck's feet.

He flung himself between the Destroyer and the two fallen mortals, using his wing as a shield. He saw the Divine's sword descend, knew it would strike him. When it did, he roared in agony as the wing was nearly sheared in two.

Furious, reeling from the unimaginable pain, Ori attacked, allowed his wings to vanish to help him maintain his balance. His strikes were hard, swift, and relentless. He narrowly blocked one sword thrust, then another, the heat of the Destroyer's weapon coming dangerously close to his face.

"You seek death," he demanded. "You seek death to atone for all you've killed." Another strike, one that sliced deep into the angel's arm, hitting bone. "I see it in your heart. You want this to stop."

"*I cannot stop.*"

"By dying, you will atone," Ori said, pressing his advantage.

The other angel fought on, but its strikes were not as strong, nor as well placed. At the same time, Ori's wounds healed, gradually but noticeably, while his foe's did not. Ori had no time to marvel at that, continuing to rain blow after blow, breaking the body and the will of his fellow Divine.

"I can make an end to this," he offered, ensuring that his voice was as persuasive as it had been when he'd seduced mortals for his infernal master. "I can end your suffering."

The instant the other angel's eyes met his, he saw the guilt. and then the decision.

"*I shall atone.*"

As Ori thrust his fiery sword into its heart, it made no effort to block the strike. Its eyes remained locked on his, acknowledging. Accepting.

He withdrew the sword, knowing it had been a killing blow, blue blood fountaining out of the wound, soaking the Destroyer's white robe. It fell to its knees, then onto its back, its sword disappearing. Slowly, its blood-drenched hand reached out in supplication.

But not toward Ori.

Trust your heart, Riley's father whispered in her mind, just like he had when she first met Isra.

She'd never understand what drove her to rise, move to the dying angel, cradling her broken arm. She ignored Beck's warning, ignored everything but the need to be by the angel's side. Ori did not stop her, for perhaps he remembered her being with him as he died. When she knelt next to this mortally wounded Divine, she took that bloodstained hand in hers. Her left clasping its left.

The Destroyer's expression was so profoundly sad that it brought tears to her eyes. As it faded from life, Ori knelt at its feet, his head bowed in sorrow. Beck, to its right, knelt and bowed his head as well.

The mental torment Riley felt through the angel's palm was more painful than her shattered arm. Deep within it was the guilt it had shielded all these millennia, its increasingly desperate rationalization that all the deaths had been righteous. Perhaps they had been, but now they were killing the angel as surely as the sword wound to its heart.

The dying Destroyer's eyes met hers now. There, reflected in the deep blue, she saw what few mortals ever saw. *Angels, so many angels.* Some had two wings, others had many. They circled around a point in the distance, one so unfathomable that her mind could not comprehend its meaning. For those few brief seconds, she felt the power of that Light, that love, even if there were so many times she didn't understand it.

The heat spreading through her palm became nearly unbearable, but she did not move her hand. If it cost her everything, then that was meant to be. This Heavenly creature would not die alone.

"Be at peace, angel."

"Be at peace," Ori whispered.

"Be at peace," Beck repeated.

With a shudder that shook its whole body, the angel whispered out loud, "*Cursum perficio. My journey is over.*"

Underneath her fingers, the body began to disintegrate. She felt it shift, become insubstantial, as the angel became millions of pieces of silver light, shimmering, wavering. Then it was no more. Once it was gone, her palm remained dusted with that silver sheen. When she blew on it, it floated away, vanishing into nothingness, leaving behind was only bare skin.

Heaven's mark, the crown she had borne for over a year, was gone.

Riley became aware again when Beck touched her shoulder. Then sounds began to reach her ears, sounds from those nearby, reminding her that there were more witnesses to this tragedy than just the three of them. It was like a mismatched choir with hundreds of people who had great voices and so many others who were absolutely tone deaf. Nevertheless, the heart of the music, the words, the intent, was one of joy. Of celebration. In some cases, outright surprise that they weren't dead.

"Hallelujah," she whispered, echoing their words.

Cheers came now. More shouts of "hallelujah," an occasional "Allahu akbar." So many languages, all thanking Heaven for their survival. Ironic, since it was Heaven who had created the deadly menace in the first place.

It wanted to die. She remembered Ori asking for the same fate and Lucifer refusing him. Why had this been allowed to happen? What was the point?

No answer came, and she felt the pain in her arm increase.

"Riley?" It was Beck, and there was worry in his voice. "Ya with us?"

She opened her eyes and gave a nod. She was in Beck's arms, Cri watching her with deep concern. Around them was a curtain of light, shielding them from view. She stared at it, trying to figure out where it'd come from.

"I am creating it," Ori said. "The Destroyer deserved to die with dignity, not with an audience."

Unlike the way Ori had.

"Thank you." Even as she said the words, the light dimmed and vanished, revealing them to the thousands who had stood witness to this moment. Her eyes trailed across the crowd— most were crying, hugging each other. Some were still singing, one massive homage to survival. And as always, there were the news trucks, the reporters sending the word out that the threat to Atlanta and its citizens was gone.

Once again, they were at the center of it all. And once again, they had lived to tell the tale.

Like someone had thrown a switch, all the pain kicked in now. Riley's back hurt, her head hurt, her right arm was sending so many waves of agony that her body couldn't even process them all.

A soothing hand brushed over her forehead. Beck. The man she loved gazed down at her. His face was bleeding, his clothes filthy, his blond hair a mess.

"I love you," she said.

"I know," he said, so softly she almost missed it.

Then she looked over at their angel. "You knew, didn't you? That it wanted to die."

"I was uncertain as to its motives, but it made sense. To kill itself would have been a sin. My guess is that your light drew it here, and it did not want to die on its own."

None of us do. Especially an angel who had spent an eternity alone.

"My crown's gone," she said, as if it wasn't a big deal,

though it was. "It vanished when the angel died."

"Yer free then," Beck said, carefully examining her palm as if to reassure himself. "They should have stopped this thing right up front. Shouldn't have let that many people die."

Ori gave no reply, cautiously letting his wings appear. The badly damaged one still looked askew, but when it extended, it looked strong enough that he could fly.

With Beck's help, Riley regained her feet, still cradling her arm. The waves of agony continued, making her nauseous.

At her sharp intake of breath, Beck grimaced. "Broken?"

"Yeah. It hurts too much to be anything else." The implications hit home. "Oh no, this really sucks. My wedding dress is not cast friendly."

"You can just cut open the sleeve. No one will care," he said, trying to be helpful.

Riley gasped. Cutting the delicate lace sleeve would amount to heresy. "Not happening. No way. Just—no." Then she sighed. Why had she thought she wouldn't be bruised or sporting a cast on her wedding day?

"Riley?" Ori said. "Maybe I can give you an early wedding gift?"

"Huh? Ah, sure, I guess," she replied, not knowing what he meant.

The angel lightly laid his fingers on her right arm and closed his eyes. With that gentle touch came the warm glow she associated with him. It sank deep into her skin, into the bones. When he removed his hand, the agony was gone.

Riley wiggled her fingers, then gingerly moved the limb. She nearly cried in relief—the arm was healed. "How can you do that?"

"Because of our . . . connection," he said, looking over at Beck, "we can share our life force, much like how I can gift you with my angelfire."

"So yer like her demi-lord or somethin'?" Beck asked, frowning.

"Hardly. I just didn't want her special day ruined," Ori said, a glint of amusement in his eyes. "Of course, she *is* marrying you, so—"

"Hey!" her fiancé said. "That's not nice." Riley broke out in hooting laughter while Beck's frown deepened. "Better she's with me than you. All those feathers of yers? They'd make a mess in the house."

It was Ori's turn to laugh. "You know, I actually like you, Grand Master."

"Good, because if you don't have fancy angel things to do on Saturday, consider yerself invited to our weddin'. It's at two o'clock at Stewart's place. You know where that is."

"Do I get to kiss the bride?" Ori teased, his eyes brighter now.

"Hell no," Beck shot back. "But we'll let you have a piece of wedding cake."

"How can I resist *that* offer?" The angel's eyes roamed to Riley now. "I will try to be there." He paused for a moment, then smiled as if something had just occurred to him. "Perhaps with a friend."

She reached out and hugged him, knowing how much they both owed him. "Thank you for all you've done for us."

"What she said," Beck added.

Ori inclined his head, seeming unsure how to respond. He walked a few feet away, then turned back toward them. Awed murmurs ran through the crowd as his wings completely unfolded, arcing out from his body. With a glance over his shoulder at all the eyes watching him he shot up into the air, then remained there for a short time, wings beating, creating a light downdraft, as if deciding his next destination.

With a sudden burst of speed, Ori zoomed up into the heavens, leaving little pinwheels of light in his wake. The crowd ooh'ed and ahh'ed, then clapped enthusiastically like it was a Fourth of July celebration.

"He sure knows how to make an exit," Riley said, grinning.

"Yeah, he's got the special effects." Beck smirked, putting his uninjured arm around her waist. "But me? I got the girl."

~~*

When Riley had warned Beck that she was going to be up before dawn and that she was headed to the cemetery alone, he'd said he'd be willing to bet money that it wouldn't happen. Especially since it was only a day after the battle and she was still sore and exhausted.

By the time she left the house, she was ten dollars richer and still smirking. Beck had wisely paid off the bet and then settled on the couch to read a book. He said he needed some downtime, as the last twenty-some hours since the Destroyer's death had been a whirlwind of commotion.

There'd been conference calls with Rome and with MacTavish, followed by meetings with the local archbishop and both Atlanta's and the state's Powers That Be. The official story given to the press was right on only one point: It had been an angel that had come to Atlanta intent on its destruction. Because no matter what—and the Vatican was insistent on this point—the world wasn't ready to learn that the Destroyer had been one of Heaven's own. As far as anyone knew, except a rare few souls, that had been a Fallen in The Gulch. An amazingly powerful one, at that. But now it was dead, so no worries.

That hadn't kept a few noted religious scholars from pointing out the similarities between Atlanta's angel and the one in Exodus, but for the most part, people were happy to accept that whatever it had been was history. They'd celebrated that Atlanta was still thriving, and insisted on making Riley and Beck the heroes of the story. Mostly because they didn't quite know who that other angel with the white wings was, the one who had fought alongside them. Knowing Ori had preferred it to remain that way, they'd never mentioned his name in any of the interviews.

Riley knew the hubbub would continue for another week or so, which was why there would be police officers stationed outside Stewart's house tomorrow to ensure that there were no gate crashers for their wedding. But that was tomorrow. This morning Riley had a number of questions, and she knew who might have the answers.

So many times, she'd hiked into Oakland Cemetery at dawn, often summoned by Ori when he'd been entombed as a statue. This morning was less crisp than the last few days, moving solidly into spring now. Flowers were blooming in a mad rush, as if they knew their time was limited. Birdsong filled the air as Riley headed down the path toward her family's mausoleum. So much had happened since her mother's death, so much since her dad's passing, yet the stone structure seemed as if it would last forever. A quick gargoyle count reassured her that there were only four. Did that mean Ori was back on Heaven's payroll? Had there been any consequences to his killing a fellow angel?

As she walked up the steps to the mausoleum, the lion heads glistened in the morning light, caused by a thin layer of frost. She unlocked the doors, swung them open, and walked inside.

She and Beck would be buried here, though he wasn't yet aware of the arrangements she'd made with the cemetery to have them placed by her mom and dad when the time came. Perhaps someday it'd be their son or daughter, or their grandchildren, who would come here, lay flowers on their parents' and grandparents' graves, and check that the supplies stored in the mausoleum were in good shape. Tradition felt even more important now.

Riley opened the lid to the raised platform in the back of the structure, and then paused. On top of the sleeping bags and other goods was a single red rose, as fresh as if she'd just picked it. Ori had given her one after they'd spent the night in this place, after he'd seduced her. She lifted the flower and took a long inhalation. Then smiled. Their morning after had been all things horrible, but at least she remembered him with great fondness.

She set the rose aside, then checked the sleeping bags and other supplies to ensure they were in good shape. They were, of course, but it mattered that she did this, just like her dad had done. Once her inspection was complete, she placed the red rose back on top of the sleeping bags and closed the lid.

After she'd locked the gates, Riley found the cemetery's angelic guardian angel waiting for her. As usual, Martha looked like a little old lady, but this time she had no knitting needles in hand.

"Riley Anora Blackthorne."

Riley hesitated. "What is your real name? It certainly isn't Martha."

"Rahmiel," the angel replied, seeming pleased that Riley had thought to ask.

"Rahmiel. I like it. It's very nice."

"Thank you." She checked Riley out, from the crown of her head to her feet. "Once again, you've survived. I wasn't sure it was possible this time."

"I'm rather stubborn about that dying thing."

"Which is probably why you're still breathing."

They drifted to the stairs that led to the mausoleum and sat side by side.

"Go on, ask your questions. If I can answer them, I will," Martha urged, flicking a piece of grass off one of her black shoes.

"Is Ori going to be punished for killing the Destroyer? He shouldn't be, because you wanted him to handle it, but then you guys like to futz with the rules whenever it suits you."

"No, it doesn't look like there'll be a problem there," was the swift reply.

"Okay." That was excellent news. "The original bargain we had—that you keep Simon from dying and I prevent Armageddon—was supposed to be it, right?" A nod confirmed that. "But for some reason, you guys changed the Terms of Service and the crown on my palm didn't go away."

Martha chewed on that for a time. "It was supposed to be a one-shot deal. You keep the world from ending, and then you're off the hook. But . . ." She thought some more. "Probably the best way to explain it in terms you'll understand is that we considered you a contract employee, hired for a specific project. However, once that was done, the decision was made that you had certain talents that might allow you to handle other projects down the line, so your contract was extended."

"Okay, that makes sense, though you did alter the contract without my approval."

"We're known to do that from time to time."

"I noticed. So you guys left the mark on me in case I'd prove useful down the line?"

"It was more than that. It gave you a degree of safety if a certain religious institution decided to make an example of you."

The Vatican.

"Well, it worked. They never could figure out why I had Hell's mark on one hand and yours on the other."

"It was a first for us, too."

"Simon's spiritual journey. Did you know where he was headed when Sartael got ahold of him?"

Martha grew pensive now and didn't answer right away. instead, she rose and descended the stairs, then tidied a nearby gravestone.

"I wasn't sure what would happen to Simon Michael David Adler. When he realized he'd been tricked so badly, I saw the immense guilt in his heart. I was afraid he'd lost his faith completely. Now . . ."

"Now he's an exorcist, and his faith is stronger than ever."

Martha nodded. "Because his test was so very hard and he overcame it."

"What about you? Why are you the angel of this cemetery?"

That question earned her a nod of respect. "Like you, I proved . . . *difficult.* This is my 'punishment.'"

"But you love it here," Riley said. "You're perfect for this place."

"I do love this place. It's more a pleasure than a punishment."

"I'll keep your secret."

Martha cocked her head. "You haven't asked the one thing I figured you would."

No, Riley hadn't. She was afraid of the answer. "Did Heaven let Ori back in?"

"That's the wrong question," the angel said with a knowing

smile. "What you should be asking is if he *wants* to be back in." She raised her head then, listening to something only she could hear. "Oh my, a jogger has twisted his ankle over by the greenhouse. I must see to him."

"Thank you, Rahmiel," Riley said. "For everything."

"Be at peace, Riley Anora Blackthorne."

Then the angel was gone, off to do her part as this holy site's guardian.

Riley walked down the steps and turned to look back at the mausoleum. Tomorrow, after their wedding, she and Beck would come here to lay flowers on her parents' graves.

"Then we'll come full circle," she whispered.

Chapter Twenty-Eight

Riley stared in wonder. The face in the mirror was so much like her mother's it was uncanny. Her eyes were bright, her makeup flawless—the latter courtesy of Simi's painstaking efforts. She'd opted not to wear a veil, so her glossy hair fell in soft waves, pulled up on the sides with pearl clips to reveal the earrings Beck had bought her in Edinburgh.

She wore her mother's cross, and tucked into a hidden pocket under her wedding gown was the pouch Ayden had given her so long ago. While some brides wore something blue, the pouch contained a few of Ori's rose petals, the locket her parents had given her, and the demon claw necklace. Though an odd combination, they all held a special meaning for her.

The champagne-tinted lace wedding gown made her skin glow while artfully hiding the scars on her left shoulder and arm. Those battle scars not under the gown were concealed by body makeup. Unless you knew what she did for a living, you'd never believe the bride was a demon trapper.

"You look amazing," Simi whispered, her reflection in the mirror revealing tears.

I look in love. "This feels right," Riley said. "Marrying Den, I mean. I have never felt like this before, so sure of myself."

"Of course you're sure. He's your guy. Who knows, maybe someday you'll be doing this maid-of-honor gig for me."

Riley met her friend's gaze in the mirror. "Peter?"

Simi became wistful. "We'll see."

"You'll know when it's right."

"I hope so."

Unlike her usually garish colors, Riley's best friend had chosen pale blue highlights, carefully accenting her coal-black hair. Since her dress was a dark blue velvet, it worked perfectly.

"My hair and makeup look incredible. You sure you want to go to beauty school? I think you've got this wired."

"No, there's so much more I can learn. You were easy because you have cheekbones." Simi glanced at the old Regulator clock on the wall in Riley's bedroom. "Come on, it's time for you to get hitched, girlfriend. Don't want Beck to think you're ditching on him."

Riley turned and carefully hugged her friend, trying hard not to mess up their makeup. "Thank you for standing by me all these years."

Simi sniffed. "Who else is going to keep you supplied with hot chocolate?"

Riley took one last look around the room, then made her way to the door. Fortunately, her choice of gown hadn't made movement difficult, as it just skimmed the floor. With a deep breath, she crossed the threshold, knowing that from this moment on, she would never be the girl she'd left behind.

As Riley made her way down the hallway, she remembered another trip like this. It'd been the night of the prom and she'd practiced going down the stairs so she wouldn't trip on her prom dress. Despite all her elaborate plans, Beck hadn't come to get her here, sidetracked by a trapping. Instead, he'd joined her at the dance. That night was branded into her memory, the moment she knew their relationship had turned serious.

Angus waited at the bottom of the stairs now, smiling up at her as she descended. He was in full Scottish regalia and beaming like a proud father.

"Riley," he said. "Look at ya, lass. Yer so brae. Yer parents would be proud of ya."

"Thank you," she said, joining him now, trying to fight the tears. It'd been a near constant battle all morning.

"Yer missin' them, am I right?" She nodded. "They're here with us now. They will always be with ya."

"I know." She felt them more than ever. "My dad would be very pleased that you're walking me down the aisle."

Angus sighed. "No one can take the place of Paul Blackthorne. I'm just honored ta serve as his second."

"Like a duel, huh?"

He grinned. "Beck's a bundle of nerves, by the way. I'm findin' it hilarious, because I was the same on my weddin' day."

"Luckily he only misplaced the ring twice yesterday."

"Probably that wee fiend of yers tuckin' it away for safe keepin'."

Riley looked at him, aghast. "You know about the Magpie?"

"Aye. He's here today, so don't be surprised if the ring is not in the best man's pocket right now."

"He'll return it. He always does."

"Honor from demons? What is this world comin' ta?" Angus replied, then laughed.

"Thank you for watchin' over me and Beck. It means everything to us."

"As you two mean everythin' ta me."

The grand master offered his arm, placed a quick kiss on her cheek, and then led her toward the back of the house and her beloved.

The rain hadn't come, and though the air was cool out in the garden behind Angus's house, Beck was warm, even in his kilt. His friend and best man, Tom Donovan, from his hometown, had helped him dress. Then there'd been a final inspection by Angus to ensure everything was "right and proper," as he put it.

Now, as he waited, Beck resisted the temptation to panic. It felt like hours since he'd taken his place, after the guests had filed into the chairs on both sides of the center aisle. The garden was just as beautiful as he remembered, the tulips and daffodils in full bloom. The trees had budded out and he heard the occasional thrum of a hummingbird winging by.

All the chairs were full—the trappers he'd expected to come were here, as well as some of the witches and necromancers.

Riley's friend Peter was in the front, smiling like he'd won the lottery.

Beck tugged at the collar of his dress shirt, staring up the aisle again. Where was she? Had she changed her mind? What if Hell had decided to steal her away from him at the last minute? What if . . .

He shot a worried look at Mortimer, who gave him a knowing smile. "She'll be here," he said quietly. "This will go just fine. You've been through too much for it to go any other way."

There was that.

Beck caught Ayden's eye and she gave him a nod. That was her signal that all the guests were here and that the protective circle would be set the moment Riley arrived.

"Here we go," Tom said.

Simi smiled as she walked sedately down the wide grass aisle. When she grew close to Beck, she took her place, giving him a wink. He dragged in a deep breath, trying to relax.

Then all he saw was the young woman on Angus's arm, his bride-to-be, the only child of Paul and Miriam Blackthorne. The little girl who'd once had a crush on him, now a master trapper and summoner who had battled Hell and Heaven. She was the one who'd taught him that he was worth more than a bottle of booze and a bad childhood. That even though he had no middle name, no father to call his own, he was worthy of her endless and fierce love.

Her gown fit her perfectly, the lace draping over her and falling gently to the ground. Her eyes were only on him as she moved closer, the promise of a life together. He'd joked and called her Princess, but he knew that was wrong. Riley was a warrior queen, and now nothing stood in their way.

When his fiancée and Angus paused a few steps away, the faint tingle of magic brushed against his skin as Ayden sealed the circle.

Since Riley had thought that having someone "give her away" was old fashioned, they'd decided to skip that part. Instead, she tipped up on her toes and placed a kiss on the old Scotsman's cheek. His eyes grew glassy and he swallowed heavily.

He looked over at Beck and said in a clear voice, "*Lang may yer lum reek.*"

It meant, "long may your chimney smoke," Angus's way of wishing them a lengthy and healthy life together.

"Thank you," Beck said.

He extended his hand and Riley walked up to accept it. Drawing her close, he whispered, "You are so very beautiful. I love you. I always will."

The smile he received made him feel like a king.

They turned toward Mortimer, who was beaming in his black robe, an ivory notebook in his hands.

"Good afternoon, my friends," he said, addressing the assembly as a few people shifted in their chairs. "And a good afternoon it is, as spring blooms around us, reminding us that we are blessed by nature's many wonders and should never take them for granted." He paused, producing a tissue and gently dabbing at his nose. "Though, to be honest, I wish the flowers were a little less enthusiastic in their mating rituals."

Chuckles came from the crowd, as some of them were allergic to the pollen as well. Mort tucked away the tissue and continued. "I have known Riley and Denver for over a year now. I have watched them go from deepest sorrow to greatest love, from powerlessness to triumph. Because of them, this city has survived, its citizens free to go about their lives.

"I am honored to unite this extraordinary couple in holy matrimony. For if ever there has been a love that transcended Heaven, Hell, and everything in between, it is *this* one."

When Beck squeezed Riley's hand, it trembled. Or maybe it was his.

"As all of you know, Riley and Denver have always done things their own way." Light laughter came now. "These wedding vows are no different. You've been warned," he said, grinning.

Mort turned a page in his black notebook. "Denver Beck, what promises and vows do you want to share with Riley today?"

Beck cleared his throat and looked deep into those beautiful eyes. "I promise to not boss you around. Well, not too much. Yer not gonna listen to me anyway, but I'll try."

That earned him a knowing smile from his bride.

"I vow to love you. No one else owns my heart, and no one else ever will. I promise to try to remember that I'm worthy of you. Oh, and that there is other food besides pizza and barbecued ribs."

"He might be lying about that part," someone called out and the guests laughed.

Then Beck grew serious again, taking a deep breath. "I promise to watch yer back when you do those dangerous things you do. But most of all, I vow to make you the center of my world, because you already are."

A light sheen had appeared in Riley's eyes now, and that caused him to blink his own.

Mort turned to her now. "Riley, what vows will you share with Denver?"

She too took a deep breath. "Well, I promise not to steal the covers. At least, not all the time. I promise to listen to your good advice. I also promise to help you create a home and a life filled with laughter, with respect, and with love."

Riley reached up and placed her left hand on his cheek. Even though Beck knew Heaven's mark was gone, he swore he could feel its power in that touch.

"I vow to remain in awe of you, Den, for all you've done, and for all you will do. You are truly an incredible man who has come so far, all because you refused to be defeated."

Beck swallowed hard. He'd received praise from others, but from Riley it meant everything.

"And finally, I vow to watch your back and love only you, for you are my heart and my soul. You are my life, Denver Beck, and I look forward to as many days and nights as we are granted together."

There was a silence now, as if Heaven was listening.

Once the moment had passed, Mort said, "Do you, Denver Beck, take this woman to be your lawfully wedded wife? To have and to hold, for richer and for poorer, in sickness and in health, unto all eternity?"

"I do," Beck said, his voice clear and strong.

"Do you, Riley Anora Blackthorne, take this man to be your lawfully wedded husband? To have and to hold, for richer and for poorer, in sickness and in health, unto all eternity?"

"I do," she replied.

"Have you brought symbols of this bond, so all will know your commitment to each other?"

Tom dutifully slipped his hand into his pocket and then he blinked. He checked the other pocket, then gave Beck a panicked look.

"The ring's gone," he said.

"Oh, little demon," Riley whispered. "That's your cue."

She'd forewarned Mort that this was likely to happen, so he wasn't the least bit surprised when a small blur zipped across the grass at his feet. With a grin, Beck held out his hand and suddenly there was a Klepto-Fiend on his palm. The demon was clad in his usual ninja clothes and the wedding ring was clutched in his hands. He grinned, displaying all those sharp little teeth. Tom stared in fascination and muted chuckles came from some of the wedding guests, at least those who knew what this was.

"Thanks," Beck said, taking the ring from the fiend. "Please don't ever steal it back."

The demon eyed him like he'd just spouted blasphemy, gave Riley an exaggerated bow, and then zipped away.

"You told me that might happen, but I really didn't believe it," Tom muttered.

Beck took Riley's left hand, and as he threaded the ring onto her finger, he cast aside all the formal words they'd planned.

"It's about time, Princess."

She was lucky he'd gotten through almost all the vows without adlibbing. And even if he had adlibbed the whole thing, she'd still love him.

When it was Riley's turn, she carefully placed her father's

wedding ring, now resized, onto Beck's finger, and threw out her prepared speech too.

"There. Now you're mine, Backwoods Boy. Never forget it."

"Not a chance," he said, grinning.

To her surprise, he didn't wait for Mort to get through the formal announcement, but pulled her into his arms and kissed her. She was vaguely aware of the summoner finishing the ceremony over the cheers and clapping of their friends, intoning the required words, "By the power vested in me by the Summoners Society and the state of Georgia, I now pronounce you man and wife." Then their friend added, "I'd say you can kiss the bride, but you're already there."

When the kiss ended, the love in Beck's eyes made her heart leap. He turned them toward the guests. "My wife," he said proudly. "Isn't she amazin'?"

Riley laughed. "And this crazy man is my husband."

"What were you thinking?" someone called out.

That love is for real. That it's stronger than any evil in this world.

Instead, she said out loud, "You got me. I'll let you know in a few years."

They were immediately swarmed by well-wishers—friends who'd made the journey right alongside them. Beck got thumped on the back so often she was sure it must be starting to ache. Riley's biggest challenge was to hold back the tears as she hugged Ayden, Rada, and then Simi. Simon delivered a very long embrace, wishing her well, as did her friend Peter.

"Many blessings on your house," Ayden said.

"I second that," Rada added. She looked over and smiled as Lord Ozymandias joined them. He was in a stylish suit, the sigil nowhere in sight.

"Thank you for helping me the other day," Riley said, and then on impulse she embraced the summoner. The shock on his face gave way to a tentative smile.

"You're ruining my image," he said as she released him.

"Good. How many more nights in the middle of nowhere

does that hug buy me?"

He raised an eyebrow. "Do you really want to know?"

"No. But it was worth it just to see the look on your face."

"You might think otherwise during our next practice session."

She grinned. "I doubt it, Your Lordship."

Mort was beside her now and she collected another hug. When it ended, she saw Ozymandias slipping away.

"He's not staying for the reception?"

"He's not good with social gatherings and avoids them if possible. The fact that he was here today says a lot about you and Beck."

Yes, it does.

As she turned to say something to her husband, she caught sight of Ori standing near a man with blond hair, but she couldn't see the man's face. Riley gave a nod to the angel and received one in return.

"I'm glad you're here."

Ori's reply immediately filled her mind. *"I am honored to be part of this day."*

Finally, she had a chance to study Beck as he chatted with Mrs. Merton, who had brought Rennie in her traveling cage, because the bunny "just shouldn't miss an important day like this." Riley suspected that Rennie was just here for the carrots, but didn't say so.

Her husband—and it was going to take a while to let that all sink in—was so striking he took her breath away. The kilt, the Prince Charlie jacket, all of it only made him more handsome. But it wasn't just the clothes. Denver Beck was unique, strong, brave, and compassionate. A man of integrity. Of all the guys she'd daydreamed about, he was the one who had won her heart. To have him by her side in this life was a gift she'd never expected.

"You married wisely," Ayden said, her eyes on Beck as well. Her friend's bright blue dress was cut low enough to reveal her tattoo. This time it was a field of wildflowers with snow-topped mountains in the distance. If Riley were to guess, she'd say it was somewhere in Scotland.

"I'm liking that one," she said, pointing to the ink. "Can you keep that for a while?"

"I wish. You know this thing has a mind of its own." Ayden looked down at it. "But I'm thinking this means it'll be quiet for a while. We all need that right now."

"Hey, wife! They say it's time for pictures!" Beck called out. He had a smile so wide she swore his face couldn't contain it.

"Duty calls," Riley said and hurried in his direction.

Chapter Twenty-Nine

Once the pictures were done in the garden, they waited until they were alone. Beck kissed her, smoothing a stray curl out of the way. "Good wedding, wife. So, what's it feel like to be Mrs. Beck?"

"Not bad. What's it like to be Mr. Blackthorne?"

He snorted. "Yer just not gonna let me have that one, are you?"

"Nope. Gotta win one now and then."

As they turned, they found Ori watching them from the end of the aisle. He wore a black suit, blue shirt, and black tie.

"You clean up nice, angel," Beck said, offering his hand.

After shaking his hand, Ori gestured at the kilt and the jacket. "So do you." He then leaned close to Riley, kissing her on the cheek. "You look radiant."

"Thank you." She hesitated, unsure if she should pose the question. "Are you back with Heaven now?"

"No." Ori shot Beck a look. "Nor am I with the infernal master, either."

"Yer free?"

The angel gave a very pleased nod. "I'm sure in time I won't find it so pleasant, but right now I'm savoring the notion that I am my own . . . boss."

"Any downsides to that?" Riley asked.

"A few, but I'll work those out over time."

"You deserve to be free," Beck said, giving Ori a clap on the back. "You've earned that so many times over."

"Thank you." Ori sobered. "I am sorry to bring sad news on

this special day, but Isra the free demon is dead. He died only a few hours after he was captured. He didn't suffer long."

Riley took a deep breath to cover the sudden lance of sorrow in her chest. At least he wasn't hurting anymore. "Thank you for letting me know. How'd you find that out?"

"One of the remarkable things about not being aligned with either realm is that certain angels and demons are willing to talk to me now. I find out the most interesting things that way." He looked past them. "There is one other thing. Since I have given the bride her gift, I believe I owe the groom one as well."

"Thanks, but I have everythin' I need right here," Beck said, looking over at his wife.

"Oh, I think this is a present you'll appreciate," Ori said. "The Prince is at his most dangerous when he has something you desperately want. Allow me to remove one of your greatest temptations." He gestured behind them, into the gardens.

The moment Riley turned and saw the face of the man waiting for them, she immediately knew who he was and what this meant. He had the same blond hair, those deep brown eyes. His posture was almost identical to her husband's.

"Grand Master, meet your father," Ori said, in case there was any doubt.

Beck's mouth dropped open in stunned silence. Because he was so shocked, he didn't reply, so Riley gave him a little nudge. "Say something," she whispered.

"Sweet Jesus," was all he could choke out.

"Does he know you're an angel?" Riley asked.

"Yes," Ori replied. "It made for a very interesting conversation."

When Beck finally regained his composure, he took Riley's hand and tugged her deeper into the garden toward the newcomer, who looked decidedly uneasy. Once they were a few feet away, Beck halted in his tracks, staring like he wasn't sure if this was for real or not. Riley couldn't imagine what this was like for him, so she took the lead. Breaking away, she walked up to the man.

"Hi! I'm Riley Blackthorne."

The man stuck out his hand and they shook. "Clinton Archer. My friends call me Clint. And congratulations! The ceremony was wonderful."

She'd hoped he'd been here with Ori all along. The handshake had also revealed that he wore a wedding ring. Did that mean Beck had stepbrothers and -sisters?

Moving in slow motion, Beck finally stepped closer and raised his hand, and the two men shook, father and son. "I look so much like you," he said, still in shock.

"Like me and your grandfather." The man looked away for a few moments, then back. "I swear to God, I had no idea I had a son until this . . . gentleman," he gestured at Ori, who'd kept his distance, "came to my door yesterday. It took some time for him to convince me, but now that I see you, I know it's for real."

"How . . ." Beck began. "God, I have about a thousand questions."

"So do I, but you have friends waiting for you and I can't keep you from them."

"Maybe you two can talk after the reception?" Riley suggested. She looked over at Beck now, judging his reaction. "We can leave for the cabin a little later. It's not that far from here."

"You sure?" Beck asked, the gratitude in his eyes telling her the suggestion was welcomed.

"If we don't get there until tomorrow, no harm done. This is far more important," she said.

How many times do you get to meet your father, the one you've been praying for all these years?

Clint's face lit up with a smile. "I'm not planning on flying back home until tomorrow, so whatever works for you. I'm sorry my wife missed the ceremony. Julianne's recovering from knee surgery, or she'd be here. She'd love to meet both of you."

Even more questions came to mind now, but Riley knew they'd have to wait. As she turned to thank Ori, she found he was gone.

But she knew he'd hear her anyway. *"Thank you. You have given him everything he's ever wanted."*

"As you have given me everything I wished for. Live well, Riley Anora."

"Don't be a stranger, dear angel. We'll always save a seat for you at our table. You're family now."

"So it shall be."

Unaware of the silent conversation, Beck took hold of her arm, his father standing on the other side of him. Seeing them together, there was no doubt that they were closely related.

"Time for some of that fancy cake you kept tellin' me about," her new husband announced, the joy in his eyes impossible to measure. Then he looked over at his father. "You like whisky, Clint?"

"I do, but not if you insist on putting ice in it," the man replied.

Beck grinned. "Yeah, we're gonna get along just fine."

~~*

His mind still reeling from Ori's surprise, Beck regained his footing once they were in Angus's ballroom. Located on the third floor of the big house, it was the height of Victorian elegance. At least that's what Riley had said. She'd decided against adding any additional decoration, so the space spoke for itself. From what Beck could see, her instincts had been correct. At present, the room was full of smiling faces, all ready to get on with the celebration.

But first, there was the matter of his father. Beck's initial impression of Clint Archer was that he was someone he could trust, and usually his hunches were on the money. He made sure to introduce him to Angus right off, including the whispered explanation as to who exactly this man was. Neither he nor his father was ready for the big reveal, especially today. Angus registered just as much surprise as he had, but promised that he'd make sure Clint wasn't on his own during the reception. He also promised to introduce him to Tom Donovan, who lived in Sadlersville and had known Beck's mom.

Once he knew that was handled, Beck made sure to be on his best behavior. He didn't jam a bunch of cake into his bride's mouth like some guys did, because there was no way he'd embarrass her like that. Besides, Riley had a very long memory and she knew magic. Never a good combination.

His bride was equally respectful of his cake portion, and then they intertwined hands and sipped a little champagne. It was all kind of silly, but he liked it anyway. After a few toasts, the attendees began working on the "finger foods," as Riley had called the spread that took up three long tables. As folks settled into chairs around the small cocktail tables, Riley and Beck did the rounds, shaking hands, collecting hugs. Beck even endured a few more backslaps. All the while, he kept gazing at the beautiful young woman by his side and wondered how he'd gotten so lucky.

He was pleased to see that Mrs. Ayers, Angus's housekeeper, had been forced to sit down and relax while people brought *her* food and drink. She'd slaved for the last few weeks to make this reception a success, and he would personally thank her when it all ended. Plus, he and Riley had already arranged for the woman to have a spa day in the next week or so. Anyone who'd thrown that much of themselves into making their wedding perfect deserved serious pampering.

Leaving Riley to talk to a crimson-robed necromancer named Lady Torin, he hunted around until he found his friend Ike. The old veteran had on a suit, though it was clearly too big for him. The smile he gave Beck said he was pleased to be here.

"Told you she was worth it," his friend said, patting the chair next to him. Beck gratefully sank into it, his feet needing the break.

"You were right. How goes it at the shelter?"

"Not bad. Seems there's a Three tryin' to chow down on some of the guys on the streets. I gave them the Holy Water just like you said, and the thing's backed off."

"Good. Let me know if it tries again and I'll go huntin'. I'd be happy to take that thing down for you."

"Ya got it."

Beck lowered his voice. "You still have that little demon?" In this case, the Magpie who'd been robbing the donation meters that the city had installed downtown.

"Nyah," Ike said. "I handed him off to another guy when I moved into the shelter. It'll keep him fed."

That it would. "Yer lookin' good. You've put on some weight," Beck observed.

"Living indoors does that to ya. Wait a year or so, ya'll be fatter too with that good woman takin' care of ya."

Before Beck could argue with that, the recorded music began. This was the other part of the wedding day that made him especially nervous, besides trying to remember the vows.

Straightening his jacket, he met his wife in the center of the ballroom, put his arms around her, and drew her in for a kiss. There were good-natured catcalls from some of the trappers, but he ignored them. When the kiss ended, he put his arms on Riley's waist and they began to dance, slow and close. She smelled of magnolias.

"This is like the prom," Riley whispered in his ear.

"I knew then that you had to be my wife. Just wasn't sure if I could talk you into it."

She grinned up at him. "You only had to ask twice."

"Yer worth it."

"Wait a year—you might change your mind."

No, that'll never happen.

Others began to join them. Simi and Peter started dancing and Kurt awkwardly led Jaye to the dance floor, while Father Harrison paired up with Carmela, the Guild's doctor. Jackson was holding his wife close, eyes closed, oblivious to the rest of the world.

So many friends, so much happiness. Looking into his own wife's eyes, he knew where it had all come from.

You. Because you never gave up on me.

~~*

The plan had been for them to retreat to Beck's house to change clothes, visit the graveyard, and then head to the cabin in North Georgia for their honeymoon. Ori's wedding bombshell had altered that timeline, but Beck didn't mind in the least. Thankfully, neither did Riley.

Once they were at his house, she excused herself, claiming that she needed a long soak in the tub, so he had Clint take a seat in the living room. Knowing Riley would need help to get out of her gown, he shut the bedroom door behind them. She turned her back to him so he could unzip her, and he took that opportunity to place a heated kiss on her shoulder.

"Kinda wish we didn't have company right now," he said, his voice husky.

"No, you don't. Not with who that guest is," she said, shimmying out of the dress.

He wasn't so sure about that. This was his wife, and he'd yet to have his honeymoon.

It took him longer to get out of his clothes than it did her. She'd pulled on a T-shirt and sweatpants, then hung her dress in the closet, running her hand down the fabric one last time.

"You gonna keep it?" he asked, stripping off his socks and flashes.

Riley turned to him, wistful. "I think I will. Maybe our daughter will want to wear it. If we have one, that is."

"We will. One of each. I have it on good authority." He really didn't know that for sure, but something told him his hunch was right.

"Then I'll keep it," she said. After placing a kiss on his forehead, and deftly avoiding his roaming hands, she headed to the bathroom.

By the time Beck returned to the living room, Clint was studying the pictures on a shelf next to the front window. Riley had framed the photograph of him receiving his Silver Star and his second Purple Heart up there. At first, he'd wanted to take it down, but now he accepted it being there.

His visitor turned, his expression hard to read. "You were in the Army. In Afghanistan. You were awarded a Silver Star."

Beck could only nod. It was hard for him to talk about that, even now.

"My oldest son, Andrew, was over there. He was in the Army too. Thank God both of you got back in one piece."

"Amen to that."

He poured them two fingers of whisky and then gestured for Clint to take a seat on the couch. Beck sat in the chair across from him. Now was when it got real.

"You probably want to know how I met your mother," Clint began after a long sip of the scotch. "I was stationed in Jacksonville, Florida—I was in the Air Force—and I met her at a bar near the state line. Sadie was funny and cute, and, well . . . one thing led to another and we spent a long weekend together. It was the week before I was deployed to Ramstein Air Base in Germany."

Beck could tell that he was uneasy having to explain this, but it had to be said.

"Sadie and I hit it off." Clint sighed. "Or at least I thought we had. I liked her a lot. I wrote her once I was deployed overseas. She never wrote me back. I sent a couple letters and then gave up because it was clear she didn't care."

It was Beck's turn to sigh. Despite all of Sadie's bitching about how this guy had screwed her over, he'd wondered if that had been the case. "Sadie had some issues."

"Did she get married?" Beck shook his head. "Did she tell you about me?"

"Not really. By the time I was old enough to ask, she wasn't willing to share that information." He leaned forward on the couch, his arms on his thighs. "I have to be honest here, Sadie had some real problems the older she got. She was an abusive alcoholic. She and I had a rocky relationship, at best."

Clint looked down at his glass now. "God, I hate to hear that."

"I survived. But when it really mattered, she was there for me. Someday I'll tell you that story."

When the man looked up again, Beck could see the anguish in his eyes. "If I'd known . . ."

"You would have done the right thing. I could tell that the moment I met you. So how's about we move forward, rather than lookin' back?"

Clint raised his glass. "I like it. Forward, not backward. You don't have to call me 'father' or 'dad' or anything. Clint is fine."

"Then that's the way it'll be."

His father left the house an hour later, after trading phone numbers and addresses. Clint had promised to bring his wife for a visit as soon as she was able to travel. And then, when he was ready, Beck would fly to New Mexico to meet his two half-brothers and one half-sister. In the matter of an afternoon, he'd gained a wife and an entire family.

He would never be alone again. Beck drained the glass of whisky, sending a mental thank-you to a certain angel.

It was time to take his wife on their honeymoon.

Reunions didn't always go well, but to Riley's relief, she could tell that this one had. Fortunately, there didn't seem to be any emotional minefields. Beck was so much more at ease now, as if he'd crossed some personal Rubicon, and she suspected much of it had to do with Clint—and the fact that there was finally a wedding ring on her finger.

When they reached the Blackthorne mausoleum, the sun was setting, gold and orange streaks in the sky to the west. The top of the mausoleum glowed, the building's original gargoyles in their respective corners. Riley knelt in front of her parents' graves, carefully placing selected flowers from her wedding bouquet on each one of them.

"Hey, look at us," she said, smiling. "We're married." Tears threatened. "I wish you could have been there but . . ." The tears fell now.

Beck knelt next to her, putting his arm around her. "They were there. You felt them, didn't you? I did. I could hear Paul's voice in my head, and your mother's laughter."

"I did too."

Beck fell silent, allowing Riley time to regain her composure. When she shifted, straightening a flower on her mother's grave, he said quietly, "I wish Sadie could have been there too, though that would have been interestin' with Clint showin' up. My momma liked you, in her own way. She never did take kindly to Caitlyn or Louisa." His old girlfriends.

"Your mother was different," Riley said, wiping away the tears.

"That's bein' kind. Truth is, I think she was too afraid to admit that she could love someone. Thought it made her weak somehow. If she'd been smart, she wouldn't have let Clint get away." He shook his head. "I don't know where she got that notion, because my grandparents weren't like that."

After a few more minutes, they rose, walking back to the front of the mausoleum, then down the path toward the bell tower. As they passed it and reached the road that led back to the parking lot, Riley could see a circle of lights to the east.

"Someone sittin' vigil tonight," Beck said.

"It might be Martha. We should drop by. Do we have time?"

"We have all the time we need," he said. "We're together. That's all that matters."

As one would expect, the circle of candles surrounded a new grave, but it wasn't an angel sitting vigil. Instead, it was a girl of maybe sixteen years, if that old. Her brown hair was in a ponytail and her matching brown eyes were as wide as they could be.

"Go away!" she cried, waving them away. "I won't sell her. I won't!"

That brought back so many memories.

"We're not here for that," Riley said. "I just thought you were a friend of ours. Her name's Martha. She guards the dead sometimes. She's the one with the serious knitting addiction."

"My brother told me about her, but she's not here tonight, I guess." The girl sighed. "I . . . just . . . there've been these people coming by. The necromancers. They keep trying to get me to sell my mother. They make my head hurt."

Riley winced. "You met Mortimer yet?"

The girl shook her head. "Is he scary like some of the others?"

"No, he's a sweetie," Riley said. "Not scary at all." *Unless you're a demon.*

Beck shifted his position next to her. "Don't you have someone to stay with you tonight?"

The girl sagged. "My brother was supposed to, but he's sick. I told him not to eat that leftover chicken, but he never listens. Now I'm here on my own."

And scared to death. That much was clear.

"Your first night here?" Riley asked.

The girl nodded forlornly. "It's creepy."

It was also chilly, and eventually she'd have to visit a restroom . . .

Riley looked over at Beck. Without speaking, the question was posed and the answer returned with a quick nod.

"You sure it's okay?" she asked quietly.

"It's fine. We can set out in the mornin'. We have an entire life together. She's alone. That's not right."

Riley tipped up on her toes and kissed his cheek. "I love you, you know that?"

"I know. I count my blessin's all the time."

She turned back to the young girl. "Would you like us to stay and keep you company?"

The girl blinked, then frowned. "How do I know you're not necromancers, that this isn't some trick?"

"Well, I'm not a necro," Beck said. "I'm a demon trapper." Riley noted he left out the grand master title.

Time to come clean. "I am a necro, but I don't summon the dead. I'm a demon trapper like Beck."

"You know how to do this vigil thing?" the girl asked, her eyes narrowing.

Riley gave her points for being cautious. "Yes, I watched over my father's grave about a year ago. He's over there with my mom, by the mausoleum."

The girl stood. "That big one?"

"Uh huh. Beck's done this too. We know what kind of head games the necros play. We'll keep you company until morning, when the next shift arrives."

"Really?" The girl seemed to work it out in her head. "You could still be messing with me."

"I like her. She doesn't trust easy," Beck said, smiling now.

"You're not helping."

Riley pointed at the booklet lying on the blanket near the girl's feet. "The last paragraph on page five is the phrase that allows us to enter the circle as long as we mean no harm. If we do intend to harm you or your mother, the circle won't let us in."

"You serious?"

"Absolutely. Read the phrase and the circle will decide if we're telling the truth or not. Trust me, if it doesn't like us, you'll know."

"I think I saw that with the last necromancer. It got really bright and he backed off."

"That'd be exactly what should happen."

The girl picked up the book and thumbed to the proper page. "'If you mean no harm, then pass within.'"

Riley stepped through the circle, then looked back at Beck.

"I'll get the sleepin' bags from the mausoleum and some of the food from the car," he said. "That way we can be warm and fed."

That was her guy—always thinking ahead. "Thanks, Den."

By the time Beck returned with the gear, Riley had learned that Mindy was only fifteen, that her mom had died from a shellfish allergy, and that her dad was in the military, trying to get back to Atlanta as soon as possible to take care of Mindy and her seventeen-year-old brother. Then Riley'd held the girl as she'd wept, evoking memories of her own losses.

Beck efficiently arranged the ground cloth, then the sleeping bags—one for Mindy and one laid out for them. He topped their makeshift beds with blankets. Then came their trapping bags and, finally, a cooler of food destined for the cabin.

"He's way cute," Mindy whispered to Riley.

"Yeah, he is." Fortunately, he hadn't heard their whispers, or there would have been some comment.

Once everything was settled and they were munching chocolate chip cookies, Mindy stared at something she'd pulled up on her phone. She looked at Riley, then back at the device, then back at Riley.

"Ohmigod, you're her! You kill demons. I thought you looked familiar."

"That's her all right," Beck said, grinning.

But he wasn't off the hook, as Mindy's attention went to him now. "Yeah, but you're that grand master dude, the one that killed that evil angel guy last year. I saw the video on YouTube. That was awesome! Well, except for the part where you got hurt. That was pretty gruesome."

"I remember that part too," Beck replied, but Riley could see he was pleased that someone had a clue who he was.

"You guys are, like, famous!" the girl gushed.

It appeared they had their very own fan.

"Comes with having Hell trying to kill you," Beck replied.

"Repeatedly," Riley added.

They talked about what it was like to be a trapper, making sure to keep the tales lighthearted, until Mort arrived. He peered at Riley, then Beck.

"I figured you guys would be headed north by now," he said.

"Mindy needed some company for the night."

Mort understood immediately. "Good deal." He doffed his fedora at the girl. "I am Mortimer Alexander and I am a summoner. I am deeply sorry for your loss."

"Uh huh," was the response.

"I know it's difficult to discuss, but would you be willing to have your mother reanimated in exchange for remuneration?"

"No way!"

He nodded again, apparently expecting that answer. "Then I wish you a good night, and once again, you have my sincere condolences." His attention shifted to Riley. "Lord Ozymandias told me the specifics of your spellwork against the death angel. You impressed him, which rarely happens. When you get back, drop by. I've got something new for you to learn."

"What now?" Riley asked, not really wanting to think about what torture that might involve.

"An advanced levitation spell. And of course, more spell blocking. You're not out of the woods yet, grasshopper."

At her groan, he gave a wave and headed back the way he'd come.

"He wasn't creepy at all," Mindy said, surprised.

"He's a good man," Beck said. "A friend of ours, too."

The next necro that showed up took one look at Mindy's companions, muttered, "Oh hell," and left them alone. The two that followed just turned on their heels and took off without a word.

"Wow, you guys are seriously badass. You scared those guys right off," Mindy said.

"We're like that," Beck said, leaning over to give Riley a kiss. "Isn't that right, Mrs. Beck?"

"I kept my last name, remember?"

"Did you really?" he said, grinning.

"How long have you guys been married?"

Riley checked her phone. "About seven and a half hours."

"What?" the girl blurted. "But you're supposed to be on your honeymoon."

"We are," Beck said. He gestured. "Fresh air, pretty stars, and good company. I'd say it's a fine way to start a marriage."

"You guys are crazy, you know that?" Mindy replied, clearly dubious.

"We've been told that once or twice," Riley admitted.

After texting her brother an update, including a photo of the newlyweds, Mindy soon fell asleep. Riley and Beck curled up in the sleeping bag. She tucked herself up against him, knowing she wouldn't be needing any additional blankets tonight.

"It was a good day, wife," he said quietly.

"It was a very good day, husband. Sorry about tonight."

"We have plenty of nights, and she needed us. It feels right being here."

"Your compassion streak is about a mile wide."

"Just keepin' up with you."

He kissed her, then rolled over so his back was to her—to avoid temptation, as he put it. While he fell asleep, Riley watched the stars. An owl hooted in the distance and the MARTA train passed on its way to Five Points Station. She felt the wind stir, then settle again.

This was their city, one filled with love and sadness, with loss and joy. Hopefully it would be the same for their children and their grandchildren. Blackthornes and Becks. Who knew, maybe one of them would become a demon trapper.

Though Heaven and Hell had turned their lives inside out, she and Den had survived. They'd learned how to love and how to sacrifice. Learned when to fight and when to bargain.

"All or nothing," she murmured, then closed her eyes.

"All or nothin'," Beck repeated in his sleep.

Epilogue

Ori watched as his fellow angel examined a gravestone near the Blackthorne mausoleum. Rahmiel always seemed to be on the move, but he saw the contentment in those mundane tasks.

"You going to hang around all night and make yourself miserable?" she asked, eyeing him as she straightened up.

"No. Just . . . remembering."

"She was never yours—you know that."

"No, she wasn't. She was never meant to be."

"What's it feel like to be free?" Rahmiel asked.

"Odd. And yet, it feels right."

"Maybe someday I'll know what that's like."

She reached down and plucked a bloom from a nearby azalea, then offered it to him. The moment Ori touched the flower, it became a red rose.

" 'In order for the light to shine so brightly, the darkness must be present.' Always remember that," she said.

Rahmiel vanished even before he could blink his eyes, off to do whatever was required of her. He had found he enjoyed her company, for she did not judge him for his many sins.

Looking toward the twinkle of candles in the distance, he smiled at the sleeping young woman, the new wife, the valiant light that had sustained him in the darkness. She had shared that light with him until he could reclaim his own.

Ori kissed the rose and laid it on the steps leading to the mausoleum. In the morning, Riley Anora Blackthorne would feel the need to visit this place again, and she'd find this token—and remember.

No matter how many he gave her, it'd never repay the gift she'd given to him, the gift of hope.

Far in the distance, he heard a familiar sound, a demon doing something cunningly evil. Eager for the chase, Ori beat his wings, ascending into the clear night sky.

It was time to push back the Darkness.

It was time to hunt.

About the Author

A resident of Portugal, Jana Oliver admits to a fascination with all things mysterious, creepy and laced with a touch of the supernatural. An eclectic soul who has traveled the world, she loves to research urban legends and spooky tales, and then write about them.

When she's not hunched over a keyboard, she enjoys photograpy, fine Scottish whisky and far too many desserts.

Thank You!

Thank you for reading *Valiant Light*. I sincerely hope you enjoyed it.

If for some reason you've never read the other books in the Demon Trappers series, please check out the following website for details:

www.DemonTrappers.com

Please tell your friends about the novel, post reviews on Goodreads and the various online booksellers' sites, etc. That's the best way to get the word out about my books.

Join my newsletter at my website! I share book news and snippets with all my subscribers.

Or follow me on social media:

Facebook: www.Facebook.com/JanaOliver
Twitter: @CrazyAuthorGirl
Instagram: CrazyAuthorGirl19
Or at my website: www.JanaOliver.com

Thank you for joining me on another Riley and Beck adventure!

The Demon Trappers Series

Be sure to check out the rest of the books in
this great series by Jana Oliver

U.S. (U.K.) Editions

The Demon Trapper's Daughter (Forsaken)

Soul Thief (Forbidden)

Forgiven (same title)

Foretold (same title)

Grave Matters (same title)

Mind Games (same title)

Valiant Light (same title)

www.ingramcontent.com/pod-product-compliance
Lightning Source LLC
Chambersburg PA
CBHW070641180626
46817CB00006B/2191